D0718886

CyberFeminism

Other Books

Susan Hawthorne and Renate Klein (co-editors)
Angels of Power and other reproductive creations
Australia for Women: Travel and Culture

Susan Hawthorne
The Falling Woman (novel)
Bird (poetry)
The Spinifex Quiz Book

Edited collections
Difference: Writings by Women (editor)
Moments of Desire (co-editor)
The Exploding Frangipani (co-editor)
Car Maintenance. Explosives and Love and other contemporary lesbian writings (co-editor)

Renate Klein
Man-Made Women (co-author)
Infertility: Women Speak Out about their experiences of reproductive medicine (author/editor)
The Exploitation of a Desire
RU 486: Misconceptions, Myths and Morals (co-author)

Edited collections
Theories of Women's Studies (co-editor)
Test-Tube Women: What Future for Motherhood (co-editor)
Radical Voices (co-editor)
Radically Speaking: Feminism Reclaimed (co-editor)

CyberFeminism:

Connectivity, Critique and Creativity

edited by

Susan Hawthorne
and Renate Klein

Spinifex Press Pty Ltd
504 Queensberry Street
North Melbourne, Vic. 3051
Australia
women@spinifexpress.com.au
http://www.spinifexpress.com.au

First published by Spinifex Press, 1999

Edited by Gillian Fulcher
Typeset in Photina by Palmer Higgs Pty Ltd
Cover design by Deb Snibson, Modern Art Production Group

Made and printed in Australia by Australian Print Group

National Library of Australia
Cataloguing-in-Publication data:
Cyberfeminism: Connectivity, critique and creativity.
ISBN 1 875559 68 X.
1. Internet (Computer network)–Social aspects.
2. Internet (Computer network)–Political aspects.
3. Feminist theory. 4. Technology–Social aspects.
5. Technology–Political aspects. 6. Women in technology. I.
Hawthorne, Susan, 1951–. II. Klein, Renate.

303.483082

Acknowledgements

The editors would like to thank all the contributors to this volume. Some waited patiently for the book to come out; others wrote contributions in record time. Many of the contributors have participated in events on the subject of CyberFeminism since 1994.

The Politics of Cyberfeminism Conference in Melbourne in September 1996—the first of its kind in Australia—included presentations by Suniti Namjoshi, Virginia Westwood and Heather Kaufmann, Beryl Fletcher and Josie Arnold. The organising of this conference was assisted by Deakin University, Victoria University and Spinifex Press. A panel on Cyberfeminism at the National Women's Studies Association Conference in Oswego, NY, in 1998, included presentations by Donna Hughes, Scarlet Pollock and Jo Sutton, while Beth Stafford had already participated in a forum at the 6th International Feminist Book Fair in Melbourne in July 1994, and Donna Hughes spoke at the Politics of Radical Feminism Conference in April 1996.

Bandana Pattanaik developed the Feminist Publishers in the Asia Pacific Website between 1996 and 1998. Virginia Westwood and Heather Kaufmann generated our enthusiam in multimedia during 1995, while Carmel Bird shared her many ideas on multimedia with us since 1996. Joan Korenman became a name we learnt first by email in 1995, as the magician at the other end of the Women's Studies ListServ. Suniti Namjoshi insisted that the Spinifex website develop in ways we had never imagined, and the *BabelBuildingSite* remains an innovative concept for publishing electronically. It is stored in the electronic archive of the National Library of Australia. The Babel site gave us the opportunity to hear Kathy Mueller speak about her research into multimedia and games.

Miriam English attended The Politics of Cyberfeminism conference along with many other well-informed participants. We have yet to meet Alesia Montgomery, and we thank her for her speedy co-operation.

Laurel Guymer has come to the rescue on many occasions, sending us information, teaching us new tools and strategies for thriving in the information age. Her enthusiasm for the electronic medium has been infectious.

We'd also like to thank three people not in the book who contributed enormously to our knowledge of the area in the early years. Dale Spender's book *Nattering on the Net* (1995) was the first book published anywhere on the subject of women and cyberspace, and we thank her for her foresight and for discussing it with us as early as 1991. Rye Senjen and Jane Guthrey co-authored *The Internet for Women* (1996) and through this increased our practical skills in the area. In 1996 Suniti Namjoshi and Beryl Fletcher were able to have an IRC link with Rye Senjen, by following the instructions in their not-then published book. Rye and Jane's work gave Spinifex the courage to enter the electronic age.

As always, many individuals have been involved in the production of this book. Liz Flynn became our Research Assistant as we tried to keep ahead of the production schedule. She kept in touch with contributors, wrote entries for the glossary, gathered the images and generally made our lives possible. Libby Fullard was responsible for developing our initial website on CyberFeminism, and in 1999 Petrina Smith has developed that further, while teaching us yet more about website design. Gillian Fulcher edited the manuscript, kept in email contact with all the contributors, and gave us critical feedback where it was needed.

Finally we'd like to thank one another, for inspiration and stamina in and out of cyberspace.

Susan Hawthorne and Renate Klein
Melbourne
June 1999

Editors' note

We have chosen in this book to use the local spellings of the contributors who come from a wide range of predominantly English-speaking countries. This is in recognition of the fact that there are a variety of accepted spellings in the English language, and it is a reflection of how these Englishes are used on the Internet.

Throughout the book you will see the marginal icon ☞ with a chapter number and a name or several names beneath it. This acts like a hypertextual link on a screen and links the underlined word(s) or themes to another essay in the book.

Many of the pieces include images. We would like to thank the following individuals or organisations for permission to reproduce these images:

- Chapter 2: Juliette Breese, first published in *Women'space Magazine*.
- Chapter 3: Softarc, Deakin University for use of FirstClass screen shots. FirstClass is a registered trademark of Softarc Inc..
- Chapter 6: Detail from 'Premenstrual in a postmodern age No. 2', cartoon by Judy Horacek, copyright 1997. Published in *Woman with Altitude*, Hodder Headline; Image of Kyoko Date, *Time Magazine*. August 26, 1996: 75.
- Chapter 10: Laurel Guymer for trapeze image; Susan Hawthorne for clowns image; Helen Killmier for POW outdoor performance image.
- Chapter 11: Josie Arnold, all images.
- Chapter 12: Miriam English for the images: girl 3, vnet, dog; Bruce Damer for image: avvys-brucel; Millennium Interactive for image: summerbg1.
- Chapter 13: Kiera Poelsma for graphics and artwork.
- Chapter 14: Virginia Westwood and Heather Kaufmann for figures and photographs.
- Chapter 17: Suniti Namjoshi for image.
- Chapter 19: Susan Hawthorne for maps.

Every effort has been made to contact copyright holders. and in some instances this has proved impossible. Any copyright holder not acknowledged, or acknowledged incorrectly, should contact the publishers. Copyright on all images, maps, photographs and figures remains with the creators.

Contents

Critique

Creativity

CyberFeminism

Susan Hawthorne and Renate Klein

CyberFeminism is not a fish
CyberFeminism is political
CyberFeminism is not an excuse
CyberFeminism has many tongues[1]

Cyber Words

'Cyber' has become a catch-all prefix in the last decade. It started with cybernetics in the 1960s (Wiener 1968), and William Gibson invented cyberspace in the 1980s (Gibson 1984). We live influenced by cyberculture. You can go cybershopping and pay all your bills through cyberbanking. Your car can be located by cybersurveillance. You can log on and have cybersex. You can become a cyborg, get involved in Cyber-Rights, cyberdemocracy, cyberpunk, cyberdrama. An entire cyberworld. And women are portrayed as cyber-Barbies, cyber-*femmes-fatales* (Millar 1998: 106) and cybersex objects. Women can call themselves cybergrrls or cyberfeminists.

Cyber comes from the same Greek (κϋβερ) word as 'governor' or 'gubernatorial'. Its original meaning is to steer, as a ship's helmsman steers a boat. Its connections to information technology are in the area of <u>navigation</u>, mapping, steering one's way through the World Wide Web. But perhaps, more sinisterly, the govern aspect should not be overlooked. And here the important issue is who is governing?

Arnold 11

---

1. These four lines are adapted from the 100 Antitheses 'What Cyberfeminism is not', developed at the First Cyberfeminist International 1997 at Documenta X, Kassel, Germany, 27 September. <http://duplox.wz-berlin.de/people/s/fem.htm>

The US military invented the Internet, allowed it into the open, no doubt initially encouraged its spread. A myth about the Internet is that it is a self-governing entity. But there are many questions to be raised about this.

CyberFeminism takes up these issues. For although cyberfeminism, itself, has many faces, there are perspectives which we have focused on in this volume. CyberFeminism is a philosophy which acknowledges, firstly, that there are differences in power between women and men specifically in the digital discourse; and secondly, that CyberFeminists want to change that situation. How precisely the power differences are played out, and which elements are highlighted depends on context. Similarly, the strategies chosen by CyberFeminists to challenge this system depends on the interests and expertise of the women engaged in the work. CyberFeminism is political, it is not an excuse for inaction in the real world, and it is inclusive and respectful of the many cultures which women inhabit.

VNS Matrix, an Australian-based group of media artists were among the first to use the term 'cyberfeminism' in the early 1990s. One of the members of VNS Matrix, Julianne Pierce, writes of their origins:

> At the same time as we started using the concept of cyberfeminism, it also began to appear in other parts of the world. It was like a spontaneous meme which emerged at around the same time, as a response to ideas like 'cyberpunk' which were popular at the time. Since then the meme has spread rapidly and is certainly an idea which has been embraced by many women who are engaged with techno theory and practice. <http://www.aec.at/www-ars/matrix.html>

Namjoshi
17

Cyberfeminism, like feminism itself, is a developing philosophy. Three years ago, when this project first started, a Web search brought up ten or twenty items. A search done a month before this book went to press turned up 300 items. Just as there are liberal, socialist, radical and post-modern feminists, so too one finds these positions reflected in the interpretations of cyberfeminism. In the 1970s Shulamith Firestone proposed that reproductive technology would free women from the burdens of childbirth. Reproductive technology, however, did not create more freedom for women, but rather made it easier for the medical profession to further medicalise women's lives (Klein 1989; Hawthorne and Klein 1991). In a similar vein, cyberfeminists such as Sadie Plant (1997: 42–43) suggest that women, because they are 'better culturally and psychologically' prepared for the work habits of the new millennium, will do better than their male counterparts in a more highly technologised world.

Melanie Stewart Millar (1998: 200) defines cyberfeminism critically as:

> A women-centred perspective that advocates women's use of new information and communications technologies for empowerment. Some cyberfeminists see these technologies as inherently liberatory and argue that their development will lead to an end to male superiority because women are uniquely suited to life in the digital age.

Thus Sadie Plant (1996: 182) gestures in the direction of political advancement through uncritical feminist encounters with the cyberworld:

> Cyberfeminism is an insurrection on the part of the goods and materials of the patriarchal world, a dispersed, distributed emergence composed of links between women, women and computers, and communications links, connections and connectionist links.

But libertarian approaches—such as those espoused by Sadie Plant (1997: 37-44)—work only for the privileged. Plant also puts forward the idea that roles defined by gender will become superfluous, resulting in a collapse of the status quo.

The VNS Matrix *Cyberfeminist Manifesto for the 21st Century* epitomises this view:

> we are the virus of the new world disorder/rupturing the symbolic from within/saboteurs of big daddy mainframe/the clitoris is a direct line to the matrix. <sysx.apana.org.au/artists/vns/>

The manifesto is reminiscent of what was euphemistically called 'central core imagery', otherwise known as cunt imagery, which began to emerge from feminist art movements of the 1970s. As Faith

Wilding (1998b) points out, our loss of historical knowledge—in this instance, the loss of knowledge of the history of feminism and of feminist activism—tends to result in repeating known patterns, whether it be Plant's reification of technology (in a way analogous to Firestone's reification of reproductive technology) or the VNS Matrix use of imagery. If cyberfeminism is to be useful politically for women from diverse cultures and regions, it will need to go further than this.[2]

Nancy Paterson takes up some of these issues in her efforts at definition:

> Cyberfeminism as a philosophy has the potential to create a poetic, passionate, political identity and unity without relying on a logic and language of exclusion. It offers a route for reconstructing feminist politics through theory and practice with a focus on the implications of new technology rather than on factors which are divisive. <http://echonyc.com:70/0/Cul/Cyber/paterson>

Similarly, Sheryl Hamilton in a 1995 essay writes:

> . . . cyberfeminism is beginning to explore, and more importantly, beginning to create new worlds, in part through, and in conversation with, digital technologies.[3]

Creativity is indeed an important component of cyberfeminism, but once again, needs further discussion.

What appears to be missing from many considerations of cyberfeminism is the critical aspect.[4] Feminism relies on the ability to critique social norms and constructs. It relies on the ability to see injustice and oppression when they occur, and, importantly, to do something to change these injustices. When sexism or racism occur, feminists expect themselves to speak up. When class, sexuality or ableness are barriers, feminists expect to go into bat for groups who

---

[2.] For critiques of Plant's position see Wilding (1998b), and Rechbach (1998).

[3.] The URL had vanished by 1999, and Sheryl Hamilton had no record of its address.

[4.] Exceptions include Wilding (1998a, 1998b), Millar (1998), Klein (1996).

are discriminated against. Cyberfeminism needs to take on all these challenges in order to become CyberFeminism.

CyberFeminism brings together a range of writers across three main fields in the cyberworld. Activists, who by linking up locally or internationally, create the possibility for co-ordinated political campaigns, or for sharing of knowledge or resources between the women involved.

Critics of cyberculture, or of particular aspects of the cyberworld, make up the middle section of the book. They look at the hype surrounding the technologies, weighing up positive as well as negative aspects. They take on post-human bodies as well as the trading in real women's bodies through electronic prostitution and electronic colonisation.

The third section includes contributions by writers and developers who reflect on the new electronic challenges for creativity in fields as diverse as poetry, virtual reality, fiction and multimedia.

Connectivity

If I had to characterize one quality as the genius of feminist thought, culture, and action, it would be connectivity (Morgan 1990: 53).

An essential component of the emerging global culture is the ability and freedom to connect—to anyone, anytime, anywhere, for anything (Conners 1997, cited in Millar 1998: 151).

Is it possible to be too connected? Perhaps. Perhaps not. But we should be the ones to decide when, how and if we become wired (Millar 1998: 173).

Connectivity is at the heart of feminism. In the 1970s we rallied around the concept of sisterhood, and challenged the patriarchal ideology of women as enemies of one another. We connected the personal to the political. We talked in consciousness-raising (CR) groups, connecting through understanding our similarities and our differences (Wilding 1998b). And despite the fragmenting forces of postmodernism (Brodribb 1992; Klein 1996), economic rationalism and globalisation, women around the world have continued to explore those issues which we have in common, while recognising our diversity. As we have come to understand, focusing on difference alone, fragments us, separates us and disenfranchises us politically.

In the era of CyberFeminism, connectivity has a new meaning. For activists and networkers it is a boon. Emails can be sent to dozens of recipients at once. Internet Relay Chat (IRC) can be used to discuss important issues without having to meet physically, while LISTSERVs can be used to spread information quickly to thousands of subscribers. On the downside, organisations can become the victims of electronic carpet bombing.

orenman 4
Pollock and
Sutton 2
Pattanaik 1

Cyberfeminists have taken to the Internet with great alacrity. Numerous guides have been written for women (Senjen and Guthrey 1996; Cherny and Weise 1996; Gilbert and Kile 1996; Penn 1997). In addition, several early general guides to Internet use were authored by women (Phelps 1995; Lowe 1996; McGuire *et al.* 1997). Some became famous for noting its potential in changing the culture (Spender 1995), some were involved in creating the culture of geekgirls,[5] surfergrrrls (Gilbert and Kile 1996) or netchicks (Sinclair 1995), while yet others were discussing the new opportunities for activists (Pollock 1996). This is because it is possible to get campaigns moving at both international and local levels. Our own awareness was prompted by its use at a conference in Bangladesh in 1993. At this stage we had heard of the Internet, but had not had an opportunity to use it. The conference covered issues raised by the forthcoming UN International Conference on Population and Development. Each day reports from the conference were posted to news groups around the world, and by breakfast the following morning there were responses from people all over the globe. We were impressed by the speed of this, as well as the ability to reach targeted groups. As anyone who has ever tried to maintain an accurate mailing list knows, reaching the right people takes dedication and time.

---

5. <http://www.next.com.au/spyfood/geekgirl.html>

Every campaign feminists have ever thought of, is present on the Internet. From what to do and who to contact for help in the case of sexual assault, to networks of women living in remote areas, to campaigns about education or violence, to networks of lesbians, Women's Studies scholars, women's organisations, environmentalists; and the possibilities are endless.

In 1996, Spinifex began a project to develop an electronic network between feminist publishers in Australia and in <u>Asia</u> (we have since extended this to include feminist publishers in other parts of the world). Bandana Pattanaik took on the task of developing the network. Initially, we faced many delays—snail mail was living up to its name. But after three or four months we began to get responses and established a Home Page on Feminist Publishing in Asia/Pacific. We put up information about the publishing houses and on any books we could get our hands on. Then, after establishing sites for particular publishing houses, Bandana began to do Internet searches and to contact people at the other end of networks focusing on Asia, and as a result the site now includes information on women's organisations in many countries. We set out to establish the Home Page because we felt the need, as feminists, to be involved as activists. Because we had had previous connections with <u>feminist publishing houses in Asia</u>, we knew that the difficulties we faced in promoting our books internationally were more than compounded for many independent publishers in Asia (Butalia and Menon 1995).

Pattanaik

Hawthorne

But there are downsides to connectivity. Information overload can become a major problem (one friend had more than 4000 emails waiting for her after a three-week holiday). Overload can mean that nothing can ever be effectively completed. Connectivity can result in disconnection from the local and the real. Your community becomes your link to virtual worlds, where you can no longer trust experience, since it is all mediated by text or image (Hawthorne 1996b).

The activist potential for the Internet is huge. Activism on a global level, and solely in cyberspace, however, is a rarefied activism if it is not connected with activism on the ground in the <u>local</u> region.

Pattanaik 1
Pollock and
Sutton 2

Without the local, one loses the connection, the heart that makes us become activists. It is comparable to the political without the personal. It is a testing ground for how things work in the real world.

renman 4
Stafford 7
Guymer 3

New information technologies can be used in ways which consciously subvert the dominant knowledge system, but it involves knowing that <u>knowledge</u> and being able to participate in it. It has its uses, but only when it is combined with politics, knowledge and passion for the local, a creative approach and an understanding that any information loaded on to the Internet is public property and can be used or misused by anyone. Such an awareness creates boundaries.

The Internet is a powerful force for networking, and for sharing of knowledge and resources. But it is also a technology originally intended for the military and for global domination. In our communities we are faced with the question of whether to use the

Mont-
gomery 5
Stafford 7
wthorne 6

technology or not. There are many benefits, so long as we bear in mind some of the <u>downsides</u>. Critical is a resistance to total immersion in the technology which results in detachment from the world, rather than an engagement with it.

When connectivity becomes the speed of your modem, or the number of Internet sites, or chat rooms or mailing lists you subscribe to, then disconnection from the real is not far away. The frustration is that just as we are beginning to consolidate the 'connectivity' to which Robin Morgan refers—the collective remembering of women —along comes a technology which threatens to annihilate it.

Critique

Cyberfeminists are offering important critiques of the medium. As Dale Spender has noted, 'for every feminist issue in the real world, the same issues apply in the cyberworld' (Spender 1996). And more. For cyberspace raises new issues as well as old. Issues to do with the

Mont-
gomery 5
wthorne 6

allocation of resources for the poor and the <u>marginalised</u>, the experience of time and space, of what is public or private, of the body, the community and global economics. And where issues overlap, cyberspace gives them a new twist.

Although cyberfeminists love their computers, they are not content simply to play with the new toys, but to make use of them for political purposes and to develop <u>critiques of their abuse</u> and problems. Bandana Pattanaik notes in her page on Networking with Asia that:

Klein 9
Hughes 8

> When I did a net search of Filipina women, all that came up was thumbnail pictures of Filipina women who 'like American men'. I was angry and disgusted. If you do a search now and get to see our pages on Isis and Gabriela[6] we would feel that our voice of protest has been heard. This is the political purpose of the project (Pattanaik 1997).

Donna Hughes analyses some of the many sites for prostitution on the Internet, and develops a critique on how these new cyberpimps operate. Her analysis points to the systematic sharing of information, spread via the Internet sometimes immediately after the man's use of a prostituted woman or child.

Developing critiques involves understanding the forces shaping the new technologies, knowing the ways in which cyberspace is being <u>colonised</u>, and knowing the ways in which these systems, like any other in global patriarchy, can be used to trace the movements of new political forces, of subversion among the citizenry, and of any individual who has ever logged into the system. Big Brother (or Sister) no longer needs to watch you with cameras, instead you type in all your personal information and they come and browse whenever they like.

Arnold 11

Another concern is the extent to which moral detachment becomes the norm, that the Internet is mistaken for the community and that the newest information is treated as 'truth'.

Detachment may be prefigured by a confusion between self and machine, a troubling confusion if it is taken out into the real world. Haraway (1991: 180) proposes that the machine is 'an aspect of our

---

6. The Isis and Gabriela pages can be found on the Feminist Publishers in Asia/Pacific website at: <<u>http://www.spinifexpress.com.au/welcomeasia/htm</u>>

embodiment' and as a result Haraway sees the machines as thoroughly benign.

This position is challenged, by us. The machines may threaten our Selves, they may require us to be other than we are. And we already have too long a history of this. The <u>cyborg</u> may not be a figure of liberation, since it does not create an embodied and localised ethic (Klein 1996). Christine Boyer asks:

Klein 9

Haw-
thorne 10

> Why, in these postmodern times have we failed so completely to arrive at a 'politicization of aesthetics'. . . ? Why have we refused to develop a new political awareness suitable to an age of electro-optical reproduction—an engaged, embodied position that would utilize our new technology in a liberating and critical manner? (Boyer 1996: 120).

Could it be because the destructive trajectory of the twentieth century war-machines and war-driven economic theories and practices (the Bretton Woods institutions of the IMF, World Bank and GATT) is taking us down a one-way path which leads to further and further fragmentation of bodies, individuals, families, communities, nations and the globe (Klein 1996; Hawthorne 1996a; Millar 1998)? Could it be that post-modernism in all its incarnations as an intellectual movement has glorified this fragmentation?

This trajectory has resulted in wholesale destruction of the environment, of knowledge systems and of people, in its disregard for heart and its valorisation of ersatz experience, simulations, virtuality, and machines which tell us of things we once gauged by listening to the body, the air, the atmosphere. Our physical lives in the well-off parts of the world are better, but the level of consumerism we participate in has its price. And immersion in the Internet, virtuality and cyberspace also have their price.

Mark Dery finishes his insightful book on cyberculture with the following reflection:

> . . . a shadow of a doubt remains, nagging at the edge of awareness—the doubt that once our bodies have been 'deanimated', our gray matter nibbled away at by infinitesimal nanomachines and encoded in computer memory, we might awake to discover that an ineffable something had gotten lost in translation. In that moment, we might discover ourselves

thinking of Gabe, in *Synners*, who unexpectedly finds himself face-to-face with his worst fear while roaming disembodied through cyberspace:

> *I can't remember what it feels like to have a <u>body</u>.* . . . He wanted to scream in frustration, but he had nothing to scream with (Dery 1996: 319).

Klein 9

Creativity

Cyberfeminism is a new concept made possible by the development of the new electronic culture. It is a field which has a huge impact on the <u>educational</u> and publishing sectors.

Guymer 3
Korenman
Westwood
and Kauf-
mann 15

We became excited about the possibilities of the electronic medium in 1991 when Dale Spender first spoke about the research which led her to write *Nattering on the Net*. By the time we, at Spinifex, had published the book we had also developed an interest in multimedia and CD-ROMs. Throughout 1995 we were part of a small group which developed a concept for a feminist CD-ROM[7] and tendered this for funding on two occasions to the then Federal government's program, Australia on CD. We were shortlisted twice, but not funded. Indeed, no CD-ROM on women was. In spite of this, the development process served as a useful learning experience as we were thrown in to come up with workable solutions. Concept development turned out to be a thrilling experience. Interactive multimedia conceptual structures were exciting and mind-stretching. It was associative, lateral, and the pathways and matrices of connections created the possibility of a <u>multidimensional</u> approach. The project had an organic feel and the group interactions and processes involved were endlessly fascinating.

Mueller 13
Bird 16
Westwood
and Kauf-
mann 15

---

7. The group consisted of Lorna Hannan, educationalist, political and arts activist; Heather Kaufmann, ESL teacher and researcher, multimedia developer from Protea Textware; Renate Klein, Women's Studies researcher and academic, activist, writer and publisher at Spinifex Press; Virginia Westwood, scientist, information technology analyst, self-taught computer programmer and multimedia developer from Protea Textware; and Susan Hawthorne, writer, arts activist and performer, academic and publisher at Spinifex Press. The project we developed was entitled, The Community of Women.

However, since we didn't get funded, the project had to be shelved and we began to think of other possibilities. We were soon convinced that Spinifex Press needed to get a Home Page operating, and to do so quickly.

In 1996 we developed our Home Page so that it would include all the titles in our catalogue, as well as news, events, and links to authors' Home Pages. In addition we had committed to presenting the final chapter of Suniti Namjoshi's *Building Babel* (1996) on our Web site.[8] This chapter invites readers to contribute their ideas and responses to the novel. The novel explores the notion that the Internet is an analogue of the process of <u>developing culture</u>. This is an important insight and one which feminists—and cyberfeminists— are constantly engaging with. It is important because the culture we develop—whether it be electronic or political or economic— determines the way we interact, and so the invitation to readers asks them to engage with the concept of culture and suggest some of its components. To date we have received poems, stories about political action, music, visuals, animated text and a range of other responses. What we hope for is a continuing stream of creativity which challenges viewers/readers to consider how they might take responsibility for the future.

Namjoshi
17, 18

The beauty of the Internet is that it allows creative responses from readers around the world, and this gives a certain unpredictability and excitement to the project.

The electronic medium opens up possibilities for new forms of writing. Hyperfiction and hypertext poetry are developing, and like any new art form the quality is still very uneven. But in our imaginations the hypertext novel already lives. As a matrix of carefully woven ideas which one could shake out like a quilt, filled with colour and detail, some of which emerges only slowly, and only if the reader/viewer/listener engages with the work, spends time following the links. There are programs such as Storyspace, Storyvision and

---

8. The Home Page can be visited at <<u>http://spinifexpress.com.au/babelbuildingsite.htm</u>>

Inspiration which can provide a structure for creativity, but Internet hyperlinks are still the most flexible and open-ended form. Or the writer can move to creating multimedia-based stories using programs such as Macromedia Director, Cosmoworld, Shockwave, Real Media, Quicktime 3.

Hypertext can incorporate text, visuals—both still and moving—sound and virtual elements. It promises to bring a new generation of art forms. The question of whether these art forms will speak to feminists depends on the extent to which we are involved in developing the electronic culture.

Hypertext allows the writer to create a multilayered, nonlinear narrative. You need a computer to read hypertext, but the writer does not need a computer to create it—it's done in the mind. The only difficulty is getting it across to others. But oral traditions—the Bible, the Talmud and fictions like those of Monique Wittig, Suniti Namjoshi, Susan Griffin, Nathalie Sarrault, Virginia Woolf—have long ago explored the terrain that hypertext is entering through a new medium. What the electronic medium allows for is <u>transparency of process</u>, not readily transmitted through other forms of text (e.g. print, spoken, sung).

Namjoshi
Bird 16
Haw-
thorne 19

There are also Virtual Reality Modelling Language (VRML) programs available on the Internet, which, with some time, we could all learn. A knowledge of VRML would allow us to put our ideas, images and representations into the virtual world. We could create the virtual worlds of our imaginations. Imaginable things could be produced: Suniti Namjoshi's (1996) <u>Babel</u> could be built,[9] or Beryl Fletcher's (1996) computer game of Alice's life as invented by <u>Pixel</u> could be developed. We could invent avatars and the worlds of our <u>imaginations</u>; we could invent games, play a wide range of <u>roles</u>, and immerse ourselves in other personae.

Namjoshi 1

Fletcher 1

English 12

Mueller 13

But even here, in the world of creativity, a critical perspective is necessary. The idea that anything goes in electronic media, is a

---

[9.] For more on this, visit the Babel Building Site on the Spinifex Home Page at <<u>http://spinifexpress.com.au</u>>

popular one. But as with any medium, it can be put to negative use. Ray Bradbury in his 1954 novel, *Fahrenheit 451*[10] imagines the possibility of every household being fitted with huge screens in which the populace immerse themselves. Their friends are screen friends, and these screen or virtual friends keep the people distracted from the real and terrifying events of their culture. That such outcomes are possible, has recently gained momentum in discussions around violence, the use of guns, and ready access to information and games on the Internet. Kathy Mueller's discussion of games and Miriam English's invention of worlds tread this line between immersion and reality, and perhaps, like Brenda Laurel (1998), they can create an alternate vision, one which does not rely on violence for its existence.

Cyberculture is only as diverse and interesting, or as violent and boring, as the people who contribute to it. It's about numbers and critical mass. In its best form it can provide direct interaction between like minds, potentially bypassing the main routes of the male-dominated media and without interference from the gatekeepers. It can promote communication across cultures, and between people of very different social groupings, because they meet as minds first, and only later, if ever, begin to reveal aspects of their identity (age, sex, country, culture, religion, race, sexuality, ability, etc.).

Connectivity provides us with the means for communicating, acting together in the real world, and for sharing information and resources. Critical engagement enables us to develop discernment, to rise above the hype and seductiveness of this new and powerful medium. And creativity should not be underplayed in the electronic culture, as it could be an important source and sustenance for social change in the future.

---

10. 451 degrees Fahrenheit is the temperature at which paper burns. Books have been banned in this dystopic society and replaced by a centrally-controlled screen culture.

References

Boyer, M. Christine. 1996. *CyberCities: Visual Perception in the Age of Electronic Communication*. New York: Princeton Architectural Press.

Bradbury, Ray. 1954. *Fahrenheit 451*. London: Rupert Hart-Davis.

Brodribb, Somer. 1992. *Nothing Mat(t)ers: A feminist critique of post-modernism*. Melbourne: Spinifex Press.

Butalia, Urvashi and Ritu Menon. 1995. *Making a Difference: Feminist publishing in the south*. Chestnut Hill, Massachusetts: Bellagio Publishing Network, Bellagio Studies in Publishing No. 5.

Cadigan, Pat. 1991. *Synners*. New York: Bantam Spectra.

Cherny, Lynn and Elizabeth Reba Weise. (Eds.), 1996. *Wired Women: Gender and new realities in cyberspace*. Seattle, WA: The Seal Press.

Dery, Mark. 1996. *Escape Velocity: Cyberculture at the end of the century*. London: Hodder and Stoughton.

Firestone, Shulamith. 1970. *The Dialectics of Sex*. London: Paladin.

Fletcher, Beryl. 1996. *The Silicon Tongue*. Melbourne: Spinifex Press.

Gibson, William. 1984. *Neuromancer*. New York: Ace Books.

Gilbert, Laurel and Crystal Kile. 1996. *Surfergrrrls: Look, Ethel! An internet guide for us*. Seattle: The Seal Press.

Hamilton, Sheryl. Not available. Pers. comm. 1999.

Haraway, Donna. 1991. A Cyborg Manifesto. In Donna Haraway *Simians, Cyborgs, and Women: The reinvention of nature*. New York and London: Routledge.

Hawthorne, Susan. 1996a. From Theories of Indifference to a Wild Politics. In Diane Bell and Renate Klein (Eds.). *Radically Speaking: Feminism reclaimed*. Melbourne: Spinifex Press; London: Zed Press.

Hawthorne, Susan. 1996b. Virtual and Real Worlds. *Metro Magazine*. No. 108, November.

Hawthorne, Susan and Renate Klein. (Eds.), 1991. *Angels of Power and other reproductive creations*. Melbourne: Spinifex Press.

Klein, Renate. (Ed.), 1989. *Infertility: Women Speak Out about their Experiences of Reproductive Medicine*. London and Sydney: Unwin Hyman.

Klein, Renate. 1996. (Dead) Bodies Floating in Cyberspace. In Diane Bell and Renate Klein (Eds.), *Radically Speaking: Feminism reclaimed*. Melbourne: Spinifex Press; London: Zed Press.

Laurel, Brenda. 1998. *Computers as Theatre*. New York: Addison-Wesley Publishing Company.

Lowe, Sue. 1996. *On-line in Oz*. Sydney: Addison-Wesley Publishing Company.

McGuire, Mary, Linda Stilborne, Melinda McAdams and Laurel Hyatt. (Eds.), 1997. *The Internet Handbook for Writers, Researchers and Journalists*. Toronto: Trifolium.

Millar, Melanie Stewart. 1998. *Cracking the Gender Code: Who rules the wired world*. Toronto: Second Story Press.

Morgan, Robin. 1990. *The Demon Lover: On the Sexuality of Terrorism*. London: Methuen.

Namjoshi, Suniti. 1996. *Building Babel*. Melbourne: Spinifex Press.

Pattanaik, Bandana. 1997. *Feminist Publishing in Asia*.
    <http://www.spinifexpress.com.au/welcomeasia.htm>

Paterson, Nancy. 1994. *Cyberfeminism.*
 <http://echonyc.com:70/0/Cul/Cyber/paterson>
Penn, Shana. 1997. *The Women's Guide to the Wired World: A user-friendly handbook and research directory.* New York: The Feminist Press.
Phelps, Katherine. 1995. *Surf's Up: Internet Australian style.* Melbourne: Mandarin.
Pierce, Julianne. *VNS Matrix.* n.d.
 <http://www.aec.at/www-ars/matrix.html>
Plant, Sadie. 1996. On the Matrix: Cyberfeminist Simulations. In Rob Shiels (Ed.), *Cultures of Internet.* London: Sage.
Plant, Sadie. 1997. *Zeros + Ones: Digital women + the new technoculture.* London: Fourth Estate.
Pollock, Scarlet. 1996. What Do Women Activists Do Online? In Scarlet Pollock and Jo Sutton. *Women'space* 4. April/May.
 <http://www.softaid.net/cathy/vsister/w-space/womspce.html>
Rechbach, Barbara. 1998, Dec 1. *What is Cyberfeminism?*
 <http://ma.hrc.wmin.ac.uk/ma.student.barbara.1.db>
Senjen, Rye and Jane Guthrey. 1996. *The Internet for Women.* Melbourne: Spinifex Press.
Sinclair, Carla. 1995. *Net Chick: A Smart-Girl Guide to the Wired World.* New York: Henry Holt and Company.
Spender, Dale. 1995. *Nattering on the Net: Women, power and cyberspace.* Melbourne: Spinifex Press.
Spender, Dale. 1996. Is the Internet a Feminist Issue? Paper presented at The Politics of Cyberfeminism Conference, Deakin University, Burwood Campus, 21 September.
VNS Matrix. n.d. <sysx.apana.org.au/artists/vns/>
Wiener, Norbert. 1968. *Cybernetics: Control and communication in the animal and the machine.* 2nd Edition. Cambridge, MA: MIT Press.
Wilding, Faith. 1998a. Notes on the Political Condition of Cyberfeminism. *Art Journal*, Summer. <http://www-art.cfa.cmu.edu/www-wilding/wherefem.html>
Wilding, Faith. 1998b. Where is the Feminism in Cyberfeminism? *n.paradoxa; international feminist art journal* #3, London.
 <http://www-art.cfa.cmu.edu/www-wilding/wherefem.html>

Connectivity

one

Home and the World: The Internet as a personal and political tool

Bandana Pattanaik

This morning there was a message on my desk from RAWA, the Revolutionary Association of the Women of Afghanistan. RAWA is the only feminist organisation of Afghanistan which is fighting for the human rights of Afghan women. They have requested us to send them a message of solidarity which will be read at their International Women's Day celebration. I look at the long list of signatures below the message. There are about a hundred women and men from practically all over the world who have signed to show their solidarity with RAWA. As I sit in front of my computer in Thailand and try to compose an email message, I have no doubt that it will reach the RAWA office in Islamabad in time for the celebration even though there is only a day left until International Women's Day. So much of my professional communication is now done via email that I am beginning to take such immediacy for granted. In the women's NGO[1] I work for in Thailand now, we receive approximately fifty emails every day and send just as many, or even more. We network with women's groups from practically every corner of the world. We exchange information, initiate signature campaigns and send letters of petition. We also visit each others' Web sites and often make new contacts through such visits. It is difficult to think back to a time when there were no such things as emails and Web sites.

And yet I started using the Internet only three years ago. Coincidentally, over the last three years I have also done some travelling. While I lived in Australia for nearly three years, a large

---

[1.] Non-Government Organisation.

part of my professional and personal life during that time depended on news from Asia. Not surprisingly, India remained the main point of reference, a place which, more than ever before, sharply defined itself as home; perhaps because I had a sense that I would be away from there for some years. But my work also made it imperative that I establish new contacts in other locations in Asia and look for hitherto undocumented information. Going against the grain of established patterns of research has not been easy for anyone. The Internet, however, proved to be an invaluable tool in my attempt at charting an alternative circuit of knowledge production. Long periods of frustration and anxiety were compensated for by moments of unexpected joy.

~

In this essay I will describe my experience of using the Internet: as a person away from her familiar world, as a technology-shy woman thrown into a job which required knowledge of new information technology, and as a researcher exploring an area on which there was little documented information.

Three years ago I was teaching English Literature in a university college in Hyderabad, India. I did not have much to do with computers at that time although I was aware of the computer craze around me. Most of my students were opting for advanced level computer courses. Every city, even small towns in India, had begun to boast several computer-training centres. Middle-class parents were buying PCs in a panic lest their children lag behind. But for most of my friends and for me, the computer was a young people's thing. As far as we were concerned, it was a machine for word processing. My friends who did a lot of writing had already acquired their PCs. Since I did not do much writing, I could see no reason for acquiring a computer and learning how to use it. It was not so much my location therefore, as my profession and personal habits which were responsible for my non-technological life.

And then, towards the end of 1995, I felt that I needed a break from full-time teaching. I also wanted a complete change of scene and toyed with the idea of living in some other country for a while.

Joining a research programme in a foreign university seemed like a viable option. There was no specific reason for choosing Australia, but no one I knew had been there and I just wanted to be different. So in March 1996, on a cold autumn morning, I landed in Melbourne.

After a break of more than a decade, I was a student again: as they say in Australia, a mature age student without any support system. I was in a new country where everything, even the trees and the sky, looked unfamiliar. There was no one I could call a friend. However, universities around the world do share many common features. Having spent a major part of my life in academia, both as a student and as a teacher, I knew, for example, that the university library could be an excellent refuge. It was wonderful to be able to read again without having to worry about teaching. But books, trusted companions though they are, could not replace the people I had left behind. I missed my friends, my students, in short the entire network which had grown around me over a period of time. I could not afford long-distance telephone calls. And because replies took an inordinately long time to come, I feared that most of my letters were not reaching their destination.

It was at this point that I got my computer account, a letter from the Information Technology Services department of the university with my email address and password. Until then, I had been putting off the visit to the computer lab, telling myself that I could go there just before the first assignment was due, that I would write everything in longhand first and then it would be just a matter of typing it out. I did know a little about emails because some educational institutions and government departments in India had already got their email connections by mid-1995; and while leaving Hyderabad, I had noted down some email addresses for contacting friends.

I took the ITS letter and a diskette and made my first trip to the university computer lab. The letter had instructions on how to set up one's own <u>email</u>—but I was hoping that there would be someone to help me out. I noticed a woman instructor in the lab that afternoon. After some half-hearted attempts to set up my own account, I went and asked if she could help me. She looked at the printed

Guymer 3

instructions—clearly wondering why I wasn't able to follow them—
and came over to set it up for me. She looked brisk and very efficient,
just the kind of woman I would have associated with technology, the
no-nonsense hi-tech kind. Within minutes my account was set up
and I was told that I could now send emails wherever I liked. I sat
down and typed a long, miserable letter to a friend in Hyderabad.

In the following days, the computer lab became a favourite
stopover. It was wonderful to open the in-box and find messages
waiting for me. None of my friends in India had their personal email
addresses at that time. I knew that, for them, the process of sending
or receiving an email was quite cumbersome: it usually involved a
trip to the local service provider or to someone whose organisation
had an email connection. Some public telephone and fax booths had
started adding emails to their list of services.[2] Often, when going
there my friends found that there was a blackout so the computer did
not work. Many of these email centres did not allow the customers to
use their machine so one just had to leave the message with them
and trust that they would both send it and then ring when a reply
arrived. Obviously there was no privacy. Despite these hassles, emails
were attractive to us because they took much less time than a letter
and cost less than a fax or a telephone call.

From the email to the World Wide Web was only a small step for
me. Homesickness was, once again, the main motive behind my
netsurfing. Using some clues like the names of universities or
research organisations in the US or the UK, I was able to renew
contact with friends I'd lost touch with. I also used to do searches by
typing in random, mostly India-related words. Those searches used
to bring up a lot of irrelevant, sometimes completely unrelated
material, but that was also how I found a mailing list to discuss
South Asian literature, a site which posted an Indian news digest

---

[2.] Until recently there was a near government monopoly on the servers in India. vsnl net (Videsh
Sanchar Nigam Limited) or ernet (Education and Research Net) were the only isps (Internet
Service Providers). In November 1998 the Indian government made a decision to give licences
to private service providers so there are possibly more players in the field now.

and the wonderful *South Asian Women's Network* (<u>SAWNET</u>): <<u>http:</u> <u>www.umiacs.umd.edu/usrs/sawweb/sawnet</u>>. Most of the India-related sites at that time had been developed in the US and were being updated there. What struck me in many of the sites, was the nostalgia of the people away from what they still thought of as their homelands, and the desire to construct identities and build communities on the basis of common interests.

Pollock and Sutton 2

While the virtual world was helping me to maintain a link with the real world I had left behind, my immediate reality was getting difficult to cope with. Given the currency exchange rates, it was imperative that I find some job to support myself in Melbourne. But nearly three months were over and I had found no paid work; I was beginning to doubt my skills and abilities. It was desperation which made me send an email to Susan Hawthorne at Spinifex. I wasn't sure what I could do there, but since I liked what they had published I thought it might be good to know them anyway. Email seemed a less intrusive mode of making contact than a telephone call, impersonal and yet immediate. A few days later I received a reply, we had a meeting and to my relief I was offered a job. So desperate was I for work, that any work would have been fine; however, not in my wildest imagination had I hoped to design a Web site!

The Spinifex project began in July 1996.[3] Initiated by Susan Hawthorne, it aimed to set up an electronic forum which small, independent feminist publishers from the Asia Pacific region would be able to use to publicise their books and communicate with each other. Although I was keenly interested in women's writing, partic-ularly those of marginalised women, I did not know much about feminist publishing houses in Asia. Most of the women authors whom I'd read were either published by mainstream publishing houses or by feminist publishing houses in the West. Kali for women was the only Asian feminist publishing house I knew of and I was not sure if there were any others in the region. I was keen to find out. From Susan I learned of a few others such as Narigrantha

---

[3.] For a detailed report on the process of this project see Pattanaik and Hawthorne (1997).

Prabartana and ASR. From talking with her, I became convinced of the political relevance of such a project. The technical aspect of the project did not make any sense to me, but I decided not to worry about it at that point. Our immediate task was to contact feminist publishers in Asia and find out whether they thought this kind of a project was relevant to them.

When months went by and we did not receive any replies, it was difficult to avoid a sense of futility. In addition to feeling personally responsible for the failure, I also started worrying about the irrelevance and arrogance of such a project. I felt that, given my background, I should have realised that an electronic network would be a ridiculously outlandish concept in the third world. I thought that it would be a long time before the women's groups in Asia started using the new information technology: I am glad that I was proved wrong.

Responses started to trickle in by the end of 1996, and when we decided to make a small beginning with whatever information we had, we received encouraging feedback from many people. The academics and activists in Melbourne whom I spoke to regarding the project, readily offered their contacts in the Asian region. They were as fascinated with the simple and small Web site as we were. Women's publishing groups in some parts of Asia—who could not even access the World Wide Web at that time—were happy to send copies of their books for use on the Web site. Their enthusiasm provided us with the moral support and the rationale to continue. In retrospect it became clear that their silence hadn't derived from suspicion of the technology or disagreement with the project's assumptions. All the factors responsible for the initial freeze in the project were, in fact, justifications of the need for such a project. As Urvashi Butalia and Ritu Menon point out:

> The very first problem arises with lack of information on what is being produced and by whom and where; currently there is no source of information on this, either within each country, or regionally (Butalia and Menon 1995: 60).

Since there was no updated directory of Asian feminist publishing groups we used a variety of sources to contact groups whom we thought might be bringing out publications. Many of our letters had not reached their destination simply because, in addition to unreliable postal services, the addresses we used were sometimes no longer valid. Some groups who replied very late told us that they were terribly short-staffed and had been unable to make time for a letter. But no one had any doubt that the Internet could be used for feminist networking.

By January 1997, the feminist publishing in the Asia Pacific section of Spinifex's homepage had a fairly good number of entries from the entire region.[4] We had been able to show that women's publishing is also active outside the developed world. We had succeeded in putting the new information technology to political use. Once the project got underway, I started enjoying the serendipitous way of finding information. A search which had brought up thumbnail pictures of Thai mail-order brides also had an entry on *Voices of Thai Women*, a feminist newsletter. There was an email address below, and that was how I got in touch with Foundation for Women, the feminist group in Bangkok. One day I found a query on the South Asian Women's Net mailing list. I didn't know the answer to the query but from the last two letters of the email I realised that the person was located in Nepal.[5] I had been wanting to get in touch with Anju Chetri and Susan Maskey, the two women who had started *Asmita*, the feminist publication centre in Nepal, but I had no contact details. I sent an email to the person who had posted a query on the mailing list. To my delight there was a reply almost instantly with the necessary contact details. This aspect of the Internet is the one which fascinates me most. No amount of technical explanation has been able to diminish the almost childlike joy which I experience

---

4. The site can be accessed at <http://www.spinifexpress.com.au/welcomeasia.htm>

5. The last two letters usually indicate the name of the country. For example, *np* is for Nepal and *in* for India. But one can also have an address ending with *org* or *com* which does not give the person's residence.

when I send an email to a remote corner of the world and a reply arrives within minutes.

Questions regarding what constitutes legitimate feminist knowledge and what role geographical locations and economic realities play in the production of such knowledge were to occupy me in the next few months. I found it ironic that, although a substantial amount of material pertaining to women's issues is published in the so-called third world, not many people know about them. And even when they do, such publications rarely find their way into academia. In order to explore the issues further, I needed to strengthen the contacts I had established with women's groups in Asia during the Spinifex project. While working on my thesis on feminist publishing in Asia, I noticed the rapid growth of Internet in the region. A large part of my correspondence could be done through email. I also noticed that there were many Asian sites that had started to be developed and maintained in Asia.[6] The mailing lists related to third world women had also started having members who were physically located there.

In March 1998 I travelled to Korea for a conference. I was amazed by the level of Internet use by women's groups there. My friends at the <u>Korean Women's Institute</u> told me that a lot of their correspondence was done via email and they also used the World Wide Web for accessing information. A couple of months later my work took me to Nepal. There I met up with Susan Maskey and Anju Chetri of Asmita Publication and Resource Centre with whom I'd had only email correspondence until then. It may sound paradoxical, but for me one of the pleasures of dabbling with the virtual world is that it has enabled me to make new friends in real life. There are some people in Melbourne I would never have got to know but for the Spinifex project. I have also been fortunate in travelling to places and meeting up with people I had contacted electronically for my research. In fact I have not been able to understand why some people

renman 4

---

6. Possibly they were already there. My ignorance of Korean, Japanese or Chinese must have made me overlook them.

are worried that the virtual is replacing the real. Nor will I ever be able to comprehend the desire of those people who want to become cyborgs. For me and for many other women I know, the Internet is a fast and economical way to communicate with others who share our interests and politics, as well as to access relevant information. And perhaps because we link up with like-minded people there is always a possibility we'll meet in some conference or workshop. We do not have the time, need or inclination to netsurf to meet people only in cyberspace.

Within Asia, countries differ greatly in the level of Internet use. For example, in Korea, Japan, Malaysia, Thailand and Singapore, it is much easier to access the World Wide Web. In Nepal, India, Laos and Burma and many other countries, on the other hand—barring a few commercial places—the World Wide Web is unavailable to most users. In these countries, email is also not very efficient. In India, for instance, the telephone lines are unreliable and blackout is not infrequent in many places which affects the immediacy. In spite of these handicaps, email is still considered a more reliable and certainly much faster mode of communication than the existing postal system. It is also very economical. A friend who lives in China tells me that it costs her almost the same to make a call from China to Hong Kong as it does to the US, and that the connections to Hong Kong are unreliable. Moreover, an email costs a fraction of the money one would spend on overseas calls.

While in India in October 1998, I found that the newspapers had started special columns related to the World Wide Web. There were also slots allocated on the television to discuss issues related to the Internet. The significant difference between the articles I read in the Western and the Indian press, was that, in the latter, most people had either technical questions or they were worried about the abuse of the Internet by criminals and undiscriminating people; I did not hear anyone talking about machines substituting people or cyber-space taking over reality. People had not started worrying about cyber obsession, perhaps simply because it was still not easy to netsurf from home. The number of email places had increased and many people now had contact with a service provider who would take handwritten mail and deliver the reply to their residence. Some people also had their own email connection from home.

Since February 1999 I have been working with a women's NGO in Bangkok. We work with women's groups all over the world. We have several collaborative projects in the Southeast Asian region and it is extremely cost-effective to use the Internet for networking. It has also proved very useful to network with people who live under media censorship. For example, using email we have been able to freely exchange information with our colleagues in Burma where telephone calls are censored (though the Internet is not completely uncensored).[7] Compared to the advantages of email, its hassles are minimal. Occasionally we do receive some silly messages. Some days ago there was an email from someone who wanted to tell us the secrets of a happy married life. We just ignore those messages. And although we use the Internet for a large part of our networking, we are not completely dependent on it. We still use all other modes of communication. Only one of our computers has a modem. One of my colleagues checks the emails, prints them out and hands them to the addressee. We all do our emails, sometimes a quick scribble on paper, or we save it on a diskette which she sends on our behalf. Instead of having everyone's computer connected to modems and forwarding mail to everyone, we let one person sort the mail for everyone. Information of general interest is posted on the bulletin board or circulated.

The Internet has had a phenomenal growth in the last few years. It is much easier to access information from the World Wide Web now. Almost every educational and research institute in the developed world, and many from the developing region, have their own Web sites. Many international NGOs have Web sites which can be used by other smaller NGOs. There are reliable databases on every

---

7. Recently there was an outrage in Singapore when users came to know that the country's largest service provider, singnet, had scanned its customers' computers in a recent anti-hacking operation without telling them.

conceivable topic. Many new countries are getting connected every day. Bhutan, for example, has its own Internet service, Druk, online now. Compared with a few years ago, cyberspace no longer feels like a North American schoolboy's playing field. I would not go as far as saying that it has reached the grass roots women and men because this technology depends on the telephone system of the country, and not everyone everywhere has a telephone, let alone a computer with a modem. But it has made networking among like-minded people much easier than any other mode. The other day I received an email from a women's group in Sri Lanka asking us if they could have a link to our Web site. Looking at the address, I realised that it was CENWOR, one of the groups I had contacted from Spinifex in 1996. They have their own Web site now, and in fact they are working on a similar project to establish an electronic network with national and international NGOs.

The Web has made it possible for people to keep track of personal and political news from every part of the world. I remember my discomfort after the nuclear testing in India in 1998. I was in Australia at that time and the media reports, both in the newspaper and on television, sounded very patronising to me. It looked as if the Big Brothers in the entire Western world were chiding and punishing the immature, irresponsible Indians. The media images were of people rejoicing on the streets of Indian cities. I was strongly opposed to the nuclear tests and I knew that there must be many people in India who shared my views. I wanted to know the reaction of those people whom the Western media had chosen to ignore. Here again, the Internet came to my aid. Someone I knew put me in touch with a mailing list which was circulating writings by several people in India and Pakistan who were deeply upset by their politicians' decision.

A few weeks ago, out of curiosity, I did a net search under *women+Asia*. I had used the same words three years ago and all I had got were <u>pornographic sites</u> advertising Asian women. This time, two similar disgusting sites came up among the first ten results. If it was a personal pleasure for me to find the *Feminist Publishing in Asia*

Hughes 8

site come up in a random search it was nothing short of a political victory to see the other Asian feminist sites. Because this technology makes authoring or creating easy there are many undesirable sites too. And if it has made networking among women activists easy, it has also brought criminals together. I think that creating relevant, women-friendly sites and linking up with each other is a very effective way of launching our protest against the anti-women sites on the Web. I do not know if it makes sense technically, but I think that if the number of feminist sites increase then the anti-women ones just will not show up.

~

I began this essay on a personal note describing how the immediacy of the electronic mode of communication had helped me get over homesickness. I have often wondered if this technology has changed the way I communicate with people. Some of my friends have been concerned that email has affected the art of letter writing. Emails, they feel, can never replace letters. In fact, some of them see the immediacy as a negative point, something that does not allow one to be reflective and serious. I prefer to see it as just one more way of communication which has its peculiarities like every other mode. I think people also vary in how they prefer to communicate. My grandmother, for example, who is a wonderful storyteller, has never written a letter in her life. She has used her literacy to read, and chosen to communicate through speech. When I left home for the first time, for higher studies in another town, she told me to write to her regularly. And for years I have written to her without ever expecting a reply. Yet when I go home on my holidays, she is the one who does not stop talking. Her eyesight is so poor now that she can not read any more. But she still waits for my letters and tells me that she always knows when a letter is going to arrive. In my childhood I had seen her coming out to the courtyard when she heard a crow cawing in the morning. She would stand in the courtyard and ask the crow, 'So are we getting a letter today? Or is it a visitor? Whose letter is it going to be?' She would then go inside and get a handful of rice and put it on the ground for the crow. She would get the answer to her queries from the way the crow pecked the rice. As a child I used to stand and watch this fascinating conversation between a bird and a human being. I really believed that they communicated with each other. And today, when the little bird on my computer says, 'You have new mail', I think of my grandmother. My mother, on the other hand, has always been a prolific letter writer. She would read the letters several times and sometimes take several afternoons to write one letter. All her brothers were overseas and she eagerly waited for their news. It might be the tropical climate which made the letters literally look as if they had travelled a long distance. The postman always arrived during midday when my mother was busy in the kitchen. She would take out a pin from her hair, open the letter while keeping an eye on the cooking pot, read it quickly and put it away under the pillow in her bedroom. Late in the afternoon, she would find time to read it again and then, again, whenever she felt like it. We did not have a telephone at home in my childhood but when we got one she did not really take to it. When I call my mother now, I do all the talking. I often tell her that I call to listen to her silences. Similarly, some of my friends use emails only for work-related communication. There are others who used to see themselves as 'not the letter writing type' but who have taken to emails in a big way.

As for myself, I do not prefer one mode over another; it works slightly differently for me. Over the last twenty years I have lived in several places, and now have a small but widely scattered group of friends. There are friends I never write to and yet we manage to keep track of each other's lives and meet at regular intervals. There are others I have not met for more than a decade, but we exchange letters on a regular basis. And there are some friends who I communicate with only through emails. Whatever the mode, the goal is to stay in touch with people. And email is terrific to say a quick hello, although I do use it for longer letters too. But as far as personal communication goes, I only write to people I already know or those whom I would like to know. Friendships which begin and end in cyberspace have no meaning for me. As for netsurfing, I do not have much time to browse and look for new Web sites any more. But I keep receiving addresses of work-related sites and do make time to check out some of them at least. Also these days while looking for information I give the net a try first. However, I do not read on the net. I still prefer the book; although I find information about books on the Web. At the end of the day I am sick of the computer screen and my back is sore. All I really want to do is look at the sky, the water and lots of trees. Or now that I am in Bangkok, I often take a ferry to have a look at the gorgeous *Wats*, the Thai temples, against the evening sky. Or just curl up in bed with a book with the sound of monsoon rain in the background. When on the road I prefer to send postcards to friends. If I need to contact someone urgently, however, I always look for a cybercafe before rushing to the telephone. If no one else, the local women's group is most likely to be connected to the Internet. That way one also has the possibility of meeting some real women, be it in Battambang or in Thimpu.

References

Butalia, Urvashi and Ritu Menon. 1995. *Making a Difference: Feminist publishing in the south*. Chestnut Hill, MA: Bellagio Publishing Network, Bellagio Studies in Publishing.

Pattanaik, Bandana and Susan Hawthorne. 1997. Building Bridges Electronically: The Spinifex Project. *Canadian Woman Studies/les cahiers de la femme*. Spring, *17* (2), 94–9.

two

Women Click: Feminism and the Internet

Scarlet Pollock and Jo Sutton

The development of women's use of the Internet has felt like Movement. It's been full of supportive acts and discussions. Women have been willing to share their ideas, experience and time with others whom they only know online. There is goodwill and growth between women. This virtual gathering together in small and not so small groups online is showing a range of possibilities for change. There is the capacity for sharing ideas for organizing and action, which some groundbreaking women have been exploring. More women are joining in and creating their own activities.

Communication Technologies Bring Change to Feminist Ways of Working

The work of feminists of the past thirty years is often the foundation from which online feminists build. Dialogue, encouraging others, listening, sharing, dealing with conflict are all brought into play. Many of the premises and assumptions made in online interaction are part of the continuity with other feminist work. To this approach, the Internet offers the possibility of working in ways feminists have often aspired to, but have sometimes had difficulty achieving: those of inclusion, diversity, and transparency in an open process which can lead to action and change.

Part of the transition comes with the new technologies. It speeds our communications, shares information on a large scale, and gives an immediacy to what we do. It can make our work more transparent and increase our accountability to women. Using the

Mont-
gomery 5
Lorenman 4
Pattanaik 1

Stafford 7

Introduction

Internet means that we have to rethink our work to see how being online can enhance what we do. We may decide that using <u>email</u> between organizations is adequate, maybe supplemented by a mailing list or two. Even this step means looking at <u>who</u> traditionally collects and processes the mail, as well as how everyone shares information.

We can use this medium, this tool, to communicate with each other and to connect over the issues that are closest to our hearts. We can reach beyond the boundaries of our neighbourhoods to exchange information and experiences with our communities of interest, and, at the same time, bring global resources to our local communities. There's much more that we can do with the Internet: such as influencing <u>government</u>, demanding accountability, promoting democratic participation. The point is to assess the possibilities and experiment in using it for our own purposes, while sharing our developing skills and experience with more women.

The voice women gain from getting online has begun to show in the range of issues, communication and information appearing both online and offline. Women and women's groups who have not always been widely supported are effectively using the Internet as a place to be heard, to listen, to be included and to make alliances. The voices of lesbian women, women of colour, immigrant women, young women, and women with disabilities, are online, and talking to each other (see Senjen and Guthrey 1996). Factors such as marginalization, distance and isolation are being tackled, so that ideas can be exchanged and more like minds can join in the discussion.

It may be that we are witnessing a further transition in how women work together. There is much to learn from the groundbreaking work being done online. Many women's groups have yet to engage in the equality struggles taking place over access to, and use of, communications technologies. Implementing use of the Internet may result in changes in the way an organization operates, as information may become more widely and easily available. Where information is power, sometimes someone's personal power, it is more likely to have to be shared. With the sharing of information and power comes responsibility. Group members who find they know more, may need to take a greater share in decision-making and organizing (see Greckol 1997; Pollock and Sutton 1997).[1]

Women Do It! The Internet as a feminist tool

Women's groups tend to talk of 'Communication Technology' rather than 'Information Technology', because communicating is central to feminist work. As Pauktuutit, the Inuit Women's Association, puts it:

> The information highway is not about computers or phones or technology—it's really about talking to each other for <u>work, for fun</u>, for talking with our families, for developing businesses, running government and for community action. It's about using whatever technology is out there to do what we have always done when we need to talk with each other to make something happen—it's about communicating . . . . Pauktuutit's role with communication today is connecting women to women IN the community, and women to women BETWEEN communities in order to work together on issues that affect women, family and community (Pauktuutit 1997: 96).

Mont-
gomery 5

Women online are participants rather than consumers. Information flow is interactive. Problem-solving in online groups ranges from the personal to the technological. This enables women to speak for themselves and develop strategies with others who are supportive or have had the same experience. It may be like a consciousness-raising group, where women debate issues, and discuss personal experiences, this time online. Mostly, it is very supportive. For example, the work of women with breast cancer involves a wide range of viewpoints and approaches, including discussions on whether or not

---

[1.] For further discussion see *Women'space Magazine* 1995–99, 1–4. Back issues at <<u>http://www.womenspace.ca</u>>

to have surgery, chemotherapy, alternative treatments, sharing experiences with drugs and support networks.

Communication can be two-way or in many directions. There is no gatekeeper to receive the information and pass it on. For women's groups and individuals who have developed ways of working which involve collecting, organizing, and disseminating information to other women, this can be a challenge to their style of operating. This process of 'disintermediation', the doing away with the information gatekeepers and putting the finding of information into the hands of individual women and the groups they belong to, means that women's groups are working together in new ways. Alliances can be short-term and very focused on the issue in hand. Actions can be discussed and passed around very quickly. These can be petitions signed by large numbers of people, sent on through email. It can be plans for a march or conference and sharing the event as it happens, both through mailing lists and on Web sites. It may be creating a sticker which is designed online by passing around ideas and designs, and placed on a Web site for downloading by all groups, who can then print them onto sticky labels for use in many cities on the same day. The potential for imaginative fun and carefully focused online organizing and action is enormous.

Women across Canada have been creating innovative ways to use the Internet. This groundbreaking work was initially largely volunteer, and often began among new and developing women's groups. As these groups have embraced the networking potential of the Internet, connections have been established with each others' work, and new possibilities for shared actions have been explored. Also, the use of the Internet to enhance offline events has been very effective. Online women set up support for actions such as the pan-Canadian Women's March Against Poverty in 1996, in the form of a *Supporting Wall* (a Web site) for messages of support arranged by the Canadian Women's Internet Association (CWIA), and in Québec, *Du Pain et des Roses* was a Web site hosted by the Montréal Daycare Workers' Union and used to organize events for the Women's March across Québec. Use of the Web site made it much easier to spread information quickly. Other Web sites linked to this organizing site in gestures of solidarity and support for the fight against poverty, brought numerous visitors to the site.

The CWIA organizes a 'Candlelight Vigil Across the Internet' in the first two weeks of December and women can download a .gif file (image) of a candle to place on their Web sites to show support. <http://www.women.ca/violence/candle.html> A visitor to any Web site displaying the image can click her mouse on it and be taken to electronic pages of information about the December 6th Montréal Massacre of fourteen women engineering students in 1989, and information about many aspects of violence against women. The CWIA's Web site is used by many women's groups as the place to start to search for links to Web sites and mailing lists, particularly those of interest to Canadian women. These important contributions to networking women and creating information have been almost entirely voluntary.

The Lesbian Mothers' Support Society, started in 1981, created their *Mommy Queerest* Web site in 1996. <http://www.lesbian.org/lesbian-moms/> Based in Calgary, Alberta, they maintain a wide-ranging site for lesbian parents, potential parents and the children of lesbians. The interest in their site and their work continues to grow, both inside Canada and around the world. A clearinghouse of information, ideas and advice, this group of women (and their kids) is a growing online community which an increasing number of women discover, and to which they know they belong. They are linked to Amy Goodloe's site *Lesbian Org*. Amy runs seven different mailing lists, the majority for lesbians.

The Beijing conference in 1995 was a fascinating example of women's networking online. We only got to Beijing virtually, but we still felt a part of it. Every morning for three weeks we received sixty to ninety emails from women at the conference. Descriptions of the opening ceremonies, of the landscape, of the events, of the difficulties and successes, of the debates and platforms. We were impressed by how we could discover so much without depending on the mainstream media: first hand accounts without the media's selection and spin. Women speaking for ourselves and being heard by many more.

Groups such as Rainbow Women's Centre have tackled the issue of poverty head on. Many in this group migrated to Canada and found that their skills were not easily accepted, which meant that they faced long-term unemployment. They have set up their own Internet access site, giving women computer and networking lessons along with other activities at the Centre. For this group, access to the Internet is not only about finding resources, but also opportunities for employment and growth which they had been unable to find elsewhere.

There are empowering possibilities in providing computer programs for women on low income, such as a place provided in a drop-in centre where women can check out their rightful benefits by filling in details and running a computer software program. The rich have accountants, why not the poor? Other examples spark new ideas; the Barrie Action Committee for Women noticed that a member's welfare cheque had stopped arriving. By connecting with other groups online they found that a very large number of cheques had all stopped the same week. They were able to gather the information quickly and then make it public, using the Internet as one of their tools. The welfare cheques were put in the mail.

Women's groups are often providers of information which can support other women in achieving the changes they wish to make in their lives, and the connections with others which will increase their capacity to make decisions and take actions. Some women's groups are now putting their work online. As the population becomes widely familiar with the new communications technologies, women will get online looking for information about sexual assault, abortion, battering, poverty, homelessness, welfare, health, sexual orientation, age, race, and disabilities. The challenge to feminists is whether we will be online and ready to greet them. Some groups are already prepared. SAWNET tells South Asian women how to get help and report assault to the police, giving telephone numbers and Web site links in many countries. <http://www.umiacs.umd.edu/users/

attanaik 1

sawweb/sawnet/violence/> The same sex violence page shows an immediate understanding of the person who has been assaulted, by starting their page 'If the one you love or used to love is using coercion, threats and physical violence to frighten you and control your actions . . . . We can help.' <http://www.xq.com/cuav/domviol. htm> In Alberta, VIOLET is working to connect women's shelters, including the women who are living in the houses. <http://www. violetnet.org> The work of groups like these needs to be emulated, so that women can collect the information online which will help them make informed decisions and know where to turn for help. This might include information such as what it's like to live in a transition house, whether to keep an emergency bag ready for a crisis, whether to take the kids when you leave (usually, yes). These are resources which have room for further developments. Women are already getting online looking for ways to connect with other women. Women's groups are able to flourish and grow because they can reach out to more women—some of whom will join and develop further campaigns and actions for women's equality.

We are involved in claiming the new space which has come with communication technologies. Here is a venue where we can exchange on a much wider scale than has been possible. Our issues benefit from the greater diversity of our community of interest than is likely to be available in each of our local neighbourhoods. Bringing global resources to local actions is a real way to widen our understanding of women's issues—whether it be a more inclusive perspective, examples of actions which have worked elsewhere, ideas for new ways of working together, and the influx of new energy and often younger women's involvement in this new forum of communication technologies.

Women'space magazine

Women'space magazine <http://www.womenspace.ca> was born out of the need to communicate, to acknowledge the work women

are doing, to share our ideas and our experiences using communications technology. We were caught by the excitement, creativity
and generosity of the women working online. By 1996 the print
magazine was attracting media interest, and a bigger readership. We
had to learn new software, and everything about the world of magazines—bar codes, distribution, appearance. Penney Kome, Denise
Østed, and Judy Michaud joined the editorial committee. Everyone
has brought her own experience and abilities, finding ways to make
the online and offline worlds accessible and welcoming for women.
Juliet Breese has shared her incredible creative talent with us from

(Image by Juliet Breese)

Both images first printed in *Woman'space* magazine, PO Box 1034, Almonte, Ontario, K0A 1A0,
Canada.
email: diamond@womenspace.ca
Web site: <http://www.womenspace.ca>

the first issue. Her illustrations have brought fun, ingenuity and clarity to previously vague ideas.

Women'space magazine has developed along with the growing awareness amongst women, that: 'There's more to this than I thought.' We changed over the first two years, from a neighbourhood newsletter to a Canadian network and an international magazine, in print and online. The magazine continues to highlight women's resources, Web sites and mailing lists, offer guides and tips, and discuss feminist issues. Importantly, we are growing with the increasing understanding of the possibilities of using this technology in a renewed struggle for equality. We are seeing feminist analyses being formulated, experiences being assessed, women creating, developing and using the Internet.

'Women'space' is about women speaking for ourselves, and bridg-

(Image by Juliet Breese)

ing the gap between the online and offline worlds. The magazine is read by women who have never touched a computer and others who use the Internet every day. Contributions come from all over the world, from women thinking and creating the Internet and its networks, by and for women.

'Women'space' addresses many of the Internet issues emerging for women: the harassment and difficulties of working online— more of the same, in another arena; the enormous resources being spent to get a whole population online without any serious attempt to ensure women and girls are included; the realization that access to the Internet is an equality issue, and that there is a long fight under way just to ensure women have the resources to get online; the need for an inclusive approach, building networks and making the Internet a welcoming and relevant place for a diversity of women where we can work together.

The Fight for Access to Resources

Women do not gain access to public resources on an equal basis with men, and that includes access to the new communication technologies. As Canada and many other Western nations go through the social transition to having a technologically skilled population, we find that education and many jobs are linked with the ability to use communication technology. If women are excluded from access now, we and our daughters will find ourselves increasingly disadvantaged in the future. To enable all of our voices to be included and heard, women are working to ensure access to communication technology is available for any woman who wants to get online.

The Canadian government is committed to providing places to use the Internet through a range of access points, such as libraries, schools and community centres. This massive programme has been implemented over the past four years, and will continue to evolve for at least another two years, with the aim of ensuring the population has the skills to use communication technologies. Not every household has, wishes to have, or can afford, a computer. Access points in thousands of communities extends people's use of the Internet. Unfortunately the planning, design, and implementation of such access points has taken very little account of the previous thirty years of work of equality-seeking groups. Public access points have, so far, had the tendency to follow the existing hierarchies of power. The problems women are encountering is that these are often places where women would not be comfortable using the computers, or where they feel that what is being offered is not relevant or appropriate to them, or where they find males step in to use the resources.

As part of their cost saving measures, many governments are putting increasing amounts of information online. For those people who live far from government offices this can be an improvement, as information can become more accessible. But information online, linked with cost saving, often means less is available on paper. Unless women gain equal access to communication technologies, government will be unable to give information to the majority of women. For example, Health Canada is putting resources into creating on-line health databases, Web sites of health information, and mailing lists for health professionals. Unless a more pro-active approach is taken by information providers only a minority of women will be able to access this health information.

Women are working to ensure that access to communication technology is equally available to all women. Setting up women's access points has largely been the voluntary contribution of women's groups. In Canada, applications for funds to set up women's access points were refused on the grounds that women were a 'special interest group' and therefore ineligible for 'public' grants (in Ontario, Newfoundland, New Brunswick and British Columbia). As long as the experiences of women, and other groups, are not taken into account, the lack of social and political awareness will cement existing divisions and hierarchies. If the ability to use communication technology is increasingly a skill needed for employment, lifelong learning, obtaining information and for the capacity to take an active part in civic life, then the difficulties women are experiencing in gaining equal access will result in their further and greater inequality.

The Women's Internet Conference/ Conférence: les femmes et l'internet

In May 1997, women activists working online and representatives from a diverse range of Canadian feminist organizations came together to share our experiences and to develop strategies for women's access to, and use of, communication technologies. Informally, the planning group became known as 'The Wedge', dedicated to opening up resources for women and forcing our way onto the social policy agenda. We addressed barriers and issues of feminist content, organizational change, resistance and motivation, as well as communications technology access for women. The meeting, and the conference which followed, were organized by 'Women'space', Women in Networking and Communication and the Ontario Women's Justice Network, and supported by Status of Women Canada, and other federal government and provincial funding agencies.

The Women's Internet Conference/Conférence: les femmes et l'internet was held in Ottawa in October 1997 bringing together one hundred and seventy-five women across the country interested in using the Internet for women's equality work. The conference was preceded by an ordinary mailout to women's groups so that everyone possible knew how to make contact—whether or not they planned to attend the event. We also set up a mailing list, conference-1, two months before the conference. This enabled women to introduce themselves and their issues. The excitement of meeting—most of us for the first time, although we knew many of the women through their online work and have worked online with some for years—launched us into three days of intense exchanges.

Over sixty presentations of women's work, discussion, debate and strategizing left us with that wonderful combination of feeling empowered, exhausted, and energized to continue our efforts. Details of the programme and report can be found at the conference Web site <http://www.grannyg.bc.ca/confer/> maintained by Judy Michaud. Because we wished to ensure as much participation as possible Judy also created a pre-conference Meep Board. Women whose only Internet access was a public place, such as a library, community centre or school, could go to the conference Web site and send a message which would become part of the Web site.

The Women's Internet Conference focused on access as a first step to participating in the Internet, and—much more—it brought together visions and experiences of how to use the Internet as a feminist medium. While our political struggles had tended to be around basic online access for women, along with information distribution and sharing, our work to develop the Internet for such things as the creation of content by and for women is growing. This is as important in encouraging women's participation, for it is clear that women are most interested in getting online when they can find useful resources for women. Those who resist the Internet as a sales medium, or as a toy for the boys, become animated when they begin to see its relevance to themselves and other women.

As women's groups engaged in political battles for equality, we were also keen to share what we are learning about increasing the visibility of women's issues through the Internet. The strength of the Internet has largely been the guides and links between the people, the work and the Web site/mailing list resources we can now share. It has been slower to develop ways of reaching out to women looking for women-centred information and services. Women's groups have much to offer here. Our understanding of equality issues and ways to offer reliable, women-friendly support and information are a vital part of developing our feminist use of the technologies.

We addressed a number of key questions around our use of communication technologies: assessing the quality of information we find and put onto the Internet, women's ways of learning, using the Internet for networking and advocacy, using Web sites and mailing lists in local campaigns and events, power shifts in organizations, incorporating the Internet into our group work practices, reflecting our diversity in our visibility and our decision-making online, crossing the language barrier, using the Internet to participate actively in social policy-making processes, developing avenues for women's employment, combining a range of communication technologies, both old and new, for increasing our effectiveness.

The conference had a communications room with twelve computers with Internet connections. We originally envisaged this as a place where women wrote email to the conference list, to their constituent groups and to individual women to share in the conference happenings. It was also planned to share and explore women's Web sites. In the course of the conference, this room became a hub of women's politics.

It started before the conference, at setup. The men setting up the computers were reluctant to let women use them and turned away any woman wanting to put a plug into a socket, attach a telephone line, or load a piece of software. Women organizers and early conference arrivals rallied immediately for our first action, to 'take back the computers' and control over the room. The technical skills of the mainly younger women kept the computers humming efficiently throughout the events, and boosted all of our confidence. This centre was enormously popular among the women attending the conference for learning, experimenting and exploring the possibilities of women's communications.

During the conference, women ran sessions in the communications centre on how to use Internet tools, and learning basic Web design. Extra demand led to additional sessions including one starting at 7 a.m. We also involved women in using Internet Relay Chat, many for the first time. Tanis Doe offered to present a session, but couldn't get to the conference. Instead, she made a video about Web sites and the needs of women with disabilities, with both a voice-over and signing. She put this up on a Web site and sent us a

VHS tape as backup. Conference participants viewed the video, then they logged on to Internet Relay Chat, formed their own 'chat room' and discussed Tanis's video with her, and others, in real time, over 2000 miles. The women with disabilities at the conference led the discussion of the online possibilities. It was an exciting new experience, and another piece of women's creativity.

Challenges to Feminists

While the Internet can help open up communications, women soon find a barrier to communications: that of language. In Canada, both French and English are the official languages, with all government department Web sites and documents equally weighted in both languages. Despite the policy, only 20% of the population speak more than one official language. Pan Canadian organizations may work in both languages but, for the majority of women, everyday communications and detailed knowledge of each other's work is difficult. So far women's mailing lists have had limited success in working in more than one language. Translating email is a time-consuming and sometimes expensive proposition. The Centre de documentation sur l'éducation des adultes et la condition féminine (CDÉACF), in Montréal, has recently initiated discussions between women's groups to look for ways to overcome the online language barrier. <http://www.cdeacf.ca/>

For native peoples in Canada, English or French is often a second (or third) language. Additionally, 17% of the population were born outside Canada's borders. On the Internet the multiplicity of languages and cultures is both a challenge and an invitation to women's groups seeking to be as open as possible. The potential for breaking down language barriers is exciting because of the innovative ideas which could be learned from other parts of the world, or even the same country, and the range of developing ways of women working together.

Low income women are unlikely to be able to afford to have access to the Internet at home, and their access to more traditional forms of education may be equally limited. Many low income women depend upon their community women's organizations for access to information and services. Those with much experience, such as the Rainbow Women's Centre and the Sunshine Coast Women's Centre, emphasize that women's organizations need to be providing access to the Internet for women in their communities, to share their resources with low income women.

Women's resources and access need to be culturally appropriate to the women using it. An increasing diversity of women using the Internet to get our voices online and raise our issues, will provide a much greater range of material for women online. Search tools for women require further development so we can improve our connections with each other. We need to continue to explore this new arena, assess what works, and how to reach a diversity of women in the context of women's community resources.

The Right have learned to use the Internet and have spent millions of dollars ensuring that they are using it effectively. Through carefully planned and integrated use of communications technology, they are able to put across their beliefs, present their platforms, find membership, chart legislation and significantly increase their outreach (Schwartz 1996: 102–7). It is important that feminists are able to monitor the Right's online activities. We need to use communications technology just as effectively to campaign and work for women's equality.

In 1998, when a Canadian Senate committee toured the country hearing views on custody and access for the children of divorcing parents, they heard an almost unified voice from fathers' 'rights' organizations. The men had used the Internet to develop their platform and to become a stronger, more effective, though minority voice. Canadian women created the Women's Justice Network which pulled together a very wide range of voices. <http://www.web.net/wjn/>

The Internet may play a key part in the generational change of feminism. It is often younger women who are at ease with the technology, and who are using it to share their experiences with many others. In some places, younger women are exchanging their knowledge and applications of communications technology with groups of older feminists who are able to pass on their organizing and campaigning experience. It is a blend which offers opportunities for mutual respect and an openness to growth and development. Young women will not just take on the issues of older feminists and become junior partners. They have their own issues and approaches. The Internet offers a greater range of possibilities for crossing generations.

When we understand the Internet to be much like our physical world, we see many parallels and opportunities. Getting online increases connections and gives us another tool and another place to grow our movement. We can place much of our ideas and developments online, where many more will have the opportunity to see our work and politics. We look forward to being able to find and read any feminist study of any issue, by an individual or a women's group, just by going online. We would love to see more of past feminist issues and debates digitized into Internet archives, so that our herstory is more widely known. We hope that the increased sharing of our politics will stimulate and facilitate the development of feminist ideas and ways of working with many more women, across many boundaries. Online women are creating a space for women where new ideas, and new approaches to old issues, have a forum.

We are still in the early stages of discovering the possibilities for feminist use of the Internet. We're looking forward to the new developments and enjoying this exploration of further possibilities for working together online.

References

Greckol, Sonja. 1997. Opportunities in Online Organizations. *Women'space*, 3(2), Fall/Winter, 30–31.
  <http://www.womenspace.ca/campaign/sitemap.html>
  The Women's Internet Campaign is a Canadian struggle for women's and

girls' equal access, equal participation and an equal voice in communication technologies.

Pauktuutit. 1997. Communicating for Change. In Scarlet Pollock and Jo Sutton (Eds.), *Women's Groups Using the Internet*. Canada: Women'space.

Pollock, Scarlet and Jo Sutton. 1997. Information Technology is a Women's Rights Issue. *Women'space* 3(1), Summer.

Schwartz, Edward. 1996. *Net Activism: How citizens use the internet*. Sebastopol, California: O'Reilly.

Senjen, Rye and Jane Guthrey. 1996. *The Internet for Women*. Melbourne: Spinifex Press.

three

Online Teaching: No fear of flying in cyberspace

Laurel Guymer

As the Internet is facilitating a revolution in teaching and learning strategies, it is important to investigate flexible modes of delivery and to compare them to the traditional fixed time and place lecture style, the land class. For most Women's Studies lecturers, how we teach is as important as what we teach. I am writing from the perspective of teaching Women's Studies in Australia and in this chapter I intend to tell the story of how I came to be flying in cyberspace—and loving it! There were three parts to this adventure. First, I had to challenge my own fears of flying in cyberspace so that I was aware of the pitfalls, the highs and lows and could ultimately become comfortable with the rapidly growing technology. Second, once at ease in the air, I learnt how to fly as cheaply and efficiently as possible. Finally, once airborne, it was important to ask the students whether they enjoyed the flight. My introduction to online teaching began well before my wings were fully developed and, like most things, 'the boys' were already launched and it seemed if I didn't run out onto the runway straight away, climb in and begin to motor, the plane would definitely leave without me.

From the outset, I had no illusion and so it was clear to me that in order to fly, hours and hours of practice would be needed. Time, money and fear of failure are often the first obstacles preventing women from even contemplating the flight into cyberspace. But unlike print media, half-baked and not fully developed ideas can be launched in cyberspace and gradually built upon. With these important guidelines in mind, I set out to develop skills with Web authoring tools such as AOL[1] press and, several months later,

---

[1] America Online.

Netscape Communicator: they offer different degrees of flexibility but generally have many similarities. Initially, the learning curve was so steep that I really questioned if I would ever take off. Unfamiliarity with the jargon—that is the computer language used in every day cyberspeak—made it necessary to learn some simple terms to assist me along the journey. These included download, html, links, jpegs, gifs. Months later I was away, enjoying the flight, my sites launched, and the students benefiting from new flexible ways of learning such as interactive Web sites and computer-mediated conferencing (CMC). In what follows I will discuss my journey through cyberspace, including the advantages, obstacles and joys for both students and educators of online teaching.

Ways of Communicating

There are several ways to incorporate the Internet into everyday teaching and learning. For example, there is email where one can send and receive messages from one computer to another; interactive Web sites using the world wide Web; ICQ[2] <http://www.icq.com/products/whatisicq.html> or IRC[3] which enables synchronous[4] chatting (see Senjen and Guthrey 1994) and CMC which incorporates both asynchronous[5] and synchronous modes of communicating. In Women's Studies, I aimed to develop interactive teaching materials using feminist pedagogical principles (Bowles and Klein 1983; Bunch 1987; Aaron and Walby 1991; Bell and Klein 1996) using a combination of ways to enhance teaching and learning (Bantow *et al.* 1997).

[2.] I Seek You.

[3.] Internet Relay Chat.

[4.] Synchronous chatting refers to discussions that take place online between two people or more at the same time.

[5.] Asynchronous refers to discussions that are not taking place at the same time. For example, one user posts a comment and another user answers several hours later, logging the conversation item by item so other students can follow the thread, in much the same way as a newsgroup works at any time.

Teaching with it?

Women's Studies has traditionally be seen as a talk, think and act subject. Therefore the concept of online teaching[6] required considerable thought. It was important to think about how women could use this technology and not just absorb or accept what 'the boys' were doing, but change it to work for us so we could use it as a tool to transform teaching and learning (Bellamy 1999). I aimed to develop a Web site that students could use, as an adjunct to the print materials, and in the process acquire some of the necessary technological skills. The site was to include three components: a) generic information for prospective students completing a major in Women's Studies—such as study day details, instructions on how to use conferencing, library resources, staff contacts and, importantly, search and research tools, and links to an electronic evaluator; b) unit material specific to each unit, and c) interactive study materials using CMC in addition to on-campus tutorials or printed study materials.

Learning to develop Web sites

Before I could launch into teaching Women's Studies in cyberspace several test flights were needed. One flight involved maintaining and updating the Australian Women's Research Centre's Web Site,

---

[6.] Deakin University prides itself on providing excellent distance learning opportunities as well as local modalities. Since 1977 these have been referred to as either on-campus or off-campus. On-campus students participate in face-to-face tutorials in a land class of fixed time and place. Off-campus students can complete their study from any location. Off-campus students receive all study materials by Australia Post, including a unit guide, study guide and Reader, plus phone calls from the lecturer. Sometimes tapes and video are included in the posted materials. Library resources are also delivered to off-campus students wherever their location. More recently, educators have aimed to offer similar learning experiences whether students are on- or off-campus, getting rid of these terms and replacing them with students or clients. This idea has increasingly encouraged me to take up the opportunity to teach in cyberspace, theoretically incorporating all students who can afford to access the technology.

<http://arts.deakin.edu.au/guymer/aworc> Experiments with different colours, fonts, tables and graphics kept me occupied for hours. It all seemed really slow, manually writing the html scripts but, with newer and faster programs developed, it wasn't long before the old manual methods were defunct and easier and quicker ways to set up sites were available. With assistance from technological witchery, specialists from Deakin Centre for Academic Development (DCAD) helped with design and development of electronic forms and templates. The Information Technology (IT) Co-ordinator in the Faculty provided unlimited advice and instructions, hard to quantify in hours, which complemented the four three-hour basic training sessions I received.

In my next test flight I began to work with templates; this was simpler than it sounded. It involved deciding where and how to place the ideas and concepts in a shell (an already made frame) with the use of graphics saved as either jpegs or gifs, and an assortment of digital photos to jazz up the sites, <http://arts.deakin.edu.au/ guymer/wshp> Thus far Women's Studies Web sites closely reflected the print copies of the Unit Guide study materials with additional links to the library (seen by some as a glorified library resource list), feminist authors, activists and publishers. Nevertheless, with many flying hours logged up, I now felt confident with the technology and ready for my first real flight into cyberspace. From months of work, in my private folder on the desktop in the safety of my office, it was time to launch my sites into cyberspace. I gave the URL to my colleagues and students enrolled in third year and together we took off.

Inspired by feminist literary lecturer Rhonda Bunbury's site <http://arts.deakin.edu.au/Manyfaces>, my next flight upgrade involved the development of more interaction for students, especially those isolated by distance or disability. Using the third year unit site, I embarked on developing a learning environment to include study guide material, that is, use text with questions and activities for students to engage with and respond to in a space where others can debate ideas <http://arts.deakin.edu.au/guymer/asw311sg>,

<http://arts.deakin.edu.au/guymer/asw333sg> and <http://arts.
deakin.edu.au/guymer/asw322sg>. In addition, I set up, adminis-
tered and moderated a cyberclassroom using a computer-mediated
conference environment called First Class to enable on- and off-
campus students to communicate and benefit from interactive tutorials no matter whether they lived five minutes from the university or
thousands of kilometres. Rosalind Resnick and Heide Anderson
(1995) investigated what women want online and found that they
want their own communities: precisely what I tried to create for
students enrolled in Women's Studies units. Janet Morahan-Martin
(1998) suggested that '[w]omen may find all-female groups allow
them a more uninterrupted online voice that is less confrontational
and more supportive.' With this in mind, I set out to create a community space for students enrolled in Feminist Research Methodology to work together using First Class. I invited on-campus
students to participate as well. Reluctantly they took to flight but,
early on, made clear their disapproval of First Class ever substituting
land classes, lectures or tutorials.

What is First Class?

First Class[7] is one way to interact via CMC. It can be accesssed via the
Web, or, for individuals who own a computer, the software can be
downloaded for everyday use. The setting up was the easy part.[8] But
once you have decided which technologies to use, technological
assistance, plenty of training and time are needed. First Class
functions much like an electronic bulletin board, with synchronous
and asynchronous ways of communicating. It is an interactive piece

---

[7.] Attached to the Women's Studies Web Site are detailed instructions on how to use First Class:
try <http://www2.deakin.edu.au/firstclass/>.

[8.] Computer Conferencing Systems Development Manager, Pam Mulready, <http://www2.
deakin.edu.au/dcad/who/mulready/default.htm> gave me all the support and practical advice
I needed to get launched.

of software designed for individual and collaborative needs. Students and teachers can post messages to the conference as this is a public forum, open to all students enrolled in this particular unit. In large classes it is possible to set up several tutorial rooms for private discussion. First Class also allows users to send and receive email. It is not the only software program available for computer conferencing but in 1999 the university I work at supports it, providing technological and administrative assistance for students and lecturers; hence my initial take off with it. The idea of First Class appealed to me as I thought it would offer something extra for both on- and off-campus students, apart from alternatives to rigid class times. In addition, I hoped that it would engage students in serious discussion and debate. Child care, disability, work, location or cost can all prohibit students from accessing traditional settings. With First Class, the cyberclassroom is open twenty-four hours a day, seven days a week.

Nevertheless, it was clear from off-campus student evaluation comments that connecting to the First Class conference sites can be intensely difficult for the first-timer. Considerable tenacity is required in order to become involved. The following email from a student may serve as a demonstration.

> email
> To: Laurel Guymer <capri@deakin.edu.au>
> Subject: Connecting online
> Date: Wed, 10 Aug 1998 23:37:48 +1000
>
> Hi Laurel
>
> I am thrilled to have overcome the trials and tribulations of cyberspace. My first encounters failed because of lack of [computer] memory to install the necessary software to communicate online. Also, the version I was trying to download was not compatible with the system I was using. Anyway, here I am and I look forward to 'real' contact with 'real' live students in the cyberclass (which will be the first time ever since embarking on my degree 6 years ago)
>
> Undergraduate Student

An eager response confirms the initial enthusiasm.

> email
> date: Fri, 9 Oct 1998 02:36:47 +1000
> To: Laurel Guymer <capri@deakin.edu.au>
> Subject: I made it!!!!!!!
>
> Hello
>
> I made it—at last. I got home from work, opened up the email and there was a message explaining that my student number is the key and that my email password will not work. Bingo! So simple when you know how. I've just now finished reading all 23 messages in the 'Women's Studies' [conference] folder, but just as I read the last one First Class cut me off to complete their daily backup which is why I'm talking to you via email—seems so primitive compared to conferencing!!
>
> Anyway, I will log in daily and check if any Women's Studies students are online but if not will work my way through the questions and post my responses. Thanks in anticipation this is going to be excellent.
>
> Undergraduate Student

How is First Class administered?

When you are the administrator of a cyberclassroom the conference space is only limited by your imagination. The top level (see SCREEN 1) shows a number of conferences, including the Women's Studies icon, and the student simply clicks this icon to open a second level (see SCREEN 2); this contains the several different conferences we use in Women's Studies, including the library (frequently asked questions are answered here) and assignment box (here students can submit assignments and evaluations electronically into a locked conference). From there the student opens the icon called Feminist Research Methodology, or the unit they are enrolled in to find where most of the discussions are taking place. The third level (see

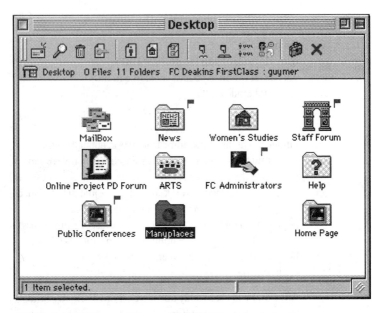

SCREEN 1

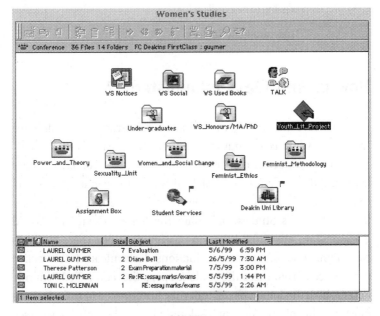

SCREEN 2

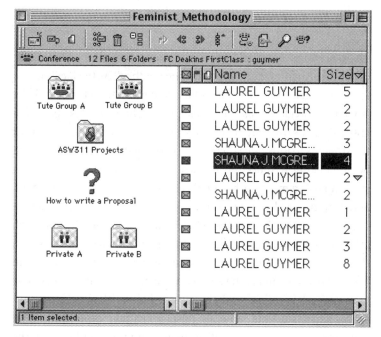

SCREEN 3

SCREEN 3) includes tute rooms, resource room (here the students find a list of the readings and questions to discuss and engage in each week), a chat facility, and private tute rooms for students wanting to work collaboratively on projects or any variation that you decide to include. All the conference spaces have permissions attached so that as the administrator you can restrict participants with a variety of functions: for example, in determining who can submit posts or modify old posts. There is also a 'read only' facility which is particularly good for assignments and evaluations because the facilitator can restrict students reading another's work. If the students agree, it is also possible to change the permissions to allow all the assignments to be open and read by all students enrolled in the subject (which is useful when all the assignments are marked to provide examples of excellent, innovative and imaginative work).

How to succeed

There are some essential ingredients in ensuring all the planes take off smoothly without crashing into one another.[9] As the facilitator or moderator in a CMC environment it is important to welcome ALL the students individually as they make it into the cyberclassroom. For many students this may be their first encounter with computers. I ask the students to introduce themselves in the first meeting. This is done by completing a short résumé which can be read each time the student posts a message, by double clicking the name of the student. Similarly, the students can read my résumé in First Class, by double clicking my name. This exercise helps the students get to know each other rapidly, and does not disadvantage students who perhaps miss the first fixed time land class. To encourage participation (even from hostile Luddites), make the space a valuable resource, include exercises using CMC as part of their assessment, and allow private workspaces where students can make mistakes without other students or educators viewing. Use incentives to encourage students to visit the cyberclassroom regularly; make yourself visible as the facilitator because you can be sure no one will turn up if the teacher doesn't. Try to attach documents regularly to assist students with their assessment tasks—for example, hints on essay and grant writing, sample budgets, ethical considerations, new Web sites to assist them, and general feedback on assignments overall. Save and post online tutorials so that students who couldn't make it to the synchronous time can read later. Introduce the students to the Women's Studies Web Site and provide the URL.[10] They can't fly without the plane.

[9.] It is important that there are alternatives for those students who do not have access to a computer and modem until the day when we are all convinced—and have the money to buy the equipment and time to learn the skills—that this method of learning is a way of life. Just like working with books and paper.

[10.] Women's Studies Web Site can be found with the following URL <http://arts.deakin.edu.au /guymer/wshp> which includes a list of all undergraduate and postgraduate Women's Studies units and their websites, study day information, staff details, instructions on how to use CMC such as First Class and an electronic evaluation tool. I also provide the students with a quick guide to the electronic educational environment (the cyberclassroom).

As well, I introduced the students to the public and private chat facility so that further communication can take place at times other than those I designated as the unit chair. It is possible to see who is online (by looking under the menu heading 'conferencing'). It is also possible to read résumés of others online. If I found any Women's Studies students online I would 'invite' them to 'chat', electronically speaking. Eventually they all got to know each other and didn't need me to 'invite' them. I posted the tutorial questions regularly, on-campus students posted their oral tutorial papers each week for further discussion and, regardless of whether I attended or not, the students took to flight and debated ideas regularly with each other in cyberspace or continued discussions that started in the land class.

Silent ones or 'Lurkers'?

Of course, similar situations arise in the cyberclassroom as they do in the fixed time and place tutorials. For example, the student who sits and never says anything exists in the virtual class as well. 'Lurkers' traditionally sit silently, and do not participate or contribute to the discussion (Cuskelly, Gregor and Zelmer 1994). Rhonda Bunbury (1999) suggests that:

> the term 'lurkers' implies that one should not be silent. But maybe there are good reasons for being silent, for example nothing much to say, yet interested in the conversation, waiting for a turn, or not yet confident

to voice an opinion. My experiences with third year undergraduates reinforced the fact that negative references to 'lurkers' were indeed detrimental to the level of participation. I received private emails from students who were worried their 'lurking' had been detected, and as a result refused even to log on.

Learning styles differ, and Pam Mulready doesn't like the negative connotations of the term lurkers either: 'they are counter product-ive' (Mulready 1999). In these environments everyone is operating at different levels of skill development, and confidence is often affected. Those who type at a 'rate of knots', or are prolific contributors can discourage the nervous newcomer.

In other words, like the silent ones who are constantly questioned or forced to speak in the fixed time and place land class, eventually the 'lurkers' will not turn up in cyberspace either. This is the challenge for educators. Do we let students know that online 'lurkers'—like the silent ones in the fixed time tutorial—can be seen? By highlighting the message in question, referring students to the drop down menu item 'message' and viewing 'history', all the names of those who have read the message are listed with a time and date. Do we withhold this information and encourage all the students to participate when they feel confident? I suppose the risk is that debates would never get up, and the planes would remain grounded.

There are a number of strategies teachers can employ to address this problem. According to Pam Mulready (1999), the best online courses build in orientation exercises, beyond posting to the conference. For example, this may involve a strategy such as collaborative exercises between two, then four people, in order to build a sense of community and teamwork up-front, so that people totally new to this online environment, don't connect in isolation. Or an activity which requires participants to input early, such as search and report exercises or something similar. In addition, the facilitator can explain the 'permissions' to all students in an introduction post. This might include the message that only Women's Studies students enrolled in the unit are able to open the conference space with a password. Also, in the cyberclassroom, students can be encouraged to read all the posts at their leisure and absorb the information before they engage. This generally improves the level of debate because ideas, concerns or fears are fully developed before students launch into uninformed critiques with one another. Of course, this way of debating doesn't improve skills for real life where arguments need to be instant. This is an important point and reinforces my belief that the cyberclass should only ever be used in addition to real time and place tutorials. The fully converted would argue that by providing synchronous tutorials online you overcome this obstacle, but I am still not convinced that the synchronous electronic environment is as 'real' as face-to-face interaction in a land class. The following undergraduate does not share my scepticism:

> Firstclass mailbox
> Date: Tues, 20 April 1999 17:16:47 +1000
> To: Laurel Guymer <capri@deakin.edu.au>
> Subject: Tute Queer Politics 20/4/99
>
> Hello All—just a short note to thank those participants for today's tute. As an off-campus student, [First class] is a stimulating environment to be in [because] when others are around in reality and virtually—the sense of isolation is not so great. The land class still has me thinking and the cyber tute is an interesting forum in which to communicate with each other—and that is an admission from a computer-technology challenged person. Good to be able to put names to people's faces as well. Thanks for trying to keep us on track—what a rowdy lot !!!
>
> Cheers and kind regards to you all,
>
> Undergraduate Student.

Nevertheless the use of First Class as a discussion tool proved rewarding as a way of:

- clarifying issues in the unit to do with the use of unit materials; for example, negotiating alternative assessment topics;
- focusing on the issues and sorting out misunderstandings of concepts underlying the unit materials, both via simultaneous discussion and asynchronous communication with the use of the message system; putting students in touch with each other and making discussion between them possible—when they lived very far apart;
- discussing the set readings;
- discussing student tutorial papers;
- enabling students and lecturers to formulate discussion questions around an article/student paper and for these

questions to be picked up during extended discussion or during the form of messages set up for asynchronous communication;

- reducing isolation for off-campus students (distance learners); and,

- in addition, this mode of learning encouraged student use of the Internet and enabled students to attend to crying babies, demanding partners, or work, and still participate in tutorials.

But for some it is not such a positive experience. Rhonda Bunbury tried to launch students into cyberspace and she received this distressing email from a student unable to get online.

email
To: Rhonda Bunbury <bunbury@deakin.edu.au>
Date: Wed, 21 Oct 1998 21:15:07 +1000
Subject: more problems and a stressed out student!

Firstly, thanks for your patience and support. I'm quite upset at the moment as it's looking like I won't be able to participate in the tutorial tomorrow. Here's why!

. . . . My off-campus subject has invited me to participate in an 'on-line' tutorial. Sounds straight forward enough. But first I didn't get sent the essential cd-rom because I'm officially an on-campus student, then the software makes my computer crash (but only sometimes—explain that?), then I can't download an alternative version of it from the net, then I try to download Netscape 4 (I only have 2), twice (it takes about an hour and a half) the first time it didn't do it properly and it disappeared, the second time it saved it OK, but it won't open it. Meanwhile I've been calling its [Information Technology Services] like crazy and doing everything they suggested and nothing works. Now, keep in mind for approx 3 weeks it's been a software problem . . . . Then last night they say maybe it's a problem with the [cd-rom], and to go to on-campus its and get a replacement, and try again and see what happens. I'm told they're only open 11am–1pm. So I nick out of teaching rounds. . . . No-one is

in the its office, door is locked. So I ring the help desk (which I
then discovered is actually located in Canberra—*??!!*) and
after lengthy discussions with a different person from whom
I'd been speaking to every other time, . . . he emphatically
tells me the problem is not the software, . . . the problem is
my machine and I'll need to get it looked at . . . by the time I
am able to get it looked at, it's time for our on-line tutorial so
I miss out once again, and maybe it will even affect my grade
. . . AAAAAAAAAAAAAAAAAAH!

Anyway, I just thought I should let you . . . know what's
going on, and if I don't appear Thursday evening, you'll
know why! But, I'll give it a go and see if time works with me
or against me. Naturally, I'll get my computer 'looked at' . . .

Regards, Student X.

Some of the difficulties expressed in the above email have been
ironed out with the free distribution to every enrolled student of the
Deakin Toolkit (which includes all the software necessary to fly safely
without any crash landings!), and with the development of the student 'kiosk' to answer frequently asked questions and for individuals
to change their password (if they lose or forget it). (The 'kiosk' is
found on all computers in the labs at the university or via ITS Web
Site if logging in from home <http://www.deakin.edu.au/its>.)

Nevertheless, enthusiasm was strong from those who did manage
to link up via First Class. For instance, the weekly chat sessions about
the unit, Feminist Research Methodology, continued after the
academic semester had ended. Throughout the semester, I had told
the students that I would not always be present but that they were to
continue without me, and if possible, make a copy of their conversations so other students, as well as myself, could contribute to the
discussion asynchronously at a later date. This worked well and
students shared the responsibility copying the chat session to the
conference site. Students also frequently responded to each other, to
chat sessions and other messages. Here are some messages from one
student to another as they help each other work out what to do.

4/9 Hi everyone Here I am in the lab at uni, not particularly convenient. I live in Fitzroy any ideas?

4/9 Reply: There is a cybercafe in Smith St with free Internet connection but beware the coffee is expensive!

5/9 Reply: Try your local community house, mine has free Internet facilities or the local library!

8/9 I want to read the attachments Laurel put up for us. What does download mean?

8/9 Reply: Ring me on . . . tonight and I will talk you through the download.

9/9 I have an idea for the research proposal but would like to discuss some ethical considerations with everyone.

9/9 Great let's talk in the private tutorial room.

Despite the highs and lows experienced in this particular teaching and learning exercise, administration and moderation required more, not less staff time, to keep the interaction happening. Because I continued to run land classes weekly and moderate the cyberclass, my workload effectively doubled. But this was an important decision I made on the grounds that, in 1999, not all students have access, so until they do cyberclasses would be an adjunct. (Pam Mulready (1999) 'would love to see a formal online orientation period for students who will be using these VERY NEW MEDIUMS, before the unit begins so that access issues, can be ironed out'. There are operational baselines that need to be communicated up-front, whether it is a version of a browser or a piece of software.) As well, the technical support required for success was occasionally beyond what I could offer. So without ongoing assistance from Pam Mulready we would have many more crash landings beyond repair.

What are the Obstacles?

For most women, there are many obstacles to getting online. These obstacles begin with issues of access and time. And importantly, these obstacles arise from the way girls are socialised in our society to view computers and technology as masculine, boring, and men's domain. Access to computers in the context of patriarchal societies is a huge challenge for feminists. A mature-aged Women's Studies student complained 'We have a computer but the children dominate the time on it,' and 'Even if I had time I wouldn't waste it sitting in the dark trying to figure out how it [the computer] works.' A third year student commented, 'My brother uses the computer mostly—I don't need it.' Comments like these raise more questions than simply obstacles of economic access. There needs to be a shift in thinking (Turkle 1988; Senjen and Guthrey 1996; Spender 1995a and b; Bantow *et al.* 1997).

Roadblock to Girls and Women entering Cyberspace

It is obvious from Sherry Turkle's (1988) study why women are so 'reticent' when it comes to online technology. She says 'for many of them [it is] best summed up by admonishment, "Don't touch it, you'll get a shock"' (1988: 41), or if you touch it and it 'crashes' you must have broken it. This was clear on observing the students on their first visit to the computer laboratory. When introducing the on-campus students to First Class technology, comments such as 'it's crashed—did I break it?' were common.

Dale Spender (1995a), using the image of the information super-highway, concurs that the main roadblock to women is economics not technofears. She says '[m]any women simply don't have the money to purchase access; [that] they aren't in a position to buy the computers, or to run accounts on the Internet'. Even for those lucky ones who have access like the girls at Melbourne's Methodist Ladies College, Spender reminds us that the reality of patriarchy is alive and well.

Again and again, the girls explained, that they couldn't get to their computers—because their brothers had taken them. And this really is the case. (In households where only the daughter has a computer, it is not unknown for parents to insist that as she has had it all day, it is only fair that her brother has it for the night!) (Spender 1995a).

However, at a Melbourne conference on the Politics of Cyberfeminism in 1996, Rye Senjen and Jane Guthrey disagreed strongly with Dale Spender; they confirmed that modems were getting cheaper and cheaper, well within the price range of many students and argued:

> If you are happy to have text-only access (no graphics, sound or video) and you have access to a reliable phone-line, $200 should buy an old 286 or 386 pc and a slow modem (Senjen and Guthrey 1995: 53).

Four years later this is not the case; older PCs are not Y2K compliant and while technology is improving, modems are getting faster and faster, and access costs are getting cheaper, hardware remains out the price range for many. But there are other alternatives: cybercafes and community houses with Internet access are slowly popping up all over town, and in rural settings, and eventually computers with connection to the Internet will be as common as colour TV is now. Students can already buy or lease the latest computer for the price of a pizza a week (so when the computer is out of date they can trade it in).

> email
> To: Pam Mulready <mulready@deakin.edu.au>
> Date: Thu, 29 Apr 1999 18:07:26 + 1000
> Subject: Student Access
>
> Terri Patterson and I conducted a study of Telecentres in remote communities late last year. (will forward a copy . . . nearly finished) . . . and it was terrific to see women . . . facilitating access. The Derby Telecentre was a fabulous example, of fundamentally Techno-newbies, establishing themselves as an isp, within what was a Community Centre, a supportive environment. It wasn't owned by a Techo, it

was shared by a community. This was a great model as were many of the Telecentres we visited.

ciao for now . . . Pam

Recent statistics in Social Work are encouraging:

Date: Tue, 13 Apr 1999 16:19:35 +1000
To: capri@deakin.edu.au
From: Lesley-Caron Veater <lveater@deakin.edu.au>
Subject: Stats re stdnts & computer access

Hi all,

Just to hand, this may be of interest to those of you looking at using the net for alternative delivery to D[istance] E[ducation] students . . .

This info was gathered from the new de enrolments in Social Work this year but they tell me it is probably pretty representative of the larger student body . . .

All students have computers

90% have cd drives & can access the Deakin Learning Toolkit

72% have Internet access

cheers Lesley

However, these figures represent eighteen Social Work students who attended three one-day sessions organised by ITS, and who are not representative of all ARTS students.

In Women's Studies, 65% of the total number of students flew into the cyberclass and participated in one form or another (all the on-campus students except one and 50% of the off-campus students).[11] For me, the effort was worth it when two students phoned me at home to let me know that they had made it, that they found the site, downloaded the attachment and printed it, and had

---

[11.] There were fifteen students enrolled on-campus and sixteen off-campus. Fourteen of the on-campus students and six off-campus participated in First Class. Of the total thirty-one enrolled, 65% flew into cyberspace.

emailed me to let me know they were launched, flying high over the roadblocks which Dale Spender talks about. At last they could participate in a world that had once belonged only to their boyfriends and brothers. They had taken off and cyberfeminism is now a part of their world.

Students reported some difficulty of access which they expressed as intial confusion regarding the two ways of opening First Class. The 1998 Web method prevented the chat facility, urging most students to download the intranet client onto their own computers (if they had one) which was time-consuming (some several hours) depending on the speed of their modem. This problem has been addressed and it is now possible to chat via the First Class Web site <http://firstclass.deakin.edu.au>

> email
> To: Pam Mulready <mulready@deakin.edu.au>
> Date: Thu, 29 Apr 1999 18:07:26 +1000
> Subject: Student Access
>
> Dale Spender articulated a projected reality (vision), exending upon the possibilities opened up by computers and networks, to facilitate education. Whilst the access and cultural issues always impact on many women, some women have been fundamental, if not pivotal, in network developments (for example if you look at the work of Roxanne Star Hiltz and Linda Harrasim, Betty Collis, Zane Berge, Sherry Turkle and Lin Thompson). The Internet is primarily a communication environment. CMC, and online collaboration produced the tools that built the WWW (HTTP/browsers), email SMTP/clients, MUDs/MOOs (Virtual worlds) . . . and this continues . . . although we can get a bit lost these days in the billboards . . . at the expense of community. It is very much early days, good luck.
>
> Ciao Pam

Regardless of the wide and often legitimate criticisms, women are overcoming enormous obstacles to learn to fly and launching themselves into cyberspace (Senjen and Guthrey 1996). Cate Kennedy's poem, 'relative complexity', reminds us that flying in cyberspace is not that difficult.

In my parent's loungeroom after Christmas dinner
I am talking to my brother the computer programmer.
He is explaining to me the principles of cyberspace.
'It is only relatively complex.' He says finally, peeling the icing off his fruitcake,
'It is mainly a system of binaries, permutations of zero and one.
So the data may be stored as, say zero, zero, one, one, one, zero, zero, one.'
My mother sighs.
She is next to us half-listening.
She is knitting a fair-isle sweater.
'I'll never understand how you get your brain around it,' she says.
'It's beyond me,' she says, and turns half her attention back to her fair-isle pattern:
Purl purl plain, plain plain plain purl purl.

(in Senjen and Guthrey 1996: 13).

Critics: Opposition to girls flying in cyberspace

In contrast to the obstacles and joys in my online teaching experiences, it is also worth noting that there are many critics of this new technology. James McDonald (1995: 537) argues that 'computer [mediated] conferencing fractures the meaning of community among a population of students who are already marginalised and isolated.' Jean Lave and Etienne Wenger (1991: 105) point out that the main mode of communication is speaking and listening rather than reading and writing. In other words, because computer conferencing asks students to communicate in a way that is relatively unfamiliar to them—using a keyboard, where they have less experience and practice—it is not surprising they become alienated and drop out because of general dissatisfaction with their learning experiences. Nevertheless, I think that McDonald underestimates students' heightened curiosity and willingness to explore new flexible ways of learning and, as I have argued above, CMC does not need to replace the other modes of delivery but can be used as an adjunct.

Susan Hawthorne's (1996: 34) fear that 'The structures of power remain the same' in the virtual world are of great concern to those of us using this new medium or developing Web sites for teaching and learning. As she puts it, 'the virtual world corresponds to a frozen image of the real world which ceased to exist decades, centuries and millennia ago'. I agree with Hawthorne that not a lot has changed in cyberspace. Random surfing reveals futuristic images of space-age women that remind us of negative stereotypes from the 50s and 60s, or 'the Virtual Valerie type who might have stepped out of the pages of *Playboy* (a 1970s image)' (*idem.*). This is precisely why feminists have to get launched to provide an alternative to dominant patriarchal images being reinforced in new ways or in old ways presented as if they are new. For instance, it isn't good enough to ignore the classism (Mahony and Zmroczek 1997), racism, ageism, homophobia and sexism (Pharr 1988) that permeate everyday life. Nor is it all right to hide these behaviours by theorising them away, encouraging new identities online and pretending that they are genderless, ageless, able-bodied etc. There are opportunities to challenge <u>patriarchal images</u>, start afresh and not have those same power relations in our future cyberclassrooms.[12] As Dale Spender puts it,

Klein 9

> Cyberspace has the potential to be egalitarian, to bring everyone into a network arrangement. It has the capacity to create community; to provide untold opportunities, exchange, and keeping in touch (1995b: 229).

Girls get connected

Dale Spender has been at the forefront of urging women to take up the challenge. While most lecturers now use email, there is still often

---

12. See Berit Ås (1996) for more detail on the Feminist University.

reluctance or even resistance to using the Internet for teaching. Also, while the use of online materials would seem to be a positive development, providing a central point of information for students, some people criticise such moves as passing the cost of printing support material onto the students assuming that they print these notes for their files, rather than read them on screen. It is also true that using the Internet for teaching Women's Studies has limitations because feminists were not among those developing the technology. Nevertheless, an increasing number of feminists are gradually setting up <u>listservs</u>, putting up Web sites, and providing access to literature online.

As a Women's Studies lecturer, Dale Spender's words ring loudly:

> The world of computers and their connections is increasingly the world of men: as more research is done in this area and more findings are presented, the more damning is the evidence. Men have more computers, spend more time with them, and are the dominating presence in cyberspace (Spender 1995: 165–6).

The obvious question is why aren't women involved? The answer is simple: girls are taught to view these technologies with suspicion and fear. Jo Sutton and Scarlet Pollock (1997) argue that women are not 'encouraged to use . . . computers, do not easily find relevant content, and are less accustomed to using computers as a tool for their own purposes'. The typical computer user is still seen by many as the twelve-year-old white, middle-class boy living in Idaho (Hawthorne 1996). If not, images of computer nerds, geeks and hackers—with thick glasses, bad eating habits and unfashionable clothing—spending countless hours isolated in dark rooms hacking into other people's computers, or some variation of the above come to mind.

Students enrolled in Women's Studies agreed that even those women who had overcome the stereotypes and were active online, typical computer nerds were thought of as 'socially dysfunctional'. These negative stereotypes reinforce myths that 'cybergeeks' relate better to their computers than to other people. Such images are alive and well, and may serve to keep many women from exploring new ways of learning. The concern about the growing inequalities in computer expertise is real and was already documented by Jo Shuchat Sanders and Antonia Stone in 1986, when they stated that 'after-school computer clubs are nearly 100% male'. Despite mainstream media not helping much to promote positive images of women using new technologies, many Women's Studies students have both ventured online and taken off in cyberspace.

I think that now is precisely the time when feminists can provide positive role models for women and encourage interest in computer learning. Many of the images used to represent women who use computers are still considered negative, and the range of characterisations in which women are shown is still very limited. Looking through a number of computer magazines, I found that the people pictured in the advertisements are predominantly male and almost exclusively white. There are very few images of women, and this lack seems to re-emphasise the perception that the field is virtually a male-realm. In addition, women who do appear in the ads are much more likely to be portrayed as sexual objects. These negative images are perpetuated in other media as well.

Movies which focus on new technologies like the Internet, virtual reality and artificial intelligence, reinforce negative stereotypes of women. In these films, the female characters are still portrayed primarily as victims of the new technology, or at best, as innocent girlfriends of the male hero(es). Even the lead character in the 1995 film, *The Net*, a woman (Angela Bennett played by Sandra Bullock) who works with computer viruses, tests software programs and spends most of her time in front of her computer screen, is open to criticism. She is portrayed negatively as a sad, lonely character with very few friends, to such an extent that when she stumbles onto a cyberconspiracy which aims to destroy the defences of major computer networks, the erasure of her identity is easily achieved. Because she has worked in isolation from home there is no one who can positively identify her. Bullock's character—depicted as isolated, never leaving her apartment and cut-off from other people—is not exactly a positive role model for girls thinking of flying into cyber-space. Angela Bennett was too attached to her computer and out of touch with the rest of life.

As lead role in the 1995 film, *Copycat*, a noted criminal psych-ologist (played by Sigourney Weaver) assists San Francisco homicide detective Holly Hunter hunt for a serial killer who has been dubbed copycat because all his crimes have been performed by famous murderers in the past. Weaver's character, like Bullock's is a recluse. Her career as a criminal psychologist lecturer was abruptly ended after she was stalked by a student and survived an attempted murder. She uses the Internet to predict the circumstances of the serial killer's next victim and this eventually leads Hunter to the killer. However, the audience is led to believe that she is nothing but a hysterical woman, eccentric, paranoid, totally controlled by her biology. Although brilliant, her character is tarnished by compulsive and melodramatic behaviour. She is cold, uncompromising and suffers from agorophobia. It is not hard to imagine that such images could encourage many women not to get involved with the Internet and computer technologies in general.

Virtual Possibilities

Nevertheless, despite the bad publicity and negative role models for women, we must acknowledge that not only can we influence cyberspace but we can develop a whole new way of using it so that women are included, interested and benefit from cyberspace. My own experiences should be a positive reminder that it's worth doing. Apart from the obvious, increasing my skills for flying in cyberspace by maintaining the Web site myself—editing, updating, and adding new material—has meant I can now see endless virtual possibilities. Future plans include a feminist library with resources that students can access or even add to via the Web Site <http://arts.deakin. edu.au/guymer/wshp> and a site that introduces students to the main concepts of Women's Studies, Why study it?, What jobs will it lead to?, and a CD-ROM for educators and careers advisers. This project follows on from research I have undertaken recently to investigate Women's Studies graduates: Where are they now? What careers have they embarked on? And, importantly, How has their Women's Studies education influenced their lives? A sample of these interviews will be included on the Web Site in several video clips.

Virtual possibilities of teaching and learning using the Internet are only limited by one's imagination. For off-campus students, the limitation is the telephone system. While current technology allows the use of text and graphics for learning applications over the Internet, the standard telephone system in Australia is not yet up to handling video of sufficient quality to be useful. Rhonda Bunbury argues that:

> not only is there a question of quality,[13] but (more significantly for most committed onliners) there is the question of download time. Onliners are not prepared to wait for large videos to download: they click onto the next fascination. Furthermore, people committed to the artistic quality of the work, are less easily satisfied, so for them animation or video online is not yet a solution (Bunbury 1999).

For all these reasons, Rhonda Bunbury (1998) ended up with six pieces of 4–6 seconds of video instead of 30 minutes, <http://arts. deakin.edu.au/slcs/diversity/multiculture.htm>

However, this will not be a limitation forever. Digital broadcasting will provide extra bandwidth to allow text, graphics and other information to be broadcast alongside the picture. While bandwidth is currently a limitation for students trying to access Internet material from home, the same applies within an educational institution. Most institutions don't yet have the financial resources allocated for IT infrastructure to provide the high speed local area networks required to bring video to every desktop. In the interim, CD-ROM may be my next test flight, it is possibly still the best medium for delivering interactive course materials. The next project proposed is a solution to a learning problem through the development of a Web

---

13. Quality can be gauged by pixels and by frames per second.

site/CD-ROM based on collaborative interactional pedagogy. Until video conferencing is a viable and affordable reality, questions of how we engage with flexible modes of delivery are questions that educators should debate at length.

Successes: What did we all get out of it?

Rhonda Bunbury (1999) sums up her online teaching experience:

> The difficulties and frustrations have been many but as a Web site has actually emerged, the experience can also be said to have been both positive and stimulating. Learning new ways of working have been demanding but engaging. Being creative as a teacher is always an enriching experience. Working in conjunction with like-minded colleagues, made possible by the Online Project, is a real pleasure. Being able to produce research insights as well as information for the wider community, satisfies a long-term goal as the plans for the development of this Web site evolved four years ago, in 1994.

Visions: Where to from here?

Time permitting, my aims are as follows: to learn how to use the Web authoring tools Frontpage, Dreamweaver and Fireworks and many more; to learn about online development through staff development sessions offered within the faculty and the wider university; to seek to participate in a joint research project which engages online teaching/learning materials and to get back to writing the regular research papers for publication which the School and University demand.

The virtual university is still in its infancy. In the meantime, technoheads and forward-thinking academics, departments and institutions are already starting to make use of Internet technologies to support and enhance teaching and learning, ignoring the critics. Virtual possibilities for students range from learning how to use email and computer-mediated conferencing, how to improve their analytic and research skills, how to download attachments and search and create their own Web Sites. As a result of the time and effort invested in Women's Studies online teaching, rich discussions took place in cyberspace and developed into some fabulous final submissions which made the time and effort invested worthwhile. Given all the obstacles, fears and criticisms, online teaching has exciting possibilities for teachers and learners. I dare you all to challenge your fear of flying in cyberspace.

References

Aaron, Jane and Sylvia Walby. (Eds.), 1991. *Out of the Margins: Women's Studies in the nineties*, London: The Falmer Press.

Ås, Berit. 1996. A feminist university: The thrill and challenge of trying to establish an alternative education. In Diane Bell and Renate Klein (Eds.), *Radically Speaking: Feminism reclaimed*. Melbourne: Spinifex Press.

Bantow, Ray, Christine Goodwin, Philip Juler, Pam Mulready, Mary Rice, Elizabeth Stacey and Lin Thompson. 1997. *Computer Conferencing*. Geelong: Deakin University Press.

Bell, Diane and Renate Klein. 1996. *Radically Speaking: Feminism reclaimed*. Melbourne: Spinifex Press.

Bellamy, Suzanne. 1999. Pers. comm. (email) (7 Feb. 1999).

Bowles, Gloria and Renate Klein. (Eds.), 1983. *Theories of Women's Studies*, London: Routledge & Kegan Paul.

Bunbury, Rhonda. 1998. *Diverse Identities ALL 330/630 Cultural Diversity and Children's Literature Study Guide*. Geelong: Deakin University.
<http://arts.deakin.edu.au/slcs/diversity/default.htm>

Bunbury, Rhonda. 1999. Pers. comm. (email) (22.02.99.).

Bunbury, Rhonda and André Czausov. 1998. Many Faces, Many Places.
<http://arts.deakin.edu.au/Manyfaces>

Bunch, Charlotte. 1987. *Passionate Politics: Feminist theory in action*. New York: St Martin's Press.

Cronon Rose, Ellen. 1998. This class meets in cyberspace: Women's Studies via distance education. In Gail Cohee *et al.* (Eds.), *The Feminist Teacher Anthology: Pedagogies and classroom strategies*. New York: Teachers College Press.

Daniels, Cherry and Rhonda Bunbury. 1998. *Blekbala Stori ALL 330/630 Cultural Diversity and Children's Literature Study Guide*. Geelong: Deakin University.
<http://arts.deakin.edu.au/slcs/blekbala/default.htm>

Eva Cuskelly, Shirley Gregor and Jennifer Zelmer. 1994. Learning on the network. *Central Queensland Journal of Regional Development*, Spring, 29–31.

Guymer, Laurel. 1997. Australian Women's Research Centre.
<http://arts.deakin.edu.au/guymer/aworc>

Guymer, Laurel. 1998. *Women's Studies: An introduction. Unit Guide.* Geelong: Deakin University.
  <http://arts.deakin.edu.au/guymer/asw101>
Guymer, Laurel and Renate Klein. 1998a. *Women's Studies Web site.*
  <http://arts.deakin.edu.au/guymer/wshp>
Guymer, Laurel and Renate Klein. 1998b. Feminist Research Methodology.
  <http://arts.deakin.edu.au/guymer/asw311sg>
Hawthorne, Susan. 1996. Real Worlds Virtual Worlds. *Metro Magazine, 108*, 31–35.
Lave, Jean and Etienne Wenger. 1991. *Situated Learning: Legitimate peripheral participation.* New York: Cambridge University Press.
McDonald, James. 1995. Te(k)nowledge: Technology, education and the new student/subject. *Science and Culture, 4* (21), 535–64.
Mahony, Pat and Christine Zmroczek. (Eds.), 1997. *Class Matters: 'Working-Class' women's perspectives on social class.* London: Taylor & Francis.
Morahan-Martin, Janet. 1998. Women and Girls Last: Females and the Internet. Paper presented at the IRISS '98 International Conference, Bristol, UK, 25–27 March.
  <http://www.sosig.ac.uk/iriss/papers/paper55.htm> (27 Feb. 1999).
Mulready, Pam. 1999. Pers. comm. (email) (29.04.99.).
Pharr, Suzanne. 1988. *Homophobia: A weapon of sexism,* Inverness: Chardon Press.
Resnick, Rosalind and Heide Anderson. 1995. Interactive Publishing Alert's 1995 survey of women online.
  <http://www.netcreations.com/ipa/women/>
Senjen, Rye and Jane Guthrey. 1996. *The Internet for Women,* Melbourne: Spinifex Press.
Shuchat, Jo and Antonia Stone. 1986. *The Neuter Computer: Computers for girls and boys.* New York: Neal Schuman.
Spender, Dale. 1995a. Roadblocks Ahead: Managing Gender Bias in Cyberspace. Keynote address, Networked Technologies for Australia's Health, Melbourne, 13–14 July, Day 2.
  <http://www.vichealth.vic.gov.au/publicat/ proceed/spender.htm>
  (21 Feb. 1999).
Spender, Dale. 1995b. *Nattering on the Net: Women, power and cyberspace.* Melbourne: Spinifex Press.
Sutton, Jo and Scarlet Pollock. 1997. Equal Access for Women [Internet]. Prepared for Universal Access Workshop: Developing a Canadian Access Strategy: Universal Access to Essential Network Services, February 6–8.
  <http://www.fis.utoronto.ca/ research/iprp/ua/gender/ws.html> (27 Feb. 1999).
Turkle, Sherry. 1988. Computational Reticence: Why women fear the intimate machine. In Cheris Kramarae (Ed.). *Technology and Women's Voices.* London: Routledge and Kegan Paul.

four

Email Forums and Women's Studies: The Example of WMST-L

Joan Korenman

'It changed my life!' Many feminists of the 1960s and '70s, myself included, said this about the women's movement. Twenty-five years later, I find I'm saying it again—this time, about *WMST-L*, an email forum that I started in 1991 for discussion of Women's Studies teaching, research, and program administration.

Through *WMST-L*, I've 'met' thousands of people all over the world who share an interest in Women's Studies. Some have become my good friends. *WMST-L* keeps me informed about what's happening in Women's Studies: events, trends, controversies, publications, films, research projects, classroom strategies and problems, new directions and developments, and more. When I need information, I have an international body of well-informed virtual colleagues to whom I can turn. And when I travel, I continually meet people whom I 'know' from *WMST-L*.

People relatively new to email may wonder why I'm making such a fuss about *WMST-L*. After all, according to the Gender-Related Electronic Forums Web site (<<u>http://www.umbc.edu/wmst/forums.html</u>>), there are now well over 500 women-related email forums, or 'lists', as they're most often called. *WMST-L* may be a fine list, but so too are many others.

That's quite true—now. But in early 1991, when I started *WMST-L*, I could count on my fingers all the women-related lists. And while many factors contributed to the proliferation of such lists between then and now, I believe *WMST-L*'s success played a significant part in spurring the growth of other women-focused forums.

In this essay, I plan to focus on my experience starting and running *WMST-L*, and on ways in which email lists like *WMST-L* have affected Women's Studies. My hope is that this account will interest both email novices and people with considerable online experience.

I ventured online for the first time in 1990, prodded by a good friend a thousand miles away who saw how easy it would be to keep in touch by email. A lifelong technophobe, I approached this experience very hesitantly, sure that one wrong keystroke would destroy my computer. But even though the first few months were a confusing jumble of new procedures, new commands, and new and old mistakes, I quickly found myself captivated by the possibilities of this new medium. The same friend who had pushed me to get an email account introduced me to email discussion lists, and I was hooked! I joined a WordPerfect list and watched in amazement as my emailbox filled with messages about this wordprocessing software from people all over the world. Whenever someone asked a question or provided an answer, copies of the message were sent automatically to everyone who had 'subscribed to' (that is, joined) the list. What an amazing resource! Until then, I had been limited to what I could learn from the WordPerfect manual or from my department's knowledgeable secretary. If neither the book nor the secretary had the answer, I was out of luck. But not any longer. Having joined the WordPerfect list, I now had access to experienced users worldwide. Was I unsure how to create a macro to perform some complex maneuver? No problem—I needed only to send my question to the list. Quite possibly, I'd have an answer within minutes.

Gradually, it dawned on me that this technology could be immensely useful for Women's Studies. At the time, I was director of the Women's Studies Program at UMBC (University of Maryland, Baltimore County). Each June, I attended the annual conference of the National Women's Studies Association and came away energized, stimulated by new ideas. Wouldn't it be wonderful, I thought, if we could have a similarly productive exchange of information and ideas not just once or twice a year at conferences but continually. The next thing I knew, I was starting *WMST-L*, an email list for

Pattanaik

Guymer 3

Women's Studies teaching, research, and program administration. A few lists already existed for discussion of gender issues, but the discussion tended to be rather wild and argumentative. I looked in vain for a place where people committed to Women's Studies could talk about problems they were encountering in the classroom, exchange syllabi and tips, track down information they needed for their research, seek help with administering their programs, or learn about relevant conferences, calls for papers, publications, and jobs. *WMST-L* would be that place.

My first task was to find a home for my proposed list. In early 1991, there was only one full-featured software program for running lists. It was (and still is) called Listserv, and in 1991 it ran mostly on IBM mainframe computers. My campus, UMBC, didn't have IBM mainframes, so I approached the computer support staff at UMBC's sister campus, the University of Maryland, College Park. They were already running a number of email lists, and once I obtained approval from the appropriate College Park dean, the computer staff was happy to create and provide technical support for *WMST-L*. Their only reservation was their uncertainty that there would be enough interest to keep a Women's Studies list going. They needn't have worried; within a couple of years, *WMST-L* was among the most active of their 70+ lists!

Once I had the dean's approval, I found myself having to make a number of decisions about the list. One was its name. I originally wanted to call it FEMINIST, which described its outlook and would just fit the 8-character maximum set by IBM mainframes. Several people advised against this name. A few pointed out that it might attract anti-feminist harassers; another noted that FEMINIST might suggest a broad discussion of gender-related issues rather than the narrower, more academic focus I had in mind. So I settled instead on *WMST-L*. 'WMST' is the acronym for Women's Studies courses at my university and a number of others; the '-L' is a convention to denote an email list, though it's used less now than in the early '90s. The only drawback I was aware of was the difficulty of pronouncing

'*WMST-L*'; sometime later, my secretary informed me that whenever she hears the name '*WMST-L*', she thinks of elephant droppings!

Another key decision involved the level of control I wished to have. Many lists are 'moderated'. That means that all messages go first to a human being, the moderator, who must approve them before they're sent out to everyone else. *WMST-L*, by contrast, is an 'unmoderated' list. No one sees the messages ahead of time. I arranged things this way for several reasons. One is that I like the spontaneity and rapid pace of an unmoderated list. You don't have to wait for someone to approve your message: you send it, and seconds later it appears. And a minute or two after that, you may already have a reply. Also, if I moderated the list, I'd feel tied to it. I could never feel free to disappear for a while, or simply not log on: the list would come to a grinding halt. Then, too, I didn't want to be put in the position of having to pass judgment on every message. What if I think a message has worthwhile content but is not well expressed— perhaps it's unclear or too snide—do I then return it to the writer with editorial comments? No thanks! In my Other Life, I'm an English professor: the last thing I need is more writing to correct! Finally, I learn more from the list because it's unmoderated. I'm embarrassed to recall the number of times I've thought, 'What a stupid message,' only to see from the responses that the message had more to it than I at first recognized. If the list were moderated, legitimate messages might be suppressed out of ignorance or prejudice.

After making these decisions, I set about publicizing the list. Many Women's Studies people were at first rather skeptical about an electronic forum. Relatively few used email. Some were afraid of computers, while others questioned whether so 'mechanical' a medium was compatible with Women's Studies' humanistic ethos. The then president of the National Women's Studies Association chided me for opening up the community to government eaves-dropping. I gave a number of conference talks and presentations designed to explain the advantages of electronic communications and to address people's hesitations. I also sent announcements to every list I knew that dealt with related matters, as well as to NEW-LIST, a list for announcing the establishment of new lists and changes to old ones (see <http://scout.cs.wisc.edu/caservices/new-list/index.html>). I made sure, too, to send printed announcements via snail mail (that is, the regular postal service) to a number of Women's Studies journals, though the announcements wouldn't appear for months.

My electronic announcements quickly produced results. In the first three days after the announcements appeared, 127 people subscribed to *WMST-L* ('subscribe' is simply list jargon for 'join'; no money is involved). By the end of May, the number had increased to 256. Approximately 30% were male, reflecting the fact that in 1991, men vastly outnumbered women as email users and were thus more likely to learn of *WMST-L*'s existence from the electronic announcements. Over time, as more women learned of the list, the percentage of women rose; currently, women make up approximately 90% of *WMST-L*'s subscribers.

I was delighted that the list was attracting so many people. One message especially thrilled me. Just a few days after the list got started, I received an email message from a New Zealand sociologist on sabbatical in Finland telling me that he had just heard about *WMST-L* from his Finnish colleagues, and that he had written to his colleagues back in New Zealand to let them know about this valuable new resource. I was blown away! *WMST-L* was only a few days old; none of my colleagues in the English department at UMBC were even remotely aware of its existence, and yet people already know about it in Finland and New Zealand. I'm not sure anyone else felt the earth shrink that day, but I certainly did!

Pattanaik 1

Though I was very pleased at how rapidly the word was spreading and people were subscribing, my pleasure soon turned to dismay. The online discussion, which had begun reasonably enough with some queries and calls for papers, suddenly moved in directions I hadn't anticipated. The atmosphere began to resemble an Abbott and Costello 'who's on first?' farce. For example, one subscriber, whom I'll call RF, asked whether his message made it through to the list. Someone else replied, simply, 'No message received from you.' Several new subscribers received this as their first message, and were understandably confused and upset. 'Do you require a minimum number of postings of your members?' one asked. 'I prefer to listen a bit before posting,' replied another. 'I just subscribed to *WMST-L* this morning and don't know RF' protested a third.[1]

A more difficult problem erupted side-by-side with the farcical confusion: gender war. A question about what to include in an 'Introduction to Women's Studies' soon gave rise to a discussion of how not to alienate the men in the class. From there, it was an easy jump to the role of men in Women's Studies more generally, especially as teachers, and from there . . . well, the battle raged.

Linguists like Susan Herring who have studied male/female participation and interaction in online discussions have observed that men often dominate these discussions by the frequency and length of their messages and by their more assured, aggressive tone (Herring 1993). Herring's observations were borne out by the early discussion on *WMST-L*. Though men made up approximately 30% of the subscribers, they posted 46.4% of the messages in May, and in the first week of June, the proportion of male-authored messages escalated to just under half (49%). The men's messages were also, in general, considerably longer, averaging seventeen lines versus the women's average of nine lines in May, twelve lines versus eight in the first week of June. The men tended to take a more assertive, even aggressive stance. 'If you are serious in this question, your ignorance abounds,' declared one man early in June. 'I have neither the time, patience, energy, nor desire to clear my screen of all the nonsense I read tonight,' proclaimed another. A third complained somewhat petulantly about another subscriber's grammar: 'Can we have an end to sentences like "if a thief breaks into a house and breaks their leg"?' Though one or two of the women seemed willing,

---

[1.] All quotations from *WMST-L* messages are taken from the list's logfiles for late May/early June 1991. I have not identified the senders for reasons of privacy.

even eager, to spar with the men, many more were turned off. One observed:

> I find it rather difficult to reply to this message (re: unreality of women's oppression and demand for proof of such) because I feel it invalidates my experience to the point that speech becomes difficult . . . . [T]he author . . . is speaking in terms that nearly silence me.

While her lament elicited sympathetic notes from some of the women, one of the men responded: 'Why are these women trying to duck responsibility for their own voices, I wondered. Why would they *choose*[2] silence, then blame *me* for it?'

Some *WMST-L* subscribers regarded the gender wars as regrettable but inevitable; others seemed to relish the battle. One male sociologist observed, perhaps tongue in cheek:

> Yeah, Steve, stick around. The folks here are fun. No one's run any of us out yet. Of course we talk too much, dominate the discourse, start fights, that's what men are for! Particularly academic men.

I couldn't share his lightheartedness; indeed, I was in despair. People were unsubscribing in droves, including many of the serious, accomplished academics I had hoped the list would attract. Some people sent me private email explaining their departure. The two most frequently cited reasons for leaving were the list's heavy mail volume (averaging fifteen messages per day) and the childish, contentious discourse. One person observed: 'If I want to fight with people, I can just go down the hall and scream at my colleagues. I don't need an email list for this!'

Desperate to move the list back on track, I started sending messages explaining my intentions in starting *WMST-L*, what sorts of messages should be sent privately or to other lists, and how to do things like unsubscribe without announcing one's desire to the world. I then reworked some of those messages into a 'welcome letter' that I sent to all new subscribers, so that they would know

---

[2]. An asterisk in email is the equivalent of italics for emphasis. ASCII email doesn't offer many ways to indicate emphasis.

from the start what the list was about and what was and was not appropriate. I also wrote a fairly extensive User's Guide to help people learn about and make use of *WMST-L*'s many resources and procedures. (The current, much expanded edition is available at <<u>http://www.umbc.edu/wmst/user-guide.html</u>>.) To my amazement, these measures worked. Within a few months, the list had turned around: it was more serious, more focused, and less contentious, and, for the most part, it has remained so. Indeed, it has been acclaimed in print as 'highly professional', 'well managed' (Hildenbrand 1995: 221), a 'rich information resource', and an 'outstanding networking resource for practitioners in the field of Women's Studies' (Muns 1994: 411).

Maintaining this sort of list has been a continual challenge, one requiring a great deal of time, attention, and diplomacy. I call myself *WMST-L*'s Official Nag. I intervene at times on the list if I think a thread is moving away from *WMST-L*'s focus. Even more often, I will send private messages to people who send inappropriate postings. I'm continually being told that *WMST-L* has many more substantive messages and much less junk mail than other unmoderated lists. I think that's one reason that the list has continued to grow and flourish. With more than 4000 subscribers from forty-eight countries, it is the largest women-related academic list in the world.

One other feature that has contributed to the list's success is its 'edited digest'. At the start of 1992, in response to frequent complaints about the list's heavy volume of mail, I created this option for those (now numbering between 550 and 800 subscribers) who would prefer not to clutter their emailbox with so many individual messages. Each day, I would take all the messages (except those that shouldn't have been sent to the list to start with) and arrange them into one or several bundles, with related messages in the same bundle and a table of contents at the start of each bundle. Eventually, the Listserv software instituted its own digest option, but its version is just one humongous bundle containing all the day's messages, even duplicates and garbage like 'hi Janie' and 'unsubscribe me'. When the Listserv version appeared, many edited digest recipients pleaded with me not to abandon the far superior edited version. I've heeded their pleas, aided by modest funding from UMBC that has enabled me to turn over the edited digest's creation to a paid assistant.

Though *WMST-L* is a large, active, highly acclaimed list, it doesn't please everyone. Some people object to my efforts to control the kinds of messages that are sent to the list. One subscriber complained about my attempts to keep the list's mail volume at a moderate level and questioned 'how useful is it to attempt to control the boundaries of discussion on a list'. She went on to say, 'Discourse must be open. Control, in cyberspace, seems unapproachable. So, by the way, do attempts to mandate behavior.' Her remarks underscore the fact that people hold sharply differing attitudes toward issues like the place of order and control in cyberspace. On the one hand, there exists a strong libertarian ethos. Many people believe that the Internet should be a place of unfettered freedom. In their view, people should be able to say whatever they want without someone else imposing restraints. On the other hand, perhaps even more people believe in the need for order and control. They want to be able to use the resources of electronic communications without having to wade through immense amounts of clutter and distraction. These competing philosophies help to shape lists.

On some lists, anything goes. The listowner may feel that the subscribers should determine the list's personality and direction. Or the listowner may want everyone to feel comfortable and completely relaxed about sending messages, and may feel that anyone bothered by high volume or an undefined focus can simply unsubscribe. Many lists have such a philosophy. One is *WORDS-L*, which was started at about the same time as *WMST-L*, ostensibly for discussion of English-language words and how they're used. In practice, however, people send messages to *WORDS-L* on just about everything— politics, jokes, finding a third cousin in Oregon, a recipe for Christmas cookies, saying hi to others on the list, etc. The list is set up so that it can distribute up to 500 messages per day (*WMST-L*'s daily limit, by contrast, is set at fifty, and that limit has never been reached). Apparently, there's a great spirit of camaraderie among *WORDS-L*'s 120 or so subscribers, and I imagine that they do have a good deal in common—lots of free time, large email quotas, and a high tolerance for the inane. It's not a list I'd want to join, but its subscribers are enthusiastic, and no harm is done if most of us decide it's not for us.

If *WORDS-L* exemplifies the 'libertarian' or 'anything goes' philosophy of listowning, *WMST-L* is a good example of a list that values order and control. But though I clearly prefer *WMST-L* to *WORDS-L*, I don't mean to imply that one philosophy of list management is right and the other wrong. A lot depends on the purpose the list is designed to serve. The 'anything goes' philosophy is fine for a casual chat list where the main goal is to establish an online community, and where it doesn't matter if most people feel compelled to unsubscribe. However, if the list is intended to serve as a professional resource, then it seems to me that the listowner should make it possible for people who need the list to remain, even if they have limited time, small email quotas, or they're on systems where they have to pay for every message they receive.

The tension between 'anything goes' and 'order and control' confronts almost all listowners, no matter what their lists are about. As the person in charge of a Women's Studies list, however, I find myself facing an additional challenge. Women's Studies has tended to oppose notions of hierarchy, the privileging of some voices above others. Authority is suspect; most feminist groups, including my own Women's Studies program, operate by consensus. Thus, many people expect that *WMST-L*, too, will be governed by consensus, and are dismayed when I insist on adhering to the policies I deem best. This is unfeminist, they charge.

I've given a lot of thought to this accusation. As a feminist, I value other women's views. Finally, though, my experience leads me to conclude that consensus is not an effective way to run a large, active email list like *WMST-L*. Consensus works well in small groups, not a group of 4000. It requires that people have time to work things out, not race through their email. It works best when people share similar backgrounds and assumptions. Even though everyone on *WMST-L* shares an interest in Women's Studies, that term means one thing to activists, another to theoreticians, yet another to program administrators, and still another to graduate students. Compounding these differences is the fact that subscribers come from forty-eight countries as different as the United States, Brazil, Pakistan, Australia, Turkey, and Zimbabwe.

WMST-L's size and diversity, coupled with its substantial mail volume, led me early on to formulate the list's most controversial policy: *WMST-L* is not the place to discuss gender-related political and social problems unless the discussion relates directly to teaching or research. Here, again, I've been accused of being unfeminist. However, if feminism involves respecting other women's needs and providing choices rather than forcing everyone into one mold, then I'd argue that the policy is eminently feminist. Other lists exist for discussing rape, abortion, domestic violence, sexual harassment, and other gender-related issues. Gender-Related Electronic Forums <http://www.umbc.edu/wmst/forums.html> makes it easy to find such lists. People can thus tailor their subscriptions to meet their needs and interests. Some people will choose to subscribe only to *WMST-L*, some will choose only issue-oriented lists, and some will choose both. No one will be coerced by another person's preferences.

WMST-L has had a major impact on Women's Studies. It has made possible international networking by people interested in Women's Studies, even those at remote institutions or without institutional affiliation. Here are some examples of ways in which subscribers have made use of the list (taken from private messages sent to me):

- A US graduate student in history wrote:
  [*WMST-L*] has enhanced my education in Women's Studies and has provided information that I share with my instructors and colleagues as well as with the students I teach. I depend on this list for information that I would not be able to access in any other format—it is like a lifeline.

- A faculty member from Nova Scotia, Canada, obtained references on homosexuality and child care that proved useful and important sources for a precedent-setting Canadian court case.

- A woman from New Zealand observed that:
  using [WMST-L] was the best way to inspire me to learn more and feel that I could belong in cyberspace too . . . . I've also found the list useful to combat academic loneliness.

- An Australian professor wrote:
  The beauty of these reference lists from the WMST-L is that they come with a comment or summary or discussion. Because of those commentaries and discussions they are even better resources than annotated bibliographies for me and my students.

  She adds:
  The discussions and references often feed directly into my own research on Cixous' deconstructive reading and writing practice, feminist pedagogy, feminist epistemology, and a feminist philosophy of humor . . . . Even though I am new to the list and a novice on the Net I already feel as though I am part of a much larger movement and intellectual community than I did before.

- A librarian in Israel wrote:
  As a librarian, I have been most interested in the discussions of new books. I have ordered quite a few books that I first heard mentioned on [the] list. I often forward bibliography lists that have been sent to the list to teachers who I think may be interested.

- The Director of Women's Studies at a Canadian university reported:
  As a director of an Interdisciplinary program, I get asked lots of questions about things way out of my competence or the competence of other people here, as there isn't a feminist scholar in every discipline. I've turned to the list on several occasions and always got prompt, useful, detailed responses.

- A professor in the US received help in identifying
  materials on Chicanas/Latinas for her Psychology of
  Women course. She added:

  > I find this network absolutely invaluable as a source of
  > teaching ideas, keeping up on some of the research others
  > are doing, and just generally as a psychological boost and
  > inspiration.

Email lists like *WMST-L* have also provided new ways for people to become known in Women's Studies. Several years ago, Pennsylvania State University professor Nancy Wyatt and I conducted a survey on *WMST-L* in which we asked subscribers whether there were people whose postings they especially valued or looked for. One of the people most often cited was someone who at that point was unemployed, but she was nonetheless making a name for herself among Women's Studies academics all over the world, and she went on to get an academic position. Also, many graduate students and untenured faculty have told me that when they go to conferences, they find they're known from their participation on *WMST-L*. This kind of recognition used to occur much later in someone's career. I've also begun to get requests for letters of support from people up for tenure who want their participation on *WMST-L* to be taken into consideration (whether it is taken into account is not yet clear).

One of the most important recent developments in Women's Studies has been the internationalization of its concerns. The Ford Foundation and FIPSE (the US-based Fund for the Improvement of Post Secondary Education) are just two of a number of funding agencies that in the last few years have encouraged projects designed to broaden the Women's Studies curriculum to be less US-focused and, indeed, less Eurocentric. I think it is highly likely that some of the impetus behind the internationalization of Women's Studies comes from the new information technologies. Email lists and the World Wide Web put us in contact with people all over the world and make us aware of the narrowness, the provincialism, of seeing things only from a national or, indeed, a <u>Eurocentric</u> perspective.

Though I've been focusing on the academic side of Women's

Pattanaik 1
Pollock and
Sutton 2
Arnold 11

Studies, email lists have also helped to enhance feminist activism. They make it exceptionally easy to find and communicate with like-minded people. A number of lists have been created to address activist issues, from local lists that combat violence against women in a single community to international lists with members all over the world working on behalf of women's equal rights or to wipe out the practice of female genital mutilation. Organizations like the Feminist Majority, the Network of East-West Women, Women Leaders Online, and the Women's International League for Peace and Freedom maintain email lists to keep their members informed about proposed legislation, right-wing backlash activities, or companies to boycott or support. (Information about women-related activist lists can be found at <http://www.umbc.edu/wmst/f_actv.html>)[1]

Email lists like *WMST-L* have helped to bring together women around the world, making possible a level of communication and networking unthinkable just a few years ago. In stressing the positive impact of electronic communications, however, I am not trying to deny that the new information technology presents problems as well as possibilities. As Cheris Kramarae (1997: 151) has observed:

> Technology not only unites, but also divides: the rich and poor, individuals and countries, upper classes and working classes, women and men.

Everything I've been saying in this essay, for example, depends on people having access to the technology, but too many people currently do not. In 1996, Patti Whaley (1996: 230) offered the following sobering statistics:

Pattanaik 1

- 95% of all Internet users are in Europe or North America;
- 80% of the world still has no basic telecommunications capabilities;
- 2/3 of the world's people have never made a phone call.

---

[1] The space between f and actv. has a single underscore which is obscured by this underlining.

These statistics may have improved a bit since 1996, but not enough. Those of us in relatively privileged circumstances must work to ensure that access to information technology is readily available to everyone.

But even universal access isn't enough; we have to ask the crucial question, 'access to *what?*' In 'Creating E-Community', Gary Chapman (1999: 20) suggests that one reason for the <u>low Internet participation among African Americans</u> across income levels is that '... there is little in cyberspace to reflect their community or reflect their concerns, and so the content issue becomes more important than people might expect'. The 'content issue' must be of paramount concern as well for people in Women's Studies. We must ask *what* information the Internet makes available. Whose theories will we study? Whose history will we learn? Women's Studies has struggled to bring to light women's experiences and accomplishments. We must be just as dedicated to making sure that women's experiences and accomplishments are fully represented in the electronic world. And we cannot do so effectively unless we participate in that world. By giving women a compelling reason to become involved with electronic communication, women-related email lists are helping to alter the Internet's once lopsided male/female ratio[3] and to make the electronic world more adequately reflect the varied realities of women's lives.

It's tempting to end my remarks on this upbeat note. But while I

Mont-
gomery 5

---

3. Statistics regarding Internet usage by gender are, for the most part, of limited reliability. Perhaps the most extensive demographic survey is the one conducted twice a year since 1994 by the Georgia Institute of Technology <<u>http://www.cc.gatech.edu/gvu/user_surveys/</u>> in the US. In their first survey, approximately 6% of Internet users were women. In the most recent (ninth) survey, completed in late 1998, this had risen to 38.7%. Among young people aged eleven to twenty, 43.8% were female. I might note that this survey looks primarily at use of the World Wide Web, while my discussion focuses primarily on email lists that precede and exist independently of the Web; however, the pattern is similar for non-Web use. In a 1994 article that does not focus on the Web, Stephanie Brail (1994: 40) estimates female Internet users (presumably in 1993) at '10 to 15 per cent', while that figure has risen in most current (1998–99) accounts to more than 40% (Peltz 1998), and, indeed, 52% of America Online's audience is now female (Krochmal/<<u>http://www.techweb.com/wire/story/TWB19980610</u> <u>S0019</u>> 06 June 1998: Female AOL Users Now The Majority)

feel enormously excited and heartened by what *WMST-L* and other women-related email lists have accomplished, I am aware that the struggle for equality and self-determination in cyberspace continues, with the site of conflict shifting from email to the World Wide Web. Business interests, which by and large have ignored email lists, increasingly see the Web as a potentially lucrative, untapped source of commerce. The commercialization of the Web poses a threat to Women's Studies in several ways. For one thing, as Crystal Kile (quoted in DeLoach 1996) has observed, these business interests often undermine the representation of women's diversity, tending instead to homogenize and stereotype women; they create 'the "woman's Internet market" to cater to the same ol' women-as-consumers, Seventeen-Cosmo-Woman's-Day market . . . .' Also, the large budgets available to commercial interests threaten not just Women's Studies but much non-profit activity on the Web. I worry that modestly-funded or free Web sites may not be able to compete successfully against glossy, high-tech, state of the art commercial sites.

Perhaps the most serious threat may come from the growing ties between search engines (the primary tools for finding information on the Web) and business interests. Currently, if you ask a search engine to identify Web sites containing information on a given topic, the search engine will provide a list of sites, often arranged according to their relevance to your query. However, the distinction between information and e-commerce is beginning to blur. At least one search engine, GoTo <http://www.goto.com/>, uses a bidding system that allows companies to determine their placement in the search results. It's as if you went to a library's card catalog and found the books listed according to the size of the fees the publishers had paid to the library. While few other search engines currently use so blatantly commercial a method of placement, the search engine Infoseek has recently joined forces with the Disney company, while Snap has paired with NBC, and AltaVista will steer users to goods on Shopping.com. According to one news account of the AltaVista deal:

. . . if a user conducts a search on AltaVista, the results also will provide a link toward the purchase of relevant products. . . . Though there will be a link to Shopping.com from the AltaVista site, it won't always be apparent whether a user is buying from Shopping.com or completing a transaction through AltaVista.
(Hu <http://www.news.com/News/Item/0,4,30818,00.html>, 12 Jan. 1999).

As increasing amounts of our information come to us online, it becomes vitally important that people who know and care about Women's Studies be able both to create that information and to assure that it can be found easily and unambiguously. Women's Studies programs should encourage their students to prepare for careers in information technology, as computer programmers, software and hardware designers, systems managers and analysts, and IT-savvy librarians or 'information specialists'. Only through such active involvement can we assure that *we* define our needs and concerns and participate in creating the technologies to meet them.

References

Brail, Stephanie. 1994. Take Back the Net! *On the Issues*, (Winter) 39–42.
Chapman, Gary. 1999. Creating E-Community. *Educom Review 34* (1), 16–22.
    <http://www.educause.edu/ir/library/html/erm9919.html>
DeLoach, Amelia. 1996. March 1. Grrrls Exude Attitude. *CMC Magazine*.
    <http://www.december.com/cmc/mag/1996/mar/deloach.html>
Herring, Susan C. 1993. Gender and democracy in computer-mediated communi-
    cation. *Electronic Journal of Communication 3* (2).
    <http://www.cios.org/www/ejc/v3n293.htm>
    Also available at <http://www.usyd.edu.au/su/social/papers/herring.txt>
Hildenbrand, Suzanne. 1995. Electronic Graffiti or Scholar's Tool?: A Critical
    Evaluation of Selected Women's Lists on Internet. In Eva Steiner Moseley (Ed.),
    Women, Information, and the Future: Collecting and Sharing Resources Worldwide. Fort
    Atkinson, WI: Highsmith Press.
Hu, Jim. 1999, January 12. Compaq's AltaVista strategy emerges. *CNET News.com:*
    <http://www.news.com/News/Item/0,4,30818,00.html>
Kramarae, Cheris. 1997. Technology Policy, Gender, and Cyberspace. *Duke Journal of
    Gender Law and Policy 4* (1) 149–58.
    <http://www.law.duke.edu/shell/cite.p1?4+Duke+J.+Gender+L.+&+Pol'y149>
Krochmal, Mo. 1998, June 06. Female AOL Users Now The Majority. *TechWeb:*
    <http://www.techweb.com/wire/story/TWB19980610S0019>

Muns, Raleigh. 1994. Appendix: List Review Service. In Tony Abbott (Ed.), *On Internet 94: An International Guide to Electronic Journals, Newsletters, Texts, Discussion Lists, and Other Resources on the Internet.* Westport and London: Mecklermedia.

Peltz, Jennifer. 1998, December 2. Women Join the Net. *PC World Today:*
<http://www.pcworld.com/pcwtoday/article/0,1510,8914,00.html>

Whaley, Patti. 1996. Potential Contributions of Information Technologies to Human Rights. *Women & Performance: A Journal of Feminist Theory 17* (9:1) 225–32.
<http://www.echonyc.com/~women/Issue17/public-whaley.html>

five

Everyday Use: Women, Work and Online 'Play'

Alesia Montgomery

Does 'cyberspace' transform women's identities and relations? Is it eroding social and geographic boundaries? To answer these questions, we must pay attention to how online use emerges in everyday life. And to understand everyday online use, we must consider the relations among paid labor, free time and online use.

Paid labor and free time *seem* like vinegar and oil—the two don't mix. Thus, the literature on women, paid labor and computers tends to focus on the working conditions of women employed to use or make computers (for example, Hossfeld 1990; Markussen 1995; Mitter 1995; Odedra-Straub 1995; Webster 1996; Zuboff 1988). A separate literature examines gendered patterns of online communication, the 'gender gap' in online use, and women's online play, organizing and care-giving—activities that occur during our free time (for example, Herring, Johnson and DiBenedetto 1995; McRae 1997; Shade 1993; Turkle 1995; Reyes 1998). Although some researchers explore border-crossing between virtual worlds and 'real life', relatively little attention has been focused on how paid labor influences these excursions. In particular, there is little research on how differences in paid labor may shape differences among women in personal online use.

In this article I examine how work identities, demands and surveillance shape when, why and how women go online. To explore this issue, I've talked to seventeen women with diverse jobs and backgrounds who live in various parts of the United States. Rather than studying a specific online group or type of play, I examine the practices of any woman with online access at her job. To understand how online ties develop—or fail to develop—we must study those who do and *do not* form new ties online. The women in my study are not a representative sample, yet they may help explain the diverse contexts of online use. All names have been changed.

~

My approach may seem unusual. The 'digital divide' is usually framed in terms of those who do and don't have online access at home. Online users tend to be relatively affluent white men in urban areas (National Science Board 1998; Hoffman and Novak 1998; U.S. Department of Commerce 1998). However, despite current disparities, Morgan Stanley analysts argue that online use may become almost ubiquitous in the US early in the next century (Meeker and DePuy 1996). Like the spread of televisions and telephones, dropping costs and rising popularity may result in just about everyone having access. However, *quality* and *place* of access may vary (Mitchell 1999; NCES 1997). For some people, online use may be centered outside the home. Even if projections of universal access are exaggerations, it seems likely that online access will become commonplace in high income countries. We cannot simply compare the digital haves and have-nots—we must examine differences in the patterns of online use.

My interest in online use at work stems from my concern about the ways paid labor shapes self-definition and voice—and how women struggle to find space for self-expression, empowerment and community in their daily lives (see Collins 1991). Too often we look only for the most dramatic breaks with conventions, the most exciting instances of play or activism. However, to see instances of personal transformation and collective organization—or processes that reproduce existing identities and relations—we must also ask quiet questions: When, why and how do diverse women take breaks in their daily routines? What do they do with their free time? Who do they talk to? How do everyday routines and resources—for example, access to communication tools—shape the nature and reach of their interactions?

Among the women I spoke with, online use does not simply reflect personal choices and resources during leisure moments at home—

differences in free time and online access on the job influence online disparities and patterns of exchange. In addition, the types of people they interact with online seem shaped by their work. For my interviewees, lack of interest and fear of 'wackos' tends to discourage online contact with strangers—with the exception of distant colleagues and clients. Paid labor does not determine personal online use, but it seems to influence the possibilities for 'play' and community. My interviewees are using the Internet to empower themselves and expand their social space, but their online excursions rarely cross economic and occupational boundaries.

Access and Time

Among the women I spoke with, those with liberal online access at work—whether or not they have home access—seem to have good opportunities for personal use. Having one's own Internet-capable computer—and working on it regularly—may be more important than whether that computer is at home or work. Public access may not be as good as having job access. Working regularly on the same computer may provide more opportunities for slipping into personal use, developing online skills and saving messages for possible use later. Regardless of whether they have home computers, almost all of my interviewees (fifteen of seventeen) describe slipping back and forth between personal and work use. Women with considerable job autonomy seem to have the best opportunities for personal online use—yet even they have concerns about electronic surveillance or nosy co-workers.

Cassie is a thirty-year-old returning student. She doesn't have a computer at home, and the library in the rural town where she lives only has one computer. Her university has a computing lab, but it is a long drive between her home and school. She mainly uses the lab to type assignments—she doesn't have time for play. Currently, she does not go online at all. Her old receptionist job seems to have provided better online opportunities. Cassie describes online use by

Pattanaik 1

her former co-workers:

> We weren't really supposed to use the web for personal reasons, but that was only verbal. So, in theory, we weren't supposed to use it for personal reasons, but in action we did . . . . The secretary [had the most freedom to go online] . . . due in part to the setup of the office and also due in part to the fact that being that she was the sole secretary, she ordered a lot of the supplies that we needed . . . . For her computer, she ordered side panels so that from the sides you can't see [her screen] . . . she had a CD [on her computer] so she'd listen to music and surf the web.

How did the secretary have time to surf the web?

> The only time [she] would be interrupted is if [she] had a . . . call . . . or if an administrator gave [her] something specific to work on and [she] needed to write a letter or something like that.

Cassie's opportunities to hide online 'play' were not as good. As 'the first person you'd see' in the office, her receptionist duties kept her busy and highly visible. Occasionally she used email to chat with a friend who worked in another part of the building:

> Even though we were supposed to be working, we were working on the computer about her wedding. . . . It's neat.

She also surfed the web to find information about colleges. Remember that Cassie currently does not go online at all. Having one's own computer—and working on it regularly—may tend to further personal online use.

Like Cassie, Chandra, a college instructor, does not *own* a computer—however, she does have her own computer at work. While taking a break from crunching numbers or writing papers, she goes online. Sometimes her 'breaks' involve surfing to web sites related to her professional interests. At other times, her online use is purely personal—for example, checking her horoscope, reading about events at a local club, looking up recipes, forwarding jokes to friends. Unlike Cassie, Chandra does not worry about being caught by a supervisor. However, she does have concerns about colleagues or students using her computer and having access to her information when she's away. While she was on vacation, someone used her

Hughes 8

computer and email address at work to subscribe to a <u>pornography</u> <u>site</u>, and so far she has been unable to stop the site from sending her mail.

Of course, online access does not always translate into personal use. For example, Wendy, a stockbroker, has much more online privacy than Chandra. She often works from home, emailing stock information to her clients. She says that her emails to clients

> never cross into personal comments—because we're in the securities industry, an email is the same as a letter going out. We have written regulations regarding what we can say.

Whenever possible, she prefers to meet face-to-face with clients. She says that they like to hear her voice, especially during times of financial scares. Although Wendy does not have anyone looking over shoulder, she tries not to slip into personal online use while working. She describes the web as a 'trap' that pulls people into 'playing on it' and 'wasting time'. For Wendy, there is little difference between the types of web sites she visits for pleasure and work: In her 'free' time, she enjoys reading the *Wall Street Journal* online.

Like Wendy, Joyce, a social sciences professor, has online access at home and on the job, and she works from both sites. Joyce's university has written policies against personal online use, but there isn't anyone enforcing the rules (at least not for professors). Although she pays some attention to the policy, she feels pretty free to do what she wants online:

> I pay attention to [the policy], in the sense that I have some discomfort doing some things, like I'm not without guilt when I do things that are real personal at work. But I don't follow it to the letter of the law. Either I figure out some way to make it work-related, or I just ignore the policy. . . . They do send us periodic memos about it . . . but nobody's over us looking.

Joyce argues that she has a *right* to talk with family and friends at work:

> They have this policy for everything—the computer, the phone, the stapler, everything, it's like, look. . . . My whole life . . . when I go home,

I'm still working for [the university.] So when I'm at work, let me make a phone call, you know, let me call check on my kids, let me call—and whatever, my car leaks—and also my friend miles away—let me call up for business and have a conversation as well.

While Joyce believes that all workers at her university should have the ability to go online for personal reasons, she recognizes that she has more privileges:

If you're comparing professors to secretaries or something, you probably would get a different thing. . . . And if you're a janitorial worker, you probably don't have the same access to computers as secretaries or professors. You know, even though you work for the institution, and you probably should have the same access to the resources. . . . Professors by and large don't have a lot of people breathing down their necks, so you know, you have more freedom. . . .

Unlike support staff, Joyce has considerable job autonomy. Although the written policy supposedly applies to all university employees, there's no one standing over professors monitoring their activities. However, Joyce avoids discussing sensitive matters with colleagues online, concerned that her emails might be used against her in 'office politics' or get seized in any legal proceedings involving the university. Also, she has concerns about email lists taking time away from her work. She unsubscribed from two <u>high volume</u> email lists related to her work.

Korenman 4

The volume of mail was so high, I just couldn't keep up, and since it was coming to my work account, it was clogging my email and I couldn't do my work. The other one, because of a time crunch also, I had to drop.

For Joyce, time demands rather than concerns about sanctions are the biggest barrier to personal online use. When she has free moments, she occasionally emails friends or surfs the web. The line between work and personal use often blurs: For example, her emails to colleagues combine chit chat and work, and she sometimes finds information on the web that furthers her research interests. She sends about 100 emails each week—she estimates that about 75% of them are work-related—and she subscribes to three email lists related to her professional interests, including a Women's Studies list. She explains that her email volume is high because she does a lot of her work online (for example, recruiting study participants within and outside the United States, collaborating with colleagues). In much the same way as Wendy, Joyce uses email to keep in touch with her far-flung contacts. Unlike Wendy's job, Joyce's work does not require a sharp distinction between formal and informal emails—there aren't any 'written regulations' regarding what she can say.

Unlike the other women, Catherine, a management consultant, moves from workplace to workplace, city to city, country to country, depending on her assignment. Sometimes she works at a client's site, other times at home or in a hotel room, and sometimes in her office at the consulting firm. Across these sites, she carries a portable computer. During a recent assignment in a small town, Catherine and another consultant had to compete for online access:

> We were both put in this tiny office, and we were always fighting over who was going to get connected, who really needed to go online. Sometimes it was kind of irrational—we just needed to go online to get our fix . . . check our stocks, check our email, read the news on the web.

For Catherine, going online helps her to stay connected to the 'richness of urban life':

> When you're stuck in some small town, and you're in a little office from 7:00 in the morning until midnight, you begin to feel disconnected from the world. You miss the richness of urban life. . . . Don't get me wrong, the people are nice, kind—they try to make you feel welcome. But in a cosmopolitan area, the people talk about things that matter to me . . . international news . . . what's going on with the economy. It's important to me to feel that I'm learning something all the time. In cities, you can lead a more intellectual life. In small towns, people talk to me about fishing. . . . A bomb could drop in New York and I wouldn't hear about it.

Although her schedule is hectic, she sometimes finds time to slip from work to personal use—for example, buying a gift for a friend online. At any rate, whether at home or at a client's site, her work and personal online use tends to blur:

Personal and work are one and the same for me. I used to go online to do the same things I'm doing now, and you'd call that personal, because I wasn't getting paid for it. Now I'm getting paid to do what I enjoy. Let's say I'm looking at company sites or financial news—I have my consultant's eye—maybe I'll see things about trends in the industry that can help my client. I also have my investor's eye—is this company going to do well? should I invest in it? And I have an entrepreneur's eye—is there a niche I could fill? Even when I'm just reading the top news stories of the day at ABC's web site, sometimes I see things that are useful personally and professionally.

While at clients' sites, Catherine has to be cautious about her online use—she doesn't want the client to walk in and catch her looking at movie reviews. Whether at home or at a client's site, she is careful about what she says online. She has concerns about her firm monitoring her email account. Also—like Joyce—she has concerns about her emails becoming part of any legal proceedings involving her firm, and cites a case in which a company's email correspondence was taken into evidence.

Having multiple places of access may help professionals juggle their home responsibilities and personal online use, while women in traditional female jobs may be less likely to have this option. Four of the seventeen women interviewed—all of the women who report having children at home—describe things that make it difficult to use their home computers. Lois, a data entry clerk, says she has little time: 'When I come home, I have things to do around the house.' Besides, her daughter has priority in using the computer, so she can do her homework. Lois's online activities at home center on helping her family: For example, she uses the web to gather information about her husband's medical condition.

Similarly, Darya, a chemist, says taking care of her small children hinders her from spending time on the computer at home. She says her husband is probably the biggest email user at home—he sometimes works on their home computer—but she tries to get all her workplace tasks done before leaving her lab. In her office, she keeps email, web, telnet, graphics and wordprocessing applications open at the same time; she switches back and forth among them, cutting and pasting, checking email, transferring files, searching for information. Almost all her online use is work-related—Darya prefers talking to friends face-to-face or on the phone. However, she occasionally exchanges personal emails at work or surfs to web pages (for example, on hairstyles) which she has heard about on television.

While multiple places of access help the three professional women juggle their personal online use, Lois does not have this option. Lois is 'wired' to an electronic network on the job that just allows her to type and check data. She says lack of Internet access at work hinders her from developing online skills:

> Most people I know use [the Internet] a lot more than I do—maybe because they get used to it at work. . . . Not having Internet access at work kind of hurts me in terms of developing Internet skills and just computer skills in general.

Lois says that her husband goes online more than she does because he has Internet access at work. His online use at work makes him more skilled and comfortable at sending emails, so he is often the one who responds to their emails at home. Among my interviewees, only three people have taken online training courses. The others have developed their online skills on their own, with some help from friends, family and the technical support staff at their jobs. Work tasks that depend upon online use seem to prod the development of online skills.

Work, Identity and Online Community

A recent commercial shows people around the world asking 'Are you ready?' . . . apparently for the new age of global communication. The women I spoke with do not seem ready to talk to distant strangers—with the exception of colleagues, clients and study 'subjects'. For example, Joyce spreads information about her projects over email:

The primary benefit is speed of communication, and the ability to communicate with people remotely and quickly. And also the breadth of distribution—it is much easier to contact people that you would never otherwise have any contact with. . . . That allows me to do national and international research . . . otherwise I'd be local.

Professionals in research and academia—and a business owner and a stock-broker who have interests and clients abroad—report going online to contact people outside the United States. Their work sometimes involves developing relations with people in the US and abroad whom they've met at conferences, know by reputation or with whom they have business dealings.

In general, the women describe ways online use has helped them to keep in touch with people they already know. For example, Chandra, a college instructor, uses <u>email</u> to keep in touch with family, friends and <u>colleagues</u> in Asia, Europe and the United States:

Korenman

> . . . you can keep in touch with <u>so many people</u> all over the world if you have their email addresses . . . when I go back to India, I still have so many friends there . . . the ones that I have email contacts with know pretty much everything about me . . . whereas the ones I don't have Internet contacts with, when I don't see them for two years it's like they know nothing about what's happened in between. . . .

Pattanaik 1

Chandra says this has implications for business opportunities:

> If you're not [online] then . . . people are less willing to be in touch with you. Like one of my friend's father, he's a writer, and I want to put him in touch with [a relative of mine who is a publisher]. But [my relative] is on email and I asked him [the writer] do you have email? He says no . . . and that's such a hassle. [My relative] is much less likely to be in contact with him than someone who has an email address. . . .

In Chandra's eyes, lack of access limits contact with existing ties and hinders the growth of new professional ties. Online access increases her ability to contact others, and it also expands possibilities for quickly getting help from informal 'co-workers'—friends who offer practical tips and emotional support:

> For example, someone can send sections of a paper they're working on

via email, then I can edit it in the body of the email. People have done that for me as well.

Like Chandra, most of the women (eleven out of seventeen) describe exchanging work-related help online with friends outside their workplace. Catherine, a management consultant, uses two personal computers—a portable supplied by her firm and her own laptop. She uses her laptop and email account to exchange work-related help with friends:

> Just in case [the firm] monitors my email, I don't want them to know I'm getting outside help. It's not an ethical problem—I don't share proprietary information. I just want [the firm] to think I'm brilliant on my own. Everyone networks, but no one says how much help they get from their friends.

English 12
Mueller 13

The women seem leery of meeting new people online—even in anonymous spaces such as <u>MUD</u>[1] game rooms. None of the women participate in MUDs. About a third have visited chat rooms, but they no longer do so. Some find it hard and time-consuming to develop online relations. Also, similar to people wary of strangers on city streets, some women express worries about being hurt or robbed online. Almost all of the women (fifteen out of seventeen) mention concern or stories about online 'wackos', 'kooks', 'axe-murderers', 'rapists', 'child molesters', 'thieves', 'blackmailers' and so on. Lois, an office worker, regards chat rooms as dangerous:

> My younger daughter goes to those chat rooms, and we're concerned about the types of people she might meet there.

Chandra voices objections to participating in any online spaces with people she doesn't know. I ask her whether online spaces are different than meeting new people face-to-face at parties. She replies:

> At a party there's a certain established social context, like my friend, the one that I met at a party twice before we began hanging out together. . . . I knew all his friends who knew him for years and years, and so there was

---

1. MUDs (multi-user domains) are online spaces in which people construct fantasy worlds and identities.

a certain amount of legitimacy and trust that he wasn't an axe murderer.
. . . Meeting someone on the Internet without having met them face-to-
face is like going to a bar and picking up someone. I think most of my
social contacts have a really established context.

Cassie's fear of online duplicity makes her hesitant about possible
online opportunities:

> You . . . hear horror stories about your name being in the computer. I
> didn't want to just be floating out there. For example, there's a very good
> friend of mine who . . . played high school football [and] he was getting
> ready to go to college. [A co-worker at my old job showed me this web site
> where] I could enter [my friend's] name for football coaches to look at
> when they were selecting players. . . . I didn't want to do that because I
> wasn't sure if I was doing the right thing and I didn't want to put his
> name in there and something bad happens.

Email lists are the only type of online group popular among my
interviewees. Of the seventeen women I spoke with, eight subscribe
to lists organized outside their workplace. With one exception, all
eight women belong to lists by, and for, people who share their
professional interests or who attended their alumni institution—
groups that share work-related information. Some of these lists are
organized by professional groups, while others are informal. For
example, Darya subscribes to four lists organized by professional
associations. She feels online access has 'greatly improved' her
connections with others in her field, making collaborations much
easier. Cindy, a software developer, belongs to a list for graduates
from her Chinese alma mater. People on the list exchange personal
news (for example, weddings) as well as work tips. Thus, a recent
graduate may ask about job openings, and others may provide help.
Joyce belongs to a list for former recipients of a minority fellowship.
People post information about jobs, events, political affairs and
media stories relevant to academics of color. Occasionally they also
share personal news or provide support:

Korenman 4

> There's some people who put personal things—like, 'just to let you know
> I got tenure or I didn't get tenure', or 'I'm having a baby' or things like
> that . . . I don't recall anyone sending a tear-soaked post or anything, but

people may say 'So-and-So had a negative experience at their job, let's send them some support.' Often it's like an advocacy thing, let's send them support, or maybe positive support, 'So-and-So just got promoted, let's congratulate them.'

Of the women who subscribe to lists, only one does not belong to a list organized for people who share professional interests. Pam, who owns a business, subscribes to a list for African Americans in, or from, her city:

I think it was started by a [college] student. . . . People on the list share information about [the city] and announce when a speaker is coming to town, and other news about social and political gatherings. For example, news about a black mayoral candidate.

Sometimes people on the list exchange help:

. . . undergraduates on the list ask for advice about graduate programs, and I help them out. Also, say someone is moving to [a particular city]—they'll ask if anyone on the list knows about good apartments. Well, someone on the list from [that city] will send them information. That kind of thing.

I ask Pam whether she knows if the people on the list tend to be professionals, students, blue collar workers . . .?

It's hard to say. . . . My impression is that most people are professionals or students. . . . I have a business in [the city], and the list helps me to keep in touch with what's going on.

The list seems to have some of the characteristics of professional lists, bringing together professionals and students who sometimes meet face-to-face and who may benefit from providing local information and support.

Faith, a programmer, is the only woman who reports never using email for personal reasons. She says that she would much rather read a book or look at art than go online, and she doesn't think the Internet is a good way to develop ties. Born in China almost fifty years ago, Faith says that she is disturbed by the lack of community she sees among people in US cities:

Our ancestors didn't have all this Internet . . . and I think they were . . . better than us. They take care of each other. . . . Look around this big city. . . . We don't even know our neighbors. What's this about the Internet, spending time on the Internet? People don't even care for each other face-to-face. . . . [laughs] . . . Our ancestors had better community than us.

Hawthorne

Faith says her co-workers chitchat too much via email, and she thinks their emails are sometimes inappropriate for the workplace. For example, her co-workers have been circulating jokes and pictures about President Clinton and Monica Lewinsky via email. She hasn't been included on the email distribution list for these jokes—she knows about them because a friend at work showed one of the emails to her.

With the exception of work identities, shared identities such as ethnicity and sexuality may draw people together online, but it may be difficult to sustain conversations unless the people share other things in common. Olga, a consultant, visited a chat room for people from Germany. She visited it because she missed 'hearing German', but it soon became boring and she left:

I mean it's so difficult to establish any sort of reasonable sustainable contact with these strangers. . . . I think you have to be very well-defined groups and I think these people have to at least talk to each other over the phone or to meet.

Similarly, Joyce joined a list for black lesbians

for social affinity reasons, because I wanted to connect with other black lesbians, but . . . when I got on it, their conversations were so evolved that I couldn't understand what they were talking about.

People didn't fully explain what they meant—they seemed to assume that everyone knew the details, perhaps because they had known each other a long time. She unsubscribed.

The women's interests in online interactions with distant others tend to revolve around their work. For example, Cassie wants to buy a computer and modem so that she can meet others online who might advance her education and career:

> I'd like to utilize email much more . . . in terms of networking. I think that there's a lot of information I'd have access to . . . in terms of jobs . . . just being able to be in contact with more people—um, ways that could help further your career or your education, things of that nature.

For Cassie, Internet access is also a status symbol and a means of keeping in touch with the 'mainstream':

> When you go to most people's houses, they have a television. If they don't, then you're thinking that's kind of abnormal, that's like in the Dark Ages. So not having access to a computer . . . makes me feel that I'm behind the times or in the Dark Ages . . . if I'm using a typewriter . . . it's so much slower and I just feel so much out of touch with mainstream reality. . . . I'd like to be aware of what's going on and to . . . be able to use things around me, even if I choose not to use them.

'Cyberspace' is often framed as a means of resisting dominant identities and lifestyles. In Cassie's eyes, online access fosters opportunity and respectability.

Discussion

Since the days of telegraph operators, workers have used electronic networks on the job to chat with friends and play games (Standage 1998). These practices seem instances of *la perruque*, which de Certeau describes as 'the worker's own work disguised as work for his employer':

> . . . *La perruque* may be as simple a matter as a secretary's writing a love letter on 'company time' . . . In the very place where the machine [the worker] must serve reigns supreme, he cunningly takes pleasure in creating gratuitous products [that] . . . signify his own capabilities . . . and . . . confirm his solidarity with other workers or his family. . . . With the complicity of other workers . . . he succeeds in 'putting one over' on the established order on its home ground (de Certeau 1984: 25).

My interviewees' online practices at work—chatting with friends, surfing the web—often exemplify *la perruque*. Yet we must be careful about framing all acts of online play as workplace subversion.

Sometimes the things my interviewees do for fun online contribute to their work: for example, Catherine's online activities serve multiple purposes. Like other professionals I interviewed, Catherine does not experience a sharp distinction between the time and space of paid labor and 'free time'—she plays at work and works at home. Work shapes her identity, interests and activities across sites. She does not see much difference between personal and work use: 'I'm getting paid to do what I enjoy'. In contrast, Cassie's job duties are unrelated to her personal online use at work (for example, chatting with a friend about her wedding, searching for information about colleges). Working as a receptionist shapes her opportunities for online use, but her job duties do not merge with her play.

Most of my interviewees engage in 'border-crossing'—slipping back and forth between work and personal online use. Yet the distance between personal and work use—and the opportunities and risks of border-crossing—vary. Surveillance may place limits on *la perruque*. Some interviewees fear bosses 'looking over their shoulders', while others are concerned about electronic monitoring. Various scholars have pointed to the dangers of the normalizing 'Panopticon' effects of electronic surveillance (for example, Poster 1984). My findings suggest diverse responses to monitoring (and the fear of monitoring): Some workers discipline themselves by limiting their online use, while others ignore surveillance. Employees whose duties and location distance them from others may slip into personal use (for example, Chandra), while those in high visibility settings are constantly kept on their guard (for example, Cassie). In some instances, status may play a role—people with high job prestige and autonomy (for example, Joyce) may feel secure from employer sanctions—but this is not always the case. If their emails involve 'sensitive issues' at their workplace, they may feel the need to censor themselves.

Work access may influence the complex ways online use is gendered: having multiple places of access may help professionals juggle their home responsibilities and online use, while women in traditional female jobs may not have that option (for example, Darya and Lois's experiences). Regularly using the Internet at work may also help develop online skills, making women more comfortable and confident when they go online at home.

Online communities explicitly organized around play or care-giving are receiving increased attention. There is also growing interest in activist networks, women's spaces and 'digital diasporas'—that is, online groups specifically organized around ethnicity or homeland. The attention paid to these groups obscures interesting statistics: a recent US survey indicates that professional groups are the most popular online 'communities'—42% of respondents who say they belong to one or more online communities describe at least one of these communities as professional (see *Business Week* 1997). A GVU survey (1998) asked respondents what types of groups they have 'become connected to through the Internet'. Hobby and professional groups were the top two US responses. Among my interviewees, work-related lists are the most popular type of online group. Whether online or offline, people with similar jobs and backgrounds tend to draw together in informal settings—'cyberspace' does not necessarily erase social distinctions.

For some of my interviewees, online groups organized around work also offer care-giving, political activity and social affirmation. However, such groups tend to consist of people who share the same economic class and occupation. Thus, these groups may help people expand the number (but not necessarily the types) of individuals in their social circle. For example, Joyce belongs to a list for academics of color, and Cindy to a list for graduates from her Chinese alma mater. Both lists provide work-related help, along with other types of news and information. In studying Joyce's and Cindy's practices, it is important to avoid technological determinism—the roots of organizing by African American college women, for example, can be traced at least as far back as the Black Women's Club Movement around the turn of the twentieth century. The interesting point to consider is not whether the technology fosters a sense of community (which probably already existed) but rather, if and how social space changes when communication among geographically dispersed

Pattanaik 1
Pollock and
Sutton 2

people with similar interests becomes quicker and cheaper. For example, does the expansion of 'weak ties' increase access to information (see Granovetter 1974)? It is not enough to study online groups organized solely around ethnicity or gender: to understand how information flows online, we must take account of the practices of professional lists.

What about the possibilities for chatting online with strangers? Lack of interest and fear of 'wackos' discourages my interviewees from interacting online with strangers. Other studies also find high rates of concern about online security (for example, see GVU 1998). Anonymous spaces where people play with identity are not popular among my interviewees. A *Business Week* (1997) survey indicates that only 5% of online users interact in MUDs/MOOs.[2] Larger percentages participate in chat groups (26%), conferences or forums (20%) and listservs or email lists (21%).

Guymer 3

Korenman 4

Compared with MUDs, why are professional lists relatively popular? Perhaps because it is easier to locate the professional lists and—in many people's eyes—there are clear benefits to subscribing. Although professionals may not have met experts in their field who live in another city or country, these colleagues may not seem as distant as the people whom they pass on the street. Within professional circles, there may be some knowledge about colleagues, so that one feels relatively certain that they are not 'wackos, kooks or axe murderers'. There may also be a common language and means of exchange. Most importantly, there may be a perceived advantage in closing the distance. In the absence of some desire—shaped by everyday contexts—there is no purpose for exchange, whether the stranger is next door or a thousand miles away.

This does not mean that MUDs—or other types of virtual communities which have relatively few participants—do not affect women's lives and the larger society (see Turkle 1995). Rather than discounting MUDs as atypical, it may be useful to explore how all types of online 'play'—including MUDs—emerge within everyday

---

2. Like MUDs, MOOs are online spaces in which people construct fantasy worlds and identities.

lives, connected by systems of production, exchange and meaning. The time, space and activities of the woman 'playing' online (chatting with a friend, reading financial news or creating a <u>MUD persona</u>) are shaped by her personal choices as well as by her social and physical location.

English 12

My study has limitations: My sample is small, and the findings may only be relevant within the context of existing online equipment and format (for example, interviewees' reluctance to visit MUDs may decrease if MUDs were to become as easy to find and watch as television shows). Also, I do not fully examine the relations between paid labor, unpaid labor (for example, housework) and personal online use. In this study, I rely solely on the women's memories: time-budget diaries would probably provide a more accurate means of comparing the length of time women engage in personal online use at various sites. In addition, future research in this area should explore whether women in particular occupations are more likely to develop online communities. Hopefully, my research may further efforts to address these issues.

Conclusion

My findings point to the importance of exploring differences among women in online opportunities which go beyond the ability to purchase computers and modems—differences rooted in work spaces themselves. Work shapes access to communication tools and the free time to engage in personal use. Work also shapes the nature and reach of online interactions. Among my interviewees, the gifts of information shared online often take on value within the context of their work. Efforts to expand women's self-expression and political activity online must take their paid labor into account.

References

Business Week. (1997 May 5). A census in cyberspace.
  <http://www.businessweek.com/1997/18/b352511.htm>

Collins, P.H. (1991). Black Feminist Thought: Knowledge, consciousness, and the politics of empowerment. New York: Routledge.

de Certeau, Michel. 1984. The Practice of Everyday Life. Berkeley, CA: University of California Press.

Granovetter, Mark S. 1974. Getting a Job: A study of contacts and careers. Cambridge, MA: Harvard University Press.

GVU. 1998. Tenth WWW User Survey. (Conducted October 1998). Atlanta, GA: Graphics, Visualization and Usability Center (GVU), College of Computing, Georgia Institute of Technology.
  <http://www.gvu.gatech.edu/user_surveys/survey-1998-10/graphs/graphs.html #control>

Herring, Susan, Deborah A. Johnson and Tamra DiBenedetto. 1995. This discussion is going too far! Male resistance to female participation on the Internet. In Kira Hall and Mary Buchholtz (Eds.), Gender Articulated. New York: Routledge.

Hoffman, Donna L. and Thomas P. Novak. 1998. Bridging the racial divide on the Internet. Science, 280 (April 17), 390–91.

Hossfeld, Karen J. 1990. Their logic against them: Contradictions in sex, race, and class in Silicon Valley. In Kathryn Ward (Ed.), Women Workers and Global Restructuring. Ithaca, NY: ILR Press, Cornell University.

Markussen, Randi. 1995. Constructing easiness—historical perspectives on work, computerization, and women. In Susan Leigh Star (Ed.), The Cultures of Computing. Cambridge, MA: Blackwell Publishers.

McRae, Shannon. 1997. Flesh made word: Sex, text and the virtual body. In David Porter (Ed.), Internet Culture. New York: Routledge.

Meeker, Mary & Chris DePuy. 1996. The Internet Report. New York: Morgan Stanley, U.S. Investment Research.

Mitchell, William J. 1999. Equitable access to the online world. In Donald A. Schon, Bish Sanyal and William J. Mitchell (Eds.), High Technology and Low-income Communities. Cambridge, MA: MIT Press.

Mitter, Swasti. 1995. Information technology and working women's demands. In Swasti Mitter and Sheila Rowbotham (Eds.), Women Encounter Technology: Changing patterns of employment in the third world. New York: Routledge.

National Center for Educational Statistics. 1997. Advanced Telecommunications in U.S. Public Elementary and Secondary Schools, Fall 1996. Washington, DC: U.S. Department of Education.

National Science Board. 1998. Science and Engineering Indicators—1998. Arlington, VA: National Science Foundation.

Odedra-Straub, Mayuri. 1995. Women and information technology in Sub-Saharan Africa. In Swasti Mitter and Sheila Rowbotham (Eds.), Women Encounter Technology: Changing patterns of employment in the third world. New York: Routledge.

Poster, Mark. 1984. Foucault, Marxism, and History: Mode of production versus mode of information. New York: Blackwell.

Reyes, Pi Villanueva. 1998. Emails on the Edge: Cutting edge, bleeding edge, and women wielding the new technologies. Women in Action:
<http://www.isiswomen.org/pub/wia/wia298/com00007.html>

Shade, Leslie Regan. 1993. Gender issues in computer networking. Presentation at Community Networking: The International Free-Net Conference, Carleton University, Ottawa, Canada, Aug. 17–19.

Standage, Tom. 1998. *The Victorian Internet.* London: Weidenfeld and Nicolson.

Turkle, Sherry. 1995. *Life on the Screen: Identity in the age of the internet.* New York: Simon and Schuster.

US Department of Commerce. 1998. *Falling Through the Net II: New data on the digital divide.* Washington, DC: National Telecommunciations and Information Administration (NTIA) US Department of Commerce.

Webster, Juliet. 1996. *Shaping Women's Work: Gender, employment and information technology.* New York: Longman.

Zuboff, Shoshana. 1988. *In the Age of Smart Machine: The future of work and power.* New York: Basic Books.

six

Connectivity: Cultural Practices of the Powerful or Subversion from the Margins?

Susan Hawthorne

> A new digital world, founded on a global information
> system run by American-based computer
> corporations, would seem to be the unstated goal of
> digital ideology (Millar 1998: 153).

Cultural Practices of the Powerful

Do you have a Power PC? A Power Mac? Are you connected to power? Do you have any power? The first two questions are power questions. They assume you are part of a culture, a race for power. They assume that you are connected to power, because even if you have a laptop, it needs recharging, and the batteries never last long enough to write anything of substantial length. If you say no to the first three questions, then chances are you don't have much power at all.

Power is a practice. It takes on a variety of forms[1] which range in effectiveness from the power of violence to the power of attitudes. Violence is a short-term and highly effective means of power, while attitudinal power is long-term, it is also effective, but only if it is not resisted. Violence is effective even with resistance.

The question of power is critical to an evaluation of cyberculture. Analyses of power have been central to the development of feminist

---

[1.] Briefly the distinctive forms of power include: the power of violence, the power of reward, the power of backlash, the power of obstacles, the power of systems, the power of attraction, and the power of attitudes. An extensive discussion of power, consequences and Dominant Culture Stupidities can be found in Hawthorne (1997b).

thought, and though these analyses have tended to be dismissed by the post-modern theorists, it is power which has brought us the digital revolution.

In turn, the digital revolution has brought about an escalation in the culture of the Powerful[2] although this too, tends to be ignored.[3] It is not surprising, since it is difficult for the purveyors of culture— the Powerful—to see the mechanisms of their own structures. And it is difficult for the Powerless to get access to the resources and education necessary to enable such a critique. Everything is ranged against it.

The Powerful are those members of a society who can gain ready access to power and who are able to exercise it without thinking particularly about what they are doing. The reason they are able to do this is because their exercise of power carries few consequences *for them*.[4]

The *culture* of the Powerful is another important force. Cultural power—the power of global domination through culture—has exploded in the last decade, to the detriment of less visible cultures,

---

[2.] By this, I mean that the culture produced by Microsoft, by Universal Studios and other huge infotainment corporations, tends to replicate the views of the dominant groups, such as whites, men, the wealthy, North American or European, as well as the able-bodied. Occasionally a token from one of these groups is included, a black man, a white woman, a disabled white man, but that does not change the overall structure of the homogenised culture.

[3.] There are a few exceptions. See for example, Millar (1998), Markley (1996).

[4.] A class analysis might give the following reading. For the Powerful there is no serious consequence on one's food intake in excessive consumption of petrol, electricity, rent, services and so on. But for the unemployed poor who may not know where they will sleep at night or how they will find sufficient money for the next meal, the consequences of every action loom large. Even more so for the poor mother with dependent children who have to be fed, clothed and housed. The consequences of poverty make her aware of her actions.

For those with privileges of mobility or ability there is a significant lack of awareness of the needs of the disabled. A single step can prove an impediment to a wheelchair, and the able-bodied will barely notice it as they lift their feet. A normative pressure to conform will create imbalances of power for all kinds of disabilities of the senses (i.e. sight, hearing, touch, taste and smell), as well as visible and invisible disabilities which affect the mind/body (Hawthorne 1996; Davis 1995). The able-bodied will also not notice the arm strength of the person who uses a wheelchair, will ignore the enhanced abilities of the senses where one or more is impaired.

cultures who have something to show us if only we had the time to listen. The culture of the Powerful is one which does not promote reflection. For the <u>Powerful</u> the culture is obvious, accessible and cut out for them. For the Powerless it is unreachable, impenetrable, high, elite, expensive and it would take an act of violence or self-violation to get in. This is nowhere more clear than with digital culture.

Mont-gomery 5

Not seeing

The unmarked category is the identifying mark of the Powerful. He is the standard by which everything else is measured. The clearest example of this is Leonardo da Vinci's Vitruvian Man, or his latest incarnation, Jobe Smith (Mitchell 1995: 26) in *Lawnmower Man*. Judy Horacek's cartoon which includes an image reminiscent of da Vinci's complete with mirror writing, sends up the idea of man as the unmarked category. On the global scale this is well represented in the informational address structures of the Internet, where US addresses are unmarked.[5] What is so clearly unmarked on the

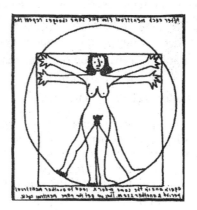

'Premenstrual in a postmodern age No. 2',
cartoon by Judy Horacek, copyright 1997.

---

5. Every other country has an identifying final term: au for Australia, de for Germany etc.

Internet, is less obviously marked in some other areas, but readily identifiable for anyone outside the category.

In discussing 'blackness' and 'whiteness' in a literary context, Toni Morrison writes:

> To notice is to recognize an already discredited difference. To enforce its invisibility through silence is to allow the black body a shadowless participation in the dominant cultural body (Morrison 1993: 9–10).

Whiteness is not visible to the Powerful, because they themselves are white. They notice bodies that are not white and they impute a difference of those imaginations. They notice them as 'cultural'. But whiteness, to the white, is the norm. It has a normative status in the same way that 'man' has a normative status.

And, within the culture of the digerati, 'American', has become so pervasive in the discourse, as to be invisibilised. Not only that, but the culture is skewed in a direction to suit the needs of elite white men.

> The average *Wired* reader is a thirty-nine-year-old male college graduate with an annual employment income of US$83,000 and a household income of US$122,600 (Millar 1998: 73).

In the development of disciplines of knowledge, what is seen, what is given importance is what is regarded as true, real, and of value. Nowhere is this clearer than in the economic systems developed under capitalism and their extension to globalised economics and digital culture in the late twentieth century.

As one practitioner of economics writes:

> Political economy . . . [is] a collection of value-free generalisations about the way in which economic systems work. (Robbins 1976: 2, cited in Hyman 1994: 30).

Only a member of the dominant culture, imbued with the belief systems of formal economics, could write the above and not feel uncomfortable, and 'experience no dissonance with the default assumptions' (Hyman 1994: 53). Economics, like all other disciplines, is value-laden, and in its latest globalised incarnation, creates a monoculture on a scale the planet has never before experienced.

As Marilyn Waring (1988: 59) points out:

> . . . much of the economic discipline is a matter of perception, and what does or does not constitute production could depend on the way you see the world. And it does.

Of digital ideology, Heather Menzies (1996) writes:

> The struggle to control the technologies of the new economy must begin with a struggle to control perception (cited in Millar 1998: 53).

Cultural Homogeneity

Digital culture is well placed to control perception. As a sometime Internet surfer, most of the Web sites which come up when I put in a search, are located in the US. Most of what we have come to see as digital culture is American in origin, even when it concerns other cultures and countries. The predominance of American cultural icons—from Barbie, to Mickey Mouse, to transcripts of trials—have the effect of mowing down the cultural icons of other cultures. An ad from *Wired* has the temerity to proclaim:

> When the digital revolution rolls over you, you're either part of the steamroller or part of the road (Millar 1998: 80).

What remains after the monocultures (Shiva 1993) of the Powerful have run over the planet's diverse cultures, is reductionism, ignorance and homogeneity of the culture. Symbolically, it is reflected in their cultural practice, and has become a powerful force in digital culture.[6]

---

6. For an example of institutional steamrolling of Indigenous culture, see Cousineau (1998. <http://commposite.uqam.ca/videaz/wg/genderen.html>).

The Local

The local is a place we can call home. It is where we live, or have lived, and have come to know its features intimately. We have a mental map in our brains of the laneways, the houses and the local businesses, or we can name all the trees or flowers, or we know the intersecting relationships between people, and their history. In the late twentieth century there is less and less knowledge of the local, except at a superficial level. Indigenous peoples, on the other hand, know their locality on numerous levels: as the source of food, medicines, spiritual renewal, art and all the trappings of culture.

Arnold 11

Our knowledge of the local progressively decreases as our knowledge of the global increases. Disconnection from the local, also increases as our knowledge becomes homogenised. Around the world we eat Big Macs, know the latest gossip about Hollywood or sporting superstars. But what do we know about our next door neighbour? This cultural knowledge has become universalised, and has seeped into every corner of the world. The danger is that it becomes important cultural currency and local knowledge loses its cultural force.

With the emphasis today on global travel—either in the real world or in cyberspace—the local is under threat. Out there, somewhere else, anywhere else, a place where one can be anonymous and unaccountable is better than one's own local community where people might know your history, your family, your weaknesses. This is a move towards disconnection from the past, from individual histories as well as community histories. The idiosyncracies of the local, which make it interesting in the long run, are disparaged, and everyone wants the global product: Coca Cola, CNN, basketball, Titanic, or a modem to link them to the World Wide Web.

Furthermore, concentrating only on what's happening on a global scale gives us no place to stand, no history of the local, no sense of community from which to launch effective campaigns or to feel as if we can have an impact on the social and cultural forces. Just as in feminism we begin with the personal and extend that to the political, so with communication, we need to find a local position in which to act effectively, in which to form face-to-face relationships, before we can become effective in the wider sphere. So much of what we hear about the Internet is what is happening out there, somewhere else, just as in the 60s outer space became the out there of the decade, in the 90s the out there is in the computer on your desk and it is no more substantial than the void of outer space.

The local, simply no longer exists. We are, as they say in the ads, 'one world' and you may not realise that the person seated next to you in the cybercafe, is one of your cybercompanions. One of the problems of new information technologies is the extent to which moral detachment becomes the norm and that the Internet is mistaken for community. The media hype portrays cyberspace as an instant community. But community cannot happen instantly, it relies on involvement, experience and memory.

'Community', in the instant sense, becomes a link to virtual worlds, where you can no longer trust experience, since it is all mediated by text or image. This in contrast to the benefits of email relationships to members of a <u>mailing list with shared interests</u>. Activism on the Internet is an aid (Hawthorne 1997a). One learns how to be an activist in the real world, in the real local settings which bring one face-to-face with discrimination, prejudice, abuse and a range of other evils.

Korenman
Mont-
gomery 5

The British, colonising Australia, declared it *terra nullius*. William Gibson's famous comment, 'There's no there there' (Gibson 1984), is a bit like the declaration of *terra nullius*, in as much as it denies that behind the screen of cyberspace, there are real people. The atopia of cyberspace implies that whatever happens in cyberspace is <u>harmless</u>. So why the rush to invest so much money and time in it? Homi K. Bhabha (cited in Boyer 1996: 20) suggests that the non-place is the template for colonial space, and I suggest that the Internet is one of the newer mechanisms of <u>colonisation</u>.[7]

Hughes 8
Klein 9

Arnold 11

---

[7]. Market research shows that the ideal customer for any computer product is a ten-year-old boy from Idaho (Barta 1995).

Colonialism, industrialisation and technological progress have transformed all our lives irreversibly. Aeroplanes, cars and trains have transformed our experience of time by disengaging from place through velocity. Cyberspace transforms our experience of space by disengaging it from time. In cyberspace there is neither time nor space. The touch of a finger on a keyboard or a mouse brings to one's own living room any place on the globe (which is networked). There is no scenery to glimpse; there is no place to be. It could be anywhere: anyone, any time of day or night, anywhere. The external velocity of vehicles has its analogue in the internal velocity of cyberspace.

The homogenisation of everything even takes in time. As Millar (1998: 90) points out *Wired* attempts 'to visually unify distinctive time periods and dehistoricize the present/future', while Tofts and McKeich (1998: 35ff) points to the dehistoricisation of the past, as cyberculture pretends that it has no history.

Knowledge

Local knowledge, Indigenous knowledge, women's knowledge, the marked knowledge of marginalised and outsider groups all face the threat of annihilation and erasure in the face of homogenised digitised western knowledge. While Outsider knowledges thrive on diversity, the dominant knowledge mandates assimilation, appropriation and homogenisation. What Vandana Shiva in looking at colonisation calls 'monocultures of the mind' (Shiva 1993), and M. Christine Boyer referring to telecommunications, describing the process of detachment, defines as 'delocalising signs of both language and sight' (Boyer 1996: 212).

The Library of Congress (and other national libraries) is digitising many of its holdings so that material can be downloaded through the new information networks. But whose knowledge will be downloaded? Melville's *Moby Dick* will probably be included, but what of Emily Dickinson? Kate Millett's *Sexual Politics* is out of print; will it be saved by digitisation, or is *Lolita* a more likely candidate? And these are the mass successes. What of the marginalised culture of women of colour, of lesbians, of the disabled, of the poor? Will Bessie Head and Keri Hulme be available in <u>digital form</u>? Of course, these issues are not new, finding and saving such works has provided a store-house of material for feminist publishers such as Virago; while writers outside the mainstream have explored these themes. Ghanaian, Ama Ata Aidoo (1977: 86) writes about the use of education as the:

Stafford 7

> Most merciless
> Most formalised
>
> Open.
> Thorough,
> Spy system of all time:
> For a few pennies now and a
> Doctoral degree later,
> Tell us about
> Your people
> Your history
> Your mind.
> Your mind.
> Your mind.

Or, as Vandana Shiva (1993: 10) explains it:

> The universal/local dichotomy is misplaced when applied to the western and indigenous systems of knowledge, because the western is a local tradition which has been spread world wide through intellectual colonisation.

Having colonised the world (and parts of outer space), it is obvious that it would not take long for the western world to begin using the Internet to advance the process of colonisation and appropriation. Katerina Teaiwa (1997) has written provocatively of the activities of the Banaban Heritage Society. The Society's Internet site, con-structed by one of the descendants of the phosphate mining indus-try, describes its mission as saving the culture of the Banabans. The problem, however, is that the Banaban Heritage Society has not consulted with the people of this Pacific Island nation, has not asked their permission to use any of the resources, and is directly promoting global marketing of the culture, its traditions, and its resources with no return to the owners of the culture.

Jane Mogina, in her research with women in Papua New Guinea on local medicines, says:

> If the women do not choose to show the plants which they use for contraceptive purpose, I do not ask. These are tabu issues in Melanesian culture (Mogina 1996: oral presentation).

Cultural transparency which results when there is 'free' or 'open' access to anyone, be they members of the community or not, has dire consequences for many Indigenous peoples. As Millar (1998: 152) points out:

> The effects of foreign businesses and technologies on indigenous cultures are not considered relevant to the larger goal of capital accumulation.

If we are to use the Internet responsibly, then issues of accountability need serious discussion. A CyberFeminism which ignores such issues, would do so at its peril.

Suniti Namjoshi, in her novel on Internet culture, raises the issue in an allegorical way. *Building Babel* (1996) explores what it means to build culture. Is it, she asks, made up of bricks, or words? And what of the people who want to come to <u>Babel</u>? In a lesbian context, Namjoshi refers to this as 'the problem of men'. When the character, Queen Alice decides to let men into Babel, she does it by decreeing that, 'Men are not men' (Namjoshi 1996: 113). This would be funny if it were not so frighteningly close to Vandana Shiva's concern about the effects of globalising culture and knowledge (Shiva 1993).

Namjoshi

17

In the process of culture building, and here I am thinking of cultures which are currently fragile or vulnerable to take over, it is sometimes necessary to create safe spaces. Hence, Teaiwa's call to the Banabans to:

> . . . talk amongst themselves, before or rather than to outsiders and to realize that we do have the capacity to develop—to grow from the fruits of our own hands and minds. Self-determination must come before global participation or we will get swept away by the tide of 'boundarilessness' (Teaiwa 1997: 8).

A similar intent is reflected in the call for separate women's spaces (Hawthorne 1976/1990), respect for Aboriginal law on Aboriginal land (Milburn 1999: 3), lesbian only spaces and so forth. But at some point in each of these political projects there is a push to open things up.[8] The positive aspect of this is getting information out into the broader public domain; the danger is that knowledge may be appropriated and misused.

Community Networking: Subversion from the margins?

As feminist activists, many of us have found email, and the World Wide Web useful for spreading information and running political campaigns. In 1996, at Spinifex Press we launched a project to create a Feminist Publishers in Asia network. In doing this we were prompted by Urvashi Butalia and Ritu Menon's complaint (1995: 60), that the biggest problem to co-operation between feminist publishers in the 'South' was <u>lack of information</u>:

In writing up the material after the project was completed in early 1997, we reflected on the process of networking across a regional electronic community.

Pattanaik 1

And the Internet isn't just an issue for the first world feminists.[9] If

---

8. All of these examples have become subject to pressure from either the dominant group or those in favour of trading with the dominant group. Separatism has fallen out of favour among feminists, but see Hawthorne (1976/1990), Wilding (1998). Yvonne Margarula, an elder of the Mirrar people, is being charged with trespassing on her own land (land which would be considered hers if Native Title were properly recognised) (Milburn, 1999: 3), and the lesbian centre in Sydney has ceased to be a place only for lesbians, as transsexual male to female, who call themselves lesbians, may now be members; for a North American example see O'Hartigan (1999: 6, 13).

9. Some other interesting developments are occurring amongst Indigenous groups. Both the Central Australian Land Council and the Ye'kuana in Venezuela are using GIS (Geographic Information's Systems) to digitally record every tree, rock and sacred place (Turnbull 1997: 560; Posey 1996: 12).

Hughes 8

sisterhood implies shared responsibilities then this is the time to protest. Are Filipinas only sex objects for American men? What are the women in the Philippines doing? In fact any feminist who is using the Web and ignores these issues is shirking her responsibilities. Women+Asia+ Publishing still does not exist as a category on the Internet. But it will soon (Pattanaik 1997, Pattanaik and Hawthorne 1997: 97).

Like Jane Mogina and Katerina Teaiwa, we may decide not to ask some questions, we may decide not to share some knowledge, for some things when displaced from the local lose their value. For Indigenous peoples and other marginalised groups this is a critical question.

When a community networking project is created using these principles, the rewards are exciting:

> That experience of the local network expanding—like the ripples of a stone thrown into water—to encompass the regional and the global is an important one in our contemporary world. What I didn't anticipate was the way it has sprung back and helped to create new networks in Melbourne.
>
> There has also been a huge perceptual change across the cultures this network touches. Different parts of Asia are plugging in . . . . It is becoming the resource we had envisioned. More importantly, however, word is getting out that feminist publishing is alive and well in Asia (Pattanaik and Hawthorne 1997: 98).

Those whom the information concerns need to be involved in its spread. Otherwise we finish up with a situation like that of the Banabans, with their knowledge exploited, misused and spread further than they wish. Without local involvement in the design, the use, the content, it becomes yet another example of cultural appropriation by the culturally powerful.

> the globalization advocated by digital ideology involves less an exchange of cultural knowledge (or information) than a self-interested extraction and commodification of subordinate cultures. . . . This extraction usually takes the form of cultural reduction and commodification based on racist western sterotypes (Millar 1998: 151).

Connectivity is a powerful force, and many groups around the world are using the Internet for all <u>kinds of purposes</u>, from political action on campaigns to sharing information and resources through Web sites, to simply keeping in touch. But connectivity is not everything. Turning off the mobile phone so that one can enjoy social activities with friends without work intruding is worth doing; holidaying without the laptop and email access ensures having a holiday in the real world.

The hype surrounding creativity and digital technology suggests that very soon we will be connected all the time, that being plugged in is important no matter where you are. Clearly, it is important to the people who make profits from digital technology. They are the Powerful. They are the multinationals who do not want local content protected so that they have free access to all markets.[10] And it will be their culture we'll be plugged into.

The Internet is an expression of our newly globalised world. It can be used for subversion and for exploitation. How we use this tool is important. Resistance to conventional misuses of power in a new 3-D, animated, full-colour form may be essential. Just as important is learning to use the tool effectively, for it is the human interaction with the technology which determines whether ethics or oppression prevail.

Pattanaik 1
Pollock and
Sutton 2
Mont-
gomery 5

---

10. The proposed Multilateral Agreement on Investment (MAI) although unsuccessful in being accepted in 1998, is still on the agenda. The beneficiaries of such an agreement will be huge international companies bent on selling US content to the world. Under threat will be national and local arts organisations, local content on television, national, state and community run health and social services. And much more. See Clarke and Barlow (1997).

References

Aidoo, Ama Ata. 1977. *Sister Killjoy, or the reflections of a black-eyed squint*. London: Longman.

BabelBuildingSite: <http://www.spinifexpress.com.au/babelbuildingsite.htm>

Banaban Heritage Society Home Page:
  <http://www.ion.com.au/banaban/stacey1.htm>

Barta, Peter. 1995. Multimedia Industry Overview. Presentation at the Australian Book Publishers Association Training Seminar, Publishing a Multimedia Title. 25 July.

Bhabha, Homi K. 1991. 'Race', Time and the Revision of Modernity. *The Oxford Literary Review*, (13) (1–2), 193–219.

Boyer, M. Christine. 1996. *CyberCities: Visual perception in the age of electronic communication*. New York: Princeton Architectural Press.

Butalia, Urvashi and Ritu Menon. 1995. *Making a Difference: Feminist publishing in the south*. Chestnut Hill, Massachusetts: Bellagio Publishing Network Bellagio Studies in Publishing No. 5.

Clarke, Tony and Maude Barlow. 1997. *The Multilateral Agreement on Investment and the Threat to Canadian Sovereignty*. Toronto: Stoddart Publishing Co.
  <http://www.citizen.org/gtw/mai.html>

Cousineau, Marie-Hélène. 1998. Gender, Ethnicity and Communication. Paper presented at Virtual Conference: The Right to Communicate and the Communication of Rights. Concordia University, Montreal. 2-8 June.
  <http://commposite.uqam.ca/videaz/wg/genderen.html>

Davis, Lennard J. 1995. *Enforcing Normalcy: Disability, deafness and the body*. London and New York: Verso.

Gibson, William. 1984. *Neuromancer*. New York: Ace Books.

Hawthorne, Susan. 1976/1990. In Defense of Separatism. Unpublished thesis (1976). Extract in Sneja Gunew (Ed.). 1990. *Feminist Knowledge Reader*. London: Routledge.

Hawthorne, Susan. 1996. From Theories of Indifference to a Wild Politics. In Diane Bell and Renate Klein (Eds.). *Radically Speaking: Feminism reclaimed*. Melbourne: Spinifex Press; London: Zed Books.

Hawthorne, Susan. 1997a. Cyberfeminism. Paper presented at the National Women's Studies Conference, Massey University, Palmerston North, New Zealand. 6 Feb.

Hawthorne, Susan. 1997b. Theories of Power and the Culture of the Powerful. In *Feminist Theory, Knowledge and Power: Study Guide*.
  <http://arts.deakin.edu.au/guymer/asw333sg/section3.htm>

Horacek, Judy. 1997. *Woman with Altitude*. South Melbourne: Hyland House.

Hyman, Prue. 1994. *Women and Economics*. Wellington: Bridget Williams Books.

Klein, Renate. 1996. (Dead) Bodies Floating in Cyberspace. In Diane Bell and Renate Klein (Eds.). *Radically Speaking: Feminism reclaimed*. Melbourne: Spinifex Press; London: Zed Books.

Lawnmower Man. 1992. New Line Productions Inc., and Allied/Vision/Lane Pringle.

Markley, Robert. (Ed.), 1996. *Virtual Realities and Their Discontents*. Baltimore: The Johns Hopkins University Press.

Milburn, Caroline. 1999. Mirrar Woman. *Age*. Saturday 13 March, News Extra, p. 3.

Millar, Melanie Stewart. 1998. *Cracking the Gender Code: Who rules the wired world.* Toronto: Second Story Press.

Mitchell, William J. 1995. *City of Bits: Space, place, and the infobahn.* Cambridge, Massachusetts and London: MIT Press.

Mogina, Jane. 1996. Oral presentation at 6th International Interdisciplinary Congress on Women, Adelaide University, 22 April.

Morrison, Toni. 1993. *Playing in the Dark: Whiteness and the literary imagination.* New York: Random House.

Namjoshi, Suniti. 1996. *Building Babel.* Melbourne: Spinifex Press.

O'Hartigan, Margaret Deirdre. 1999. Post-modernism Harms Women. *Off Our Backs.* January 6 and 13.

Pattanaik, Bandana. 1997. *Feminist Publishing in Asia.*
<http://www.spinifexpress.com.au/welcomeasia.htm>

Pattanaik, Bandana and Susan Hawthorne. 1997. Building Bridges Electronically: The Spinifex experiment. *Canadian Woman Studies/les cahiers de la femme,* No. 17, special issue on 'Bridging North/South: Patterns of Transformation.

Posey, Darrell A. 1996. Protecting Indigenous Peoples' Rights to Biodiversity. *Environment, 38* (8) October, 6–13.

Shiva, Vandana. 1993. *Monocultures of the Mind.* Penang: Third World Network.

Teaiwa, Katerina Martina. 1997. Body Shop Banabans and Skin Deep Samaritans. Paper presented at the VIII Pacific Science Inter-Congress, Women, Science and Development Symposium, University of the South Pacific, Suva, Fiji, 17 July.

Tofts, David and Murray McKeich. 1998. *Memory Trade: A prehistory of cyberculture.* Sydney: Interface.

Turnbull, David. 1997. Reframing Science and Other Local Knowledge Traditions. *Futures* 29, 6, 551–62.

Waring, Marilyn. 1988. *Counting for Nothing: What men value and what women are worth.* Sydney: Allen and Unwin.

Wilding, Faith. 1998. Where is the Feminism in Cyberfeminism? *n.paradoxa #3,* London.
<http://www-art.cfa.cmu.edu/www-wilding/wherefem.html>

Critique

seven

Information for People or Profits?

Beth Stafford

Introduction

My experience as a Women's Studies librarian for approximately twenty years informs the following observations regarding libraries, cyberspace, information resources and services on women and gender issues, and women's knowledge. For the purposes of this chapter, 'cyberfeminism' is taken to mean feminist responses to computer-mediated communication.

I have seen the birth and development of the two multi-disciplinary fields of <u>Women's Studies</u> (WS) and <u>women in international development</u> (WID). (Very roughly, WID includes women and gender issues in all developing areas of the world.) During that time I have built a collection and provided reference service for faculty, graduate students, undergraduate students, many visiting international scholars, and the general public.

Korenman

Pattanaik 1

On a daily basis I see the effects of the hyperbole and mythology about information technology (IT) and Internet on those seeking information about women and gender issues—particularly on undergraduates. Because of the hyperbole and myths about computers/IT many people have unrealistic expectations that everything they are looking for will be instantly accessible in exactly the form they need. Largely because we live in a sound byte communications culture, many, especially the young, cannot fathom the need to invest time and effort in the pursuit of what they need.

That is, it appears to be difficult for many to understand that they might need to consult more than one source to do research on a topic such as media images of women or how a mother's working outside the home affects children. More peculiar to many is the notion that, in some cases, the sources that would be most helpful to them are actually available only on paper(!), thanks to the myth that anything found on a computer is more valid and more up-to-date than anything found on paper.

In general, people tend to take the path of least resistance (or effort) when seeking information. As a result, of course, most will research those subjects that are easiest to find. A grave concern is how well new, online products and services really include journals and other literature that would be most valuable to those conducting research on women and gender issues.

Background of Information Technology (IT)

The confluence of three factors shortly after World War II began a process that has resulted in a mentality that is in direct contrast with traditional library values; these hold that a primary goal is open and free access to information for all. US federal spending on research and development was continued at an accelerating rate during the postwar period and generated an enormous amount of data. Concurrently, computer technology was undergoing rapid development and refinement in order to facilitate access to the flood of new data. Congruent with these developments was the growth of private corporations now moving into the international market, becoming powerful multinational conglomerates. A private information industry emerged to capitalize on the commercial potential in the processing and distribution of data. These three interactive forces have had a profound impact on the nation's economic and cultural life (Schiller 1989: 69–73). In short, information has become a commodity.

awthorne 6

A shift in the political climate in the United States has further affected developments. In 1980 the White House Conference on Library and Information Services declared:

Information in a free society is a basic right of any individual, essential
for all persons, at all age levels, and all economic and social levels . . .
Persons should have free access without charge or fee to the individual, to
information in public and publicly supported libraries (1980: 42).

The Reagan-Bush years resulted in a series of legislative acts and
executive orders that converted the profit-seeking objectives of the
private information sector into national policy. By 1982 the
Public/Private Sector Task Force of the National Commission on
Libraries and Information Science (appointed by the President)
issued a report that included the principle that

The federal government should establish and enforce policies and
procedures that encourage . . . investment by the private sector in the
development and use of information products and services . . . that
private enterprise should be encouraged to 'add value' to government
information by repackaging it and otherwise enhance it so that it can be
sold at a profit (1982: 7–8).

In other words, private enterprise was encouraged to repackage
information that consumers had already paid for with their taxes
and turn around and charge consumers for access to that
information (Blanke 1996: 61).

IT's Effects on Libraries and Librarianship

There is much debate within the library profession on the effects of
information technology/the cyber world on libraries, the profession,
and the roles of both. Libraries have always incorporated new technologies into their work and are obviously incorporating IT into
their work now. What is not known is the degree to which IT will
ultimately affect libraries and library services and what roles
libraries and librarians will play in the future.

On one side of the debate are those who embrace without
question a view of information as a commodity and concentrate on
being 'competitive' by providing high quality service only to those

they consider 'primary user groups', that is, those who can pay fees (Blanke 1996: 63)

Many others in the profession question the ethics and wisdom involved in the near-frenzy to digitize huge numbers of resources, leave print behind, and to make libraries into 'information service centers'.

Libraries are not wholly or even primarily about information. They are about the preservation, dissemination, and use of recorded <u>knowledge</u> in whatever form it may come so that humankind may become more knowledgeable, through knowledge reach understanding, and, as an ultimate goal, achieve wisdom. One could say they have always been and will continue to be knowledge service centers, with the emphasis on service.

Klein 9

Knowledge, not information, is power. Civilization is the keystone of enlightenment and understanding. Records of civilization began with the image and the text, and, since that dawning, human beings have striven to create and preserve recorded knowledge for <u>future generations</u>. Librarians owe a duty to posterity to preserve the records of our time, in whatever form they are created and issued, because knowledge, taught and recorded, is the essential prerequisite to understanding and wisdom. Libraries can and will use technology intelligently to carry on their historic mission (Crawford and Gorman 1995: 5–6).

amjoshi 17
Fletcher 14
wthorne 19

Libraries exist to collect, give access to, and preserve knowledge and information in all forms, and provide instruction and assistance in the use of resources. What IT has brought is an information explosion. We can have all the information in the world but be totally powerless unless we have the ability to analyze and interpret this mass of information (Crawford and Gorman 1995: 3).

The public sphere has been defined as

those arenas of social life . . . where dialogue and critique provide for the cultivation of democratic sentiments and habits. Schools, libraries, museums, and other public institutions are constructed around forms of critical inquiry that dignify . . . the discourse of public association and social responsibility (Giroux 1984: 192).

Those on this side of the debate see the 'information-as-commodity' side as discarding the ideal of provision of library service as a public good. Those wary of treating information as a commodity warn of a corrosion of the values that allow libraries to contribute to an enlightened public discourse, a corrosion that amounts to a form of censorship. With the growing economic prominence of information has come the encroachment of corporate capitalism into the public information realm and a concomitant distortion of information issues and policies to serve private interests. At stake is the future vitality of democratic public spheres of independent art, inquiry, discourse, and critique (Blanke 1996: 67).

> [This] growing economic prominence of information and the intensifying commercialization of cultural activity have generated forces, both within and outside of librarianship, that threaten to undermine the ideal of knowledge as a public good . . . Marketplace forces, rather than individual needs, drive the development and introduction of new information products (Blanke 1996: 60).

In addition, the future of Internet itself is uncertain. With all its potential to be 'the basis of a free social information facility, it is being divested of its public character' (Schiller 1989: 64). The *New York Times* says that:

> the rush to commercialize . . . the Internet has created an investor frenzy not seen in the technology industry since the early days of the personal computer
>
> and privatization of the Internet appears to be inevitable (Zuckerman 1995).

'In a political system grounded in an informed citizenry', the American Library Association (ALA) Code of Ethics espouses an explicit 'commitment to intellectual freedom and the freedom of access to information' (*ALA Policy Manual* 1996: 46).

The death of print has been predicted several times before—at the advents of film, television, and microfilm, to name a few. New technologies don't necessarily replace old as much as they enhance them. The efficient use of technology lies in applying it intelligently and appropriately to improve and enhance library services: to replace inefficient manual processes, and to deliver data and information when that delivery is more cost-effective than 'traditional' means. While information services will be best supported by electronic technology, the knowledge services libraries offer will best be supported by physical collections supplemented by electronic resources (Crawford and Gorman 1995: 180).

Librarians need to learn the culture of technical personnel who develop and maintain information systems in order to communicate with them more effectively as the two groups collaborate on systems development. At the same time, librarians need to teach technical personnel about library culture so that the systems being developed will further their values of free inquiry and universal access. Librarians are working with computer center personnel and information system vendors to design information systems that meet library constituents' needs, that are easy to use, and that help them judge the relevance of the information they retrieve through those systems (Ford 1998: 4–5).

Graduate schools of library and information science are training their students in such areas as systems design and analysis, networks, information policy and computer operations as well as organization and preservation of information and information storage and retrieval. Librarians are researching and teaching human-computer interfaces, human-computer interaction, and information transfer in order to get a better understanding of how to organize and present information and how people use that information once they have it.

Effects on Libraries and Library Users

The public, including many in the academy, is frustrated, in large part because they have accepted several troubling myths about online information. One is that all information is now available electronically. Just as dangerous is another, that all information is or soon will be available for free somewhere on the World Wide Web. With some futurists predicting that some day it will be possible to read everything that has ever been written on one's own screen, people get the impression that print will or should be abandoned altogether.

In at least one instance, in 1996 a state legislator informed a state university library director that his library no longer needed a budget for library materials because Harvard University had digitized its entire library collection and was making it available to the entire world at no charge. Such an undertaking would take billions of dollars, involve identifying thousands of copyright owners and negotiating for payments to them, and an enormous degree of generosity to make the <u>materials available</u> to everyone for free. Common sense dictates otherwise. And, the truth is that much of what is on the Web is plain junk—not current, objective, or trustworthy (Miller 1997: A44).

Hawthorne

The concept of the 'virtual library' predicted by many futurists also confuses the public. Print is and will remain an important medium of communication for the indefinite future. Electronic publishing and dissemination will grow and replace print in the cases in which print is inferior—primarily compilations of data and short packages of information.

The future means both print and electronic communication. Libraries will continue to build and maintain strong collections of both print and other media in order to serve the essential needs of their users. Libraries will rely more heavily on access to materials they do not own, and they must find ways to share the risks, costs, and benefits of such access. In reality there are no monolithic solutions for libraries. Particularly absurd is the notion that all library resources will and should be available as text in electronic form (Crawford and Gorman 1995: 180–181).

Total dependence on electronically accessed information would further disadvantage those who are already disadvantaged, from the level of the individual to the national and international levels. That is, clearly the gap between the haves and have nots, individuals, groups, and countries alike, would only grow wider. Libraries must be careful not to end up serving only an elite population.

Abandoning print altogether would mean producer/vendors of electronically accessed resources would be the only ones to own the complete resources. With buyouts and mergers being common, vendors simply cannot be depended on to archive resources, and they certainly wouldn't make them available without charges, which they could then raise to astronomical levels at will.[1] Already some producer/vendors program their CD-ROMs to become unusable at a predetermined date.

> The virtual library is a concept of remote access to the contents and services of libraries and other information resources. It combines an on-site collection of current and heavily used materials in both print and electronic form, with an electronic network that provides access to and delivery from, external worldwide library and commercial information sources (Ford 1998: 3).

In a recent article, David Rothenberg (1997: A44) says that, in point of fact, students' use of the Web is making their research papers worse. Among other things, materials retrieved from the Web are 'curiously out of date', and depending on the Web for research makes research look too easy. He thinks that, when libraries divert funds from books to computer technology that will soon be obsolete, they send a message to students not to read but just to connect, download, <u>cut and paste</u>. (He does take some responsibility for not being more careful to teach his students how to read, to take time with language and ideas, to work through arguments, to synthesize various sources to come up with original thought.)

Klein 9

Too frequently student use of Internet leads to superficial research papers that are full of data—some of it suspect—and little thought. Students literally get lost in cyberspace. As one faculty

---

1. This means that a library can pay thousands of dollars each year for ten years to acquire a CD-ROM or online access to a cumulative resource, but if it cannot afford the subscription price the eleventh year it does not have even the ten years' worth that it has paid for—or actually 'rented'. Librarians are engaged in intense negotiations with producer/vendors over such issues.

member at the University of Wisconsin puts it, 'One of the things you're missing on the Web is a reference librarian' (Knowlton 1997: 18). Academic research involves three steps: finding relevant information, assessing the quality of that information, then using appropriate information 'either to try to conclude something, to uncover something, to prove something, or to argue something'. The Internet is useful for the first step, somewhat useful for the second, and not at all useful for the third (Knowlton 1997: 21).

Increasingly, information found in cyberspace can be most effectively used only with the assistance of knowledgeable, technically competent librarians. Increasingly, librarians need to help users to evaluate materials found in cyberspace. If librarians working with information on women and gender issues are to be effective, they must be aware of the pitfalls of the variety of available products and services. That is, they must be aware of what types of materials are not included online as well as those that are.

Information technology affects different types of libraries in different ways. For most public libraries, access to Internet and other electronic resources such as CD-ROMs greatly enhance services to users, opening up resources previously unobtainable to them.

Some special libraries in some industries or businesses such as law firms have been nearly eliminated. In such settings, swift responses to questions have traditionally been more important to library users than assistance from a librarian showing a user how to find answers her/himself. (The vast majority of library transactions are of the latter type.) It is not surprising then, that some companies have decided to 'outsource' some or all functions previously performed by library staff. It remains to be seen whether, in the long run, such practices will be more or less beneficial to the firms than maintaining in-house libraries.

Academic libraries are struggling to find the right balance between print and electronic sources that will best serve the needs of their clientele. Just some of the difficulties they face include diminishing budgets; price gouging by publishers of journals (especially those in science and technology fields); and enormous

costs for equipping and training personnel to use IT, constant
upgrading of hardware and software to serve their clientele more
effectively through public access online catalogs, a wide range of
database services and digitized and image databases to enhance
their collections and services. In addition to that, there are
numerous difficulties negotiating with vendors over frequently very
steep prices and overly restrictive licenses for packages of
information sources whose contents are determined by the
vendors.[2]

Accessing Information

In cyberspace we are even more dependent on terminology than we
are in print. This means that feminists, perhaps especially feminist
librarians, must have some impact on the shape and structure of
cyberspace if people are to have access to information on women
and gender issues. Just as feminists must create 'a room of (their)
own' in cyberspace, so must feminist librarians be involved in the
enterprise.

Feminists, both in and out of the library profession, have caused
substantial improvements in accessibility methods used by libraries
all over the world. Past classification schemes (call numbers) and
bibliographic structures (systems of cross references) used in
libraries traditionally made information by and about females all but
invisible. One of the critical issues in coping with access to information by/about women and gender issues is that the terminology
employed by libraries has been expressed in language overwhelm-
ingly based on male experience only. For example, the very word
'sexism' and phrases such as 'body image' did not exist thirty years
ago. The most widely used system of terminology used in libraries is

---

2. One instance of the outrageousness of this practice is the fact that one vendor has attempted to
   charge one large, well-endowed US university library over $250,000 per year for a 'package' of
   resources that include resources in disciplines that university does not offer.

the one devised at the Library of Congress in the United States (Library of Congress Subject Headings, or LCSH) or national adaptations of it.

Recognizing the many limitations and biases in LCSH and other schemes, feminist librarians, scholars, and others have created thesauri of terminology based on language expressing female experiences and perspectives. *The Women's Thesaurus* was published in the US in 1987. At approximately the same time the National Women's Education Centre in Japan published *Thesaurus on Women and the Family.*

We need to continue the work of such projects with updates and additions. The largest bibliographic database search service in the world, OCLC, (Online Catalog Library Center) has included terminology from The *Women's Thesaurus* for years, but the *Thesaurus* needs to be updated.[3]

A study on how well general online tables of contents services cover Women's Studies journals indicates that the paper-only *Feminist Periodicals*, although not indexed, is more complete than any of the online services because it includes entire tables of contents of over one hundred Women's Studies journals. The online services provide selective coverage and completely omit many significant journals in the field (Krikos 1994: 65–78, 82).

While a few new, commercially available products are beginning to fill some of the gaps in electronic access to materials on women and gender issues, several questions remain about which materials are being made accessible. A recent article exemplifies the types of work that librarians will increasingly need to do. It evaluates four recent products providing unprecedented fast access to vast amounts of information, comparing the qualities of two databases having bibliographic citations and two that are fulltext—that is, that

---

3. A commonly-used controlled language is needed in order to make information findable. For example, it is much easier to find information about the families of Americans of African heritage if all materials in a collection or network are consistently labelled as 'African-American families' rather than having some with that label and others called 'Black families' while still others are called 'Afro-American families' or 'Negro families'.

contain entire articles from various types of sources (Dickstein *et al.* 1998: 59–84).

Feminist librarians need constantly to question to what extent materials such as Women's Studies journals are included in the flood of mainstream online and other electronic products and services being produced—and even in those devoted to Women's Studies. They need to have meaningful input into decision-making processes in libraries as they struggle to select which resources to purchase. (Fees for individual online resources range from a few hundred dollars a year to several tens of thousands each year.)

Feminist librarians, particularly those in research settings, must also pay attention to such questions as whether materials with a lesbian or international focus are included in any online product or service, or if materials in languages other than English are included. (In fact, to date, even the few databases devoted to Women's Studies badly neglect journals with a lesbian focus.) With the needs of big business driving the content of what's available online, what other forms of censorship, intentional or not, do or will take place?

Feminism, Cyberspace, and Libraries: Now

The first effort to address the difficulties connected with electronic accessibility of information on women was *Women Online: Research in Women's Studies Using Online Databases*, edited by two US librarians (Atkinson and Hudson 1990). It provides an overview of coverage of women and gender issues in extant online resources. At that time such information could be had only through searching a variety of resources organized by broad subject areas such as law.

The first CD-ROM on women was *Women's Indicators and Statistics (WISTAT)*, produced by the United Nations in 1989, giving vital statistics about women and girls in over 140 countries in a form that enables one to produce one's own spread sheets on a particular country or group of countries for comparison. The 1996 edition will be replaced by an online-only version in 1999.

Other early CD-ROMs devoted to women and gender issues were those produced by CD Resources (New York) in 1990. *Women: Partners in Development* and *Women, Water, and Sanitation* provide full text to hundreds of United Nations agency documents.

An outstanding resource available in cyberspace is *Contemporary Women's Issues* (CWI), produced by Responsive Database Services, in Beachwood, Ohio, (in collaboration with feminist librarians). It is available online or on CD-ROM only by paid subscription. Excellent international coverage of English-language titles includes many from over 130 countries in all.

CWI provides full text access to journals, hard-to-find newsletters, reports, pamphlets, fact sheets, and guides on a broad array of gender-related issues such as violence, economic development, law, health, the military, and more. Over 25,000 entire articles in the database can be downloaded to disc or printed. Information is available at <http://www.cwi>

Also available only by paid subscription on CD-ROM or via Internet is *Women's Resources International* (WRI), a bibliographic resource. That is, it includes only citations to materials on women and gender issues. The most comprehensive in scope of currently available online resources of its type, it includes citations from a variety of databases. Today it includes an estimated 140,000 citations from the following ten different databases:

- *Women Studies Abstracts* (WSA), which indexes periodicals that are feminist or woman-focused. WRI's coverage starts in 1984, with semi-annual updates.
- The *Women's Studies Database*, based on the Women's Studies collection at the University of Toronto. Its coverage starts in 1972 and includes mostly journals, newspapers, popular magazines, and newsletters.
- *European Women's History from the Renaissance to Yesterday: A Bibliography*, includes book citations from 1610 and periodical citations from 1810.
- *Women of Color and Southern Women*, produced by the

University of Memphis Center for Research on Women from 1989 through 1996.

- Popline Subset on Women, which emphasizes the health and social concerns of women in developing countries, includes journals, reports, books, unpublished and published papers.
- *Women's Health and Development: an Annotated Bibliography* from the World Health Organization.
- Four published bibliographies compiled by the University of Wisconsin Systems Women's Studies Librarian's Office make up the balance of materials in WRI. They include non-mainstream materials and those not covered in published indexes.

Subscription to WRI includes no ownership rights (see footnote 1, p. 144).

One of the finest library resources on women and gender issues available in cyberspace is the website for the University of Wisconsin System Women's Studies Librarian, at <http://www.library/wisc.edu/libraries/WomensStudies/>

This site includes numerous bibliographies and core lists of Women's Studies resources prepared by feminist librarians and links to hundreds of other websites. In addition, it has online versions of the 'Computer Talk' columns from *Feminist Collections*, a quarterly publication of that office.

Another truly fine library-based resource in cyberspace is WSS Links: Women and Gender Studies Web Sites. Developed and maintained by the Women's Studies Section of the (US) Association of College and Research Libraries' Collection Development Committee; its URL is: <http://www.library.yale.edu/wss/> It also maintains a listserv called *WSS-L*. Its purpose is to provide access to a wide range of resources in support of Women's Studies. Different feminist librarians maintain links to women's information online, organized into fourteen broad topics. Sample topics include General Sites, Health, Archives, and Politics. The exemplary link for International Women includes bibliographies, general sites for international women's issues, and resources organized by region. *FEMINIST-L* is the listserv of the American Library Association's Feminist Task Force.

In the spring of 1997, the African Gender Institute at the University of Cape Town, South Africa, hosted a pan-African workshop for librarians and documentalists with the aim of exploring ways to share gender information and resources throughout Africa. Two results of that workshop have come to fruition. First is a listerv for librarians and documentalists in Africa connecting all interested people in the field—to be expanded later to include those outside of Africa who are interested in gender issues in Africa. Second is the African Gender Institute website, still under development, at <http://www.uct.ac.za/org/agi>

In mid-1996 experts from women's information services in Europe met together in Amsterdam to discuss progress in constructing a European database for Women's Studies. They formed a group called Women's Information Network Europe (WINE), to set up a network for documentation centers, archives, and libraries that have expertise in the provision of information services on the position of women and Women's Studies in Europe and to facilitate exchange among these groups.

One member of WINE is the International Information Centre and Archives for the Women's Movement (IIAV) in Amsterdam, which has clearly taken the lead in developing access to women's information. An English-language version of their website is at <http://www.iiav.nl/homeeng.html>

In 1998 IIAV hosted an international conference for librarians and documentalists working with materials relevant to women and gender issues. Approximately three hundred women's information specialists and representatives of government agencies from over eighty countries and territories attended the 'Know How Conference on the World of Women's Information' to highlight their projects and activities—employing cyberspace as well as other means. Topics covered included, among others, indexing women's information on Internet, new women's information resources on Internet, designing new online resources, disseminating information via Internet, and using women's information in public policy decision-making processes.

One of the most impressive elements of the 'Know How' conference is the 'Mapping the World of Women's Information Services: project, available at <http://www.iiav.nl/mapping-the-world/index.html>

It is an online guide to collections of women's information in all types of organizations, from government agencies to activist groups to academic libraries, everywhere. This guide provides keyword and geographic access to the content of collections literally worldwide and is a continuing service of IIAV. In addition, a listserv of conference participants continues to facilitate exchange of information and experience.

One goal of the Round Table on Women's Issues of the International Federation of Library Associations and Institutions (IFLA) is to support the information needs of women as users in communities at all levels. The Round Table has a website to network like-minded librarians all over the world and plans to provide links to selected collections and information sources. Its website is: <http://www.ifla.org/VII/rt14rtwi.htm>

Pattanaik 1

The Women's Information Center at the Korean Women's Development Institute in Seoul has numerous online databases and provides English translation services to exchange information with women in other countries via Internet. Its website is <http://www.intermusic.co.kr/webip/kwdi/>

One online library resource now available is at the University of Illinois Library in Urbana (UIUC). Co-sponsored by the National Women's Studies Association, it is a continuing searchable database on Women's Studies programs, mostly in the United States. Via keyword searching it accesses course titles, individuals teaching Women's Studies, degrees offered, majors, minors, etc. With it one can find quickly, in one source, which institutions and individuals in a particular geographic area offer specific degrees and fields of specialization. It is at <<u>http://www.library.uiuc.edu/wst/search3.htm</u>>

Another UIUC Library resource is a database on videos relating to women and gender issues worldwide that is searchable by subject and geographical area, at <<u>http://www.library.uiuc.edu/wst/wst vdb.htm</u>>

A third UIUC Library resource is a database on women in science, engineering, and technology. It includes text of the title pages and tables of contents of books on these subjects in order to give more visibility to the links between feminist scholarship and women in these three fields. It is at <<u>http://www.library.uiuc.edu/wst/ tocs/ index.html</u>>

Feminism, Cyberspace, and Libraries: The future

Women's Studies has been called the academic arm of the women's movement. It has contributed entire reconceptualizations of theory and practice in nearly all traditional disciplines in the academy. Feminist scholars have proven gender to be a crucial factor of analysis in both teaching and research by questioning long-held assumptions. Combining research with activism, they have given visibility to cultural beliefs and practices that were formerly unacknowledged or unknown. For example, violence against women has been taken out of the closet and is being taken seriously from the local to the <u>international level</u>. An example of previously unrecognized phenomena feminists have made visible is ways in which classroom teachers can unconsciously treat girls differently than they treat boys. Another previously unrecognized phenomenon is the fact that traditional economic analyses have ignored many of women's unpaid contributions to the economic welfare of nations. These include production within the household, housework, child

Hughes 8

care, and emotional labor (nurturing children, spouses, personal relations) (Waring 1992: 307).

Feminists both in and outside of the academy have long pointed out existing obstacles to obtaining information on women, gender issues, and women's recorded knowledge. It has been the job of librarians to make information and knowledge accessible in whatever form it exists, to disseminate and preserve it.

At the present time, various search engines on Internet and other online sources can lead to an unwieldy number of irrelevant results, causing a good deal of exasperation because there is little control.

Librarians are working on ways to link the Web's coding language to structured systems of information retrieval. Michael Gorman suggests that

> if all useful documents on the Net were to be assigned subject headings the potential for searching would be so great that the present aimless surfing ... would be replaced by purposeful, powerful search and retrieval systems that would produce results high in relevance and recall (1997: 4–5).

He proposes that each country or linguistic group review subject heading terminology in each subject area, propose changes, and use the power of online systems to replace outdated and anomalous terms in online catalogs.[4] He also suggests that all elements of the terminology be made equally searchable and retrievable.[5] Thirdly, he suggests that links be made to work both from the broad to the narrow topic (as most links are currently) and from the narrow topic to the broad.[6]

Obviously the key word in Gorman's plan is 'useful'. That not-

---

[4.] Fifty years ago, a book written on single mothers would have been assigned the subject headings 'Woman—Social and moral questions' and 'Unwed mothers'.

[5.] A subject heading 'Women heads of households—In-service training' would be searchable (findable) under 'In-service training', and 'Training' as well as under 'Women . . .'.

[6.] An example of linking a broad term to a narrow would be to link 'Genital mutilation' to 'Clitoridectomy'. A narrow term linked to a broad term would be linking 'Clitoridectomy' to 'Genital mutilation' or 'Chicanas' to 'Hispanic American women'.

withstanding, the principle thing that librarians have always contributed to the pursuit of information and knowledge is structure. Online database systems, CD-ROMs, and Internet have all made vast quantities of information available more quickly than previous access methods, but there is nearly no structure on Internet.

In designing a more user-friendly interface to their online catalog, librarians at the national library of Denmark have done some very promising studies on data mining and fuzzy logic. Results from a Web-based test model convincingly support the conclusion that fuzzy logic is a very relevant tool in user-friendly search interfaces (Andreasen 1997).

It has been pointed out that the future belongs to those who control the filtering, searching, and sense-making tools we will rely on to navigate cyberspace. Librarians evaluate, analyze, organize, and package information, adding value as they make it usable, and, as their roles evolve, they might well be the search tools of the future. Libraries are in a position to provide expertise on information organization and retrieval, public service, and access for the broadest range of information users (Ford 1998: p 2).

An excellent example of the type of enterprise feminist librarians must pursue is the *European Women's Thesaurus* published by IIAV in 1998. It is a 'professional tool for indexing and retrieving women's information in databases, on Internet and in the collections of libraries, documentation centres and archives' that provides a common terminology for these functions (*European Women's Thesaurus* 1989: i).

Working closely with feminist scholars and activists, feminist librarians must continue with their efforts to create and apply terminologies that can best access information on women and gender issues in cyberspace as well as in print and other forms of communication. They must also work with those creating online resources to provide access to women's recorded knowledge in all forms, inside and outside libraries.

References

American Library Association. 1996. *ALA Policy Manual*. Chicago: American Library Association.

Andreasen, Troels. 1997. DanBib: a Union Catalogue Applied for User Friendly Flexible Querying. Paper given at 63rd Conference of International Federation of Library Associations and Institutions (IFLA), Copenhagen.

Atkinson, Steven D. and Judity Hudson. 1990. *Women Online: Research in women's studies using online databases*. New York: The Haworth Press.

Blanke, Henry T. 1996. Librarianship and Public Culture in the Age of Information Capitalism. *Journal of Information Ethics*, 5(2), Fall, 54–69.

Crawford, Walt and Michael Gorman. 1995. *Future Libraries: Dreams, madness and reality*. Chicago: American Library Association.

Dickstein, Ruth and Marcia Evans, Lisa German, Jessica Grim, Sandra A. River. 1998. From Zero to Four: a Review of Four New Women's Studies CD-ROM Products. *The Serials Librarian* 35 (1/2), 59–84.

European Women's Thesaurus. 1998. Amsterdam: International Information Centre and Archives for the Women's Movement. (Translation and adaptation of Vrouwenthesaurus: lijst van gecontroleerde termen voor het ontsluiten van informatie over de positie van vrouwen en vrouwenstudies. Amsterdam: IIAV, 1992.)

Ford, Barbara. 1998. Building Bridges: Librarians as Leaders in the Age of Information Technology. Speech at various venues as President, American Library Association, 1997/98.

Giroux, Henry. 1984. Public Philosophy and the Crisis in Education. *Harvard Educational Review*, 54, 186–94.

Gorman, Michael. 1997. The Future of Cataloguing and Cataloguers. Paper given at 63rd Conference of International Federation of Library Associations and Institutions IFLA, Copenhagen.

Knowlton, Steven R. 1997. How Students Get Lost in Cyberspace. *New York Times Supplement*, pp. 18 et seq. November 2.

Krikos, Linda. 1994. Women's Studies Periodicals Indexes: an In-Depth Comparison. *Serials Review* 20 (Summer) 65–78, 82.

Miller, William. 1997. Troubling Myths About On-Line Information. *The Chronicle of Higher Education XLIII* (47) A44.

National Commission on Libraries and Information Science. 1982. *Public/private Sector Interaction in Providing Information Services*. Report to NCLIS from the public/private sector task force. Washington, D.C.: Government Printing Office.

Rothenberg, David. 1997. How the Web Destroys the Quality of Students' Research Papers. *The Chronicle of Higher Education. XLIII* (48) A44.

Schiller, H.I. 1989. *Culture, Inc.: the Corporate Takeover of Public Expression*. New York: Oxford University Press.

Thesaurus on Women and the Family. 1987? (date uncertain) Saitama, Japan: National Women's Education Centre (in Japanese only).

Waring, Marilyn J. 1992. Economics. In Cheris Kramerae and Dale Spender (Eds.), *The Knowledge Explosion: Generations of feminist scholarship*. New York: Pergamon Press (now Teachers College Press).

White House Conference on Libraries and Information Services. 1980. *Summary*. Washington, D.C.: Government Printing Office.

Zuckerman, 1995. With Internet Cachet, Not Profit, a New Stock Amazes Wall St. New York: *New York Times*, August 10, A1, D5.

eight

The Internet and the Global Prostitution Industry

Donna Hughes

The Internet has become the latest place for promoting the global trafficking and sexual exploitation of women and children. This global communication network is being used to promote and engage in the buying and selling of women and children. Agents offer catalogues of mail-order brides, with girls as young as thirteen. Commercial prostitution tours are advertised. Men exchange information on where to find prostitutes and describe how they can be used. After their trips men write reports on how much they paid for women and children, and give pornographic descriptions of what they did to them. New technology has enabled an online merger of pornography and prostitution, with videoconferencing bringing live sex shows to the Internet.

Sexual Exploitation on the Internet

Global sexual exploitation is on the rise. The profits are high, and there are few effective barriers at the moment. Because there is little regulation of the Internet, the traffickers and promoters of sexual exploitation have rapidly used the Internet for their purposes.

Traffickers and pornographers are the leading developers of the Internet industry. *PC Computing* magazine urged entrepreneurs to visit <u>pornography Web sites.</u>

Pattanaik 1

> It will show you the future of online commerce. Web pornographers are the most innovative entrepreneurs on the Internet (Taylor and Jerome 1997).

The pornographers and other promoters of sexual exploitation are the Internet leaders in the developing privacy services, secure payment schemes and online data base management.

The development and expansion of the Internet is an integral part of globalization. The Internet sex industry has made local, community, and even, national standards obsolete. Nicholas Negroponte, Director of the Media Laboratory at the Massachusetts Institute of Technology, and founder of *Wired* magazine said:

> As we interconnect ourselves, many of the values of a nation-state will give way to those of both larger and smaller electronic communities (Negroponte 1995).

The standards and values on the Internet are being set by the sex industry and its supporters and users. This economic and electronic globalization has meant that women are increasingly 'commodities' to be bought, sold, traded and consumed.

Newsgroups and Web Sites for Men Who Buy Women and Children

The oldest forum on the Internet for promoting the sexual exploitation of women is the newsgroup alt.sex.services (later renamed alt.sex.prostitution). Its 'aim is to create market transparency for sex related services'. Postings from this newsgroup are archived into a World Wide Web site called 'The World Sex Guide', which provides 'comprehensive, sex-related information about every country in the world' (Atta and M. 1996).

The World Sex Guide
Where do you want to fuck today?

Web Site for Finding Women to Buy

The guide includes information and advice from men who have bought women and children in prostitution. They tell others where and how to find and buy prostituted women and children in 110 countries from seven world regions (Africa, Asia, Oceania, Europe, North America, Central America and the Caribbean, and South America). The following are a few examples of men's opening lines for their reports:

> I have a good knowledge of brothels in Brazil, due to my frequent journeys during the last 5 years (Anonymous 7 Oct. 1995).

> Having some experience with the scene in New Zealand I would like to offer the following advice (Anonymous 30 Aug. 1995).

> Another of my 'catching up' reports on present knowledge of hot spots around the globe, this time from Bristol, England (an370191@anon. penet.fi, Bristol 15 Sept. 1995).

Details of the men's reports of their prostitution tours and buying experiences include: information on where to go to find prostitutes, hotel prices, telephone numbers, taxi fares, cost of alcohol, the sex acts that can be bought, the price for each act, and evaluations of the women's appearances and performances. One man includes a rating scale on the likelihood of getting mugged in that neighborhood. The men go on to describe, often in graphic detail, their experiences of using women and children. The scope and detail of this exchange is without precedent. The women are completely objectified and evaluated on everything from skin color to presence of scars and firmness of their flesh. Women's receptiveness and compliance to men buyers is also rated.

The men buying women and posting the information see and perceive the events only from their self-interested perspective. Their awareness of racism, colonization, global economic inequalities, and of course, sexism, is limited to how these forces benefit them. A country's economic or political crisis and the accompanying poverty are advantages, which produce cheap readily available women for the men. Often men describe how desperate the women are and how little the men have to pay.

The postings also reveal that men are using the Internet as a source of information in selecting where to go and how to find women and children to buy in prostitution. Men describe taking a computer print-out of hotels, bar addresses and phone numbers with them on their trips, or describe how they used the Internet search engines to locate sex tours.

> This three day trip happened in June 1995. On the flight I read all the information I had printed out from The World Sex Guide—I had a lot of expectations of the City of Angels [Bangkok] (Anonymous, Short Trip, date unknown).

There is extensive information on legal prostitution in Nevada, USA, including photographs of the brothel entrances and road signs leading to the brothels (Bashful, 'Reno and Carson City', 1995). One man calling himself Cybersuck provides a list of legal 'whorehouses' in Nevada with detailed driving instructions on how to get there (Cybersuck 1995, 1996).

Photograph of Legal Brothel in Nevada

This rapid publishing electronic medium has enabled men to pimp and exploit individual women. Now, men can go out at night, buy a woman, go home, and post the details on the newsgroup. By morning anyone in the world with an Internet connection can read about it and often have enough information to find the same woman. For example, in Nevada, one man bought a woman called 'Honey' and named the brothel where she could be found. Within a couple of weeks other men went and bought 'Honey' themselves and posted their experiences to the newsgroup. Within a short period of time men were having an orgy of male bonding by describing what each of them did to this woman. The men are keeping a special Web site on the Internet for men to post their experiences of buying this one woman (Bashful, Honey, 1994, 1995, 1996). Additional Web sites have been created for other identifiable women. To my knowledge this is completely unprecedented. The implications for this type of public exchange in a fast-publishing easily accessible medium like the Internet are very serious for the sexual exploitation of women in the future.

The most voluminous coverage is on Bangkok, Thailand. The men give information on everything from currency exchange rates to how to run a bar tab. The names, addresses and phone numbers for 150 hotels where men will feel comfortable are listed (baguio@ix. netcom.com 1995, March). All the city sections and their sexual specialties are listed and described. Does the man want massage? Discos? Escort services? A lady house? Japanese clubs? A short-time hotel? A blow job bar? At these Web sites the men are presenting an etiquette and buyer's guide on how men should behave and solicit in all of these places.

One colorful page on the Web promotes special shows in Bangkok where men can pay to see women smoking cigarettes with their vaginas. Another Web page provides a description of the razor blade show in which a woman dances and pulls two dozen razor blades connected by a string from her vagina. A color photograph of the act is shown (Odzer 1995). A woman named Cleo Odzer owns this web site. She did her PhD research on prostitution in Bangkok and presents herself as an objective researcher, but on her Web site she refers to the women in the bars as 'my prostitutes'. She has a picture of herself with a pimp named Choo Choo Charlie. The caption to the photograph reads:

> Choo Choo Charlie the tout says, 'Psst . . . you want prostitute? Step right this way into the Patpong Bar. Female, male, katoey . . . fill all your dreams in the PatpongBar.

She seems to have taken on the role of pimp on her web site. At another site a man describes a show in Bangkok in which a woman dances with two pythons and inserts the head of one into her vagina (Anonymous 15 Jan. 1995).

Author Cleo Odzer with Pimp in Bangkok

Some of the men posting information on the alt.sex.prostitution newsgroup are quite straightforward about their misogyny and sadism. Other men, who I'm sure, would deny that they have ever abused a woman, reveal quite inadvertently their abuse of women. The reader can get a glimpse of the humiliation and physical pain most of the women endure at the hands of men who buy them by reading accounts of men's 'bad experiences'. To the men who buy women and children, a 'bad experience' means they didn't get their money's worth or that the woman didn't keep up the act of enjoying the men. It means she let her true feelings of pain, desperation, and hopelessness show.

The men exchange information on child prostitution. One man says, in Bangkok 'there is child prostitution. I have been offered 9-year-olds, and 14-year-olds are not uncommon'. His solution: 'If child prostitution turns you off, be careful when you select your girl' (Anonymous, Bangkok, Date unknown). Another man described which street corners are the best for finding pimps who can supply pre-teen girls. He said not to worry if you ask the wrong guy, he will probably just direct you to the right one. The men assume that the whole town is there to serve their demand for women and children.

> Outside _____ is the best chance of finding guys selling very young girls-pre-teens. You strike contact with the guy, he asks you to meet him somewhere close in an hour, and he will then bring one or two school girls for you to look over (Anonymous Bangkok, Date unknown).

Some men describe finding and buying young girls for sex. Although they are clearly seeking and raping children, they always include a comment in their writings that later they found out the girl was really much older than she looked. The men believe that this statement will legally protect them from being accused of buying under-age girls. One man wrote a long description of finding and buying a young girl. This is an excerpt:

> My helper [bar attendant—pimp] suggested that perhaps I would be interested in some young ones. . . . Inside the other room sat about twelve little girls watching TV. On a command from my attendant, they all sat back up on the couches and smiled at me. It was obvious that these young things had not yet matured into ladies. . . . their giggles and squirming quickly gave them away. No dummies either, the establishment had made no attempts to dress them sexy, but rather clothed them in young girl outfits befitting their age. My attendant assured me that all of them were suitably trained. I couldn't restrain myself! I had to have one of them (Anonymous Jan. 1995).

This man continues with a graphic description of the sex that is so pornographic and abusive I will not reprint it. It includes many references to her 'tiny' mouth and vagina and her 'grimace of pain' when he had intercourse with her.

We know that many of the girls and women in Bangkok's prostitution industry are virtual slaves. The men who buy them know that. Slavery is accepted and exploited by these men, and their comments prove that. One man on the Internet newsgroup said, 'Yes there is slavery in Bangkok. Some girls work against their will.' He then goes on to describe where the 'kept' women are most likely to be found. He says:

> if this is a problem for you, simply stay away from [these hotels]. Another
> way of handling this is, of course, to be gentle and gentlemanry [sic] and
> give the girl a good time whether she is a slave or not (Anonymous
> Bangkok, Date unknown).

On this newsgroup, the men tell each other that they can exploit the women and girls held against their will for sadistic practices.

> The hotel girls are usually younger than most other 'available' girls in
> Bangkok, fourteen–fifteen years old being rather common. They are in
> effect 'owned' by the hotel, which means that you can treat them more or
> less any way you want—and many men do. Hotels like this should be like
> paradise for those of us who are into S&M [sadomasochism]
> (Anonymous Bangkok, Date unknown).

Although the basis of prostitution is economic exploitation for the pimps, brothel and bar owners, the men who buy the women and girls engage in enslaving them for purposes of sexual gratification and domination. The following selection, from a man's report on his prostitution tour in Thailand, reveals in his own words, how the women are constrained and forced to perform sex acts for basic survival:

> You can go to an island. . . . You and a buddy or two go to a beach resort
> . . . and talk to any of the boat owners in the harbor. He agrees to meet
> you at a specified time the next day. Then you spend the evening storing
> up on good books, rented scuba gear, frisbees, things like that—and go
> bar hunting. There are bars, and there will be bar girls, and some of them
> will agree to join you the next day. Come the next day, your party (two or
> three guys, five or six girls, perhaps) transfers to the ship and is taken to

one of the thousands of small paradise islands off the coast of Thailand. It will be deserted, maybe with a hut or a bungalow, but with no people at all. Then you agree with the skipper to come by every day with fresh food, and to pick you up again in a week. It is a great way of getting both a good tan, a good relaxation, and all your sexual fantasies fulfilled. Last time I did this, we quickly established a house rule that no girl was ever allowed to wear any piece of clothing except her sandals. That, plus our other rule that every girl had to in some appropriate way or another earn her food before every meal, turned the stay in a rather pleasant one.

The following is another example of a man's self-report of forcing a prostituted woman to stay with him and submit to sex when she did not want to. He felt entitled to twenty hours of ownership because he paid for that amount of time to the brothel owner. This man is writing about buying a woman in Phnom Penh, Cambodia.

At my last stop I do find a Khmer girl. She's thin with small breasts and a very attractive girlish figure to go with her cute face. I settle on $15 to have her for the night and until noon the next day. This I make clear with the papasan,[1] but it is apparently not clear with the girl.

Her name is Mao and the two of us take a moto-taxi back to my hotel. I quickly have her undressed, with her attempting to conceal her body within a towel. She turns out to be another okay screw, not especially passionate, and absolutely refuses to let me [perform oral sex.] Her other difficulty is her insistence on watching TV, which I will allow [only as] a tradeoff, if she allows [oral sex]. She has a childish inability to seek compromise, though, instead kicking her feet in a tantrum of sorts, and the TV remains off.

We do manage a shower together to go with the sex, and the next morning we wash each other's hair and she shaves me. As the morning proceeds, though, her restlessness increases, turning at times into tantrums, pouting, and even a few tears. Having already got a read on her early on, I don't buy any of this, and later on she just as easily allows me another screw with her.

Finally, at a little after 11 am I decide I've had enough fun and we both dress to go out. We go outside to hale a moto-taxi and from across the street comes what I guess is one of the mamasams.

---

1. Papasan and mamasan are terms often used to refer to the men and women controlling the women in the brothels.

Even from the man's perspective this woman wants to leave, and is resisting, but he feels entitled to temporary ownership for the time he has paid.

Prostitution Tours

Centers for prostitution tourism are also the sources of women trafficked for purposes of sexual exploitation to other countries. For centers of prostitution tourism in European countries, women from poor countries are imported legally and illegally to fill the brothels. One of the largest sources of trafficked women today is the countries of the former Soviet Union. Advertisements for prostitution tours to these sights appear on the Internet, usually described as 'romance tours' or 'introduction tours'.

Advertisement for Sex Tours

Prostitution tours enable men to travel to 'exotic' places and step outside whatever community bounds may constrain them at home. In foreign cities they can abuse women and girls in ways that are more risky or difficult for them in their hometowns.

As prostitution has become a form of tourism for men, it has become a form of economic development for poor countries. Tourism was recommended by the United Nations, the World Bank and

United States advisory boards as a way to generate income and repay foreign debts (Lee 1991). Nation states set their own tourist policies and could, if they chose to do so, prevent or suppress the development of prostitution as a form of tourism. Instead, communities and countries have come to rely on the sale of women and children's bodies as their cash crop. As the prostitution industry grows, more girls and women are turned into sexual commodities for sale to tourists. In the bars in Bangkok, women and girls don't have names—they have numbers pinned to their skimpy clothes. The men pick them by number. They are literally interchangeable sexual objects.

Sex Tour Advertisement for Amsterdam

Prostitution tourism centers in industrialized countries are receiving sites for trafficked women from poor countries. The Netherlands is the strongest international proponent for legalized prostitution. Its capital, Amsterdam, is the leading prostitution tourism center in Europe. In 1997 the Netherlands legalized brothels. The result has been increased trafficking to Amsterdam from all over the world.

Advertisements for prostitution tours appeared on the Web in mid–1995, when Alan J. Munn, New York City, USA, launched PIMPS 'R' US. He arranged prostitution tours to the Dominican Republic and Nevada, USA. In his Dominican Republic tour he offered four days and three nights in a 'wonderful setting' which includes 'many female prostitutes'. A tour guide on the trip provided 'practical information about how to find and deal with prostitutes and how to arrange group orgies'. On one night, courtesy of the tour, 'oral sex (fellatio) is provided by an attractive female whore chosen by the tour guide.' Participants are also given PIMPS 'R' US baseball caps (Munn Summer 1995). Alan J. Munn also arranged group tours to legal brothels in Nevada, USA. Alan J. Munn provided information on 'prevailing prices, what influences how much whores charge, and reputations of the various whorehouses'. The package price included 'round trip transportation from the hotel to one whorehouse daily for a total of four different whorehouses chosen by the tour guide' (Munn Summer 1995).

There are many advertisements for prostitution tours to Central America and the Caribbean. An advertisement for Erotic Vacations to Costa Rica quotes a price which includes double occupancy rooms and intra-country flights, booked for two. 'Your companion [a euphemism for prostitute] will meet you at your hotel. . . .' If the tourist chooses a longer tour his 'companion' is changed halfway through the trip, so the man gets to buy two women in the longer sex tours (Travel Connections Fall 1995). The fees for the 'companions' are paid directly to the tour operator, not the women, although the men are encouraged to 'tip' the women if they are pleased with their services.

Bride Trafficking

Mail-order bride agents have moved to the Internet as their preferred marketing location. The Internet reaches a prime group of potential buyers—men from Western countries with higher than average incomes. The new Internet technology enables Web pages to be quickly and easily updated; some services claim they are updating their selection of women weekly. The Internet reaches a global audience faster and less expensively than any other media. One mail-order bride agent explained why he preferred operation on the Internet.

> So when the World-Wide Web came along, I saw that it was a perfect venue for this kind of business. The paper catalogs were so expensive that their quality was usually very poor; but on the Web you can publish high-resolution full-color photos which can be browsed by everyone in the WORLD (Toms, Santa Barbara International 1996).

The agents offer men assistance in finding a 'loving and devoted' woman whose 'views of relationships have not been ruined by unreasonable expectations'. The agencies describe themselves as 'introduction services', but a quick examination of many of the Web sites reveals their commercial interests in bride trafficking, sex tours and prostitution.

The catalogues offer women mostly from Asia, Eastern Europe and Latin America, although in mid-1998 special catalogs of women from Africa appeared. They are called 'African Queens', and 'Brides of Nubia'. Pictures of the women are shown with their names, height, weight, education and hobbies. Some catalogues include the women's bust, waist and hip measurements. The women range in age from thirteen to fifty. One of the commonly promoted characteristics of women from Eastern Europe is that they 'traditionally expect to marry gentlemen that are ten to twenty years older' (Toms 1995). The women are marketed as 'pleasers', who will make very few demands on the men, and will not threaten them with expectations in their relationships, as women from the US and Western Europe are said to do. The mail-order-bride Web sites rely on racial and sexist stereotypes about the women in order to attract men from the US and Western Europe.

In 1990 the Philippines government banned the operation of prostitution tour and mail-order bride agencies in the Philippines. One mail-order-bride trafficker lamented this new law, and told his

Filipina Girl from Catalog

customers that now he was operating out of the United States with his computer. He sent his own Filipina wife back to the Philippines to make contact and recruit women and adolescent girls for his web site.

One mail-order bride trafficker complained that the Philippines government banned the operation of sex tour and mail-order brides agents in the Philippines. He said,

> The Philippines government is ... definitely working against the interests of their own people. These girls want and need to leave that country.

The same agent also complained that the US government will not allow his youngest 'brides' on offer into the country.

> The service itself is not restricted by the American government, although they are real picky about getting your bride into the states—they won't give a visa to a bride under age sixteen (World Class Service 1996).

In his catalog of potential brides there is one girl, named Hazel, aged thirteen; another girl, Eddy Mae, is aged fourteen. There are a total of nineteen girls in his catalog aged seventeen or younger.

The bride traffickers sell addresses to men. Later they offer to arrange tours for the men to go to meet the woman with whom they have been corresponding, or to meet as many women as possible.

Men can pay for these services over the Internet with their credit cards.

Bride Traffickers Accept Credit Cards

There are some catalogues which list women with young children. One Web site asks if men want women with or without children. On another Web site there are pictures of naked children playing. I think children are being trafficked also in this way. The men are being subtly shown ways of acquiring women and children—all in one package.

Sexual Exploitation and Organized Crime

Sex tourism, bride trafficking and prostitution are different forms of sexual exploitation. An examination of advertisements on the Internet reveals the links among these types of sexual exploitation and enables us to see that the agents are using women in any way that is profitable.

Most of the mail-order bride agents on the Internet also offer tours. Men pay for the addresses of the women in the catalogues, later the tour/bride agent sets up a group tour for men to go to meet the woman or women with whom they have been corresponding.

> The Moscow trip is a logical conclusion to your correspondence efforts. The purpose of the tour is to meet as many lovely ladies as possible as soon as possible.

Men going to either Russia or the Philippines are assured of getting a wife to bring home, if that is their desire, or they are assured of the

Mail-order Bride from Russia

availability of many women. Men don't want to believe they are taking home a prostitute as a wife, so the men are assured that they will be introduced to marriageable women, as well as other 'available and willing' women. A man is usually offered the option of paying for an 'escort' for each day. 'Each and every day you will be escorted by your choice of lovely, elegant ladies.' Men are assured that if they have not established a correspondence with a woman, they can still go on the tour to 'try out' the women.

I will take a series of advertisements from a US-based agency, describe what is offered, and show the connections among the forms of sexual exploitation.

A picture of a Filipina tops the first page of Travel Philippines. She invites the men to 'Come explore the Philippines with me!' The advertisement describes the Philippines as an 'exotic and interesting place to visit'. Information is given on tickets, lodging, food and water, money changing, nightlife and the tour schedule.

Prostitution is briefly mentioned as being 'everywhere', and a price range for prostitutes is listed. Men are told, 'You can partake or not, it's up to you. Most do partake.' Marriage is also briefly mentioned:

'Come explore the Philippines with me!'

As most of you know, the Philippines is the happy hunting ground for men seeking a wife. There are all kinds of women of every description. It's hard to go to the Philippines and not get caught up in the idea of marriage. The whole lifestyle seems to revolve around love, marriage and kids (Craven Come Explore, Fall 1995).

On the next linked page the man is asked 'Would you like to have a beautiful female companion as a private tour guide?' or 'Would you like to have introductions to "decent" marriage minded ladies?' (Craven Tour Philippines, Fall 1995). If he chooses the private tour guide he is directed to the X-Rated Escorted Tours. At the top of this page a picture of the same Filipina from the introductory page appears, this time with her breasts exposed. The woman invites the men to 'Come explore the Philippines and Me!'

Much of the same travel information is repeated, but here the man finds out how much it costs to have an 'escort' during his trip. The fee is paid to the travel agent-pimp, not the woman. The agent-pimp suggests that the tourist-buyer tip the woman, although it is not required (Craven Come Explore Me, Fall 1995).

If the man chooses the marriage option he is directed to the linked page on Over Seas Ladies. There he is asked if he is tired of watching TV and having women make him jump through hoops. He is told

Come explore the Phillipines and Me!

that the women for sale here 'respond to every gesture and kindness, no matter how small'. He is reassured that these women are not concerned about his age, appearance, or wealth. Thirteen pages of pictures of women from which he can choose follow (Craven Over Seas Ladies, Summer 1995).

The agent pimps sells the addresses of the women to the man. For an extra fee the buyer can have a lifetime membership which entitles him to the addresses of all the women, those currently available and those in the future. (If the man is seeking a permanent relationship, why he might want or need a lifetime membership is not explained.) The whole sexual exploitation racket comes full circle with the next linked page on Escorted Wife Seeking Tours. The man is told:

> You will meet a lot of beautiful women there. Your pen pals that you have been writing to will be happy to see you. The new women you meet will be generally 'good' girls, but there are plenty of bar girls there too and you will surely encounter some (Craven Escorted Wife Seeking Tours, Fall 1995).

Bar girls, X-rated tours with 'private tour guides', mail-order brides—all are forms of sexual exploitation organized by the same agency for the profit of pimps, hotels and bars.

Even from the advertising it is apparent that these men are operating or dealing with prostitution rings. I'm sure that police investigations will show that these agents are most likely involved in trafficking of women from country to country as well.

Live Videoconferencing

The most advanced technology on the Internet is live video-conferencing, in which live audio and video are transmitted over the Internet from video recorder to computer. This advanced technology is being used to sell live sex shows over the Internet. Real time communication is possible, so the man can personally direct the live sex show as he is viewing it on his computer.

The only limitation on this type of global sex show is the need for high-speed transmission, processing and multimedia capabilities. The software required is free, but the most recent versions of Web browsers have these capabilities built into them. As more men have access to high-speed multimedia computer and transmission equipment, this type of private sex show will grow. There are no legal restrictions on live sex shows that can be transmitted over the Internet. As with all Internet transmissions, there are no nation-state border restrictions. With Internet technology a man may be on one continent, while directing and watching a live strip show, a live sex show, or the sexual abuse of a child on another continent. There have been several documented cases of live transmission of the sexual abuse of children through live videoconferencing.

The first live videoconferencing prostitution industry site I saw on the Web was Virtual Dreams in October 1995, running off the CTSNET server in San Diego, California.

Virtual Dreams uses cutting-edge technology to bring you the most beautiful girls in the world. Using our software and your computer, you can interact real time and one-on-one with the girl of your dreams. Ask her anything you wish—she is waiting to please you! (Virtual Connections, October 1995).

By November 1995, 'live nude video teleconferencing' was being touted on the Internet newsgroup alt.sex.prostitution. Derek Hamilton said:

> Here's something that will make your modem sizzle! I was sitting at home—my *Penthouse* subscription had run out, when I stumbled across 'Video Fantasy' on the net. This is one of the most interesting 'adults only' services I've ever seen. With Windows, my 486 and their software, I called a pretty girl's studio with my modem and watched her undress. All of this was live and in color on my computer monitor. What will they think of next. Sitting at home being entertained by a beautiful girl. Talk about 'safe sex'! I love it! Check out their website at <<u>http://www.videofantasy.com</u>>. This is lots of fun' (Hamilton alt.sex.prostitution, 21 November 1995).

Who buys women over the Internet? According to the Internet Entertainment Group (IEG), the largest pimp on the Web, the buyers for live strip shows are 90 per cent male, 70 per cent living in the United States, and 70 per cent are between ages 18 and 40. The buyers are young men in college, and businessmen and professionals who log on from work. This information was obtained from analysis of credit card usage (*Wired*, December 1997).

Growth of the Commercial Prostitution Industry on the Internet

In the mid-1990s, the hottest place for commercial development was the Internet. In early September 1995 there were 101,908 commercial domains on the Web, which was 26,055 more than the end of July, and 72,706 more than the end of 1994. The sex industry was leading the way.

At the beginning of 1995, there were just 200 businesses on the World Wide Web selling 'erotica services' and products, from condoms to pornographic videos (Strangelove Internet Business Journal, January 1995). I did a search on Yahoo, a popular search engine, in August 1995 and August 1996. In August 1995, the category Yahoo: Business and Economy: Companies: Sex had 391 listings for phone sex numbers, adult CD-ROMs, X-rated films, adult computer software; live videoconferencing, sex tours, escort services and mail-order bride agencies. In August 1996 there were 1676 listings—a four fold increase in one year (Yahoo August 1996).

By mid-1995, strip clubs set up advertising on Web sites. Stripclubs from New Jersey, New York and Delaware, USA, had their own home pages where they advertised their shows. They featured pornographic photos of strippers, they called their 'cyberstars' of the week. One Web site for a club in Delaware included pornographic images of women engaged in the types of legal prostitution offered at that club, including couch dancing, table dancing, shower shows and dominatrix acts (Fantasy Show Bar, Summer 1995).

The price of magazines, videos, CD-ROMS—any item produced by the sex industry—is always much higher than similar non-pornographic materials. The high prices and profit margins of pornographic materials keeps the revenue and profit high for the sex industry. In 1996 Americans spent more than US$9 billion on pornographic videos, peep shows, live sex shows, pornographic cable programs, pornographic magazines and computer porno-graphy. That amount is more than many other entertainment businesses, such as film, music, and theater (see Table 1). To put that amount in some context, according to War on Want, US$9 billion is enough to provide debt relief for the world's twenty worst affected countries (*The Guardian* November 1997). These revenue figures don't include the millions of dollars made illegally through the sale of women in brothels, massage parlors, or on the street, or the sale of illegal materials, such as child pornography.

Table 1 1996 US Entertainment Industry Revenues

New books	$26.10 billion
Magazine publishing	$11.18 billion
Sex industry	$9.00 billion
Recorded music	$8.15 billion
Film industry	$5.90 billion
Theatre, ballet, opera	$1.69 billion
Computer gaming	$1.10 billion

Sources: Motion Picture Association of America, The National Association of Music Merchants, The Magazine Publishers of America, Live Broadway, Opera America, and Dance USA (as cited in *Wired* (online) (Dec, 1997)

The highest revenue for legal materials produced by the sex industry was for the sales and rentals of pornographic videos at US$5 billion dollars, followed by strip clubs at US$2 billion. Sex industry sites on the Internet earned US$925 million in 1996 (See Table 2).

Table 2 1996 US Sex Industry Revenues

Adult CD-ROMs	$75 million
Cable (pay-per-view)	$325 million
Phone sex	$750 million
Online sex sites	$925 million
Strip clubs	$2 billion
Adult video sales, rentals	$5 billion

Sources: Adult Video News, U.S. News and World Report, Naughty Linx (as cited in *Wired* (online) (Dec, 1997)

In 1996, that amount (US$925 million) could be subdivided into subscription fees at US$490 million, advertising at US$269 million and merchandise at US$167 million (see Table 3). Estimates of the amount of money being made on the Internet by the sex industry vary widely between sources. The only thing analysts agree on is that a lot of money is being made and the rate of growth is exponential. According to David Schwartz, a phone sex business operator who switched to the online sex business, 'The Internet is where the big money is right now' (Said November 1998).

Table 3   1996 US Online Sex Site Revenues

Merchandise	$167 million
Advertising	$268 million
Subscription fees	$490 million

Surces: Adult Video News, U.S. News and World Report, Naughty Linx (as cited in *Wired* (online) (Dec, 1997)

The popular mainstream pornographic magazine *Playboy* was quick to jump on the Web. In 1994, *Playboy* made its debut. *Playboy*'s Web site content differed from the print magazine. The content of the Web site was designed to appeal to a younger, wealthier audience, the majority of whom (75 per cent) did not subscribe to the print *Playboy* magazine (Runett October, 1998). In 1996, *Playboy* magazine's site was the 11th most visited site on the Web (Simons August 1996). Since its debut on the Web, *Playboy* has been one of the most popular Web publications. In 1997, the Web site generated US$2 million in advertising revenue. Many of the advertisers are exclusive to the Web site and do not buy advertising in the print publication. In mid 1998, *Playboy*'s CyberClub had 26,000 subscribers paying US$60 per year (Runett October 1998).

In April 1996, another popular pornographic magazine, *Penthouse* went online. Its web site recorded the highest number of visits for publication sites on the Web in that month (Nielsen *Wired* Survey 1997).

A 1996 survey found that 20 per cent of the users of the World Wide Web said they regularly visited pornographic sites (Simons 1996). By 1998, another survey indicated that 30 per cent of American households with Internet access visited online sex industry sites at least once per month (*Seattle Post-Intelligencer*, April 1998). In the same year, one report estimated that the Web had 600 commercial pornography sites, which were expected to generate revenues of US$51.5 million. This does not include the amateur sites, or those that have free sites, but make money only by advertising. Only computer products and travel exceeded pornography sales on the Internet (Simons 1996). Some single commercial pornography and live sex show Web sites became very profitable in 1996. Danni's Hard Drive, named after Danni Ashe, a former stripper who runs the Web site, was selling pornographic videos, digital images, and magazines. She started videoconferencing to create video peep shows on her Web site. In mid-1996 her site was being visited 1.5 million times per day, and was expected to bring in US$1.2 million in 1996 (Simons August 1996).

The estimated number of pornographic web sites varies widely. In late 1997, according to Naughty Linx, an online index, there were 28,000 'sex sites' on the Web with about half of them trying to make money selling pornography, videos, or live sex shows (Rose 1997). Another study estimated that there were 72,000 pornographic Web sites on the Internet (Patriot Ledger 1997). At the end of 1997, Leo Preiser, the Director of the Center for Technology at National University estimated that 60 per cent of the electronic commerce on the Web was pornography (PR Newswire 1997).

At the end of 1997, the online sex industry was estimated to be making US$1 billion a year, just in the United States (Said 1998). In findings from a 1997 survey, *Inter@ctive Week* magazine reported that 10,000 sex industry sites were bringing in approximately US$1 billion per year (*Chicago Sun Times*, June 1997). A midsize site that was accessed 50,000 times per day, made approximately US$20,000 each month. Established sex industry sites could expect to make 50 to 80 per cent profits (*The Guardian* May 1998). A

Sacramento, California firm that handles online credit card transactions said that in 1997, the largest sex industry sites had revenues of US$1 million per month; while the smaller sites took in approximately US$10,000 per month (Said 1998).

Forrester Research, an Internet analyst firm, estimated that the Internet sex industry would make close to US$1 billion in 1998. 'We know of at least three sites doing more than US$100 million a year. And there are hundreds of sites out there' (*Seattle Post-Intelligencer*, August 1998). Although sex industry sites are only estimated to be one per cent of the Internet content, aggressive advertising using banners, spam and search engines gives the sex industry much more visibility (*Seattle Post-Intelligencer*, April 1998).

Regulation

The new technologies of the Internet have leapt over national borders and have left lawmakers scrambling to catch up. Internet users have adopted and defend an unbridled libertarianism. Any kind of regulation or restriction is met with hysterics and predictions of a totalitarian society. Even the most conservative restrictions on the transmission of child pornography are greeted with cries of censorship. The December 1996 issue of *Wired*, the leading professional publication on the Internet, stated that a new state law in United States, which made it illegal to transmit indecent materials to minors, was censorship. The Internet libertarianism, coupled with United States free speech absolutism, is setting the standard for Internet communication.

Expressions of concern or condemnation of forms of sexual exploitation of women and children on the Internet are minimized by claims that pornographers have always been the first to take advantage of new technology—first photography, then movies, then VCRs, now, the Internet. Those concerned about the use of the Internet for sexual exploitation are chastened with history lectures on new technology and pornography.

The solution that is being promoted is software programs that will screen out sexually explicit material. President Clinton just announced that he supported a rating system on the Internet, so pornography would be rated and software programs will screen it out. This is seen as a way to protect children. Most adults are only concerned that their children may see pornography on the Internet. They aren't concerned about the women who are being exploited in the making of the pornography. In any search for a solution to pornography and prostitution it is crucial to remember that sexual exploitation starts with real people and the harm is to real people.

We need international judicial and police co-operation in regulating the Internet and ending the trafficking and prostitution of women and girls. If it is illegal to run a prostitution tour agency or mail-order bride agency in the Philippines, then it should be illegal to advertise these services on a computer in the US. The countries that send the men on tours and receive the mail-order brides should also ban the operation of such agencies and prohibit the advertisement of these services from computer servers in their country.

The European Union defines trafficking as a form of organized crime. It should be treated the same way on the Internet. All forms of sexual exploitation should be recognized as forms of violence against women and human rights violations, and governments should act accordingly. Although the Internet offers open communication to people throughout the world, it should not be permitted to be dominated and controlled by men's interests or the interests of the prostitution industry, at women's and children's expense.

References

Anonymous. Date unknown. 'Bangkok' The World Sex Guide, <http://www.paranoia.com/faq/prostitution/bangkok.txt.html> (29 Aug. 1995).

Anonymous. 15 Jan. 1995. 'Bangkok Story', The World Sex Guide. <http://www.paranoia.com/faq/prostitution/bangkok_story.txt.html>

Anonymous. 30 Aug. 1995. Wellington, New Zealand, The World Sex Guide, <http://www.paranoia.com/faq/prostitution/Wellington.txt.html>

Anonymous. 7 Oct. 1995. Recife, Brazil, The World Sex Guide, <http://www.paranoia.com/faq/prostitution/Recife.txt.html>

Anonymous. 11 Feb. 1996. A travel report from Boca Chica, Dominican Republic— It's True!! The World Sex Guide, <http://www.paranoia.com/faq/prostitution/Boca-Chica.txt.html>

an370191@anon.penet.fi. 15 Sep. 1995. Bristol, UK, The World Sex Guide, <http://www.paranoia.com/faq/prostitution/Bristol.txt.html>

Atta and M. (an48932@anon.penet.fi) The World Sex Guide (Updated Jul. 1996). <http://www.paranoia.com/faq/prostitution>

baguio@ix.netcom.com. Mar. 1995. A primer on what is happening in the city of Angels, Version 1.2 The World Sex Guide, <http://www.paranoia.com/faq/prostitution/bangkok.faq.txt.html>

Bashful (bashful@paranoia.com). 1994, 1995, 1996. Honey's Page, <http://www.paranoia.com/~bashful/faq10p03.html>

Bashful (bashful@paranoia.com) 1995. Reno and Carson City Brothels, <http://www.paranoia.com/~bashful/nevabrot_366230.html>

Chicago Sun Times 1997. X-rated sites pace online industry, 24 Jun.

Craven, J. Fall 1995. Come Explore the Philippines With Me! World Wide Web <http://www.conline.com/~dad/phil_gen.html> (18 Nov. 1995).

Craven, J. Fall 1995. Tour Philippines. <http://www.conline.com/~dad/trip_ind.html> (18 Nov. 1995).

Craven, J. Fall 1995. Come Explore the Philippines and Me! <http://www.conline.com/~dad/phil_x.html> (18 Nov. 1995).

Craven, J. Summer 1995. Overseas Ladies <http://www.conline.com/~dad/oversea.html> (29 Aug. 1995).

Craven, J. Fall 1995. Escorted Wife Seeking Tour—Philippines <http://www.conline.com/~dad/phil_wif.html> (18 Nov. 1995).

Cybersuck. 1995, 1996. Cybersuck Consumer's Guide Legal Whorehouses Home Page, <http://www.panix.com/~zz/ex2.html>

Guardian. 1997. The land of the free. 26 Nov.

Guardian. 1998. Surfing for sex. 14 May.

Hamilton, Derek (derek1@free.org) 21 Nov. 1995. alt.sex.prostitution.

Lapin, Todd (Ed.), 1996. New York's CDA, Cyber Rights Now, *Wired*, December, p. 94.

Lee, W. 1991. Prostitution and tourism in South-East Asia. In N. Redcliff and M.T. Sinclair (Eds.), *Working Women: International perspectives on labor and gender ideology* London: Routledge.

Markoff, John. 1998. Indictment says mob is going high-tech, Six men arrested in alleged Vegas computer scheme. *New York Times*, 17 October.

Mob seen in Las Vegas sex trade. 1998. Associated Press, 17 October.

Munn, Alan J. Summer. 1995. PIMPS 'R' US Goes to the Dominican Republic, The World Sex Guide (Updated 7 Aug. 1995), World Wide Web
<http://www.panix.com/~zz/exDR.html>

Munn, Alan J. Summer. 1995. PIMPS 'R' US Goes to Nevada Whorehouses, The World Sex Guide (Updated 7 August 1995), World Wide Web
<http://www.panix.com/~zz/exDR.html>

Negroponte, Nicholas. 1995. *Being Digital*. London: Hodder and Stoughton, p. 7.

Nielsen Survey. *Wired* [Online] Dec. 1997, Issue 5.12.

Odzer, Cleo. 1995. The Razor Blade Show.
<http://sensemedia.net/sprawl> (29 Aug. 1995).

Patriot Ledger. 1997. Sex-oriented E-mail is increasing rapidly. 10 Oct.

PR Newswire. 1997. Money to be made on the web, National University adds three technology degrees. 17 December.

Rose, Frank. 1997. Sex Sells—Young, ambitious Seth Warshavsky is the Bob Guccione of the 1990s. *Wired*, Issue 5. 12, December.

Runett, Rob. 1998. Hefner highlights Playboy transitions to TV, Web. *Connections @ the digital edge*,
<http://www.digitaledge.org/connections98/hefner.html> (8 Oct. 1998).

Said, Carolyn. 1998. Adultdex Trade Show: Sex sells on the Net. *San Francisco Chronicle*, 19 November.

Seattle *Post-Intelligencer*. 1998. Wired for sex—A growing cyberporn empire in Seattle takes a new twist on an old trade, 27 April.

Seattle *Post-Intelligencer*. 1998. Some cybersex companies weaving webs of deceit, 28 August.

Simons, John. 1996. The Web's dirty secret; Sex sites make lots of money, *US News and World Report*, 19 August.

Strangelove, Michael W. 1995. Internet advertising review—The Internet has hormones, Selling Sex in Cyberspace, *The Internet Business Journal*, January, p. 10.

Taylor and Jerome [sic]. 1997. Pornography As Innovator, *PC Computing*, February, p. 65.

Toms, Bruce W. 1995, 1996. Santa Barbara International Center.
<http://www.rain.org/~sbintl/ourstory.html>

Travel Connection. Fall 1995. A tropical paradise vacation is waiting for you! World Wide Web
<http://www.travelxn.com/fer/fer2.htm> (18 Nov. 1995).

Virtual Connections, Live Nude Video Teleconferencing.
<http://www.cts.com/~talon> (29 Oct. 1995).

Wired (online) (Dec. 1997).

World Class Service. 1996. Be A Mail Order Husband (For Men Only),
<http://www.filipina.com/FAQ.html>

Yahoo
<http://www.yahoo.com> (8 Aug. 1996).

nine

The Politics of CyberFeminism: If I'm a Cyborg rather than a Goddess will Patriarchy go away?[1]

R e n a t e   K l e i n

Introduction

Over the past three years I have been pondering the developments of
cyberculture and its relationship to CyberFeminism both in practical
and theoretical terms. In my daily work teaching Women's Studies,
together with my colleague Laurel Guymer, I have become an
enthusiastic learner and promoter of <u>online teaching</u> and computer-
mediated conferencing (CMC) in an otherwise sceptical environment of Arts academics. In my activist work (for example, as a
member of FINRRAGE and CATW)[2], I value the swiftness of global
information sharing as well as the possibilities of campaigning
against social injustices '@the speed of thought' (to paraphrase Bill
Gates 1999). In my research, however, looking at the increased
(western culture induced) fragmentation of bodies, minds and souls
through post-modern writing (still) infecting academia and much of
cyberwriting,[3] in conjunction with my criticism of reproductive
technologies and genetic engineering, I remain profoundly ambiva-
lent. Some of the assumptions in and about cyberculture, as well as

Guymer 3

[1.] I am grateful to Susan Hawthorne and Laurel Guymer for many constructive comments on this
chapter and for being radical feminist cybersisters in real and virtual life.

[2.] FINRRAGE stands for Feminist International Network of Resistance to Reproductive and
Genetic Engineering and CATW is the acronym of The Coalition Against Trafficking in Women.

[3.] For detailed criticism of post-modernism see Brodribb (1992) and Section Three 'Radical
Feminists "Interrogate" Post-modernism' in Bell and Klein (1996).

actual IT developments trouble me. Put differently, it is the *ideologies* behind cyberlife that bother me a great deal and I am worried that what is hailed as the virtual techno-paradise of the new millennium remains as woman hating as does much of real life at the end of the twentieth century.

My question is simple: can the theories and practices of cyber-culture[4] amount to a CyberFeminism which leads, in one way or another, to a feminist future? A future, as Diane Bell and I have defined it in *Radically Speaking*, '. . . of justice, dignity and above all safety from all forms of violence' (1996: xx)? Does cyberculture contribute to a feminism that combines passion and politics—a feminism of the heart, as Australian *Real* feminist Zelda D'Aprano has put it so well (D'Aprano 1977/1995)? If the answer is yes, does cyberculture benefit *all* women and if so, in what ways? If no, is it a 'not yet': in other words will increasing number of feminists as multimedia and online producers, consumers, educators, watch-dogs and theorists turn cyberspace into a powerful tool that will serve (cyber)feminists in the quest to improve women's socio-economic as well as physiological and psychological wellbeing? In short, does the theory and practice of information technology contribute to women's liberation? Or, to put it polemically, para-phrasing Donna Haraway's (in)famous words from her *Cyborg Manifesto* (1991): If I'm a cyborg rather than a goddess will patriarchy go away?[5]

---

4. I use 'cyberculture' interchangeably with 'cyberlife' in which I include Internet features such as e-mail, e-commerce, bulletin boards, MUDs, IRCs, the World Wide Web, personal web pages, cybersex, CD-ROMs—as well as more esoteric technologies such as virtual reality and becoming a 'cyborg'—or even 'post-human'.

Hawthorne

10

5. A 'cyborg' is an organism that is part-human, part-machine. Cyborgs became fashionable in the 90s (see Hawthorne, this volume and *The Cyborg Handbook*, Gray 1995 for a good overview) but it was feminist historian of science and post-modern theorist Donna Haraway who wrote one of the first articles on this topic. Published initially in 1985 and republished many times since then, her 'Manifesto for Cyborgs: Science, Technology and Socialist Feminism in the 1980s' (changed to 'in the late Twentieth Century' in later editions, for example, 1991), catapulted cyborgs into the limelight as the new feminist icon for 2000 and beyond, that were clearly superior to women. As she put it 'I would rather be a cyborg than a goddess' (ibid p. 181).

In order to find (partial) answers to these (big) questions I will critically look at some of cyberspace's promises, voice my doubts, and confront nightmares. Critical questions leading my inquiry include: who has access to these technologies?; who holds power and is in control?; in whose interest is cyberlife developed?; how does the fragmentation of cyberculture fit within the framework of know-ledges of Indigenous and other marginalised peoples?; and, import-antly, what is happening to women's bodies/minds/souls in real and cyberlife—is technology serving women—or are we serving it?

I Promises

Oppressed groups which include all those not part of the dominant group in power—the twenty per cent heterosexual and middle/upper-class men, predominantly Caucasian although increasingly elites from the developing world who are in charge of 'globalisation' through their transnational companies—are often said to remain marginalised because of their lack of resources. By this I mean, on the one hand, *material* resources which make it possible through earning money (under humane conditions) to enjoy a 'good'—or at least decent—life, even if not as part of the dominant group.[6] On the other hand I am considering the repression of *political and cultural* resources—including art forms such as painting, dancing, story-telling and poetry—to inform the world about conditions of social injustice, the suppression of human rights, and the torture of the body and/or soul. Importantly, I am also thinking of the exploitation and appropriation of Indigenous peoples' knowledges and practices of subsistence—particularly how they affect women—which are so often destroyed by the transnational colonisers' 'monocultures of the mind', to use Indian ecofeminist and physicist Vandana Shiva's words (Shiva 1993, see also Mies 1986/1999).

[6.] Given the 'free' international trade instigated by the World Trade Organisation that shamelessly does away with tariffs in the non-powerful part of the world but keeps or raises them in the USA, raising the material life circumstances does not look too rosy for the people in Asia and Africa (Chossudowsky 1998: 62–63).

Listservs and email which enable networking with like-minded allies around the globe by distributing information, asking for political solidarity and exposing ruthless machinations of the powerful are hailed by cyberenthusiasts as the new 'democratic' medium destined to break the information monopoly of the powerful and resist its colonising effects. And indeed the very convenient use of electronic mail, that for many of us has already become second nature, makes it possible to circumvent barriers of space and time by 'chatting'—and/or exchanging crucial information—be it for business transactions, cultural productions, political actions, or simply friendship and fun, often in almost 'real time' between, say, Suva in Fiji and Helsinki in Finland or Dhaka in Bangladesh and Melbourne in Australia.[7] Also, it is suggested by liberal techno-optimists that such information equals knowledge which in turn equals power. And indeed the hundreds of thousands, probably soon millions, of websites on the World Wide Web are a liberal's el dorado of 'free', 'uncensored' mingling of minds. There is no doubt that <u>international e-listservs</u> such as *Women'space* diamond@fox.nstn.ca, *WMST-L@UMDD.UMD.EDU* and the e-magazine AVIVA (Burke 1999), as well as feminist librarians establishing virtual <u>Women's Studies libraries</u>, create incredibly useful networking tools for those lucky enough to make it online. Websites from educational institutions, environmental and Indigenous groups, famous feminists such as Mary Daly, Andrea Dworkin, and Dale Spender,[8] women's businesses and special interest groups ranging from groups dealing with violence against women to women's health and lesbian e-listservs to the feminist group ISIS based in the Philippines and the Spinifex Feminist Publishers in Asia Homepage <<u>www.spinifexpress.com.au/welcomeasia/htm</u>>—not to mention dog lovers of every

Pollock and
Sutton 2
Korenman 4

Stafford 7

---

7. Or indeed in real time using the free ICQ software (the drawback is being sent invitations to check out pornsites!).

8. The URLs are:
    Mary Daly, <<u>http://www.womenbooks.com/mary_daly/index.html</u>>
    Andrea Dworkin, <<u>http://www.igc.org/Womensnet/dworkin/</u>>
    Dale Spender, <<u>http://www.espc.com.au/dspender/</u>>

known breed!—do indeed create an opportunity for information exchange and solidarity. The first Australian Women's Human Rights Tribunal organised by the Women's Rights Action Network Australia was transmitted in real time over the web (1999, May 21, <<u>http://www.nwjc.org.au/wrana</u>>), as was an international symposium to end violence against women (1999, March 8, <<u>http://webevents.broadcast.com/unifem/women</u>>).[9] And feminist cyberpoets and novelists contribute <u>hypertextual fiction and cyberpoetry</u> to the growing range of electronic cyberarts on the web.

Bird 16
Fletcher 14
Hawthorne
Namjoshi 1

But are such feminist treasures really what makes up the thousands of megabytes stacked up in the servers around the world? What about the ubiquitous porn sites that without even trying, one lands on,[10] the services for <u>mail-order brides</u> and <u>trafficking</u> in women? What about the MUDs (multi user dungeons)—inhabited fantasy places—and IRCs (inter relay chat rooms) where people play around assuming multiple selves and enjoying cybersex with or without S/M? Is this the safe and healthy twenty-first-century way to have relationships and make love without catching infectious diseases? Is the information created, or fun experienced, in any way new and does it liberate women from patriarchal norms? Is digitally created curvaceous and silicone lookalike Lara Croft with two pistols in her hands a feminist icon? Will 'netchicks' lead the way in the next wave of women's liberation? Is total twenty-four hour immersion in virtual reality the way to cope with the feminisation of poverty and violence against women? Is dabbling in nicknames—'coldturky, pashnfrut, amazo, smellycat or tommigirl' (Szego 1999: 15)—or assuming a dozen identities in one evening just so much fun that it drowns out the pain of the remote control war in Kosovo? Or Ethiopia?

Hughes 8

---

9. See also Wendy Harcourt's (1999) international collection of women's activities, *Women@Internet*.

10. When using a search engine to find the Lara Croft Tomb Raider Website, it took only two clicks to land, inadvertently, on an adult pornsite!

I could provide many more positive examples including the use of the World Wide Web as an educational resource from primary schools to universities, the gist of the exciting promise remains the same: the cybersky is the limit—a wealth of resources will be at our fingertips ready to transgress all boundaries and make the twenty-first century equal and fair for all! And we will all be so clever: the information rich! Eerily though, such hype sounds like the old promise of the 'frontier'—the 'Wild West' of the US, for instance—just waiting for the cowboys and then settlers to appear on the horizon with their horses, guns and wagons. Not only fun to be had and 'survival of the fittest' (cleverest?) is promised, but there is electronic gold to be made on the net as well.

II Doubts

While undoubtedly there is merit in some of the promises outlined above and I strongly believe that marginalised groups—including Indigenous peoples, the poor, the disabled, lesbians and gay men as well as women from all parts of the globe—need to be active in cyberspace and influence its development as users and content producers (Spender 1995; Senjen and Guthrey 1996), I have my worries and doubts about cyberculture's promises of fortunes and the good life for all. After all, where are the native populations in the new scenario? And what happens to them?

We know what happened to Native Americans and Indigenous peoples in other countries whose souls, minds and bodies were destroyed in 'catch-up' developments (Mies 1986/1999). Genocide and stealing of children may not (yet) happen online (paedophilia and <u>trafficking in girls</u> does), but assimilation in style and form does and can result in dispossession. A computer screen is flat and neither laughs nor cries nor smells, and when you touch it, it feels like a hard board which of course it is. In an email message there are only so many fonts one can use, the header is the same every time when a message is sent or a message received: X-Sender, Mime-Version, To, From, Subject, X-Status, X-Keywords, X-UID. As for the funny or sad

Hughes 8

faces :–) :–(they never did much for me. 'You have new mail . . .'
'Eudora could use some help . . .' 'you have some messages waiting
to be sent . . .'—the same signs flash up on the screen everywhere in
the world. (Worse, on some programs a never changing mono-
tonous computer voice even announces these commands.) Monocultures of the mind: is this the McDonaldisation of cyberculture?
This may seem a trivial comment in the light of the many benefits
enumerated above, but given the fact that computersavvy children
write many more emails than letters these days, one can only hope
that software developers have mercy on us soon. Reflecting on her
email correspondence, Australian writer Julie Szego comments
(1999: 15):

> I smile inwardly when I communicate with my distant friend, but e-mail
> has changed our relationship. We write only when in the mood, never
> talk over each other, never make faces or engage in rapid verbal
> combat. . . . In cyberspace, she is one message in the in-box that lets the
> jewels ride in with the junk; one user-friendly information-bringer on a
> super-highway that lets you wave as you pass, but never lets you pull over
> to the side and get your feet wet.

And later she states: 'I can't gauge the state of her soul from the
intonation in her voice, as in a telephone conversation' (*idem*).

The cyberphile might reject such comments as old-fashioned, not
with it—and what about faxes? didn't we get to like them too?
True, but what about the euphoria about cybersex—supposedly the
hottest thing under the sun? Here is how cultural critic Mark Dery
describes one such odd occasion (1996: 200–201):

> Inevitably you and your partner decide to retire to the virtual boudoir.
> After activating the CREATIVE PRIVATE ROOM program, you zap the
> bedchamber's name and password to your partner via private message;
> within seconds, both of you have rendezvoused onscreen. Hunched over
> your computer keyboards, separated by a sea of wires, you tap out erotic
> messages that materialize, like spirit writing, as glowing characters on
> each other's screens. Soon, you find yourself typing with one hand.
> Coitus in cyberspace, like intercourse in the physical world, progresses
> from foreplay to climax; orgasms are signaled by cartoony exclamations:

"ohhhhhh," "WOW!!!" and the perennial favorite: "I'mmmm Commmmmmmminnngggggggg!!!!!!".

While I find it difficult to take any of this very seriously, netsex is apparently engaged in by thousands at the very minute I type this text. And women as well as men are into 'cyber addiction' as Carol Parker, in the *Joy of Cybersex*, calls it: 'I felt I had had the wildest sex of my life and it had seemed so intensely real . . . the cyberslut was born. I threw myself into this new role with gusto' (1997: 4). Mary's story in the 'Kiss of the Web Woman' (1999) sounds less ebullient. It is her husband who engages in cybersex and Mary feels her privacy invaded and despairs in net-induced isolation (p. 30):

> I have no control who comes into my sanctuary; no protection from a persistent presence destroying intimacy in our home, reducing me to a nonentity in my own space. . . . A shadow, a kind of stalker, is in my home.

And she continues, 'A decade ago, I could be disempowered by lipstick stains, late nights, different perfumes. Now, early morning 'Intercourse', an inaccessible password . . . and a letterbox lock are ominous signs of email infidelity' (*idem*).

So, shrugs the insisting cyberphile, what's different? We've had phonesex, and stalking before—there's just some technological value adding, that's all! Perhaps this is exactly the point: 'value adding' to already alienating, soul-less behaviours. Email stalking that happens @the speed of touch: 'An incumbent contained in the computer' (Mary 1999: 31). Surface sex that can be switched off with a click, interactions at a distance, love without touch. Instant gratification guaranteed or else you flame the unwanted and log out. The added 'value' has no depth. Men donning female avatars (on-line personas) that imitate the worst of 'feminine' stereotypes—from dominatrix to subservient coy blonde—what is really new in this exciting cyberworld? That would-be transsexuals don't even need the operation? It's so easy to become a woman in cyberspace— meanwhile, in real life, woman hating continues.

Mueller 13
English 12

Thus my doubts persist. I worry about a generation of boys growing up with the switch and click mentality of assumed control that delivers Playmate Virtual Valerie or <u>Kyoko Date</u>, the Japanese 'virtual idol' who is 'a hybrid of three real life women: one provided her speaking voice, another provided her singing voice, and the other was the model for her computerised movements' (Garran 1997: 8): fake women who exist to obey every (sexual) whim of their masters.

Hawthorne
10

Another obvious doubt is access, paralleled by the question: who is in control of cyberspace? Apart from needing resources for the equipment and for paying your service provider—not as cheap as usually advertised—as to who is in control the answer is certainly neither women nor Indigenous peoples—nor any other of the not-powerful groups. And when an email message appears on your screen 'from your mailmaster: this message might be for you' (Klein spelt Kline) you know that big brother is watching you. Or, when surfing on the World Wide Web, before you know it, your search engine results come up in a bookseller's animated multicoloured window (no, not amazon.com!) you know that 'free' cyberspace=big business.

Technical know-how is a further precondition that does not transcend barriers of race or sex. Recent statistics are difficult to obtain, but Dale Spender's 1995 statistics of the Internet as a masculine space with women comprising only between 10 to 30 per cent of its users now, on America-On-Line (AOL) seem to have improved to <u>52 per cent</u> (Spender pers. comm. 1999, see also Herman 1999: 200, who mentions a survey's results as 38.7 per cent of female Internet users). While service providers, home page 'owners' and users continue to be predominantly US, Canadian and European, it is possible to argue that, given time and *all* governments' determination to make *all* children cyber-literate and to accord access to the net, the same importance as was previously accorded to the telephone (still of course not realised in many so-called third world countries), these are barriers that in time might be overcome.

Korenman 4

Nevertheless, the question remains about the purpose of '<u>flying in</u>

Guymer 3

cyberspace': girls/women for education and research, boys/men for playing games and downloading pornography? (And there are, of course, always exceptions.) In a world in which it is reported that in March 1999, in one single week, 60,000 men spent AUD$7 million on visits to prostituted women in Melbourne (Forbes 1999: 1), is it a surprise that the virtual world imitates the real?

Another of my doubts concerns the relationship between information and knowledge and, importantly, wisdom. The millions of 'bytes' floating around in cyberspace do not, emphatically not, constitute knowledge, nor do they all hold the same weight. In other words, because the net is so 'free', all sorts of 'truths' can be posted with no one to check their factual merit. Libertarians are not concerned about this: 'what is truth anyway?' they say, or, 'there is much written in books that is factually wrong, in spite of its passing the desk of an editor'. Although there is merit to this argument, the difference is the incredible ease of access as well as the sheer volume of information that is at the fingertips of the technologically adept. This enables students to write cosmetically beautiful essays with an impressive bibliography (obtained first through their use of search engines and then <u>cut and pasted</u> from their direct access to the library's catalogue). But when queried about their understanding of the subject matter, their faces remain as blank as a screen that has just crashed. So the question of whether to be 'information rich'—a catchcry of the advertisers—amounts to being able to describe, analyse, and really understand an issue in its specific local as well as global context, must be answered in the negative for the large majority of current users. This is worrisome because without an understanding of (inter)connections, relations of power, and, importantly, historical developments of, for instance, colonisation, exploitation and appropriation of ideas, peoples and lands, the technological 'ease' of producing a text without context does not in any way fulfill the promise of the 'new land' as paradise for all. Importantly also, how does such unchecked cut-and-paste information fit within the framework of knowledges of Indigenous and marginalised peoples which is rooted in a deep connection of all

Stafford 7

things organic and inorganic—body as well as mind, soul as well as spirit? How will the 'whole woman' (Greer 1999) fare in the cyberage?

III Nightmares

It is the fragmentary nature of cyberspace that turns my doubts into nightmares as it builds on the extreme celebration of fragmentation in post-modern ideology as well as in reproductive and genetic enginering: both concerned with the (re) fashioning of what constitutes 'bodies' in the post-modern age. What rules supreme is the mind, thus connecting to man's (*sic*) past, present and future longing for control, and, even more so, transcendence and immortality. Cybergurus' dreams are to achieve what religious believers have piously put their faith in for centuries: eternal, bodyless, life. Before this ultimate solution, however, the body/machine organism —the cyborg—offers partial liberation from messy bodies that leak blood, guts and gore.

Post-modern ideology . . .

Post-modern thinking revels in idolising multiple subjectivities and borderless transgressions. It abhors (universal) truths, connections, identity and, at its extreme, proclaims that 'the author is dead'[11]— all that counts are texts without contexts, words without flesh. Post-modern theorists are particularly keen to deny, destroy, disown, 'disembody' and fragment the body. Indeed it is not overstating the case that real live bodies—anything that breathes, smells, sighs, laughs and has a heart—are loathed in post-modern writing. Labelled 'essentialist'—and thus banned as the ultimate of sins and replaced by representation only—bodies *are* no longer; bodies exist

---

[11.] Ironically, these intellectual feats are attributed to a chorus of prominent, predominantly French men (see Brodribb 1992), and, in the feminist version, a group of US women—a hypocrisy that I think also pertains to power relations on the net: it is supposed to be democratic and equal-for-all, but it is really the authority of Bill Gates and his competitors that determine our supposedly limitless access to cyberspace.

only 'discursively' and are 'reconfigured'—the production of texts that in jargonistic language dissect and 'disrupt' the body, in sheer size and volume is beyond credibility. Without doubt, post-modern body writing has been the growth industry in cultural and literary studies as well as the sociology of the body since the late 80s.

. . . and reproductive technologies

Post-modern (wet) fantasies about fragmented, leaking bodies oozing from the pens of thousands of academic theorists are mirrored by the actual feats—and fantasies—of cutters with knives who also revel in fragmentation and alienation: medicos and scientists engaged in <u>reproductive and genetic engineering</u>. Under the guise of helping infertile couples to alleviate their pain of involuntary childlessness, the search is on for the womanless child from the glass: made to order by the 'gods' in the labs. Immature eggs are taken from the ovary of a woman or fetus—dead or alive—matured in vitro, then fertilised with easy-to-get sperm. The resulting embryo is placed in a womb—as of yet still that of a real life (other) woman though the artifical womb has long been under development—and the designer baby, so the theory goes, makes its sex-selected, disease-screened, monitored and controlled entry into the technoworld.[12]

Fletcher 14

I do not criticise cut-and-paste baby-making because these technologies tamper with 'nature' (the accusation of essentialism again), but rather because they constitute medical violence against

---

[12.] I have written at great length elsewhere about my criticism of reproductive and genetic engineering as well as other medical miracles which reduce women to living laboratories (Klein 1989a, 1989b, 1992; see also Rowland 1992). Whilst embryo research and testing has been the raison d'être for reproductive scientists since the beginning of their mission to conquer the process of reproduction and take it away from real women, a big infertility industry built on hope and despair has certainly aided their quest. Nevertheless, more than twenty years after Louise Brown was born in 1978, the IVF failure rate is still close to 90 per cent per individual woman, which means that the procedure rarely works for more than ten women out of 100. In order to improve these statistics, in 1999 male infertility accounts for up to half of all clients in fertility clinics. Put differently, a few or only one sperm is injected into an egg of a perfectly fertile woman whose health and indeed life may be jeopardised in the drug-heavy torturous IVF procedure.

women's bodies/minds/spirits/souls, and will, if continued unabated, remove the decision-making power of whether to have children or not—and how many, and of what sex—from women. It will be 'technodocs' who are in control, and women's consciousness will be bent to see this as the post-modern responsible way of baby-making.[13] Importantly, also, by means of conjuring up any disability as monstrosity—but as preventable—only the 'perfect' child will be allowed to be 'born': the one whose genes have been checked for existing genetic diseases as well as predispositions to, say, diabetes, manic depression, homosexuality,[14] and, no doubt, the 'correct' race and sex. Similar to cyborg enthusiasts reproductive and genetic engineers conjure up the illusion that bodies are technologically alterable—a cut or a click away—and the motto is 'enhancement' and, above all, 'choice'. Worryingly, at the end of the twentieth century these techno-fix cultures are gaining ground as they mix nicely with the ubiquitous 'do it yourself' ideology of individuals which rules supreme.

Still Our Bodies—OurSelves?

Body altering technologies also encompass cosmetic surgery which deconstructs and then reconstructs supposedly imperfect bodies of predominantly (western) women to fit with stereotypes of the masculine idea of femininity. These bodies are perceived—and scorned—as objects: never good enough, never thin enough. Worship of alienation—be it through words or through knives—has overcome women's determination from the end of the 1960s to reclaim our bodies, best expressed through the slogan of the then

---

13. A developing gynaecological specialty—adolescent or children's gynaecology: for girls only!—is keen to investigate hormonal and other developmental changes in girls from birth to puberty. To this end it is suggested that girls as young as seven be required to attend yearly gynaecological exams. This of course instills early in the girl's mind the idea that 'doctor' (the expert) knows best. For an illuminating expose see Schüssler and Bode (1992).

14. As I have discussed earlier (Klein 1989a), I do not for one moment believe in the existence of a gene for homosexuality. Rather, in the age of 'geneticisation' (Lippman 1993), sociobiology gets revisited: homophobic pseudoscientific myths browbeat people into accepting science's gospel about their socially constructed sexuality.

newly emerging western Women's Liberation Movement: 'Our Bodies—Ourselves'. Today, more breasts, bellies, noses than ever are augmented, reduced, filled with silicone, chiselled away. 'Reconfigured'—just like texts! In spite of radical feminist theory and practice advocating to overcome the western male tradition of divide and conquer, mind versus matter, self versus 'other' and exposing and resisting global patriarchy's systematic use of racism, sexism, classism (see Bell and Klein 1996)—the objectification of bodies and parts thereof continues.

Multiple Identities

These bodies are not Selves, but in this post-modern cyberage, the idea of a holistic Self with a solid identity [15] has become, at best, a thing of the past, at worst, abhorrent. Where the pleasures and pains of uncertainty, slippage and transgressing boundaries occupy the discursive spaces of high theory, the concept of both Self and 'identity' is said to be in crisis. The creation of multiple identies by engaging in cyberactivities is encouraged and celebrated. US cyberenthusiast and psychoanalyst Sherri Turkle informs us about a midwestern college student named Doug and his adventures on the net (Turkle 1995: 13). Doug plays four characters in three dfferent MUDs which include a seductive woman, a macho, a cowboy type, a sex-neutral rabbit and a character called carrot. He plays all these characters in windows which allows him to 'turn pieces of [his] mind off'. As Doug further elaborates (*idem*):

> I split my mind. I'm getting better at it. I can see myself as being two or three or more. And I just turn on one part of my mind and then another when I go from window to window. I'm in some kind of argument in one

---

[15.] Lest I be misunderstood, having lived in many countries and changed from heterosexual to lesbian, working-class to educated middle-class, ablebodied to disabled, young to old(er), medium thin to medium fat, etc. etc., and speaking/thinking in German/English/Spanish/French, a post-modernist might tell me that I have (had) many identities/Selves. In contrast I would argue that what has changed are surfaces/appearances, but not my core identity. Of course I've changed personal and political views, but I see this as part of learning—associating and synthesising the experiences of growing older and wiser (hopefully)—and not to the detriment of a 'me' that is my own ontological Genuine Self.

window and trying to come on to a girl in a MUD in another, and another
window might be running a spreadsheet program or some other
technical thing for school . . . And then I'll get a real-time message [that
flashes on the screen as soon as it is sent from another system user], and
I guess that's RL. It's just one more window (my emphasis).

Real life (RL) is just one more window? Are these really parallel
realities? Parallel lives of equal significance? The boy's voyeuristic
fantasy life might be closer to home than we would like to believe. If
Post-human Bodies co-editor Ira Livinston's wish '. . . bodies to be
secreted, bodies not inert but becoming strung into loops' (1995:
101), comes true, the 'real life' of the increasing number of dis-
located women and children refugees, as cheap labour and trafficked
for prostitution into market-driven corners of the world under the
guise of the much touted 'globalisation', is indeed not worth much.
Or perhaps, if we follow Doug and other cyberaficionados, such RL
experiences might even be glorified as 'liberation' because our
bodies/minds/spirits/souls have become texts without contexts and
minds without matter—just one more window, it really doesn't
hurt.

There are startling similarities between such net fantasies of
wilfully indulging in playful body 'dissociation' and 'splitting off'
described by survivors of sexual assault. For them the development
of a fragmented identity is often the consequence of sexual abuse,
rape, prostitution, or indeed a *survival* mechanism during these
assaults. As therapist Judith Lewis Herman puts it in her book
Trauma and Recovery: From Domestic Abuse to Political Terror (1992),
'The traumatic event thus destroys the belief that one can be oneself
in relation to others' (p. 53), and 'Doubt reflects the inability to
maintain one's separate point of view while remaining in connection with others' (*idem.*). The sense of connection between individual and community is broken, and, as a survivor put it, '. . . my body
would float into space like a balloon' (p. 102). One need only read
one of the biographies of people suffering from multiple personality
disorder (now called DID, dissociative identity disorder) as a result of
sexual abuse, to despair about the mindless 'mind' celebration of

those 'choosing' parallel multiple identities in contrast to the sheer terror of RL living with twenty-four multiple personae that developed out of despair (West 1999).[16]

Body Art

Real Life is also reduced to a series of windows by post-modern artists, amongst them French performance artist Orlan's 'radical' body transformations in which she 'inscribes' her body as celebration and art. Over the past five years she has had her face surgically changed in operation after operation—to-date there have been seven of them—which were all videotaped and later displayed at conferences. Orlan starts from the post-modern premise that there is no such thing as a 'natural body', but that it is entirely socially constructed. She sees bodies as 'nothing more than a "costume", a "vehicle", something to be changed in our search "to become who we are" ' (Davis 1995: 173–4). Orlan's body art—or should we call it mutilation?—is a good example of the post-modern fascination with bodily fragmentation, which, in the opinion of post-modern theorist Elizabeth Grosz, is to be celebrated. As Grosz puts it: '. . . human bodies have the wonderful ability to . . . produce fragmentation, fracturings, disclocations. . . .' (1994: 13). The term dislocation could be taken only too literally in Orlan's case. The question needs to be asked what continuous pain and indeed long-term health consequences will Orlan suffer due to her many operations, as part of which foreign bodies are inserted under her skin (such as, for instance, silicone implants), or her ear is severed from the rest of her face? But these are questions that post-modern writers do not consider important; instead the 'transgressive potential' of such performativity is seen as boundary-breaking. Orlan's body is not considered as the body in which she lives every minute of her life—it is an object to be fragmented at will. This, Orlan sees also as

---

16. Far from being a feminist account (and indeed often determinedly anti-feminist), Cameron West's autobiography nevertheless makes it clear how desperate the struggle of a person with DID is to regain a sense of Self and to create a 'safe' place for the many alter egos that range from self-mutilating to assaulting other family members and friends.

changing her identity—thus the question to be asked is whether in post-modern performativity a person's identity is confined to her bodily looks. Put differently, has a woman ridden with arthritis and suffering from continuous pain a different identity from her 'Self' before the illness manifested itself? What happens in cases of remission? Does she revert to her former Self? Has she been permanently changed? In Orlan's case, is she 'better' now because her 'identity' has been enhanced and multiplied by technology? For post-modernist thinkers these questions present no problems, since they see bodies as 'discursively produced'—they are but texts that can be written, rewritten and undergo continual change.

Compared with ordinary women's daily realities of living with beauty norms, inflicted physical and emotional violence and/or the burdens of poverty, to be a post-modern bundle of changing identities might seem like a happy scenario come true—or having a trip without actually needing any drugs! But what about the pain suffered during and after the operation—pain, that to some extent, may become permanent? Multiple identities will collapse into one: the one that is woken up by sharp pain. A rude awakening for post-modern/cyberspace devotees of multiple identities who, too, have but one body—at least for the time being.

Although one might shrug off Orlan's experiment as a bit of self-aggrandised artistic over-excitement, theories of post-modernism underlying body performativity have their counterparts in cyber-space: the rapidly expanding theories of cyborgs and cyberbodies in robotics and cyberscience.

Cyborgs

The fascination with physically changing people's bodies either in real life or in cyberspace has been seized by theorists who have invented the '*cyborg*', an organism that is part-human, part-machine. As Donna Haraway put it: 'The cyborg is a kind of disassembled and reassembled, post-modern collective and personal self. This is the self feminists must code' (1991: 163). Thus Haraway's self is a cut-and-paste body, 'rejoicing in the illegitimate

Hawthorne I

fusion of animal and machine' p. 176). A self that adds—and
sheds—machinic bits so that, according to Haraway, 'communications technologies and biotechnologies are the crucial tools
recrafting our bodies' (p. 164). The cyborg is clearly superior to
human bodies. As Haraway puts it starkly: 'We don't need organic
holism to give impermeable wholeness, [producing] the total woman
and her feminist variants (mutants?)' p. 178). While Orlan is bound
to agree—perhaps a voice-activated computer implant is on the list
for future operations—Germaine Greer might raise her eyebrows.
How did political feminism turn into mere 'lifestyle' where, independent of gender, class, race, ability and age hierarchies, bodies can
be reconfigured—continuously 'updated' (in the same way we
update our computers)? In this destabilised post-modern world,
power has become a meaningless concept. It is easy to see how it
might pose a bit of a problem to decide which of one's multiple selves
should join the protest march. So much better to stay home all of
us—where it is dry and cosy and we can pretend to be superheroes
on the net. Patriarchy, meanwhile, is laughing: so much better to
rule where everyone is kept busy—and divided!

In post-modern and cyberthinking, the categories of 'women'
and 'men' (or young and old, or white and black) have lost any
meaning. The cyborg world is built on '. . . permanently partial
identities and contradictory standpoints' (Haraway 1991: 154). In
other words, it is up to the individual to be whatever s/he desires—
including donning the body/ies s/he wishes to appear in, at a given
time—some sort of an eternal fancy dress ball, one might think.
Perhaps contemporary goddesses are not too dissimilar from
cyborgs? Perhaps patriarchy has co-opted them both?

It is time for a good dose of realism about the fate of 'real' women
and men. For instance, who will it be that decides who—of which
country, sex, race, age—will get the latest electronically wired body,
and who will miss out? The electronic revolution has already created
the information-rich and the information-poor, and the rampant
individualism inherent in post-modern cyborg-thinking reinforces
this trend. As Susan Hawthorne puts it succinctly, 'Once again the
coloniser colonises' (Hawthorne p. 217).

Eroticised technobodies

Many cyborg fans believe that the addition of prosthetic devices is a first step towards 'cyborg consciousness' (Haraway 1991: 148). Zachary Nataf (quoted in Hawthorne this volume, p. 218) goes even further and posits that rather than using prosthetic devices in order to overcome an accident or improve on a disability, we should use the whole gamut of body modification to joyfully enhance our (lacking) bodies—and our eroticism.

Hawthorne

The notion that cuts, gash marks and wounds—augmented with prosthetic devices—lead to a cyborg existence and add erotic pleasures has become fashionable in post-modern body writing. Real, flesh, 'lived' bodies are accorded so little value that it is only through (technological) modification that they appear redeemable (or will be disappeared, see Hans Moravec's ideas, below).

In 1995, in an article entitled, 'Beating the meat/surviving the text, or how to get out of this century alive', US film and media theorist Vivian Sobchack resolutely queried the assumptions behind post-modern writers' romanticising of body mutilation and techno-logical 'enhancement'. Having undergone major cancer surgery on her thigh followed by a later amputation of her leg, Sobchack was outraged about well-known French theorist Jean Baudrillard's praise of the pornographic science-fiction novel *Crash* (by J.G. Ballard; also the subject of a movie). She accused Baudrillard of wilful misreading of a work whose pathological characters 'get off' on the erotic collision between the human body and technology, and celebrate sex and death in wrecked automobiles and car crashes (Sobchack 1995: 205). She wishes him 'a car crash or two, and a little pain to bring him (back) to his senses (Sobchack 1995: 207). It is the loss of the 'lived' body in much of post-modern body writing that Sobchack questions. Also, she is critical of the importance given to mechanical devices (for example, a leg prosthesis), labelling it a 'technobody' or cyborg and deeming it superior to the mere 'meat' (for example, the organic body). In Sobchack's words:

What many surgeries and my prosthetic experience have really taught me is that, if we are to survive into the next century, we must counter the millennial discourses that would decontextualize our flesh into insensate signs or digitize it into cyberspace . . . (p. 209).

Cyberminds

Digitising our flesh into cyberspace—precisely what Vivian Sobchack has been warning against—is the aim of eminent US computer scientist and robotics specialist, Hans Moravec. Detailed in *Mind Children* (1988) and followed in *Robot* (1999), in Moravec's vision, real bodies are relegated to irrelevant 'meat' and 'wetware' (the brain). The dream of eternal life consisting of ever-changing mind molecules, without the flesh, is writ large. In the 'post-biological' age, we will leave behind our organic bodies made out of proteins (encoded through DNA and RNA). Instead, electronically wired machines of far superior quality—faster and with much more storage and selection/combination capabilities—will take over. In Moravec's words (1998: 4):

> Our culture will then be able to evolve independently of human biology and its limitation, passing instead directly from generation to generation of ever more capable intelligent machinery.

This, Moravec argues, is immense progress as it will do away with the 'uneasy truce between mind and body . . . [when it] breaks down completely as life ends' (1988: 4). The mind, as he goes on to say, will be 'rescued from the limitation of a mortal body' (p. 5). The resulting 'mind children', in Moravec's view, will be perfectly suited to an ever faster pace of life on this planet—and others. The computer as 'head' of a robot body could update the contents of its own mind continuously, adding and deleting, testing components in all kinds of combinations, to keep up with changing conditions (p. 5).[17] Of

---

17. In chapter Four 'Grandfather clause' (1988), Moravec describes in (gruesome) detail how a human mind is 'downloaded' into its new mechanical 'body'. Other writings by Moravec can be found at <http://www.ix.de/tp/english/special/vag/6037/2.html> or <http://www.ashbrook.org/books/moravec.html>

course these minds could be copied and sold, patented and leased;
and cloned—to keep young and fresh on ice—all leading to a
burgeoning 'mind industry':[18] think not only of the technological
experts needed, but of the instruments and endless gadgets in
addition to booming global business for lawmakers and ethicists (the
gold in the cyber wild west tempts again). In 'Simulation' (1998)
Moravec elaborates on his idea of downloading a brain:

> The brain would be sustained physically by life support machinery, and
> mentally by connections of all the peripheral nerves to an elaborate
> simulation of not only a surrounding world, but also a *body* for the brain
> to inhabit (my emphasis).

What fun, the body restored and the fashion industry re-invented.
(More gold!) Bodymorphing from one avatar to the next? Orlan
might not need to suffer pain. Cyberbliss!

It is important to emphasise that Moravec is an established
scientist who backs up his assumptions with mathematical and
computational details, but also adheres to sociobiological theory
which is antithetical to feminism through its blatant anti-feminist
assumptions. In 1999 he expanded his original vision in *Robot: Mere
Machine to Transcendent Mind*. An online review published by the
John M. Ashbrook Center for Public Affairs at Ashland University
(1999, February 1) states that 'Machines will attain human levels of
intelligence by the year 2040', predicts robotics expert Hans
Moravec. 'And by 2050, they will have far surpassed us.' This does
not worry Moravec. As the reviewer puts it, he embraces this
development and contends that intelligent robots will be our
evolutionary heirs:

> [m]achines, which will grow from us, learn our skills, and share our goals
> and values, can be viewed as children of our minds.' . . . In a bid for
> immortality, many of our descendants will choose to transform into
> 'ex humans', as they upload themselves into advanced computers. We

---

[18.] I am indebted to Susan Hawthorne for the concept of leasing and duplicating one's
downloaded mind which came out of her own old-fashioned protein mind which I hope will
never be replaced!

will become our children. (<<u>http://www.ashbrook.org/books/moravec.</u> <u>html</u>>)[19]

Cyber- and reproductive technology happily married! (I wonder if lesbians will be allowed to have 'mind children'?) The annihilation of the organic human body 'of woman born' is enthusiastically advocated. By downloading the brain it is hoped, 'we' (which we?) will achieve transcendence. In some way, this is of course a rather old-fashioned dream as science writer Margaret Wertheim points out. In *The Pearly Gates of Cyberspace* (1999), she draws attention to many analogies between the new (male) cybergurus and old (male) religious thinkers. All have in common that 'the better life' is achieved when the unclean, dangerous, imperfect body is left behind, and, as Wertheim puts it, 'the "sins of the flesh" will be erased and men [sic] shall be like angels' (Wertheim 1999: 259). And she continues: 'Repackaged in digital garb, this is the dream of the "glorified body" that the heavenly elect can look forward to when Judgment Day comes' (Wertheim 1999: 261).

Will it be the 'heavenly elect' again or will the cybermiracle happen for all? Brain-downloading democracy across the globe? Certainly, religious and secular thinkers alike continue to ascribe the most impure, most sinful and most dangerous bodies to women. Cybergurus such as Moravec and Kurzweil do not problematise female and male bodies, but in their so-called gender 'neutrality' reinforce the male as the norm. Others, quoted in critic's Mark Dery's *Escape Velocity* (1996), are more forthcoming and project the worst of sexist, racist and ageist images in their visions of cyber-space. Given the current configuration of cyberspace as overwhelm-ingly macho, pornographic, (hetero)sexualised, and imbued with 'cyberselfishness' (Paulina Borsook in Wertheim 1999: 281)— libertarianism rules supreme—it is quite likely that it will be a white

---

19. Ray Kurzweil, author of *The Age of Spiritual Machines* (1999) offers scenarios similar to those of Moravec. Science fiction fans should consult Claudia Springer's *Electronic Eros: Bodies and Desire in the Postindustrial Age* (1996) for references and feminist criticism of the excesses of eroticised technobodies.

male 'cyberelite' who will invest in cyberimmortality for themselves. Yet at the same time they will need women as real and virtual sex objects as well as menial workers/emotional supporters for their travails/travels in cyberspace.[20] But then, who knows, with cloning and the artificial womb perfected and the need for 'hardware' (the hard disk, also called matter, mater, and womb in contemporary cyberwriting, see Dery 1996) diminished, the idea might be to remove women's consciousness from their mat(t)er altogether and have it reside in the cyberskins of robot bodies floating in cyberspace. Cybermatricide on the next millennium's horizon as the final solution to the woman question?

It is difficult to assess how much of these (farfetched?) scenarios will come true. Like so many other male fantasies, the dream of the bodyless mind that has rendered the body/matter/matrix/mater obsolete might remain just that—a cyberdream. On the other hand, it cannot be denied that computer power is doubling every year, and, that through the use of the World Wide Web, information is made available at an increasingly rapid rate. Similarly, post-modern body theorists—including some feminists—continue to push their 'transgressive boundaries', alienating women (and men) further and further from their own bodies/minds/Selves. And uncivil, greedy and selfish globalisation rules supreme. Ever the feminist optimist, I will nonetheless leave my Nightmares and return to my initial question what a CyberFeminism might look like so it can contribute to social justice and a feminist future for all.

[20.] Films such as *Gattaca* (1997) paint a disturbing picture of a future which, although not in cyberspace but inhabited by genetically engineered people, is mercilessly hierarchical and mirrors the past and the present. It is not too difficult to imagine who will populate the underclass of 'unworthy' people—and who will form the elite: a rather gloomy scenario for Indigenous, other marginalised and poor people who would not be accepted into the genetic engineering (cyberspace) laboratories in the first place. See also Marge Piercy's *He, She, and It* (1991) for an equally disturbing 'utopia'.

IV CyberFeminism: Holistic Strategies for Social Change

In a CyberFeminism that encourages the development of Cyber-Selves, the *real* bodies/minds of *real* women connected to the environment they live in, have to remain at the *centre* of our theory and praxis. It is the 'lived body' of Vivian Sobchack who sits in front of the computer (with a stiff neck and a gin and tonic!)[21] that must insist on its continued presence in the mind-heavy domain of cyber-space. German philosopher Annegret Stopczyk (1998) has developed her theory of 'Leibsinn', a term which resists translation: the term 'bodysense' sounds heavy and not very elegant. Yet in a way it is precisely this 'bodysense' that we need to rescue and nurture, a grounded whole/self, resisting fragmentation and dissociation. This does not imply that 'bodysense' is static and something that we are born with (the essentialism accusation refuted again!). Quite to the contrary, 'bodysense' changes as we grow, learn, and get older, and there is no reason why we cannot avoid developing—and indeed must develop—a CyberSelf that takes the groundedness in its various guises into cyberspace.

The memory of connectivities of body/souls has been lost for many western women but survives in some Indigenous cultures. It may be the way ahead to thrive and survive in the cyberage. In her ethnography detailing the lives of the South Australian Ngarrindjeri peoples, *Ngarrindjeri Wurruwarrin: A World That Is, Was, and Will Be* (1998), Diane Bell was told how in Ngarrindjeri culture land and body are fused. The term 'ruwi' means land and the word 'ruwar' means body. Thus damage to the land is damage to the body in a very

Arnold 11

---

21. Lack of space prevents me from talking more about the real life bodies who sit in front of the computer screen. It is interesting though, that when computers first began to be used in offices, problems about electromagnetic emissions and injuries to hands and backs were widely discussed. These days, when millions play on the net for hours, including very young children, these health concerns curiously seem to have lost centre-stage.

visceral sense (Bell 1998: 262). Women speak of pegs driven into the land as spiritual wounding (Bell 1998: 267).

Given the many advantages that cyberspace offers for (feminist) activism, for the exchange of information, online teaching and learning, and for creative activities making use of multimedia as well as for personal friendships across the globe, a pragmatic Cyber-Feminism will insist on being embodied even when we are engaged in cyberactivities (our bodies are as [non] 'present' in a letter, a fax, or on the phone). It is crucial that women are not left behind as the communications revolution accelerates.

Women have complicated relationships with their/our bodies. From an early age, the patriarchal messages we get, differing in nuances but not intent—and depending on culture, race and social status—are that our bodies are wanting: they are never good enough and thus in need of ongoing control. Always promoted as 'for our own good', throughout our life-cycle, women are medicalised, body-down-sized, disabilities hidden. And we body-modify from diets to anorexia, from cosmetic surgery to body cutting. There exists an enormous hatred and loathing of female bodies, especially in western cultures around the world, and women are amongst those who hate their own bodies most. There are always resisters though, perhaps victims first, but through sheer willpower and insistence—and often theoretical and bodily insight—they are survivors in the end. And there are some individuals who manage to live harmonously as theirSelves bodies/minds/souls.

In order to survive with our real bodies in cyberspace we must develop feminist *CyberEthics* which take as their starting point that embodied bodily integrity has to be upheld in cyberlife, precisely *because* cyberlife is no less 'real' than the world the computer worker inhabits since *they are the same*. In practical terms, this would mean an end to assuming stolen identities, from pretending to have a different gender, a (dis)abled body, different age or race. On the topic of cyborgs it would mean taking the glamour out of this icon, and welcoming technological developments as possible improvements in our 'real' lives, but never as the dominating, indeed more 'spiritual' machine part (Kurzweil 1999).

Finally, should the technical feasibility of scanning one's brain activities onto a computer indeed become possible, we might do well to remember that 'the man (*sic*) on the moon' has not become the norm for women; and that if we like and enjoy being our bodies through their life cycle, then the majority of women might not rush to the action.[22] The post-modern and cyberenthusiasts' disembodied mind-dreams sound a warning bell and need to be critiqued as a twenty-first century attack on 'whole' women and men.

CyberFeminism can be the answer to both cyborg fantasies and cybergoddess yearning. As icons they reinforce techno-patriarchy rather than displace it. Those of us who are concerned about the future of the oppressed and marginalised, of women as a social group as well as Indigenous peoples, and other groups that have kept connections with their mind/body/land/soul, might want to go for the pragmatic 'low' ride on the net (see also Douglas 1996) and use its potential to connect and improve lives through its spider-like web. Disregarding the 'high' disembodied theories that currently plague the minds (maybe even the bodies!) of post-modern cybernerds, we have to trust that we will find the answers within our bodies—ourSelves.

References

Ashbrook, John M. Center for Public Affairs. 1999. On-line review of *Robot: Mere machine to transcendent mind* by Hans Moravec, February 1.
<http://www.ashbrook.org/books/moravec.html>
Bell, Diane. 1998. *Ngarrindjeri Wurruwarrin: A world that is, was, and will be.* Melbourne: Spinifex Press.
Bell, Diane and Renate Klein. (Eds.), 1996. *Radically Speaking: Feminism reclaimed.* Melbourne: Spinifex Press; London: Zed Books.
Brodribb, Somer. 1992. *Nothing Mat(t)ers. A Feminist Critique of Post-modernism.* Melbourne: Spinifex Press.

[22.] But then, as discussed earlier, most women might indeed be barred from joining the cyberelite in their brainlives and instead be forced into sex or other maintenance labour.

Burke, Kate. 1999. AVIVA. The Women's World Wide Web. In *Liberating Cyberspace. Civil Liberties, Human Rights and The Internet*, edited by Liberty. London: Pluto Press in association with Liberty (The National Council for Civil Liberties).

Chossudowsky, Michel. 1998. *The Globalisation of Poverty. Impacts of IMF and World Bank Reforms*. London: Zed. Books.

D'Aprano, Zelda. 1977/1995. *Zelda*. Melbourne: Spinifex Press.

Davis, Kathy 1997. 'My body is my art': Cosmetic surgery as feminist utopia? In Kathy Davies (Ed.), *Embodied Practices: Feminist perspectives on the body*. London: Sage.

Dery, Mark. 1996. *Escape Velocity: Cyberculture at the end of the century*. London: Hodder and Stoughton.

Douglas, Carol Anne. 1996. I'll take the Low Road: A Look at Contemporary Feminist Theory. In Diane Bell and Renate Klein (Eds.), *Radically Speaking: Feminism reclaimed*. Melbourne: Spinifex Press; London: Zed Books.

Forbes, Mark. 1999. Sex Boom Fuels Super Brothel Bid. *The Age*, February 28, p. 1.

Garran, Robert. 1997. The Cyber Chick Most Likely To . . . *The Weekend Australian*. May 31–June 1, p. 8.

Gates, Bill. 1999. *Business@The Speed of Thought. Using a Digital Nervous System*. Melbourne: Viking.

Gattaca motion picture. (1997) Written and directed by Andrew Niccol. Columbia TriStar/Jersey.

Greer, Germaine. 1999. *The Whole Woman*. London: Doubleday.

Gray, Chris Hables. (Ed.), 1995. *The Cyborg Handbook*, New York and London: Routledge.

Grosz, Elisabeth. 1994. *Volatile Bodies: Towards a corporeal feminism*, Bloomington: Indiana University Press; Sydney: Allen & Unwin.

Halberstam, Judith and Ira Livingston. 1995. *Post-human Bodies*. Bloomington: Indiana University Press.

Haraway, Donna. 1991. Manifesto for Cyborgs: Science, Technology, and Socialist-Feminism in the Late Twentieth Century. In Donna Haraway *Simians, Cyborgs and Women. The Reinvention of Nature*. New York: Routledge.

Harcourt. Wendy. 1999. *Women @Internet. Creating New Cultures in Cyberspace*. London: Zed Books.

Herman, Clem. 1999. Women and the Internet. In *Liberating Cyberspace. Civil Liberties, Human Rights and The Internet*, edited by Liberty. London: Pluto Press in association with Liberty (The National Council for Civil Liberties).

Herman Lewis, Judith. 1992. *Trauma and Recovery: From domestic abuse to political terror*. London: Pandora.

Klein, Renate. 1989a. *The Exploitation of a Desire: Women's experiences with in vitro fertilisation*. Geelong: Women's Studies Summer Institute, Deakin University.

Klein, Renate. 1989b. *Infertility: Women speak out about their experiences with reproductive medicine*. London: Pandora Press; Sydney: Allen & Unwin.

Klein, Renate. 1992. Reproductive Technologies, Genetic Engineering and Womenhating. In Cheris Kramerae and Dale Spender (Eds.), *The Knowledge Explosion: Generations of feminist scholarship*. New York: Pergamon Press (now Teachers College Press).

Klein, Renate. 1996. (Dead) Bodies Floating in Cyberspace. Post-modernism and the Dismemberment of Women. In Diane Bell and Renate Klein (Eds.), *Radically Speaking: Feminism reclaimed*. Melbourne: Spinifex Press; London: Zed Books.

Kurzweil, Ray. 1999. *The Age of Spiritual Machines: When computers exceed human intelligence*. Sydney: Allen & Unwin.

Lippman, Abby. 1993. Prenatal genetic testing and geneticisation. Mothers matter for all. *Fetal Diagnosis Therapy*, 8 (suppl. 1), 175–88.

Mary*. 1999. Kiss of the Web Woman. *The Weekend Australian*. March 27–28, pp. 30–31. (*a pseudonym).

Mies, Maria. 1986/1999. *Patriarchy & Accumulation on a World Scale. Women in the International Division of Labour*. London: Zed Books; Melbourne: Spinifex Press.

Moravec, Hans. 1988. *Mind Children: The future of robot and human intelligence*. Massachusetts and London: Harvard University Press.

Moravec, Hans. 1998. Simulation.
   <http://www.ix.de/tp/english/special/vag/6037/2.html>

Moravec, Hans. 1999. *Robot: Mere machine to transcendent mind*. New York and Oxford: Oxford University Press.

Parker, Carol. 1997. *The Joy of Cybersex*. Melbourne: Reed Books.

Parker, Carol. 1997. How Cybersex Destroyed My Marriage. *The Weekend Australian*, May 3–4, pp. 1, 4 (extract from *The Joy of Cybersex*. Melbourne: Reed Books).

Piercy, Marge. 1991. *He, She, and It: A novel*. New York: Knopf.

Rowland, Robyn. 1992. *Living Laboratories: Women and reproductive technologies*. Sydney: Macmillan.

Schüssler, Marina and Kathrin Bode. 1992. *Geprüfte Mädchen—Ganze Frauen. Zur Normierung der Mädchen in der Kindergynäkologie*. Zürich and Dortmund: eFeF Verlag.

Senjen, Rye and Jane Guthrey. 1996. *The Internet for Women*. Melbourne: Spinifex Press.

Shiva, Vandana 1993. *Monocultures of the Mind*. Penang: Third World Network.

Sobchack, Vivian. 1995. Beating the meat/surviving the text, or how to get out of this century alive. *Body and Society*, 1 (3–4), 205–14.

Spender, Dale. 1995. *Nattering on the Net. Women, Power and Cyberspace*. Melbourne: Spinifex Press.

Springer, Claudia. 1996. *Electronic Eros: Bodies and desire in the postindustrial age*. Austin: University of Texas Press.

Stopczyk, Annegret. 1998. *Sophias Leib: Entfesselung der Weisheit*. Heidelberg: Carl-Auer-Systeme Verlag.

Szego, Julie. 1999. Friends On-line. *The Age*, Melbourne, June 11, p. 15.

Turkle, Sherry. 1995. *Life On The Screen: Identity in the age of the Internet*. New York: Simon & Schuster.

Wertheim, Margaret. 1999. *The Pearly Gates of Cyberspace: A history of space from Dante to the Internet*. Sydney: Doubleday.

West, Cameron. 1999. *First Person Plural. My Life as a Multiple*. Sydney: Macmillan.

ten

Cyborgs, Virtual Bodies and Organic Bodies: Theoretical Feminist Responses

Susan Hawthorne

> *Reality is more fantastic than any product of the imagination.*
> (Christa Wolf 1968: 184)[1]

Reality is up for grabs. Whose reality? What sort of reality? Does reality exist? And our bodies. Are they simply wet ware? Meat? Are they post-human? Transcendent? Immaterial? The bodies of women are central to any cultural or political discourse, and bodies have been central to feminist activism and theory.

Likewise, 'reality' is a central word for feminists, because our 'reality' as lesbians, poor, black, working, disabled, old, young, marginalised women has been ignored. Whose voice is it you hear when you read the newspaper, academic articles, a high percentage of novels, poetry, even more of film, and 99% of computer games? What we see is constructed by who we are and our experiences in the world.

Marilyn Frye (1983), in a marvellous essay called 'To See and Be Seen: The Politics of Reality' defines reality in terms of the word's historical connections with royalty. She traces real to the Spanish 'real' which is equivalent to the English 'regal' or 'royal'. And she traces reality to the eye of the king. Real estate—the property of the king; reality—what the king can see. And she finishes with:

[1.] An extraordinarily prescient essay in which she asks the question: 'Are we really waiting impatiently for the complete model of our brains that the cybernetic experts dream about?' (Wolf 1968: 183).

To be real is to be visible to the king.
The king is in his counting house (Frye 1983: 155).

Indeed. These days the developers of computer hardware and software are king. And they are certainly in their contemporary counting houses (stock exchanges). And what they say is real goes.

No longer 'real estate' but unreal estate, virtual estate, the estate where:

'. . . there is no there there' (Gibson 1984: 270).

And:

Objects in this virtual world are only surface; they have no weight or mass (Holtzman 1994: 195).

In the real world, Beryl Fletcher has her character Pixel, a young nethead say of her body:

Fletcher 14

I hate <u>living in the body</u>, it's too demanding, too there (Fletcher 1996: 111).

Virtual reality keeps bringing us up against such paradoxes, and I am puzzled by the feeling of familiarity.

To be real is to be visible to the king (Frye 1983: 155).

What does the king *not* see? Does he see poverty? Does he see women? Does he see anyone cast beyond the edges of his sight? Does he deny anyone's reality?

Given the difficulty the king had in seeing 'real' things and people in the 'real world', one wonders how he will go in a world where there's no physical reality, only abstractions.[2] How will he make laws about the new kinds of people? Are cyborgs citizens? What of virtual citizens? And then, what of the old-fashioned organic body? Will it work? Is it worth supporting them in ill-health and old age?

---

2. As I point out elsewhere (Hawthorne 1996a), the king probably suffers from Dominant Culture Stupidities, which means that he frequently sees less than those around him who inhabit multiple real worlds. And children in these circumstances are quite capable of noticing the emperor (or king) without clothes, and perhaps without a body.

Cyborg Bodies

> *Cyborgs, the burning signs of our illumination*
> (Deborah Staines, *Now Millennium*).

The word '<u>cyborg</u>' is derived from: cybernetic organism—'an entity comprising organic as well as machinic parts and information systems' (Sofia 1995: 154).

Klein 9

Donna Haraway defines the cyborg:

A cyborg exists when two kinds of boundaries are simultaneously problematic: 1) that between animals (or other organisms) and humans,[3] and 2) that between self-controlled, self-governing machines (automatons) and organisms, especially humans (models of autonomy). The cyborg is the figure born of the interface of automaton and autonomy (Haraway 1989: 139).

Anne Balsamo in *Technologies of the Gendered Body: Reading Cyborg Women*, writes:

Cyborgs are hybrid entities that are neither wholly technological nor completely organic, which means that the cyborg has the potential to disrupt persistent dualisms that set the natural body in opposition to the technologically recrafted body, but also to refashion our thinking about the theoretical construction of the body as both a material entity and a discursive process (Balsamo 1996: 11).

In practical terms the cyborg is a body which crosses the boundary between human and machine. This is achieved when there is an insertion into the body of, or surrounding of the body by, a mechanical or informational device. Some examples used frequently

---

[3.] Although this essay deals only with human/machinic cyborgs, the issue of animal/plant cyborgs needs to be addressed. Briefly, GATT has created the preconditions making possible widespread use and misuse of animal/plant cyborgs through the universal application of US patent laws, the development of genetically engineered plants and animals, and the further dispossession of the world's Indigenous and poor peoples whose lives depend, in many ways, on the maintenance of traditional knowledge which is now being capitalised and commodified by the developed nations of the world. See Hawthorne (1996a: 496–501), Mies and Shiva (1993), Shiva (1996)

throughout the literature include people with heart pace-makers, deep-sea divers, people with artificial limbs, speaking or hearing devices, or the quintessential cyborg: Stephen Hawking.

Describing Hawking, Sandy Stone writes:

> Sitting as he always does, in his wheelchair, utterly motionless, except for his fingers on the joystick of the laptop; and on the floor to one side of him is the PA system microphone, nuzzling into the Vortrax's tiny loud-speaker (Stone 1995a: 4–5).

A number of writers compare the female body with cyborgs which I find puzzling. Anne Balsamo, for instance, writes:

> . . . the female body historically [has been] constructed as a hybrid case, thus making it compatible with notions of cyborg identity promulgated by more recent cultural theorists (Balsamo 1996: 19).

And N. Katherine Hayles:

> . . . there is essentially no difference between a cyborg and a woman (Hayles 1995: 311).

I suspect the reason for this is that women, under patriarchy, are perceived as incomplete. Freud saw it, medical doctors have tried to rectify it, religions have tried to stamp it out. It is, as radical feminist Robin Morgan so clearly stated, that 'I am a monster' (Bell and Klein 1996: xv).

And yet.

David J. Hess when posing himself the same question answers that Arnold Schwarzeneggar4 is a clear example of a cyborg (1995: 371).

Klein 9

But perhaps this is just the ability to hold <u>contradictory stand-points</u>, for Donna Haraway is perfectly happy for people in a cyborg world to not be 'afraid of permanently partial identities and contradictory standpoints' (Haraway 1991: 154).

Haraway, among others, has proposed that the addition of prosthetic devices results in what writers have called 'a cyborg con-

---

4. Hess is referring to the role played by Schwarzeneggar in the film, *The Terminator*.

sciousness' (González 1995: 269), where he points out Haraway's allusions (1991: 148, 153, 180) to such a consciousness.

And literary theorist, Hayles writes:

> Standing at the threshold separating the human from the posthuman, the cyborg looks to the past as well as the future. It is precisely this double nature that allows cyborg stories to be imbricated within cultural narratives while still wrenching them in a new direction (Hayles 1995: 322).

This Janus vision of cyborgs reminds me of Janice Raymond's two-sights seeing (1986); of the way in which the straight mind, as proposed by Monique Wittig, tends 'to immediately universalize its production of concepts into general laws' (Wittig 1980/1992: 27); or of my own concept of 'dominant culture stupidities' (Hawthorne 1996a). Chela Sandoval (1995: 408) at least recognises '. . . that colonized peoples of the Americas have already developed cyborg skills'. Perhaps the concept of *cyborg* gives white men and other dominant culture individuals something to feel different about.[5] Once again the coloniser colonises.

I also dispute the existence of cyborg consciousness. The definitions of cyborg are too inclusive to be useful. What are the limits of the set? If it includes the cane of a blind person—and some extend it to include the spanner in the hand (Sofia 1995)—then does that mean when I ride a bicycle or drive a car, I become a cyborg? Similarly, roller blades are extensions of legs, trapezes make it possible to overcome one's destiny as a featherless biped, stilts artificially increase one's height. Where does it stop? Its all-inclusiveness results in the conclusion that 'we are all cyborgs'. The problem with this reification of cyborg identity is that the writers appear to forget the real body inside or outside the cyborg. They appear to forget the

---

5. The problem here is appropriation. The dominant culture is always quick to appropriate any advantage the oppressed gain either through struggle (for instance, men's health centres when women's health centres are being defunded), or which the oppressed have by nature of their oppression. The latter includes an appropriation of difference (Cubism developed out of appropriating African art, see Hawthorne 1989/1990), as well as an intelligence about the nature of the dominant culture (see Hawthorne 1996a; Hawthorne 1997).

years of activism by disabled peoples, instead they reify the mechanisms of dildos,[6] artificial wombs, bionic and genetic body parts without questioning in whose interest this is done. The other side-step which is taken, is to refer to mythical traditions to support all manner of theoretical positions. Nataf (1997: 187–188), for example, refers to the Dogon story of Ama, whose progeny were firstly, a hermaphroditic jackal, and secondly, hermaphroditic twins. He makes no comment on the mythical justification of genital mutilation[7] which recurs throughout the story. Instead the transgendered, cultural shaping of flesh is highlighted as the most salient feature of the story. His conclusion, that 'Biology is ideological' (Nataf 1997: 188) is not in dispute. But to suggest therefore that just because the body *can* be modified, that that is, socially or politically, the best outcome, is in dispute. The idea of the cyborg has proven fruitful for those espousing polymorphous perversity, along with commodified sexual practices. He writes:

> S/M or non-genital eroticism captures the charge and diffuses it across the surface, causing the whole body to resonate. Surgical mutation can create new orifices or types of genitals. A proliferation of new erotogenic zones can be made available simply by cutting and stitching the flesh, piercing, tattooing, branding, with prosthetics to increase and enhance the receptivity of the body's surface and interiority (Nataf 1997: 188).

Cyborg territory provides a nice home for transsexuals.[8] Best known among cyborg theorists is Sandy Stone who describes his work as a series of provocations (1995b: 393), and as someone who 'Fell in love with my Prosthesis' (1995a: 1 and 1995b: 393).[9] And in writing of Stephen Hawking, he asks, 'Where does he stop? Where are his edges?' (1995a: 5, 1995b: 395). He might well ask the same question of *himself*.

---

6. For more on this see Jeffreys (1993) and Hawthorne (1991).

7. For a heart-wrenching depiction of what happens to girls see Rioja and Manresa (1999).

8. For an insightful discussion on transexuality see Raymond (1994).

9. In keeping with cyborg practice, since Sandy Stone is simply a man with a prosthesis, I will continue to refer to him as male, although strangely he refers to himself as she/her.

In spite of Haraway's (1991: 178) claim that 'machines can be prosthetic devices, intimate components, friendly selves', 'an aspect of our embodiment' (1991: 180), machines, prostheses and other devices are neither gender- nor race-, nor age-neutral, nor are they free of political importance.

Audre Lorde, in her important work *The Cancer Journals*, points out that:

> Prosthesis offers the empty comfort of 'Nobody will know the difference' (1980: 61).

As activists around disability and ageing know, this is not the path to well-being, either individually or socially. A prosthesis flies in the face of the post-modern push for difference. Rather than allowing us to face the differences and accept them, prostheses disguise difference, forcing a move towards 'normalisation'.[10] Indeed, Lorde writes:

> I believe that the socially sanctioned prosthesis is merely another way of keeping women with breast cancer silent and separate from each other. For instance, what would happen if an army of one-breasted women descended upon congress and demanded that the use of carcinogenic, fat-stored hormones in beef feed be outlawed? (Lorde 1980: 16).[11]

Acceptance, argues Lorde, and 'decency' demand that women who have had mastectomies use a prosthesis in order to look 'right' or 'normal'. And there is nothing about a prosthesis for Lorde to make it signify a new consciousness. Rather, a prosthesis perpetuates the same old prevailing body myths.

> But where the superficial is supreme, the idea that a woman can be beautiful and one-breasted is considered depraved, or at best, bizarre, a threat to 'morale' (Lorde 1980: 64–65).[12]

[10.] For a longer discussion on this see Hawthorne (1996a).

[11.] This is a particularly pertinent question with the outbreak of Mad Cow Disease, an outcome of transgressing the boundaries (Shiva 1996) between herbivore and carnivore. This is cyborg farming in its maddest incarnation.

[12.] Oddly, cyborg theorists quote Audre Lorde at length on difference, but ignore her work in *The Cancer Journals*. Is it because she refused to join them, to become a cyborg?

Nataf's theory that 'surgical mutation' (1997: 188) leads to 'new erotogenic zones' (ibid.) is not borne out for women recovering from mastectomies and being straightjacketed into prostheses (Batt 1996: 230–232).

Another important theme for cyborg theorists is that '. . . cyborg identity is predicated on transgressed boundaries'. (Mitchell 1995: 32). This is familiar territory for anyone with a nodding acquaintance of queer theory or post-modernism. The distinction between inside/outside is destabilised (Fuss 1991), bodies become volatile (Grosz 1994) and Mitchell (1995: 31) goes so far as to query whether this represents a new relationship between the carbon/ silicon divide. But who, asks Vandana Shiva (1996), do the new boundaries serve? Globalisation is a transgressing of boundaries, as is the feeding of carnivorous foods to herbivorous animals, as in the case of the transmission of Creutzfeldt Jacob's Disease and Mad Cow Disease through beef production. Transgression is not inherently positive. The transgression of colonisers on the lands of Indigenous peoples, breaking the connection between land and people, is not in the long-term interest of social justice. Nor is the breaking of the food chain (Shiva 1996). It makes me ask, why break the connection with the organic body in exchange for a machinic one?

Cyborg is built upon the fear of a body outside the norm, a body out of control. Instead of developing knowledge about one's body, about what makes it function well, feel well, create happiness or stress, the goal of a cyborg theorist is something like this:

> Think of yourself on some evening in the not-so-distant future, when wearable, fitted, and implanted electronic organs connected by bodynets are as commonplace as cotton; your intimate infrastructure connects you seamlessly to a planetful of bits, and you have software in your underwear (Mitchell 1995: 31).

Or:

> The machine is us, our processes, an aspect of our embodiment. We can be responsible for machines; *they* do not threaten us. We are responsible for boundaries; we are they (Haraway 1991: 180).

Without the origin stories of human culture, the cyborg machinic culture pretends it has no origin (see Haraway 1991: 173–181). It ignores the obvious: that machines and cyborgs are precisely originated by human minds and their genealogy can be traced through the scientific literature.[13] Cyborg theorists ignore the culturally determined origins of these machines, predominantly controlled and owned by white, elite male cultures.

The information revolution will not stop with your brain or your body. It includes the whole communications and biological sciences' search for a solution to:

> —*the translation of the world into a problem of coding*, a search for a common language in which all resistance to instrumental control disappears and all heterogeneity can be submitted to disassembly, reassembly, investment and exchange (Haraway 1991: 164).

Back in the world of organic bodies, this is precisely what the Human Genome Project is about. The Human Genome Project seeks to disassemble, reassemble, invest and exchange bits of bodies and information about those bodies (Klein 1996). How much simpler their task will be when we don body nets and surf the Internet. Everything they need to know about us will be relayed directly from our body and our computer to theirs. Simple really. This search for the 'whole explanation' has an extraordinarily universalist ring to it. As does the inclusivity, polymorphous perversity and commodified diversity. Similarly, these theorists of the cyborg constantly appeal to essentialism. In spite of Haraway's dismissal of essentialism, she falls into it herself, creating oppositional and essentialised cyborgian descriptors such as, 'without gender' (1991: 150), 'partiality', 'perversity', 'completely without innocence' (1991: 151) and speaking 'a powerful infidel heteroglossia' (1991: 181). These heterogeneous terms reflect the essential commonality of cyborgs: a diversity of exciting combinations of plant/animal/human/machinic components.

[13.] For the beginnings of an analysis of the prehistory of cyberculture, see Tofts and McKeich (1997: 22–24).

Cyborgs provide a haven for all those dominant culture theorists who have suddenly been left behind by their own reification of difference? How can you claim *difference* if you are a white (fe)male heterosexual cash-rich American? Answer: you claim your cyborg identity. You claim a cyborg consciousness derived from bodily extensions such as prostheses, guns, muscle building steroids, you can even use your wheelchair as a weapon. This is a new form of essentialism taken into the machinic body.

Cyborg consciousness is sanctioned, even fostered, and yet women organising as women (essentially speaking) and claiming a feminist consciousness, is not. The differences between cyborgs— and they are greater than the differences between women—are acceptable: from Arnold Schwarzeneggar to Stephen Hawking, on the one hand, to the new born baby with spina bifida and the elderly lesbian with a pacemaker, what could it be that they share that might be politically useful? My view is in sharp contrast to Haraway's notion that (1991: 150):

> . . . we are cyborgs. The cyborg is our ontology; it gives us our politics.

The cyborg is a redundant notion stripping us of politically useful categories. The word tends to obscure discussions around misuses of power instead of clarifying and giving us a key to work with. For, if we are all cyborgs, where do we locate the structures of oppression?

The greatest limitation of the idea of the cyborg, ultimately, is its meaninglessness. If, as these writers suggest, we are all cyborgs, then we might as well return to saying, we are all 'man' and from that 'all men are equal' but women, blacks, the disabled, lesbians, the poor, the aged just don't happen to be quite so equal. The so-called 'provisional difference' (Mitchell 1995: 31) is a matter of context.

Virtual Bodies

Virtual bodies exist in virtual reality. Virtual reality is generated through the use of graphics programs to create a three-dimensional computer-generated space that a user/participant interacts with and manipulates via wired peripherals (Balsamo 1996: 117).

The organic body wishing to manoeuvre in cyberspace must put on a headpiece with wired goggles which track the movement of the head. This, in turn, is connected to a computer with software which creates a simulation of 'reality', known as <u>virtual reality</u> or VR.[14]

English 12
Klein 9

It is instructive to look at the meaning of the word 'virtual'. It's a word made in heaven for the advertisers: the first part, *vir*, comes from the Latin word for man (the primary audience at this stage); then there's the shadow of *virtue* in the word, meaning all things good; and finally there's the effect part of the meaning: virtually there, all but there; as good as, says my dictionary. But this is where the age of my dictionary is showing. There's an advertising slipperiness to this word, because although the claim is that it is as good as, ('as white as'?) it isn't the thing, or the place it claims to be. Virtual truth is a lie. In virtual flight your feet are firmly on the ground.

Let's look further at virtual reality games, portrayals of virtual reality and a creeping phenomenon from the virtual to the real world, and see how they measure up.

I 'experienced'[15] one of these VR games in a game parlour in Adelaide. I was given a helmet and an object to hold in my hand. The woman showing me how to use it, pointed out that the bit I pressed with my thumb would make me go up and down (I was virtually flying) while the forefinger trigger was precisely that. I would be able to shoot at the virtual figures attacking me. I asked if there was a game without a gun. There wasn't. So I flew about, up and down, round about, constantly aware of the cord tangling around my feet (although I could not see this, I could feel it). I shot at three figures,

---

[14.] Most VR experience at this time is limited to using headgear not bodysuits, resulting in mental rather than physical experience.

[15.] I use quotes around the word 'experience' because it is not experience in the sense we are used to using the word. Unlike dream experiences there are no physical sensations of flying. In this sense, it is not an experience but rather a form of ersatz voyeurism. For more on cultural and spiritual voyeurism see Hawthorne (1989/1990; 1994/1995).

dressed like men(?) in armour. I 'killed' them and did quite well at the game for a novice. But two things mattered to me: 1) I wanted to 'experience' flying; but what had more impact on me was the 'experience' of shooting; 2) I'm not sure I could have 'shot' them, had these virtual figures been women. I found the experience deeply disturbing.

This <u>game has a context</u>. It also has a political meaning.

Mueller 13

In the classic representation of a body in virtual space, the character Jobe Smith, in *Lawnmower Man*, is in fact much the same body as Leonardo da Vinci's Vitruvian Man. Jobe is a blonde-haired, blue-eyed Aryan (and clearly a reincarnation of the Biblical Job). Both bodies, Leonardo's and Jobe's, are white western men. Imagine a man from the Congo forest, a Japanese woman, a Polynesian man, an Aboriginal woman, or indeed an old lesbian or a disabled body, in the place of this white western male body? Could the audience[16] identify with this representation? Could such a movie gain cult status?

Interestingly, in *Lawnmower Man 2: Beyond Cyberspace*, Jobe has lost both his legs and initially also his mind. What is the point in creating such an anti-hero? The Biblical roots of the story give us a clue. Think of it as a Bible class. In the film the character who runs the Virtual Light Company (he's the baddie—the devil—Lucifer,[17] if you like!) says:

> Since the superhighway has left people feeling isolated, the Virtual Light Company will create a continuous cultural flow.

Such have been the promises of evangelist Christians setting out to convert the world to one homogenised religion, a universalist fantasy. Not only that but Jobe refers at one stage to:

> . . . the womb of cyberspace.

---

16. Mark Slouka points out that that unlike the effect of real experience, the effect of represented experience, including virtual experience, is an 'homogenizing force' which turns us 'from individuals to an audience' (Slouka 1995: 148).

17. Lucifer comes from the Latin for light.

This is rather like the birth of Jesus: of woman born, but not of woman made.

And he promises transcendence,[18] bodilessness in saying:

> The material world will fly away.

At the climax of the film, Jobe says of himself:

> I've become the chip.[19]

Then he engages in a sword fight. This is so clearly an image for fans of *Dungeons and Dragons* games (a very materially-based, medieval style game that is the basis of MUDs), that one wonders where the cyber- went.

So here we have two movies, each claiming to represent a new world, falling back on clichés, images and retellings from the Bible, the medieval period and the renaissance.[20]

None of this feels very new.

William Mitchell (1995: 37) describes the relationship between the virtual world and the real world as one in which it is now possible to 'experience' phenomenal motion without any actual motion. That is, experience of motion is disconnected from physical movement. Mitchell claims that this is a loophole in Newton's laws. But the experience is virtual. Newton was talking of real world laws.

Virtual reality, it is claimed, is more than simple simulation. Virtual reality is presented as potentially liberatory:

> The ability to represent oneself—if only virtually—as another kind of body may be liberatory for those who have been traditionally defined only as feminine and natural bodies (Sofia 1995: 158).

---

18. For more on *Lawnmower Man* and transcendence, see Springer (1996). Springer notes how the figure of Jobe changes, he is transformed from an unmasculine figure into a hypermasculine one '. . . once his mind has been detached from his body in virtual reality'. (1996: 93)

19. William Mitchell (1995: 31) describes this as a crossing over of the 'carbon/silicon divide'.

20. The Renaissance is ill-named, as many feminists have pointed out: men had a renaissance; women had a witch-burning.

Mueller 13
Mitchell, excited by the possibilities of VR claims that <u>immersive</u> multimedia will be equivalent to 'being there' (1995: 20).[21] Or perhaps it will become a new form of shapeshifting.[22]

> Postmodern bodies can shapeshift. In many cyberspace games, players are invited to configure their bodies and identities themselves from a selection of parts. In some games the most interesting body parts cost more. Art reflects life (Clarke 1995: 147).

One must ask, precisely what kinds of body parts are the most interesting? And is it surprising that this point was made to Clarke by Sandy Stone, a man who chose to replace his male body parts with female ones? But loss and replacement of body parts is not always the result of choice: breast cancer, for example, and victims of road accidents who incur the <u>loss of limbs</u>, create very different experiences.

Klein 9
One of the persistent themes of virtual reality and cyberspace existence is that genders are flexible, perhaps even non-existent. A great deal of discussion focuses on gender bending and its power for good or evil. But what is the difference between gender swapping electronically and masked actors in a Greek, Japanese or Shakespearian theatre? One must ask, how is this any more subversive? It can happen only in certain circumstances (electronically/ theatrically); it is intended to subvert peoples' expectations. Nor is it significantly different from the make-up used in *Planet of the Apes* or indeed in any film where an actor ages noticeably. This is grandstanding hype and not useful.

While Zoë Sofia claims that email reduces the self to text (1995: 159), Anne Balsamo says that it makes no sense to ask 'whose reality or perspective is *represented* in cyberspace' (1995: 14). But

---

[21.] From my experience of multimedia, virtual reality and the interactive edge of the Internet, it has always been very clear to me where I am. For the technology to create a sense of 'being there' it still has a long way to go.

[22.] Shapeshifting is about power. In its mythical use, shapeshifters possessed power. Zeus transformed himself into a swan in order to rape Leda. Shapeshifting, like transgressing boundaries, is not always a force for good.

who has created the space of cyberspace?[23] Cyberspace and virtual reality are no more gender-, race-, sexuality-, ablewise-neutral than the real world. If one takes a Lawnmower man-style-trip through virtual reality as an example: who put the asteroids and meteors there? Some programmer who grew up watching *Star Trek*? Why is it that all virtual spaces that I have seen to date are composed of grids? Is this simply a matter of the limits of the technology at present?[24] I can create more interesting visual worlds in my own mind, why would I want to inhabit someone else's world when it is less rich?

Jaron Lanier, one of the key developers of VR has said: 'whatever the physical world has, virtual reality has as well' (Balsamo 1996: 117).

Including rape and violence against women.

> . . . in *Night Trap*, a video game recently popular among prepubescent boys, vampires drill holes into the necks of barely clad female victims and hang them from meat hooks (Slouka 1996: 6).

So what's different? *Hustler* and other pornographic magazines have used images of this kind in their magazines.[25] Slouka continues:

> Virtual reality (coming soon to a modem near you) will allow you to be the vampire. To inflict pain [to have the virtual experience of power]. Without responsibility. Without consequences.[26] The punctured flesh will heal at the touch of a button, the scream disappear into cyberspace. You'll be able to resurrect the digital dead [is this another Jesus tale?] and kill them again (Slouka 1996: 6).

What is not clear is why the incorporeal world of the Net is so good? If we had no bodies, could we understand the metaphor of the Net?

[23.] It is wellknown that the Internet is a by-product of the US military, and the military visits sites which it identifies as 'subversive'.

[24.] It seems unlikely that the technology is limited in this way, since Roehl *et al.* in *Late Night VRML 2.0 with Java* describe how to create curved surfaces (1997: 373–406).

[25.] To take another mythical sidetrack, the ancient Sumerians had a myth about the goddess Inanna who enters the underworld, is stripped of everything and hung from a meat hook for three days.

[26.] For more on inconsequential behaviour see Diamond (1994).

Cyberspace depends for its existence on real space, real time, real bodies. Without space/time/bodies the cyber- is inconceivable. It is a metaphor—not a place. Similarly, immersive spaces are not real, and the body's 'experience' is not real. Rather, when immersing ourselves in virtual space 'we actively create belief' (Murray 1997: 110), just as we do when attending the theatre or reading a novel. And, as Balsamo concludes, the:

> *conceptual* denial of the body is accomplished through the *material* repression of the physical body (1996: 123).

Perhaps more disturbing for optimistic feminists who believe that men can effect changes in their own lives, is a report in *Time* magazine where the 'repression of the physical body' has been taken to an extreme.

English 12
Klein 9

I thought I was reading about a real woman, <u>Kyoko Date</u>.[27]

The Ideal Dream Girl turns out to be a 'virtual date' and 'virtual data' created by:

> More than a dozen computer graphic (CG) artists [who] have toiled for 20 months to perfect different aspects of the Date character—the way she moves, speaks and sings. By borrowing cutting-edge CG technology perfected in the US for recent movies like *Casper*, Date's creators plan to superimpose her on film and in videos used in stage shows (Kunii 1996: 75).

Date has grown out of an '$11 billion-a-year arcade and software game market' (Kunii 1996: 75). The games, developed by Gainax, have already had their first-generation run of 'virtual relationship games' and have sold over 200,000 copies since 1991. The producers are predicting 'no shortage of boyfriends' for Date. 'Real ones' (Kunii 1996: 75). The potential boyfriends:

> Know what they are going to get: a babe with short-cropped reddish-black hair who will *never grow old*, never be caught with drugs and *always do as she's told* (Kunii 1996: 75, my emphasis).

[27.] The Japanese are well aware that American boys will read 'her' last name as 'date', but the word is acceptable Japanese pronounced da-te (rhymes with bla-sé). It could also be read as 'data', which is precisely what 'she' is.

The Ideal Dream Girl: Japan's next pop starlet has perfect pitch and looks—and a virtually assured future (Kunii 1996: 75)

And what will this mean for the 'real' girlfriends of boys who learn about relationships from a computer screen by relating to someone who will 'always do as she's told'?

Some men have just begun to learn new skills in the area of emotions. Just when they begin to, along come such games which promise to emotionally deskill them.

Mueller 13

And it's not just in the area of emotions that this is happening. Proponents of VR claim that the audience authors the experience and that it 'holds great promise for enhancing visual thinking' (Rheingold 1992: 251). But there seems to be no knowledge of prior traditions of visual thinking which we can create simply by closing our eyes, using our minds—and there are a number of frequently used gateways for such experiences such as meditation, use of drugs and visualisation techniques.

Are we being deskilled in yet another area? Mentally and emotionally deskilled through the widespread use of VR technologies. What might be the purpose of this deskilling? Perhaps one of them is the crisis in capitalism. VR is the commodification of the mind's processes. No more free lunches for you. No more daydreaming allowed. Put on those goggles and headgear, pay $5 and slip into someone else's trip. VR, of course, will make much more money than ordinary old real world methods of thinking, relating, visualising.

As Robert Markley, a critic of Virtual Reality, points out:

> . . . the experience of Virtual Reality is intended to send us back to the real reality with a heightened appreciation of the exploitability of our environment. Cyberspace is the ultimate capitalist fantasy (Markley 1996: 74).

This brings us back to the issue of context. If we become so out of touch with ourselves—our bodies and our minds—and we become completely fragmented psychologically—all that swapping of identities and genders—and further that we hardly move from our computer screens inside the house, let alone into the garden or the wilderness—who and what will we be? Where will our feminism be?

What of our notions of ecological sustainability? Will we know anything about the 'real world'? Will we know what sand, mud and snow feel like? Will we know the wide expanse of blue sky, or the curve of the horizon at sea, and what of the intricate processes of birth, growth and death that happen all around us every day?

Instead, we will see the inside of an ant's nest with programs developed from cameras that have travelled down the tunnels to the queen's chamber; we will know how many teeth a tiger has; we will be able to take a virtual tour of Jupiter (Holtzman 1994: 207); and see how photosynthesis occurs in a rainforest. But will we recognise the ant or tiger when it bites us? Will we have any rainforest to stand in, or Earth to live on? Perhaps, by staying out of 'nature' it will have time to regenerate, but what impact this will have on our psyches.[28] As Michael Heim has described the symptoms of Alternate World Syndrome (AWS), after three hours in VR the body experiences:

> . . . an acute form of body amnesia which can become chronic Alternate World Disorder (AWD). Frequent virtuality can lead to ruptures of the kinesthetic from the visual senses of self-identity (Heim 1995: 67).

The experience he describes means that VR will not put us more in touch with ourselves and our bodies, but rather rupture the engagement of the body with itself. The extent to which such symptoms can be modified will depend on how expendable people become.

Likewise, just as aeroplanes, cars and trains have transformed our experience of time by disengaging from place through velocity, cyberspace transforms our experience of space by disengaging it from time. In cyberspace there is neither time nor space. The touch of a finger on a keyboard or a mouse brings to one's own living room any place on the globe (which is networked). There is no scenery to glimpse, even; there is no place to be, no there there. It could be anywhere: anyone, any time of day or night, anywhere. The external velocity of vehicles has its analogue in the internal velocity of cyberspace.

[28.] A newspaper article appeared in late 1996 with the title 'Save your habitat with virtual nature' (Lovell 1996: 3).

And Boyer notes:

> ... it becomes increasingly difficult to extract oneself and to gain perspective on or acknowledge the mundane reality of here and now. 'The virtual' represents a complete world: it saturates one's imagination. There is a kind of violence that 'the virtual' exercises on the user's sensibility (Boyer 1996: 55).

This reflects my experience in a simulator which I happened upon at a local community festival. It involved sitting in a darkened capsule which tilted in time to the visual program. The visuals simulated the experience of riding a big dipper through the Grand Canyon.

Walking out from the experience of a simulator there is a sense of disorientation in the external world. The body which has been simulated into experiencing the acceleration of a big dipper wants, on exiting, to move at a fast pace and yet this pace has no context or purpose in the real world.

It is obvious from this that cybernature will not easily replace real nature as a place of relaxation, regeneration, or even ecotourism. Indeed, the presuppositions of cyberspace are in direct conflict with those of VR developers. As Robert Markley points out Virtual Reality is 'antiecological' (1996: 75). It presupposes 'infinite productivity' (*ibid.*) and in its desire for bodilessness and transcendence it aims for immortality.[29] The structures of power remain the same, and, as we have seen, so do the prevailing images and narratives. The world being made in cyberspace, the virtual world, corresponds to a frozen image of the real world which ceased to exist decades, centuries and millennia ago. None of the CG artists involved in the development of these technologies seem to have any understanding of history, of politics, of power, let alone of feminism. They are creating a world without consequences (Slouka 1995), and—despite the hyperbole —a world without a future.

[29.] Steven Holtzman (1994: 220) writes about 'creativity after death' and of the film *Brainstorm* (1993) in which a 'recording of making love is edited and looped for the experience of a continuous orgasm.' He then comments, '*The ultimate recorded experience is of transcendence after death*' (1994: 209).

> . . . what these VR encounters really provide is an illusion of control over[30] reality, nature and especially over the unruly gender and race-marked, essentially mortal body (Balsamo 1996: 127).

If we begin to spend all our time in the atopic environments of cyberspace, and we ignore what is going on in our local communities, we will lose all connection to the things that make us who we are: knowledge of our own particular local conditions; personal 'interactive' knowledge of real people; knowledge of our own and our local histories. Without these distinguishing features we run the risk of becoming the 'grey people' Ursula Le Guin writes about in *The Lathe of Heaven*.

Direct experience has become passé, the ideology of the future suggests that in some future time all experience will be mediated, either by virtual <u>immersion</u>[31] or by donning body suits (Mitchell 1995: 31) which will tell us our body temperature, heart rate, level of perspiration or stress. We will no longer have to listen to our bodies, no longer know the feel of a cool breeze on perspiring skin, no longer need to be aware at all; instead machines will do the listening and telling for us. But if learning is based on experience, direct experience, then we will be lesser beings, perhaps we will no longer feel sympathy for the refugee who is starving. We will become submissive to the noise of the machine, responsive only to electronic messages, ignorant of emotion.[32] The fake recuperability of virtual characters (Slouka 1995) will desensitise us to real suffering and pain. We will be silent and silenced.

English 12
Mueller 13

Boyer has referred to this process of detachment as 'delocalising signs of both language and sight.' And Italo Calvino has referred to the corruption of our imaging through

---

[30.] For more on the illusion of control and especially over unruly and wild bodies see Hawthorne (1996a); for further discussions of control see Diamond (1994), Hawthorne and Klein (1996), Klein and Hawthorne (1995) and Klein and Hawthorne (1996).

[31.] For an extensive discussion of some of the possibilities see Murray (1997).

[32.] For more on emotion see Hawthorne (1996b) and Kunii (1996).

. . . a flood of prefabricated images . . . We are bombarded today [1988] by such a quantity of images that we can no longer distinguish direct experience from what we have seen for a few seconds on television (Calvino 1988: 75).

And this was before the Internet, multimedia, cyberspace, virtual reality and simulators.

The most interesting program I have encountered in the literature is Brenda Laurel and Rachel Strickland's *Placeholder*. Unlike other VR, where disembodiment is the key feature, this one:

> requires the user to choose one of four totemic animals[33] in which to be embodied. If the user chooses Crow, she negotiates the virtual terrain by flying; if Snake, her vision shifts to infrared as she moves by crawling (Hayles 1996: 35).

And:

> if a woman in the crow's body spreads her arms she sees her crow wings extend and her perspective changes as her crow body lifts off the ground. By swooping and banking appropriately she can take a flight along a waterfall (Murray 1997: 61).

The simulation is complex, requiring ten computers and some suggest that it will never make it to a marketable product.[34] This is odd talk for the VR industry who are usually taken by big products. Could it be that the marketers are more interested in disembodiment than embodiment? In passivity rather than engagement?

It appears that VR research is not focused on replicating the complexity of reality or even the possibilities of complex play. No one mentions modelling economic systems. It's the complexity of our real lives—real worlds, reality—that makes life interesting. Virtual worlds *must* ignore complexity in order to keep the experience of distance (Murray 1997: 100). But VR should not be confused with reality.

---

33. I worry, however, about the appropriation of Native American culture.

34. The VNS Matrix interactive, ALL NEW GEN, found financing their product difficult. The Idaho boy again? See VNS Matrix: 1998.

I can see uses for the technology in designing women-friendly cities and houses, for practising a foreign language, for simply having access to new experiences, including having fun. Certainly a different focus for VR has been suggested. Firstly by Brenda Laurel, and secondly by interactive narrative theorist, Janet Murray. Murray writes that with increasing advances in the technologies (including a more varied content, beyond fighting and killing games), flexibility, and reduced encumbrances (such as cords):

> interactors will be lured into worlds where they float and tumble, and arc through thrillingly colored spaces, fly through imaginary clouds, and swim lazily across welcoming mountain ponds (Murray 1997: 263).

But even with the dream or projection of increased technological sophistication, how far can it really take us? Will the new emperor be without clothes *and without a body*? Immateriality (Woodward 1994: 50) is a dream of progress, transcendence of the body an old story, nearly always male-centred. What would a virtual reality constructed along woman-centred lines be? What if the virtual world were populated by gynoids instead of androids? What would a virtual reality constructed according to an Aboriginal perspective be? What could virtual reality constructed by a blind or deaf or physically disabled person be? These are questions needing to be asked, and answered.

As Balsamo (1996: 131) points out:

> Cyberspace offers white men an enticing retreat from the burdens of their *cultural* identities.

Organic Bodies

With the advent of the women's movement in the 1960s and 1970s women organised politically around their bodies. The areas where activists have worked hard to change the culture include rape and all kinds of violence against women, the building of knowledge and respect for women's say in when and how they reproduce, building strength around sexuality, wellbeing and physical health. The women's movement has also been a place where women who did not fit, or who had rebelled against, feminine or cultural norms, were accepted and respected. This extended to differences of skin colour, culture, class, ability/mobility, age, sexual preference, body shape and size, body hair.[35] Landmark books have been written in all these areas, including the now iconic, *Our Bodies, Ourselves*.

The last decade has seen a widespread move in academic circles to undermine the importance of the *organic* connection women have developed in feminist theory. The charge of <u>essentialism</u> has been used as a mechanism to silence activists and radical feminists, a fear tactic which went hand-in-hand with representing those groups who built projects on commonality across cultures, ages, sexualities as 'dinosaur' politics, and being presented as exclusionary and divisive. The Lesbian Space Project in Sydney had to specify that membership was open to women-born lesbians[36] and with a subsequent inclusionary definition (including transsexuals), the Project failed as lesbians stayed away in droves.[37] Post-modern theorists are fascinated by the transgression of boundaries in theoretical bodies. Queer theorists pursue polymorphous perversity, and VR buffs just wish they could get rid of that 'excess baggage' (Balsamo 1996: 125), the organic body.

Theorising the body is not new, Mary Douglas in *Natural Symbols* wrote:

Klein 9

[35.] My own experience with an invisible disability informs this claim (see Hawthorne 1996 and 1999). With my own involvement extending back to 1973, I was constantly amazed at the diversity of the movement in its early years. The first meeting in Melbourne was organised by four women, three with working-class migrant backgrounds and one middle-class Anglo woman (D'Aprano 1995). Aboriginal women took the lead in a number of issues of critical importance to them, including childcare and health (Hawthorne and Klein 1994).

[36.] Transsexuals are perfectly free to raise their own money for their own space, rather than gatecrashing the lesbians' party.

[37.] For documentation of similar events in North America, where the word woman is erased, see O'Hartigan (1999). She makes the interesting comment:

. . . the actual oppression of real women is minimized by means of an almost psychotic break with reality in which the physical nature of sex is overwhelmed by the theoretical 'deconstruction' of gender (O'Hartigan 1999: 9).

The social body constrains the way the physical body is perceived. The physical experience of the body, always modified by the social categories through which it is known, sustains a particular view of society. There is continual exchange of meanings between the two kinds of bodily experience so that each reinforces the categories of the other (Douglas 1978: 93).

Indeed, it was these very constraints which feminists perceived and acted upon in order to change the cultural norms. In spite of this, epidemics of anorexia/bulimia ravage populations of teenage girls; cosmetic surgery is offered to women whose bodies sag in all the usual places; magazine diets, beauty tips and body decorations are offered as the latest fashion accoutrements to all women and now we have the possibility of a bodyless body in cyberspace.

Members of the Performing Older Women's Circus (POW Circus)[38] have decided to keep their bodies. POW's members are women over forty years of age and the circus was established in Melbourne, Australia in January 1995. The members learn skills at their own pace and are limited only by the availability of trainers, the cost of equipment and the constant shortage of funds. Women in their sixties have learnt clowning, have learnt to walk on stilts, do inverted double balances, base or fly in three high group balances. In addition, others in the circus—the young forty and fifty-year-olds— have learnt to climb ropes and do tricks on them, have learnt aerials routines and sequences on trapezes and cloudswings, group bicycle riding, roller blading, juggling, clowning and manipulation of flags, sticks and fire clubs. And the entire group participates in theatrical performance. A dedicated group of musicians provides an eclectic range of musical scores.

[38.] The aims of POW Circus are:
  To challenge ageism and ageist assumptions.
  To promote wellbeing and fitness for women over 40 regardless of ethnicity, class, previous experience or physical abilities.
  To provide a supportive environment for older women to learn new skills.
  To uphold feminist principles.
  To recognise lesbian visibility.
  To have fun and work safely.

But perhaps POW Circus needs to redefine itself, with stilts, roller blades, ropes and trapezes as cyborg extensions: is it really a cyborg circus?

Our bodies may be culturally inscribed, even limited by our previous opportunities, but that doesn't mean that we cannot set out to subvert and challenge those cultural determinations. As Catherine Itzin points out:

> Ageism is usually regarded as being something that affects the lives of older people. Like ageing, however, it affects every individual from birth onward—at every stage putting limits and constraints on experience, expectations, relationships and opportunities.[39] Its divisions are as arbitrary as those of race, gender, class and religion. (Itzin 1986, cited in Woodward 1994: 47).

Ageism, and a persistent denial of mortality, can be found in some of the hip post-modern writings on cyborgs. Hans A Scheirl (1997: 49), for example, in his 'Manifesto for the dada of the cyborg-embrio', writes: 'Age is dispersed & reversed'. Such fantasies of immortality are not unusual in cyberculture, and they do not serve to change prejudicial attitudes towards ageing, particularly attitudes towards women's ageing. It is at this locus that the women in POW Circus do challenge conventional attitudes. Without seeing POW Circus one might imagine a group of highly athletic older women who are in denial about ageing, and who fear the crumbling and disintegration of the human body. Nothing could be further from the truth. The members of POW cover a huge range of physical abilities and disabilities. While illness—including terminal illness—is something many members have confronted.

POW Circus members do not set out to change their bodies into something reminiscent of youth culture, and although fitness is valued it is not a prerequisite. Nor is any prior experience of circus skills. Unlike the singularly physical culture of bodybuilding (see

---

[39.] As Bangladeshi feminist, Farida Akhter (1996), has pointed out, childhood development has been so commodified that every six to twelve month period is marked by new toys, as though the tooth won't come out on its own.

POW Circus Acrobalance,
Lee Williams and Claire Warren
(Helen Killmier)

POW Circus Clowns:
Maureen O'Connor
and Mary Daicos

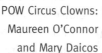

POW Circus Aerials:
Claire Warren and
Susan Hawthorne

Balsamo 1996: 41–55), where women pose in tiny skin-hugging bikinis and are judged by men who define whether they have gone too far (Bev Francis) or that they remain 'powder puffs' albeit 'a really strong powder puff' (Rachel McLish), (Balsamo 1996: 49) women in POW Circus define their own limits and their own abilities. The community theatre aspect of POW Circus means that the audience is particularly responsive, and effort often gets as much applause as technique. In one instance, a forty-seven-year-old per-former climbing a rope in the show was encouraged by cheers and whoops from both audience and co-performers to reach the roof. Each night she climbed higher, breaking her own personal bests and culminating a year of consistent training which shifted her from ground dweller to climber.

Circus combines physical culture with theatrical culture. It draws together disparate and conflicting 'norms'. Add to that a good dose of feminist irreverence and anti-ageist intentions and you have a powerful and challenging outcome.

The culture of athleticism is sometimes subverted in the shows by POW. This is particularly so in the clowning sequences where physical prowess is undermined by humour in mimed weight-lifting routines, olympics which favour the ridiculous over the competent, or overcoming the fear of heights associated with climbing ladders. In the group balances, humour is generated when the whole structure built by the performers collapses as the last woman is about to add herself to the well-balanced edifice. The collapse is in turn undermined by the fact that the last woman is standing on the shoulders of another woman. This is not how 'old women' are expected to act.

The first show put on by POW was called 'Act Your Age'[40] and used chants of 'act your age' and 'don't act your age' throughout the show as a way to underline and subvert the dominant expectations.

[40.] Performed at the Footscray Community Arts Centre, Melbourne on 8 and 9 March 1995. Footscray is an inner-West suburb in Melbourne with working-class and recent migrants making up much of its constituency.

The second[41] documented the history of the women's movement from the 1960s to the 1990s. Through the use of a skeleton narrative, fleshed out by movement, light, sound and humour. Both shows took the ageing body as their starting point, on the one hand looked at synchronically, on the other, diachronically. Recent shows[42] have looked at the history and rituals of women, and of lesbians,[43] using movement and metaphor to carry the momentum of the show. In 1999, the International Year of the Older Person, POW will once again be exploring the theme of falls and debility in old age in a show entitled 'Balancing Acts'.

Every show done by POW ends with an age-line: each member steps forward and calls out her age. Beginning with the youngest member (currently forty-one) and ending with the oldest (currently sixty-nine), this part of the show frequently brings tears to the eyes of the audience.

The representations of age and women in our culture are subverted by the sheer existence of POW Circus. It counters the forces which tell us that our bodies are 'excess baggage', imperfect, uncontrollable, unruly and our feminism essentialist and founded on organic connection. Furthermore, engagement with one another and with the physical and mental self is highlighted. When you are participating in a pyramid with four or ten or twenty other women, everyone has to be 'wholly present to one another' (Case 1996: 156). You cannot afford to be a dissipated self, a self so disunited as

---

[41.] 'Still Revolting'. Performed at the Footscray Community Arts Centre, Melbourne on 29 February and 1, 2, 6 and 7 March 1996.

[42.] 'Every Witch Way'. Performed Melbourne on 28–30 November, 1996. 'Unstopped Mouths' Performed Melbourne on 30 and 31 October and 1 November, 1997. The script of 'Unstopped Mouths' can be found in Hawthorne, Dunsford and Sayer (1997). 'Tarot over the Top'. This show was dedicated to a founding member of POW who died just before the show's season began. Performed Melbourne, 24–26 September 1998. All Performances of the annual show have been at the Footscray Community Arts Centre. Other shows have been taken to suburban and rural centres.

Hawthorne
19

[43.] Lesbian visibility is one of the aims of POW and it informs the style and content of the shows. POW includes heterosexual performers and their experiences and needs are also incorporated into shows.

to be incapable of being 'present to itself' as Iris Young (1990: 310) argues. When two women are performing a sequence of tricks on a trapeze three metres above the ground, both have to be 'wholly present to one another' (Case 1996: 156.). Indeed, the importance of engagement, respect, and complicity[44] cannot be underrated. An increasing awareness of the body accompanies training which takes the woman past previous experiences of her body. Overcoming fear, even terror, as well as performance anxiety and self-consciousness are hurdles which most members who participate for any length of time have to confront.

Learning to be *in* the body is one of the advantages of circus skills training. Learning to be *with* other bodies, in an engagement of trust is one of the advantages of improvisational theatre techniques. Put the two together and you have an emotionally powerful, physically charged combination. It is one where intimacy is taken for granted through close physical contact with others, while social contact proceeds in much the same mosaically rich way, with some women becoming friends, others retaining a more distant relationship.

The approach to physical activity taken by POW members is in stark contrast to commodified exercise provided in commercial gyms. Community[45] is central for POW, and engendering respect for one another whatever the limitations is another. The intention is to work in safety and have fun. This is very different from the aims of some commercial gym owners who envisage extending VR applications for sport and fitness.

The design of cyberspaces for sports is based on market forces, so that sporting decks will generally have sophisticated props, like recombinant bicycles and inclined treadmills, and sporting houses will make money by renting time on those decks. The purpose of cyberspace for sports is not just to help people have fun and stay fit. It is also to help keep sporting

---

[44.] Complicity is an important element in any kind of theatre which incorporates some improvisation. Women's Circus Artistic Director, Sarah Cathcart has influenced POW, some of whom are members of both circuses.

[45.] For more on community circus, see Liebmann *et al.* (1997). It was the Women's Circus which first gave impetus to the founding of POW Circus.

houses in business, by keeping their decks full of players (Randal Walser cited in Balsamo 1996: 121).

So, the gym will be a place where one continues to walk the tread-mill, but perhaps through a virtual environment such as mountains, deserts or shopping malls, purchasing as you walk. The cyberbody can only get fit if it is actually exercising the real life muscles. The prospect of cyberexercise on, say a trapeze, would help the exerciser learn some new tricks. But even if she can learn through a process of virtual visualisation or virtual simulation, her real life muscles also need training or she simply won't have sufficient strength to do the things she'd like to do. And with the starting price for a VR home installation at around US$250,000 there won't be many of us with a virtual rowing machine or bicycle in our homes, or even in our local community centres! This is elitist culture, often also escapist. But unlike the ingestion of hallucinogenic drugs, which at least are generated by one's own chemical processes, VR is someone else's trip. And at this time, that trip is male-defined, male-generated and male-limited. In contrast to the hype that VR is 'focused primarily on the subjective and expressive dimensions', it is, in fact, neither sub-jective nor expressive. It is packaged entertainment for the mainly male market.

For my own money, I'd rather go and have fun with a group of old organic bodies, who can laugh and clown and encourage me to go that one step further.

Virtual and cyborg bodies glorify <u>cosmetic and transgressive surgery</u>. Sex-change operations lead the charge and it opens up the possibility of age-change operations (Woodward 1994: 57). Such man-made operations and bodily determinations will do nothing to eliminate sexism, racism and ageism (among others) in our culture. They lead, instead, to the notion of disconnectedness from the world, from the limitations of a non-expanding planet, and to a collective awareness of our connections to other forms of organic and inorganic elements. The subversive use of our bodies, on the other hand, challenges the norms which dominate our global culture.

Klein 9

Conclusion

Cyborg bodies and virtual bodies are bodies moving in the wrong direction. The cyborg may be 'unnatural and aberrant' (Hayles 1995: 323), it may incorporate male and female subjects, it 'unites' Black and white, hetero- and homo-, rich and some lucky poor by focusing on the machinic elements, while white-washing organic and culturally determined differences. Like queer, it contains a grab bag of identities, polymorphously perverse. Cyborg theory sidesteps the issue of disability, seeing the prosthesis rather than the person. It heightens the fashionableness of transsexualism, and pays no attention to politics. So inclusive is cyborg, that it ceases to have any use or meaning. As I sit here at my computer screen, I am a cyborg (see Hayles 1995: 322).

Virtual reality, we are told:

> will represent the greatest event in human evolution. For the first time mankind [sic] will be able to deny reality and substitute its own preferred version (J.G. Ballard [cited on the back of *Virtual Reality* by Howard Rheingold]).

So we 'will be able to *deny reality*'. We will be able to deny the processes of growth and ageing which are the fate of any organism. We'll be able to deny nature, stay young forever, imagine we are the powerful conquerors of the latest mainstream computer game. Is this all there is? Ballard avoids the issue of whose 'preferred version' will be available, by using the innocuous 'its'. But we know from decades of feminist analysis whose version will be available globally and at the cheapest price.

With virtual reality, 'we are offered the vision of a body-free universe.' (Balsamo 1996: 127). A universe created from the culturally determined imagery of elite (mostly) white (mostly young) men. The virtual world is a pale imitation of the real world.

> Virtual bodies have no status in the real world, light cannot pass through a virtual body, can have no impact on it. Nor is the virtual body affected by heat, rain, the smell of a rose. It is a body without heart (Klein and Hawthorne 1996: 90).

Indeed, it is a bodyless body. In Latin, real women's bodies were the *matrix*, the mother word doubled—*mater* with a feminine ending (Walker 1993: 619), the connecting tissue, the organic matter which provided humans with life. Once a direct term, now a metaphor for any kind of connectivity or for words to do with measurement. A mathematical matrix is one made up of numbers, and in computers of the binaries, one and zero. Virtual bodies are imaginary bodies transformed by metaphor into numbers!

Can you imagine the day:

when you get up and put on your headphones and sensor gloves?
when you'll wear wear smart sneakers to circus practice?
when you will inhabit your own private digital environment?
when you'll wear a new kind of body matrix?
and finally have a room of your own in cyberspace?

But there is still one problem: the real world—the world where the free market holds sway; where poverty, starvation, homelessness and refugee status afflict many women and children; where women in the so-called Third World are paid appalling rates to make the electronic appliances used to create cyborg and virtual selves; where elites ensure that the marginalised will never have the resources to topple them—the real world permeates every aspect of the virtual world we can think of. And so, if social justice does not prevail in the real world, how could we be so naïve as to think it might just happen in cyberspace?

References

Akhter, Farida. 1996. People or Population. Oral presentation, 'People or Population', University of Melbourne, 30 April.

Balsamo, Anne. 1996. *Technologies of the Gendered Body: Reading cyborg women.* Durham and London: Duke University Press.

Batt, Sharon. 1996. *Patient No More: The politics of breast cancer.* Melbourne: Spinifex Press; Charlottetown: gynergy books, 1994; London: Scarlet Press, 1994.

Bell, Diane and Renate Klein (Eds.), 1996. *Radically Speaking: Feminism reclaimed.* London: Zed Books: Melbourne: Spinifex Press.

Bender, Gretchen and Timothy Druckrey (Eds.), 1994. *Culture on the Brink: Ideologies of technology.* Seattle: Bay Press.

Boston Women's Health Collective. 1984. *The New Our Bodies Ourselves.* New York: Simon and Schuster.

Boyer, M. Christine. 1996. *CyberCities: Visual perception in the age of electronic communication.* New York: Princeton Architectural Press.

Case, Sue-Ellen. 1996. *The Domain-Matrix: Performing lesbian at the end of print culture.* Bloomington and Indianapolis: Indiana University Press.

Clarke, Adele. 1995. Modernity, postmodernity, and reproductive processes, ca. 1890–1990, or 'Mommy, where do cyborgs come from anyway?' In Chris Hables Gray (Ed.), *The Cyborg Handbook.* New York and London: Routledge.

D'Aprano, Zelda. 1995. *Zelda.* Melbourne: Spinifex Press.

Diamond, Irene. 1994. *Fertile Ground.* Boston: Beacon Press.

Douglas, Mary. 1978. *Natural Symbols.* Harmondsworth: Penguin Books.

Fletcher, Beryl. 1996. *The Silicon Tongue.* Melbourne: Spinifex Press.

Frye, Marilyn. 1983. To Be and Be Seen: The Politics of Reality. In Marilyn Frye *The Politics of Reality: Essays in feminist theory* (152–174). Trumansburg, NY: The Crossing Press.

Fuss, Diana. (Ed.), 1991. *Inside/Outside: Lesbian theories, gay theories.* London and New York: Routledge.

Gibson, William. 1984. *Neuromancer.* New York: Ace Books.

Golding, Sue (author/editor), 1997. *The Eight Technologies of Otherness.* London: Routledge.

González, Jennifer. 1995. Envisioning Cyborg Bodies: Notes from current research. In Chris Hables Gray (Ed.), *The Cyborg Handbook.* New York and London: Routledge.

Gray, Chris Hables. (Ed.), 1995. *The Cyborg Handbook.* New York and London: Routledge.

Grosz, Elizabeth. 1994. *Volatile Bodies: Toward a corporeal feminism.* Sydney: Allen and Unwin.

Haraway, Donna. 1989. *Primate Visions: Gender, race, and nature in the world of modern xcience.* New York and London: Routledge.

Haraway, Donna. 1991. A Cyborg Manifesto. In Donna Haraway *Simians, Cyborgs, and Women: The reinvention of nature.* New York and London: Routledge.

Hawthorne, Susan. 1989/1990. The Politics of the Exotic: The paradox of cultural voyeurism, *Meanjin, 48* Vol. (2) Australia; also published in *NWSA Journal*, USA, *1*, (4), Summer 1989; translated into German as Die Politik des Exotischen: Das Paradoxen des kulturellen Voyeurismus. *Beiträge 27: Geteilter Feminismus*, 109–119. Köln, Germany.

Hawthorne, Susan. 1994/1995. A Case of Spiritual Voyeurism. Review of *Mutant Message Down Under* by Marlo Morgan. *Feminist Bookstore News*. November; translated into German as Spiritueller Voyeurismus. Review of *Traumfänger* by Marlo Morgan. *Virginia*, Nr. 18, March.

Hawthorne, Susan. 1996a. From Theories of Indifference to a Wild Politics. In Diane Bell and Renate Klein (Eds.), 1996. *Radically Speaking: Feminism reclaimed*. Melbourne: Spinifex Press; London: Zed Books.

Hawthorne, Susan. 1996b. Virtual and Real Worlds. *Metro Magazine*. No. 108, November. 31–36.

Hawthorne, Susan. 1999. *Bird and other writings on epilepsy*. Melbourne: Spinifex Press.

Hawthorne, Susan and Renate Klein. (Eds.), 1994. *Australia for Women: Travel and culture*. Melbourne:Spinifex Press; New York: The Feminist Press.

Hawthorne, Susan and Renate Klein. 1996. Feminist Ethics, Sexuality and Population Control. In Margaret Winn, Mary Spongberg and Jan Larbalestier (Eds.), *Women, Culture, Sexuality*. Sydney: Women's Studies Centre, University of Sydney.

Hayles, N. Katherine. 1995. The Life cycle of cyborgs: Writing the posthuman. In Chris Hables Gray (Ed.), 1995. *The Cyborg Handbook*. New York and London: Routledge.

Hayles, N. Katherine. 1996. Boundary Disputes: Homeostasis, Reflexivity, and the Foundations of Cybernetics. In Robert Markley (Ed.), *Virtual Realities and Their Discontents*. Baltimore: The Johns Hopkins University Press.

Heim, Michael. 1995. The Design of Virtual Reality. *Body and Society: Cyberspace/Cyberbodies/Cyberpunk: Cultures of technological embodiment*, 1 (3–4) 65–77.

Hess, David J. 1995. On Low-Tech Cyborgs. In Chris Hables Gray (Ed.), *The Cyborg Handbook*. New York and London: Routledge.

Holtzman, Steven R. 1994. *Digital Mantras: The Languages of Abstract and Virtual Worlds*. Cambridge, MA: MIT Press.

Jeffreys, Sheila. 1993. *The Lesbian Heresy: Feminist Perspectives on the Lesbian Sexual Revolution*. Melbourne: Spinifix Press.

Klein, Renate. 1996. (Dead) Bodies Floating in Cyberspace. In Diane Bell and Renate Klein (Eds.), 1996. *Radically Speaking: Feminism reclaimed*. Melbourne: Spinifex Press; London: Zed Books.

Klein, Renate and Susan Hawthorne. 1996. Reclaiming Sisterhood: Radical Feminism as an Antidote to Theoretical Embodied Fragmentation of Women. In Magdalene Anj-Lygate, Chris Corrin and Milsom S. Henry (Eds.), *Desperately Seeking Sisterhood: Still challenging and building*. Washington: Taylor & Francis; London: Taylor & Francis, 1997.

Kunii, Irene M. 1996. The Ideal Dream Girl. *Time*. August 26: 75.

Lawnmower Man (motion picture). 1992. Written and directed by Britt Leonard, written and produced by Gimel Everett. New Line Cinema. Film.

Lawnmower Man 2: Beyond Cyberspace (motion picture), 1995. Written and directed by Farhad Mann. First Independent/Allied Entertainments/Fuji Eight. Film.

Le Guin, Ursula. 1980. *The Lathe of Heaven*. London: Granada.

Liebmann, Adrienne, Jen Jordan, Louise Radcliffe-Bown, Patricia Sykes and Jean Taylor. 1997. *Women's Circus: Leaping off the edge*. Melbourne: Spinifex Press.

Lorde, Audre. 1980. *The Cancer Journals*. San Francisco: Spinsters Ink.

Lovell, Glenn. 1996. Save Your Habitat with Virtual Nature. *Australian: Computers.* Tuesday 8 October, 3.

Markley, Robert. (Ed.), 1996. *Virtual Realities and Their Discontents.* Baltimore: The Johns Hopkins University Press.

Mies, Maria and Vandana Shiva. 1993. *Ecofeminism.* London: Zed Books; Melbourne: Spinifex Press.

Mitchell, William J. 1995. *City of Bits: Space, place, and the infobahn.* Cambridge, Massachusetts and London: MIT Press.

Morgan, Robin. 1972. Monster. In Robin Morgan. n.d. *Monster.* Melbourne: Radicalfeminists. Quoted from Diane Bell and Renate Klein (Eds.), 1996. *Radically Speaking: Feminism reclaimed.* Melbourne: Spinifex Press; London: Zed Books.

Murray, Janet H. 1997. *Hamlet and the Holodeck: The future of narrative in cyberspace.* New York: The Free Press.

Nataf, Zachary I. 1997. skin-flicks. In Sue Golding (author/editor), 1997. *The Eight Technologies of Otherness.* London and New York: Routledge.

O'Hartigan, Margaret Deirdre. 1999. Post-modernism Harms Women. *Off Our Backs, xxix,* (1), January. 6 and 13.

Planet of the Apes (motion picture). 1968. Written by Michael Wilson and Rod Serling. Directed by Franklin Schaffer. Deluxe Panavision TCF/Apjac. Film.

Raymond, Janice G. 1986 *A Passion for Friends.* Boston: Beacon Press.

Raymond, Janice G. 1994. *The Transsexual Empire: The making of the she-male.* New York and London: Teachers College Press.

Rheingold, Howard. 1992. *Virtual Reality.* London: Mandarin.

Rioja, Isabel Ramos and Kim Manresa. 1999. *The Day Kadi Lost Part of her Life.* Translated by Nikki Anderson. Melbourne: Spinifex Press.

Roehl, Bernie, Justin Couch, Cindy Reed-Ballreich, Tim Rohaly and Geoff Brown. 1997. *Late Night VRML 2.0 with Java.* Emeryville, CA: Ziff-Davis Press.

Sandoval, Chela. 1995. New Sciences: Cyborg feminism and the methodology of the oppressed. In Chris Hables Gray (Ed.), 1995. *The Cyborg Handbook.* New York and London: Routledge.

Schierl, Hans A. 1997. Manifesto for the dada of the cyborg-embrio. In Sue Golding (author/editor). 1997. *The Eight Technologies of Otherness.* London and New York: Routledge.

Shiva, Vandana. 1996. Keynote address at Subversions Conference. University of Melbourne, 27 April.

The Shorter Oxford English Dictionary on Historical Principles. Vol II. 1977. Oxford: Oxford University Press.

Slouka, Mark. 1995. *War of the Worlds: The assault on reality.* New York: Basic Books.

Slouka, Mark. 1996. The Unreality Trap. *Australian: Weekend Review.* 16–17 March, 6.

Sofia, Zoë. 1995. Of spanners and cyborgs: Dehomogenising feminist thinking on technology. In Barbara Caine and Rosemary Pringle (Eds.), *Transitions: New Australian feminisms.* Sydney: Allen & Unwin.

Springer, Claudia. 1996. *Electronic Eros: Bodies and desire in the postindustrial age.* Austin, TX: University of Texas Press.

Staines, Deborah. 1993. *Now Millennium.* Melbourne: Spinifex Press. (Published jointly with Sandy Jeffs. *Poems from the Madhouse.*)

Stone, Allucquère Rosanne (Sandy). 1995a. *The War of Desire and Technology at the Close of the Mechanical Age.* Cambridge, Massachusetts and London: MIT Press.

Stone, Sandy. 1995b. Split Subjects, Not Atoms; or how I fell in love with my prosthesis. In Chris Hables Gray (Ed.), 1995. *The Cyborg Handbook*. New York and London: Routledge.

The Terminator (motion picture). 1984. Written by James Cameron and Gale Anne Hurd. Directed by James Cameron. Orion/Hemdale/Pacific Western.

Tofts, Darren and Murray McKeich. 1997. *Memory Trade: A prehistory of cyberculture*. Sydney: Interface.

Turkle, Sherry. 1996. Who Am We? *Wired*. 4.01, January.

VNS Matrix. 1998. ALL NEW GEN. In Joan Broadhurst Dixon and Eric J. Cassidy (Eds.), 1998. *Virtual futures: Cyberotics, technology and post-human pragmatism*. London and New York: Routledge.

Walker, Barbara G. 1983. *The Women's Encyclopedia of Myths and Secrets*. San Francisco: Harper & Row.

Walker, John (Ed.), 1998. *Halliwell's Film and Video Guide 1999*. Revised and Updated, Fourteenth Edition. London: HarperCollins.

Wittig, Monique. 1980/1992. *The Straight Mind and other essays*. Boston: Beacon.

Wolf, Christa. 1968. The Reader and the Writer. In Christa Wolf. 1977. *The Reader and the Writer: Essays, sketches, memories*. Translated by Joan Becker. New York: International Publishers; Berlin: Seven Seas Books.

Woodward, Kathleen. 1994. From Virtual Cyborgs to Biological Time Bombs: Technocriticism and the Material Body. In Gretchen Bender and Timothy Druckrey (Eds.), *Culture on the Brink: Ideologies of technology*. Seattle: Bay Press.

Young, Iris Marion. 1990. The Ideal of Community and the Politics of Difference. In Linda J. Nicholson (Ed.), *Feminism/Postmodernism*. New York and London: Routledge.

eleven

Feminist Poetics and Cybercolonisation

Josie Arnold

> According to Wired, 'the cyber is . . . [t]he terminally
> over-used prefix for all things online and digital'
> (Hale 1996: 66).

Colonising cyberspace

> Cyberspace is the electronic equivalent of the
> universe. William Gibson (1983) describes cyber as
> 'consensual hallucination'. It can only be reached
> through computers.

is the challenge that we are facing at the end of the 20th century.
How we do this so as to include women and women's business is the
crucial question. There is much *'boy-talk'*

> Yet the feminisation of language demands that such
> phallogocentric discourse be re-shaped:

>> After our oppressive and inflexible era,
>> I would like to live in a time in which
>> language would not be bound, castrated,
>> intimidated, obliged to obey the false
>> scholars who are true ignoramuses. But
>> sometimes I am stopped by the word-police.
>> Interrogated and counter-interrogated.
>> Sometimes I am the one who stops . . .
>> (Cixous 1988: 50).

about *superhighways,*

> All western-style societies have utilised the car both
> personally and commercially. It has become the

dominant leitmotif of the consumer/capitalist economy and has developed a cultural iconography that is powerful and immediate. The great autobahns that have provided untrammelled vehicular movements have played a central role in the shrinking of distance and the lessening of local isolations. The individual's familiarity with the car culture gives an immediate point of reference in which to place the implications of travelling a superhighway. Not only does it evoke a sense of personal empowerment as the driver of a fast car going where they have determined their destination to be, it also reminds us of the speeding along that occurs on the freeways. A superhighway is no place for uncertainty, reflection, or going back over the steps in a journey, or even of slowing down. It is a place that rushes forward towards a common major destination that has, in many ways, been predetermined, as have points of access or exit.

The electronic superhighway, then, acts as a seductive and non-critical metaphor. It implies up-to-dateness, speed, manufacturing dominance and individual driving skills. However, all feminisms problematise rather than accept and hence reinforce 'givens'. In critiquing the iconography of the superhighway, might we not fruitfully 'read' it from multiple feminist perspectives? Might it not, for example, also imply thoughtless exploitation of resources, the de-centering of <u>local societies</u> and the pressure of stress-related social and personal ills? What might we learn about technology-driven cultures if we pull over and take a reflective opportunity to critique them, or if we put the local onto the global agenda?

Hawthorne
6
Namjoshi
17

and much of the potential of these is modelled upon the masculinist society from which we will '*launch*'

the ejaculative penis?

ourselves into cyberspace. This colonising society, which, without

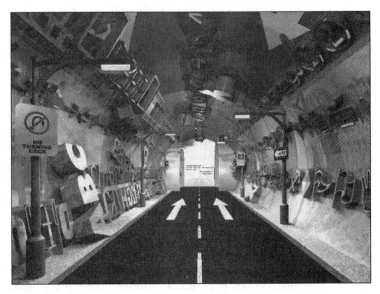

Corridor (CD-ROM Oz 21 Australia's Cultural Dreaming)

irony, we call 'the first world', has a very specific view of cyberspace: it is a place in which we will practise and expand Western capitalist cultural imperatives.

Our earthspace experience of Western colonisation tells us that we will take our prejudices and beliefs with us into cyber-colonisation. So we may safely assume that human strengths and weaknesses pertinent to Western post-industrialist societies are implicated in the construction of the emergent electronic culture. This might seem to be a self-evident point, yet it is ignored in the superhypeway talk about the inevitability of the 'advances' offered by a global cyberculture.

Print, mainly in the highly structured form of prose, has domin-ated the ways in which the masculinist culture in which we live has formed and sustained itself. Indeed, that part of cyberspace which has already been colonised consists mainly of electronically de-livered print/prose. Until now, our main means of communication, particularly long-distance, and particularly through the colonising power of print, has been **words.**

> **We first learn the geography of words . . . the way they fit together, the patterns they make, the pleasures they give and the pitfalls there are in using them . . . through our hearing. As the poet Gerard Manley Hopkins said to explain his own 'sprung-rhythm' of speech in poetry: 'read with the ear and all will be well'. As well he might:**

> I caught this morning morning's minion, king-
>   dom of daylight's dauphin, dapple-dawn drawn Falcon, In his
>   riding
> Of the level underneath him steady air, and striding
> (from The Windhover)

> **By the time most of us begin primary school, we have a good idea of how words work: we have a pattern into which we can fit, for example, action words, describing words, naming words and connecting words. We know how plurals and sentences work and how stories hang together in chunks or paragraphs. More than this, we are aware of the melodies of our language: we know that Australian is not Japanese or French, and is sometimes only loosely related to standard English, much less to American. We also know the most common words we will use for the rest of our lives–about 4,000 of them. This is a very sophisticated skill and one which underlies all our spoken, written and reflective communications. Most people use a slightly broader vocabulary of about 10,000 words, but can recognise about 40,000. There are approximately 600,000 words in the English language!**

> **These are the words which we will bring to writing on/for the electronic medium. I believe them to be the essential building blocks of any text, even a visual one, because they are the way in which we articulate what we are doing, seeing, thinking, feeling and responding. In writing for the new technologies, then, we should not ignore the old skills that come to us from a**

> **sensitivity to the expressiveness of words. At the same time I recognise the urge for universality rather than context-specific meanings that words represent.**

At this stage, most of the writing in the new spaces consists of prose, and I believe this makes it necessary for us to remind ourselves of the implications of both print and prose in the masculinist hegemony which has controlled our tools of expression.

As the American feminist Andrea Dworkin says, 'I speak in the words of the oppressor, but it's the only language I have.' Some feminists have resisted this by taking ***feminist***

> **There is, of course, no one feminist position even though 'feminists' are spoken about as though they are one homogenous-femogenous?-group.**

poetics

> **Poetics being writing in a way which is more closely aligned to the storytelling aspects of poetry than to the sortive and functional elements of prose. For Cixous, the feminist poetic is:**

>> **... the style of live water, where thirst quenches, since to be thirsty is already to give oneself drink. This style of water gives rise to works which are like streams of blood or water, which are full of tears, full of drops of blood or tears transformed into stars (Cixous 1988: 25).**

as the ways in which they express themselves.

When we are writing with words for placement in cyberspace, we are transporting much of what we practise when we write on the blank page as paper. Let's think about how that impacts upon the blank page when it's a computer screen. ***Scrolling, scrolling, scrolling.***

> **Scrolling, scrolling, scrolling. Will I be bored to death? Will my eyes drop out? Am I getting cancer from the electromagnetic field of the computer? Is this another**

Paper (CD-ROM Oz 21 Australia's Cultural Dreaming)

part of the fiendish masculinist plot to get us all in front of computers instead of television screens/ away from nature and subjected to technology? Will Oprah Winfrey soon appear to help my psyche?

The screen orders me to be user-friendly in a way which might be thought patronising on the page:

- Small chunks of information so that they can be put up on powerpoint;
- Pretty colours in the background;
- As many fonts as I like to mix and match the visual impact;
- Some sense of movement . . . are those words really moving towards me? Are they growing? Is this the excitement of a verbal erection?
- Don't use too complex a vocabulary, or if you must (show off) have an arrow, a hot word, a box to simplify it;
- Show off the technology and how you can use it . . . does this make the content secondary?

- Bring in your own personality by comments shooting across the page that show what a wit you are;
- Have an inert audience.

Yet written text is becoming a smaller and smaller part of how we are now enabled to think creatively about colonising cyberspace. Words are a very tiny part of what you can do in the new electronic superworld. The new <u>interactive multimedia</u>, which is only beginning to be understood, much less colonised, by anyone not a *'techno-head'*,

Westwood
and
Kaufmann
15

> This refers to the most dominant players in the reductionist methods of programming to control the new technologies through 'in-group' technical know-how.

Interactive multimedia

Namjoshi
18
Hawthorne
19

> The possibilities of the text are extended in the multi-layered <u>cybertext</u> through the use of audio-visuals, interactivity, three-dimensionality and animation.

offers us a new textuality and discourse and highlights the ways in which *semiotics*

> The relationship of words with their meanings. Much of this, which appears transparent, is in fact a cultural construction of meaning. In colonising cyberspace, we now need to take into consideration new ways of constructing meaning. Cybersemiotics? Part of feminist poetics is to interrogate the accepted relationship of words and their meanings to display the constructed nature of meaning which has led to the master narrative being valued over other meanings and narratives.

>> By interrogating what have been called the master (that is, white, European, male) narratives which have legitimized and naturalized Western thought, and which have excluded, repressed, spoken for and

> about women of colour, white women, Jews, lesbians, and gays, those with phys- ical and mental disabiities and other, poststructuralists have helped denaturalize what has historically been constructed as 'natural', 'normal', 'seamless', 'real', and 'live' by the master narratives (Orner 1992: 78).

have led us to an understanding of the fragile relationship between words and meanings.

Now we have a screen which can provide us with visuals that are not merely add-ons to print in the rather inert way of photographs and diagrams, but that are a moveable and interactive part of the text in a totally new way. This is an opportunity for us to develop new ways of thinking about textuality which alter the masculinist paradigm that has developed from/via prose and print. When we think about working on/for the very smallest screen, the ***visual choreography***

> We see the world around us long before we try to put that vision into words. So we have an enormous reservoir of visuals to apply to the new media. This has been emphasised not only by painting, film and photography, but also by the pervasive influence of television. TV has provided us with multiple examples of visual as well as verbal literacy. If we are no longer trying to record the seen mainly in words, then we are dipping into the visual acuity that has been seen as decorative or for entertainment in the prose- dominated arena of knowledge, disciples and genre. Linda Dement's CD-ROM, 'Cyberflesh Girlmonster', gives us an insight into this. 'I wanted the piece to be non-linear and more cyclical in nature.' <http:// geekgirl.com.au/geekgirl/003broad/dement.html>

> Cixous imagines such a space as I am recom- mending occurs for feminist poetics in cyberspace:

> > What would become of logocentrism, of the great philosophical systems of world

order in general if the rock upon which they founded their churches were to crumble? If it were to come out in a new day that the logocentric project had always been, undeniably, to found (fund) phallo-centrism, to insure for masculine order a rationale equal to history itself? Then all the stories would have to be told differently, the future would be incalculable, the historical forces would, will, change hands, bodies, another thinking, as yet unthink-able, will transform the functioning of all society (Cixous 1985: 361).

It is, I think, instructive that TV is not seen as an educative space within its own terms and used as such. Yet, TV is a cultural text which:

- schoolaged children watch for more hours (an average of 23 plus hours a week) than they attend school;
- adults watch for more hours (an average of 23 plus hours a week) than many other activities in their lives;
- has been demonised as 'dumbing down' viewers;
- is widely available to the most privileged and the most underprivileged in almost all cultures;
- students can view critically, analytically, creatively and knowledgeably provided we stop seeing it as content delivery and start unpeeling some of the concepts and ideas that can be learnt from it;
- leads to a kind of visual and aural literacy which we should value;
- leads into the small screen of electronic deliveries which will underpin the emergent electronic culture;
- is a central player in the convergence of electronic technologies.

and acuity that we have developed through art, photography, cinema and television has a place, will act as a starting-point for our understanding of this.

Prose and print provide us with an opposition between authors and readers, with a dominant pattern of working towards a point of focus and with a text having an authoritative purpose which is indicated from its title, its table of contents, its beginning, middle and end, its references. These devices have given us a model of textuality that clarifies aims and purposes and provides information and data. This model has its zenith in the academic world where it describes itself as *knowledge.*

> **Once we see knowledge as a cultural construction, we understand that woman and women's business has been largely locked out of its construction. A deconstructive reading shows knowledge to be a construction of the powerful in the culture.**

> > **Woman's relation to knowledge, to education, and to professional life has been manifested within the bounds of a regulating discursive system that insists on defining her as inverse, the opposite of man. What is more, women's attempts to disprove the evidence against them, to assert legitimate claims to knowledge, are caught up in the same terms of discourse, the same conditions of truth. Women have entered the battle on the grounds laid out by male science and remain 'the other of reason' (Martusewicz 1992: 152).**

Electronic space provides a challenge for all writers to develop an entirely new *geography or <u>topography</u> of writing.*

> > **Writing has its own melodies, its own ways of displaying itself. The language that we know to have a tenuous connection to reality is nevertheless the main way in which we have constructed meaning. That this**

Hawthorne
19

has been dominated by a particular perspective needs to be identified and changed. It is very difficult to achieve this within the established domains, I think that electronic textuality and discourse offers an opportunity for the feminisation of multiple possibilities within language and meaning structures, rather than the

> ... truth-constituting, legitimising and deeply hidden validifying function of the genre, prose (Richardson 1993: 103).

Westwood
and
Kaufmann
15
Mueller 13

Even thinking about the ways in which a text might be prepared for interactive multimedia challenges our known writing and reading practices. An interactive multimedia text has multiple layers of experience as well as information. To bring these together to form knowledge, or even to make it a personal experience, the reader must be an active co-navigator of the text. There is no other possibility, because it is absolutely inert unless it's being *'played'*.

> Interactivity–particularly as practised in computer games–enables us to see very clearly that the balance of power in reading and writing has moved from the author to the reader/enactor. Interactive texts, and especially the world wide web, enable the navigator to make a specific journey of her or his own which may never be replicated.

Namjoshi
18
Hawthorne
19

A *cybertext*

> This refers to the endless possibilities of writing for the world wide web. It can also be called a hypertext to indicate that the nodes of connection from one site to another can be followed by the reader/player on an individual navigation.

is a navigation of possibilities, a series of choices and movments which are outside the confines of the author-as-director. In a very real sense, we experience Roland Barthes's theoretical understandings of *'the death of the author'*

> In this powerful concept, Roland Barthes articulated the breaking down of the master narrative that underpins the authoritative nature of prose. He opened up the possibility that the text can only come to life through the reader and can only be 'understood' in the cultural reference terms of that reader. So he proclaimed the 'death of the author' as the definitive authority and announced the empowerment of the reader.

whenever we are involved in a cybertext. We also experience the theoretical ideas that Derrida has called *'deconstruction'*

> meaning is not imposed upon us through the power of words, rather it is a construction into which we enter. Like any construction, it can be seen as its constitutive parts, or deconstructed so that we can understand how meaning is culturally produced

and *'bricolage'*

> There is no final text, thus each text is always under construction or being made as it went along by someone who was not an authority but who was undertaking a building-up of meaning with the culture and the reader. Bricolage is performed by a handyperson rather than an expert and is a 'one-off' rather than following/establishing a pattern

and Irigaray's *'jouissance'*

> which attacks the 'serious' nature of knowledgeable writing and calls upon the authoritative to be replaced by fun, joy and pleasure instead of the *gravitas* of determinist textuality and discourse

and Barthes's *'readerly-writing'*

> Such 'readerly-writing' places the power in the hands of the reader and alters forever the relationship of the reader, the writer and the text. As a text is no longer authoritative, but is made or constructed by each reader, the concept of the singular master narrative

no longer remains sustainable. Chatrooms are a good example of this.

The *mindsetshift*

Alice Jardine discusses how, while the feminist will welcome the rejection of 'man's truth',

> . . . she will also understand that it is not enough to oppose man's truth; the very conceptual systems that have posited it must be undermined (Jardine 1985: 153).

involved in participating in the creation of cybertexts is huge. We are being asked to change a cultural mindset that has been developed and made central to our understandings of communication, knowledge, learning and information over the entire history of Western civilisation. Like the Imperial thrust of the colonising European cultures, prose is orderly, sortive, focused and definitive; it calls for models and repetitions. It has an AUTHORitative voice. Interactive multimedia provides a tool for us which is deceptive, many layered, and open to multiple constructions, navigations and manipulations on the part of the user.

There is resistance to this view and/or use of electronic textuality and discourse, of course. The technology for entering cyberspace came from the military. Even the ways in which programs are set up, their interactions, the language we use to talk about them, are part of the most masculinist aspects of the establishment. This leads to a desire to make the technology available to initiates: to have authoritative and paradigmatic ways of using the flexibility offered by cybertextuality and harness it for example in training, replication, and a kind of *'Yes/no', 'right wrong' educational experience.*

> It is my proposal that a feminist colonisation of cyberspace, a feminist writing of cybertexts, would confound that movement to provide programmed paradigms/templates for electronic experiences, and cyberfeminists would show that these might best be found in the practice of feminist poetics. All feminists

ask the culture to recognise and alter how gender is politicised within it. A group of French intellectuals concerned with textuality and discourse has been called 'l'écriture feminine' or feminine writers. One such writer, Luce Irigaray, is concerned about the writing of feminist texts.

> ... how can women analyze their own exploitations, inscribe their own demands, within an order prescribed by the masculine? *Is women's politics possible within that order?* What transformation of the political process does it require? (Irigaray 1985a: 81).

Women, having been marginalised from the accepted practices of the dominant white, middle-class, **masculinist hegemony**

> Querying the construction of culture asks us to identify and then interrogate those things which we have most seen or had presented to us as 'natural' or 'normal'. 'Male dominance exists in any system in which men as a group oppress women as a group, even though there may be hierarchies among men (and women). Typically in male-dominated societies, men have access to and control over the most highly valued and esteemed resources and social activities (Flax 1990: 23).

have also been ascribed certain 'abilities' by that group which are undervalued by that hegemony and hence suppressed by/in them. These attributes, which the hegemony devalues, suppresses or even regards as unnatural, might also be described as 'poetics' for they are involved with understanding the intricacies of the holistic nature of our species and with valuing a full range of human activities.

These 'abilities' open up new cybercolonising performances and possibilities. In doing this, the binary opposites which provide power for the 'right' way of enacting our culture give way to multiple possibilities, all acceptable. Thus, for example, 'emotions' are no longer seen as a lesser human experience than 'reason'; nor are emotion and reason seen as pitted against one another. In this construction, which recognises and practises difference, the potential for feminist poetics resides in all forms of textuality and discourse. This potential Audre Lorde calls the **'black mother'**.

> **The black mother is the poet who exists in every one of us. Now when males or patriarchal thinkers (whether male or female) reject that combination, then we're truncated. Rationality is not unnecessary. It serves to get from this place to that. But if you don't honour those places, then the road is meaningless. Too often, that's what happens with the worship of rationality and that circular, academic, analytical thinking. But ultimately, I don't see feel/think as a dichotomy. I see them as a choice of ways and combinations (Lorde 1984: 103).**

Poetics can draw together old binaries such as feel/think since they can provide a freer and more roving view of what a text is like, how it can be read, and the kind of information it conveys as important. Thus, poetics offers us something very different from prose/book.

By its nature, **the book**

> **Catalogued, entitled, with an author, enclosed between covers ... the book is didactic, taxonomic. There is a publisher, table of contents, chapters which lead from an Introduction to a Conclusion in a linear progression.**

is part of the authoritative paradigm of the dominant masculinist Western culture. Underpinning this authoritative nature of prose is the taxonomy of **genre.**

> **Such types of writing as scientific, romantic, fact, fiction, intellectual, junk-science, women's magazines and so on.**

Furthermore, the book has an author or authors. Prose itself is sortive: it seeks to be directive, critical, maybe even *didactic.*

> **You are trying to convey something to your audience out there, you are the performer; you are in control. You have the knowledge and by placing it in print others will be drawn to your insights and/or standards. You are confronting the blank page and when you have finished your MASTERpiece will be revealed as a way of leading others to greater heights.**

Some genres are culturally constructed as serious and important, others as less so or negligible. Phallogocentrism has a strong impetus to make hierarchies based on *prioritising lists.*

> **Western dominant culture and hegemony-based in a desire to categorise and to order. It relies upon lists which ascribe importance from best to worst. In writing, genre is clearly a part of this urge to list, to give value, and to control by categorising. Scientific writing is seen as an important genre. It is full of factual data. It claims to be disinterested as though its practices are outside the culture itself and are fully inclusive . . . that is, it does not choose what should be researched or why or who should be the subjects or who should provide the money. 'Pure' science is probably at the top of the genre list, women's magazines towards the bottom. This is instructional, because the latter are full of advice about how to dress, eat, run relationships, bring up children, or make things. Clearly such everyday activities are low on the scale of importance.**
>
> **Low, too, is non-prose. Writing for the theatre, film or television and writing poetry is a lesser genre than writing 'serious' academic, intellectual or scientific texts. Yet writing for cybertexts is closer to scripting than anything else.**

By utilising poetics, particularly elements of *scripting,*

> **The cyberscript is a multilayered investigation of the possibilities offered by dialogue, sound, film,**

Panel (CD-ROM Oz 21 Australia's Cultural Dreaming)

English 12

animation, three-dimensionality and interaction. It gives us opportunities to take the written word as a planning space to establish the architecture, topography, geography and choreography of the new poetics of cyberspace. The multilayered script of film is instructive. Dialogue, camera, sound, action, characters, music, setting. It's extended, of course, by interactivity and <u>virtual reality</u> as well as three-dimensionality and animation. The script will have horizontal layers of directions to the actors, the director, the long list of credits we see after a film, and also the progammers, telling them what else you need to make a cyberscript into a cyberpresentation.

Hawthorne

19

cybertexts can transcend genre. They can move outside the expected and draw together elements of entertainment as well as information and knowledge-production; elements of <u>poetics</u> as well as prose; elements of group production rather than solitary authorship; and elements of fun and emotion as well as analysis and criticism. They are a perfect vehicle for breaking down the old dominance of genre as either 'fact' (good, useful, researched, reliable, checkable) or fiction (emotional, unstable, unreliable, unresearched, non-replicable).

We live in a time when critical and cultural theories are questioning our models of textuality and discourse. Perhaps feminism has carried these insights furthest. Ferenc Feher sees women's struggle to confront masculinist ways of knowing and their powerful impact upon our cultural realities as:

> ... the single *long durée* revolution of our age which has proved not only increasingly successful, even irresistible, but which also brings many gains and very few losses. Its participants cannot help but have a very strong awareness of where they are coming from and what direction they are heading (Feher 1990: 174).

The new reading and writing spaces offered by cyberculture are fully explored through *interactive multimedia.*

> **The new aspects of such a text, consisting as it does of written and spoken words, sounds, and both still and active images, are three-dimensionality, virtuality, global immediacy and animation. Even interactivity has been prefigured by the bringing to 'life' of a book through lifting it off the shelf and reading it, by the choice of television viewing, or by playing games. Future interactivities could involve holograms, changing TV and film presentations through computerisation so as to readerly write, to explore one aspect or character, to change endings, to add material, to interweave music etc. to enact within the context of the virtual.**

> **Animation may now be undertaken by the navigator rather than the author. Three-dimensionality means that a cyberworld is becoming more and more like our experience of the real world. Interactivity means that the player may enter the cyberworld and effect what is happening there. This is becoming more**

apparent as ways to produce cyberexperiences are being developed.

As well as calling on new areas of discourse, interactive multimedia draws together many skills which we already have, and in doing so it is clearly more than the sum of its parts. As a writer I actually felt my brain shift into another space when I had to think about writing for interactive multimedia. Clearly, writing prose, poetry, drama, film and a PhD thesis had given me a lot of skills, but they were not enough to take me readily into interactive multimedia. I learnt that writing for a CD-ROM is closer to writing for film, drama and poetry than it is to writing prose and that the process relies more on laterality than linearity. In teaching our Media and Multimedia courses at the Lilydale campus of Swinburne University, many of my ideas about the theory and practice of electronic textuality and discourse were enacted in making the ***CD-ROM and building the navigation nodes for the dynamic peripheral.***

Guymer 3
Westwood
and
Kaufmann
15
Bird 16

Over two years, we have successfully taught more than 2,000 students using the core <u>CD-ROM</u> and associated websites. Writing for the CD-ROM used all the preliminary laterality of mindmapping. We set up the supportive architecture for delivery of the users' journeys as a museum walk through exhibition spaces. There are multiple layers and choices. These include Australian white history, Aboriginal Dreamtime and a main exhibition 'Cruising the Superhighway: Australian Culture on the Move'.

'The Future' gallery enables players/readers to use the computer within theirs, to discover hotspots which range from the introduction of print to Indigenous contemporary science and technology. The CD-ROM has been extended, revised and reburned four times. It provides a stable base for jumping off points to specific subject websites containing information and a navigation of relevant nodes of interest on the world wide web. They can be surfed or individually extended into a cyberjourney. There are discussion threads and chatrooms, but print is still the dominant

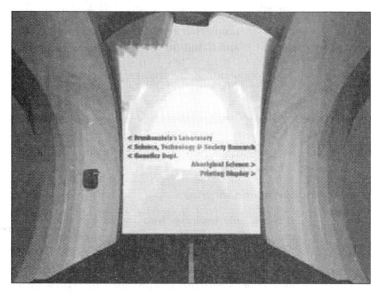

Doors (CD-ROM Oz 21 Australia's Cultural Dreaming)

mode. We have dealt with this ironically on the CD-
ROM by making interactive 'books' with hotwords and
page-turning.

Like genre, knowledge (instructively) is broken into ***disciplines.***

In all the disciplines, one finds evidence of
the underlying assumption that society is
rightfully described from the perspective of
those who have the authority to speak on
behalf of those who have no legitimate
voice of their own. Deviance has been
associated with those who have rejected
the authoritative spokesmen of society.
Exclusion of women from seats of authority has been accomplished by rewarding
women for compliance with the hierarchical gender-relation paradigm and by sys-
tematically excluding those who refuse to
comply. The institutionalized invisibility of

> women has provided the context for prior
> unqueried gender bias in research (Tomm
> and Hamilton 1988: xv-xvi).

Thus, disciplines are similar to genre: they are part of the taxonomy
of knowledge.

> Genres evolve through human purposes, reflecting and reproducing
> (through the various systems in which they are implicated) what is
> culturally relevant and significant for the human community
> (Swingewood 1986: 104).

The power of print and/as prose

> It is not only feminists who see the powerful sortive
> and taxonomic influence of printed texts. The
> contemporary French Philosopher, Jacques Lyotard
> (certainly no feminist), also sees the need for a new
> approach to textuality and discourse to free it from old
> constraints:

>> The complicity between political phalla-
>> crocy and philosophical metalanguage is
>> made here: the activity men reserve for
>> themselves arbitarily as fact is posited
>> legally as the right to decide meaning. The
>> social groups of distributors, that is,
>> citizens, becomes confused with the prin-
>> cipal that there is something like distrib-
>> utive reason, matter upon which reason is
>> inscribed or written, and that there is a
>> distinction between matter and reason
>> (Lyotard 1989: 119).

has reinforced the dominance of the patriarchal society. Feminist
writings and poetics act against this dominance. Patriarchy may be
viewed as Irigaray defines it:

> . . . the appropriation of nature by man, the transformation of nature
> according to 'human' criteria, defined by men alone; the submission of
> nature to labour and technology; the reduction of its material, corporeal,
> perceptible qualities to man's practical concrete activity; the equality of

women amongst themselves, but in terms of equivalence that remain external to them; the constitution of women as 'objects' that emblemize the materialization of relations among men, and so on (Irigaray 1985: 184-5).

The nonlinear possibilities of computer textuality and discourse

An excellent print example of a project based on feminist methodologies is Professor Diane Bell's *Ngarrindjeri Wurruwarrin: A World That Is, Was, and Will Be*. Here, in her study of the Hindmarsh Bridge application to join, and develop for housing, an island off the South Australian coast, she tells of her discourse with Indigenous women on 'women's business'. She questions the ways in which the episteme has been built by specific masculinist knowledge models and proposes an alternative knowledge based on Indigenous orality and story-telling traditions.

> . . . the stories which are nourishing this generation draw heavily on a distinctive body of knowledge and practice which is more than the product of resistance to oppressive policies. It is grounded in oral traditions passed from generation to generation, albeit traditions which have accommodated change, absorbed new ideas, and thus survived (Bell 1998: 14).

There is still contention about this and the appropriation by academics, particularly anthropologists. <http://www.spinifexpress.com.au/nwdiss.htm>

provide an opportunity for lateral and singular and hence non-masculinist models of knowledge.

. . . the main battle is to destroy the hegemonic phallocentric system. The demand should not be for exclusively female society, but for a society where men and women share the same anti-logocentric, anti-hierarchical values (Przybylowicz 1987: 155).

In many ways, feminist poetics fits into postmodernist or poststructuralist views of the immediacy and individuality of each piece of information, story or happening. It acts against the established episteme of scientific methodology and its influences on how stories about people are recorded. Rosemary Tong sees the potential of postmodernist feminism as positing the potentials for a new start for all people.

> Whether women can, by breaking silence, by speaking and writing, overcome binary opposition, phallocentrism, and logocentrism, I do not know. All that I do know is that we humans could do with a new conceptual start (Tong 1989: 233).

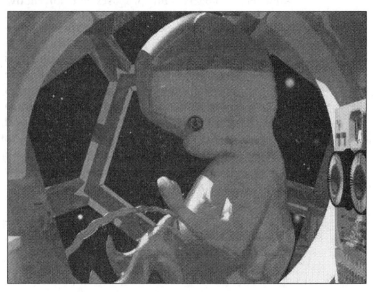

Foetus (CD-ROM Oz 21 Australia's Cultural Dreaming)

Cybertexts

> The electronic text itself provides multiple voyages which empower voyagers to participate in the textual experience as writers/readers. In doing so they enact much of the postmodernist moment. More importantly they participate in the movement BEYOND the postmodernist moment of the dispersal of certainties: they are voyaging to where such textual freedoms might take us.

and cybercolonisation offer this. As critics of the present cultural construction, feminists are well placed to enact alternatives.

Of course, *__colonial and post-colonial practices__*

> There is a great interest in realearth in deconstructing the impact of colonial values upon the colonised peoples. These studies are very relevant to the colonisation of cyberspace. Leela Gandhi says that:

Fletcher 14
Hawthorn
19
Namjoshi
Pattanaik

>> ... postcolonial studies claims that the entire field of the humanities is vitiated by a spurious universality ... to disguise its political investment in the production of 'major' or 'dominant' knowledges (Gandhi 1998: 44).

have continued to oppress and supress all but the dominant modes of discourse in research. Bell's exemplar is worth studying for those thinking of opening old paradigms and showing them to be less fruitful than alternative research methodologies. Like feminist poetics, the Ngarrindjeri world in which she learns from their knowledge patterns:

> spell out an epistemology in which 'feelings' are central and they detail the 'respect system' which underwrites the authority of the elders (Bell 1998: 36).

Moreover, this storytelling is not linear, replicable, sortive and taxonomic:

Ngarrindjeri, it seems, have always tolerated, perhaps even delighted in, ambiguity and shifting emphases in story-telling (Bell 1998:37).

Such a lack of focus and precision is a basic element of poetics and can be seen to be particularly apposite for the practice of <u>feminist poetics</u>. Indeed, the feminist educationalist Jane Flax says of feminist textuality and discourse that it acts to:

Namjoshi
17

> . . . tolerate, invite and interpret ambivalence, ambiguity and multiplicity, as well as to expose the roots of our need for imposing order and structure no matter how arbitary and oppressive these may be. If we all do our work well, 'reality' will appear even more unstable, complex, and disorderly than it does now (Flax 1990: 183).

The sailing ships that set off from Europe to colonise the 'New' world had no place on board for women much less women's issues and ideas. The highly masculinist nature of Western realworld colonisation is still being felt in the struggle for postcolonial identity. If we are to have a new way of colonising cyberspace with cyberfeminists then women need to be aware of the power of feminist poetics in the new electronic textuality and discourse.

Realworld colonisers did not value what they found there. For example, the Aboriginal mode of mapping and communication is totally pictorial as well as verbal. The ways in which we communicate mapping are extremely linear, didactic and grid-like. Yet the Aboriginal mapping sustained an environmentally sound way of life for over 40,000 years on the Australian continent <<u>http:// libfind.unl.edu:2020/alpha/Links_to_Aboriginal_Resources.html</u>>

Often this mapping was ephemeral and personal. It might be done as body painting, dance, songlines or carvings. Only now are Australia's white colonisers beginning to ask how we might learn from Indigenous people rather than tell Indigenous people to do as we do. Even so, Aboriginal 'mappings' are regarded as commercial art rather than modes of discourse. (Benterrick et al. 1984). Roslyn Haynes, in *Seeking the Centre: The Australian desert in literature and*

[1.] The three spaces in this address each have a single dash which is obscured by the underlining.

film, discusses this very thoroughly, and her quotation of the poet George Tinamin, responding to the demands of the dominant culture, is apposite:

> 'One land, One Law, One People'
> Ngangatja apu wiya, ngakyuku tjamu-
> This is not a rock, it is my grandfather.
> This is a place where the dreaming
> comes up, right up from inside the ground.

Feminist poetics provide us with a new way of entering into cyberspace in which women are not banned or even tolerated but their lack of hegemonic power becomes a plus for new ways of exploring the new territories of cyberspace. In urging feminists to colonise cyberspace, I give Irigaray the last word:

> It is already getting around–at what rate? in what contexts? in spite of what resistances?–that women diffuse themselves according to modalities scarcely compatible with the framework of the ruling symbolics. Which doesn't happen without causing some turbulence, we might even say some whirlwinds, that ought to be reconfined within solid walls of principle, to keep them from spreading to infinity (Irigaray 1985: 106).

Landing (CD-ROM Oz 21 Australia's Cultural Dreaming)

References:

Arnold, Josie, Kitty Vigo and Daniel Green. 1997/8/9 CD-ROM Oz 21 *Australia's Cultural Dreaming*.

Barthes, Roland. 1977. *Image-Music-Text*. London: Fontana/Collins.

Bell, Diane. 1998. *Ngarrindjeri Wurruwarrin: A World That Is, Was, and Will Be*. Melbourne: Spinifex Press.

Benterrick, Kim, Stephen Meucke, and Paddy Roe. 1984. *Reading the Country: Introduction to Nomadology*. Freemantle, Western Australia: Fremantle Fine Arts Press.

Cixous, Hélène. 1988. *Writing Differences. Readings from the Seminar of Hélène Cixous*. Edited by S. Sellers. Milton Keynes: Open University Press.

Dement, Linda. 1995. CD-ROM. *Cyberflesh Girlmonster*.

Derrida, Jacques. 1978. *Writing a Difference*. London: Routledge & Kegan Paul.

Feher, Ferenc. 1990. The Historical Novel and 'Post Histoire'. In Andrew Milner et al. *Discourse and Difference: Post-structuralism, feminism and the moment of history* (177–190). Monash University.

Flax, Jane. 1990. *Thinking Fragments: Psychoanalysis, feminism, and postmodernism in the contemporary West*. Berkeley: University of California Press.

Gandhi, Leela. 1998. *Postcolonial Theory : A critical introduction*. Melbourne: Allen and Unwin.

Gibson, William. 1983. *Neuromancer*. New York: Arc Books.

Hale, Catherine. 1996. *Wired Style: Principles of English use in the digital age, from the editors of Wired*. California: Hardwired.

Haynes, Roslyn. 1998. *Seeking the Centre: The Australian desert in literature and film*. Melbourne: Cambridge University Press.

Hopkins, Gerard Manley. 1953. *Poems and Prose*. Selected and edited by W.H. Gardner. Harmondsworth: Penguin Books.

Irigaray, Luce. 1985. *This Sex Which Is Not One*. Ithaca, New York: Cornell University Press,

Jardine, Alice. 1985. *Gynesis: Configurations of woman and modernity*. Ithaca: Cornell University.

Lorde, Audre. 1984. *Sister Outsider*. New York: The Crossing Press.

Lyotard, Jacques. 1989. *The Lyotard Reader*. Edited by A. Benjamin. Oxford: Basil Blackwell.

Martusewicz, Rebecca. 1992. Mapping the Terrain of the Postmodern Subject. Post-Structuralism and the Educated Woman. In William Pinar and William M. Reynolds (Eds.), *Understanding the Curriculum as Phenomenological and Deconstructed Text* (131–8). New York: Teachers College Press.

Orner, Mimi. 1992. Interrupting the calls for student voice in Liberatory education: a feminist poststructuralist perspective. In Carmen Luke and Jennifer Gore (Eds.), *Feminisms and Cultural Pedagogy* (pp 54–73). London: Routledge.

Przbylowicz, Donna. 1987. Contemporary Issues in Feminist Theory. In Joseph Buttigieg (Ed.), *Criticism without Boundaries: Questions and crosscurrents in postmodern critical thinking* (pp. 129–160). Indiana: University of Notre Dame Press.

Richardson, Laurel. 1993. Poetics, Dramatics and Transgressive Validity: The Case of the Skipped Line. *The Sociological Quarterly*, 34 (4), 695–710.

Swingewood, Alan. 1986. *Sociological Poetics and Aesthetic Theory.* London: Macmillan.

Tomm,Winnie and G. Hamilton. 1988. *Gender Bias in Scholarship: The pervasive prejudice.* Waterloo, Ontario: Wilfrid Laurier Press for The Calgary Institute of Humanities.

Tong, Rosemary. 1989. *Feminist Thought: A comprehensive introduction.* USA: Unwin Hyman.

Zupko, Sarah. Homepage <http://www.mcs.net/~zupko/cs-criti.htm>

Creativity

twelve

W hy Virtual Reality?

Miriam English

Why on earth should women be interested in <u>Virtual Reality</u>? The very name conjures up images of boys sitting in dimly lit rooms with bizarre headgear and gloves on. But I believe the technology will actually be appropriated largely by women in the near future.

Fletcher 14

Not long ago everybody thought the next generation of telephone would be the videophone. Much more useful, in my opinion, is VR.

You have just got out of the shower to answer the phone. You stand there—naked, and dripping wet—talking on the phone, glad it does not transmit pictures. It sends a description of your gestures and expressions so that the computer at the other end is able to reflect your actions in a 3D image of your choice. The other person sees you as you would have them see you. You can have any shape, appearance, skin colour, and choose whether you're using a wheelchair or are able-bodied.

Can you see?

The headgear most people associate with VR will disappear or shrink to almost nothing in the future. People simply do not like to wear large clumsy devices. You will see VR using either something like ordinary spectacles (but most likely much smaller), which project the images directly into the eye, or something more like Star Trek's holodeck, where the images appear around you without requiring you to wear any equipment. The tiny headgear is almost here now. The holodeck exists only as special rooms called CAVEs (Computer Aided Virtual Environment) in a few places around the world. The walls are simply large projection screens. (There is actually another route to VR, but I don't think people will be making <u>direct connections to their brains</u> for a few decades yet, unless someone can come up with a non-invasive method.)

Klein 9

At the moment most VR is just seen as a picture on a computer screen and viewed without any special devices. Many people do not think of this as VR, but it is, and it is the most rapidly growing form.

One of my avatars.
(Miriam English)

See me move.

In a shared, 'multi-user' world, the other people need to be able to see you. What they see is your avatar—the body you 'wear' in VR. Avatars are just models like the rest of the virtual world is and are created in exactly the same way (more about this later). You need to be able to make the avatar move, do things and express body language. Currently, navigating the world is generally accomplished by moving a mouse or pressing the arrow keys on your keyboard. Giving the avatar body movements has been done using cumbersome and expensive gloves and suits, or using the keyboard or mouse to trigger painstakingly pre-programmed, standard actions (walk, run, wave, etc.); however some people are developing computers with eyes which intelligently interpret your actions and move your avatar accordingly. My bet is that this is how we will communicate our actions in VR in the future.

What does it feel like?

I was surprised to learn (thanks Jed) that heat and cold may be relatively simple to reproduce, but movement (kinesthesia) and touch (tactile sense) are very difficult problems to solve, and—apart from some fairly unsatisfactory gloves with vibrating pads in them, or moving platforms or seats, or robotic actuators which resist your actions—nobody has come close to a general solution to this. For the moment we just have to use the fact that most of the cues we take from the world are visual.

The sense of smell is an odd one. There have already been Smellorama movies and you may have seen (smelled?) a scratchit book. In the 1960s Morton Heilig designed and built the Sensorama, an arcade size virtual reality machine which included smell with 3D vision, stereo sound, and vibration to give a sense of movement, but he was never able to get financial backing. Apparently there are only seven distinct odours that mix to produce the spectrum of smells—it should be easy to mechanize . . .

Recent History

The following is a brief, and personally slanted, history of some of the amazing recent developments in VR.

Virtual Reality Modelling Language (VRML) was developed by a small number of people during 1994/1995. VRML is a major milestone because it is a simple way of creating complex virtual worlds with nothing more than a text editor. For the first time, VR was open to any person interested enough to invest a small amount of time in learning it. The specifications are freely available to anyone on the World Wide Web, and the program used to display your worlds inside your Web Browser is free also. In fact if you obtained your Web Browser recently, and it is a full version (not a 'cut-down' version), chances are that it already has the ability to display virtual worlds because the major browsers now include world-viewing capabilities as standard.

The development of such a simple and effective standard attracted a lot of people, and the development during 1997 of VRML97 (also called VRML2.0) was a much bigger affair. It was conducted almost entirely over the Internet by several thousand individuals (though less than a hundred were active participants at a time), and extends greatly the functionality of VRML because now VRML has become interactive and dynamic.

Now the next generation of VRML is under development. Great things are afoot. This is an enormous co-operative effort by people all over the world. Development of VRML and discussion of its directions takes place almost entirely over the Internet via email.

Around the same time as the initial development efforts for VRML, the appropriately named AlphaWorld was created. In 1997 it was purchased by Circle Of Fire, a small team of artists and programmers who were responsible for much of the content of AlphaWorld. They renamed it ActiveWorlds. The original AlphaWorld still exists and is enormous, but there are now over four hundred worlds in the ActiveWorlds universe, which is certainly the biggest multi-user system on the Internet. You can become a citizen of Active-Worlds by subscribing—and there are hundreds of thousands of citizens. An annual subscription of just under US$20 gets you the ability to stake a claim to any plot of 'land' not already owned and build whatever you want there. Citizens also get to use custom avatars, whereas visitors may use only standard male or female 'tourist' avatars. There are some utterly gorgeous worlds in the ActiveWorlds universe. Each time I have been there I have met people from dozens of different countries. And in late 1998 the awesome Avatars98 was held in there . . . but more of that below. ActiveWorlds does not use VRML.

In 1995, and hot on the heels of AlphaWorld/ActiveWorlds was Blaxxun (back then, they were called Black Sun in honour of a place in a virtual world in Neal Stephenson's novel *Snow Crash*). They hoped for their worlds to be of more use than simply places for people to meet, and they adopted the new VRML standard to make their worlds more open-ended. They have made shopping worlds and places for corporate clients to hold international staff meetings and conferences. But it seems that in spite of all their success at commercializing them, socializing is still what their worlds are mostly used for. And they are impressive worlds.

Sony started up their own group of multi-user worlds as Community Place. It never seemed to get the attention that the others did outside Japan. It uses a slightly altered variant of VRML, extended to give more capabilities.

On 8 September 1997, Kathy Rae Huffman had arranged a conference at the Ars Electronica in Linz, Austria. She and I had earlier talked about the possibility of putting a virtual world on the Internet for women to meet in during the conference; this way, even women who were unable to physically attend, owing to financial or other reasons, could still take part in the event in some (small) way. I built a small world and some of us met in there from time to time over those few days using a few simple avatars I had built.

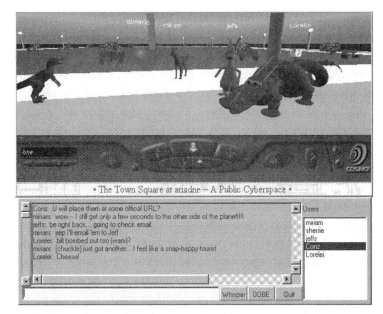

A meeting in Jeff's VNet world. There are five avatars in this picture.
The glowing yellow point in front of the dog avatar is a firefly avatar
being used by Sherrie. The OOBE button activates Out Of Body
Experience mode. That is how I managed to take the picture
with my avatar in the shot. (Miriam English)

The world's first live performance of Shakespeare's *A Midsummer Night's Dream* inside a virtual world was broadcast to the world over the Internet on 26 April 1998. It was the pet project of Bernie Roehl and Stephen Matsuba at the University of Waterloo in Canada, and they named it VRML Dream. The performers operated avatars representing the characters in the play. Often more than one person was required to operate each avatar so that the performers were more like puppeteers than actors. The audience was able to point their Web browsers at the address where this landmark performance was taking place and watch the play by moving around within the action. Members of the audience didn't have avatars— they were invisible. VR presents some very interesting possibilities

The view from near the front of the audience at the climax of the
Avatars98 Awards ceremony. The more distant avatars in this picture
appear to have the standard tourist avatar here but actually had various
avatars. Near top, centre, MyTwoKeys (Victoria D'Onofrio) was actually
wearing her winning avatar, a rather distorted picture of which can be
seen on the main screen. (Reproduced ourtesy of Bruce Damer)

for an audience. They could wander freely around the action or even
ignore it completely. They could take on the viewpoint of any of the
characters, or see the play from the director's 'camera'. There were
also many preset positions around the scene that the viewer could
jump to.

In mid 1998 Stephen White gave his VNet to the world. VNet is a
small program which can be embedded in a Web page which gives a
window onto a VRML97 multi-user virtual world. Now anybody can
create a virtual world in which groups of people can meet and
socialize on their Web page! There is a small proviso however: the
person or organization owning the server from which the virtual
world is served up to the Web must consent to VNet running there.

Many commercial service providers will not allow this. You will have to look for small operators who are enthusiasts. My VNet world lives on a machine owned and operated by a generous net-friend of mine in California. (Now a new player in the field looks set to get around even that problem. Using VRTelecom's Holodesk, anyone will be able to host multi-user virtual worlds.)

As soon as Stephen White released his code several people put VNet worlds up on the net. The best known and most used of these is Jeff Sonstein's Town Square. Since his world has opened there have been many special meetings held in there.

Steve Guynup has been experimenting with virtual poetry readings in Jeff's VNet world. He was able to do things there that are totally impossible in reality. To illustrate and accompany his poetry he metamorphosed his avatar at several points during the reading. He started with a title page which simply stood there for a little while before the reading began, then changed to a couple of photographic pictures, then an enormous, dizzily spinning avatar larger than the main part of the world we were in, then a little ball-like object which bounced randomly around. These meshed perfectly with the sense of his poem and enhanced it in a way which is difficult to describe.

Earlier, I briefly mentioned Avatars98 (affectionately called the Avvys). On 21 November 1998, for the first time, it was held entirely in several virtual worlds, with more than 4000 people attending the events over the 24 hours. The Avatars awards—the climax of the event—was held in the ActiveWorlds universe in the AV98 world built specially for it. It was a wonderful occasion, buzzing with excitement. People came from many countries in the real world to parade their avatars, display their works of art in the art gallery, attend the seminars, and exhibit their business wares. It looked and felt like a real-world exhibition, except that you were not limited to walking along the floor; at any time you were able to fly, or if you knew the coordinates of your destination, teleport. Another thing which set it apart from a real life exhibition, was the fact that visitors were quite at ease, stopping and chatting with the people around them at any time. It was a very friendly atmosphere, and was crowned by a thrilling final ceremony where the avatar awards were made. 'Summer', the winning avatar, was made by Victoria D'Onofrio (MyTwoKeys) and Rodolfo Galeano (Netropolis). 'Summer' is exquisite in detail; a beautiful woman wearing flowers and flapping butterflies. She holds a rabbit (George) which she pats from time to time as she moves, looks around, and fidgets—even the rabbit moves and changes expression! An extraordinary work of art. They certainly deserved to win.

VR Avatars' 'Summer and George the bunny'.
(Reproduced courtesy of Millennium Interactive Co.)

Like much virtual design and development, the collaboration between Rody and Victoria was conducted over the net—Rody lives in Argentina and Victoria in Texas. The following is some of what Victoria had to say to me of her experience in designing 'Summer'.

Most people think that I have had a long history of training and design experience using 3D modelers but Rody and I started with RWX [Renderware text file format] scripting about $2^1/2$ years ago, making models for our projects. Jasmine (the runner up best humanoid, last year) was my first true experience using a 3D modeler, so I have about $1^1/2$ years experience in this area.

The Renderware scripts contain the geometry definition of the model. Basically it's a list of vertices (x, y and z coordinates) and a list of polygons (connecting the vertices and containing the surface settings). We use a 3D modeler for the design and then convert the model to RWX. After the conversion, some text editing is always needed.

I animated 'Summer and George' (as a single model), using Life Forms [a 3D animation program]. The animations took me a full six days, and that was working almost around the clock on them. I was making animations up to the day of the Avvys! :)

Rody was responsible for fixing all the technical problems that cropped up . . . The conversion process is always a pain . . . You have polys [polygons] missing and sometimes I have to redesign the model because the 'camera' in ActiveWorlds has a tendency to exaggerate the bust line (as was the case with 'Summer'). And we had problems getting the textures to download correctly.

'Summer' was supposed to be part of a series of avatars (spring, summer, fall, winter) . . . but when I started designing her, I kept throwing in other 'aspects' that I felt meshed better with one of the other seasons or something that wasn't my idea of 'summer'. I almost gave up on the seasons concept, but I'm stubborn when I have one of my 'inspirations'. :)) So, I remade her costume almost into a Greek Diana . . . The Diana came about because I wanted to add young animals (at that point, there was no 'George') . . . great design, but wasn't 'summer' enough :)) so I threw the whole thing out again and went back to the seasons . . . and a naked model :)) I finally achieved what was in my mind when I started . . . although I still cannot say she is a 'true expression of summer' :)

Technically, once I had the direction, modeling her was not hard for me. I do have to say though that the joints, especially the knees, were quite difficult. I spent days perfecting the knee joint, so that when she sits, walks, kicks, or bends them, they look natural. Summer's knees can be rotated 90 degrees and they will still look natural. When you are restricted to a very low poly count it's extremely difficult to do.

Rody and I fought about George :)) One of his jobs is to make sure that the model stays low poly count . . . but I wanted to incorporate all the tags. I wanted Summer to look young, innocent . . . a part of nature . . . but I wanted to show off the body design, I WANTED (I felt she desperately needed) a fawn, or a bunny (they are so cute!).

'Summer' was finished for all intents and purposes in TrueSpace [a 3d modeling program in which objects are 'sculpted'] . . . It was 2 weeks before the Avvys, and I still hadn't done her animation sequences. I kept telling Rody 'I want to add an animal' and he kept saying 'No, no, the poly count! . . . you don't have time to animate her now!! :))'

Well, I'm stubborn, and I modeled George without telling him, in one day . . . made the textures the next . . ., stuck him in the crook of her arm . . . and then showed Rody :)) George was so cute, he almost couldn't refuse but he did! Same argument, told me I was crazy, and couldn't possibly animate the combination of Summer/George before the Avvys . . . I still didn't listen and made him convert the Summer/George combination for animation in Life Forms. I did the 'wait' sequence (the animation she assumes repeatedly, when the user is not initiating a sequence). Summer petting George and George enjoying it sometimes, struggling in her arms at others . . . It was SO CUTE he couldn't refuse any longer and George stayed :)

Winning the Avvys was overwhelming . . . My goal was to win, of course, but I never really could convince myself that I had a chance to win the 'most realistic humanoid' category, let alone the 'Grand Prize'. When they displayed 'Summer' on the big screen, Grand Prize Winner . . . I started jumping up and down, and then broke down and cried for at least an hour :)) I can't describe that feeling, all I can say is that winning the Avvys for an avatar designer is like winning the Oscar!

Using computer generated VR for socializing and interacting extends what the telephone, low cost travel, and the postal service have done before it. The present telephone system uses incredibly complex computer networks which even make use of space technology to link people via satellites in orbit around our little planet. With the advent of mobile phones it has become even more complex, with small, hand-held computers communicating via radio with various base stations, automatically selecting the best one to send your voice message through. But how many people think of all this when they phone a loved one for a chat? In the same way, as the newness of the technology wears off and people come to take it for granted, they will see it less as something to do with computers and more as just another way of socializing.

What can we use it for and why would I even want to?

There are major openings right now in VR work for people who like to sculpt with computers. VR is being used commercially as a tool for visualizing difficult or impossible-to-see things. There is a real need for people with the interest and ability to do this kind of stuff. VR holds many attractive possibilities beyond what I expect to be its most common use as the future telephone. Here are some of them:

- 3D models are often the only way to get a handle on numeric data. Business people, researchers, statisticians, mathematicians, engineers, all need to be able to interpret what are often large, complex number sets, and our brains are marvellously adapted to interpret 3D patterns.
- Research chemists, molecular biologists, particle physicists all need to be able visualize and understand things which are impossible to see. VR has been a very useful tool for coming to grips with such unseen forces and objects.
- Designing new products (for example, cars) in VR makes the same kind of sense that writing using a wordprocessor does; making changes is straightforward, and you can view the final result no matter how big it is before committing to producing the finished, solid product.
- VR is also used to visualize things that no longer exist, like archeological ruins, or the layout of a modern city a hundred years ago.
- Using VR you may no longer need to work in a local company. The office you work in may be inhabited by people from anywhere on the planet. When VR hits its

stride you may be able to work with or for somebody regardless of where you live. If you live in an area where there is no employment—no problem, in VR everywhere is close.

- I work for myself from home over the Internet right now. I don't have to get dressed for work in the morning if I don't want to, and I don't need to travel to and from work. This saves me a lot of money and time. Soon I hope to be able to do much of my business in VR. Of course nothing will ever replace real, face-to-face contact with people, but when I do meet people face-to-face I prefer it to be for pleasure rather than being thrust into the company of people when I'm tired or under pressure.

My favourite avatar. (Miriam English)

- Throwing a masquerade party in VR would be unlike any normal party. You wouldn't be limited to donning a costume; you could come as an elephant, a mouse, Wonder Woman (with the ability to fly), an alien, a machine, a cloud, a jar of yoghurt, or anything you might design. And no one can physically hurt you in VR.

- Exhibitions held in VR have distinct advantages over those in the real world. (See below for descriptions of Avatars98.) There is no physical limitation on the size of a VR world. If you want to display a building you have designed, it is as easy as if you wanted to show a small gallery of pictures. The rental of space is likely to be measured in fractions of dollars per hour instead of thousands. Visitors are not only those who were able to be in town that day; they can come instantly from all over the world. Sculptures in VR don't even have to obey the law of gravity—or any other natural laws if you so desire. They can move through each other, and even grow and reproduce like living things.

Guymer 3

- <u>Conferences</u> in VR can enable people to do things which are impossible in reality. For example, in the real world, if someone is demonstrating something then only a couple of people could see that thing from the demonstrator's angle—by looking over their shoulder. In VR it can be arranged that a crowd standing around the object all see the object from the same angle as the person demonstrating it—totally impossible in the real world! Also people are not restricted to just floor space; they can quite happily float in the air.

- Theatre in VR. (See below for descriptions of VRML Dream, and Steve Guynup's poetry readings, both of which were held recently in virtual reality.) Virtual theatre opens up a wealth of possibilities! Leaving aside the <u>actors</u> and their capability to easily take on any form desired, let us consider the audience for a minute. They are no longer sitting in rows of seats. They may wander about, through the action. They need not have bodies at all,

Mueller 13

though out of respect to the actors they might become little points of light so that the actors may still be able to play to their audience. And the sets! They can be whole worlds. Some stories may become more open-ended where the audience is able to take part in the action. How would one write such a story? What are the 3D equivalents for cuts, pans, and dissolves?

- Film and stage directors can use VR to storyboard their productions in an easily manipulated and interactive way. Sets built in VR would allow crew, set constructors, and camera to walk through the action together without even having to be in the same country! Scenes can be recorded to be played back on a laptop anytime later.

- VR would allow schools to add immediacy to distance-education. At present a very few lucky people are able to use <u>video conferencing</u> occasionally, but this requires special, expensive equipment. VR will work on any reasonably fast computer over a normal phone line using an ordinary modem. There are a lot of people currently exploring the possibilities for teaching through the use of VR.

Guymer 3

- Some doctors are already beginning to use simple VR to view things like 3D CAT scans of patients. VR might be particularly useful in consultations if patient and doctor(s) are separated by great distance. There has been some use of VR in helping people overcome phobias, particularly acrophobia (fear of heights).

- Architects and engineers have been using VR for some time now to allow them to walk potential customers through as-yet-unbuilt structures. This gives customers more control over the design of what they are buying. The designers benefit by having more satisfied customers.

- <u>Game players</u> (this is the application most people initially think of) can have worlds which would combine the visual immediacy of arcade games with the intellectual and

Mueller 13

social challenge of MUDs. (Multi-User Dungeons or Multi-User Dimensions are text-based, online imaginary worlds used for socializing and gaming. They actually have nothing to do with dungeons and can be set in space stations or medieval worlds, anywhere or anywhen that their writer fancies.)

- Advertising on the Internet, in the form of banner ads, can be made much more interesting while making them download faster. Many people consider advertisements on the net to be an annoyance, ignoring the fact that very often it is these ads which pay for the pages or search engines that we use. An animated gif banner ad can quite easily be 10k bytes in size. That will just be a simple two- or three-frame picture. Linda Hahner and her company Out Of The Blue have pioneered the use of banner ads which are little virtual worlds playing a short movie lasting several minutes. Most surprising is that their file size is no larger than an animated gif!

- Of course the new art forms of World Building and avatar sculpting, just now appearing, will grow, and proud artists will display their latest creations for all to explore.

As with all new fields, this work will be certain to open up unexpected vistas of human endeavour . . . and to support them, many new industries are bound to spring up.

The downside

Every technology has its downside and the use of VR by the military is one sad note. But VR is no good as a place to do the actual fighting—you can't physically hurt anybody in VR. In fact, that is one of the aspects which makes it so useful for the military; real-world training exercises can be very dangerous and there are often casualties. It has to be noted that one by-product of that work is the commercial aeroplane flight training simulator, which has made air travel so much safer for all the rest of us. But the Military are no longer the greatest source of funding for VR. Entertainment and tourism have become the biggest money-spinners in the world and now drive VR research and development. I expect that as the possibilities for communication via VR become more widely appreciated, the communications industries will become more involved too.

For many people, their only exposure to VR is the <u>shooting</u> and racing games in game parlours. My only answer to critics of VR who point to the violent nature of these games, is to ask if they condemn all books for a few which glorify battle. Do they dismiss the value of film and theatre because of the many violent shows? Most VR is as distant from these parlour games as *Rambo* is from *Fantasia*.

Hawthorne
10

There is the problem that only a minority of people in the world have access to this wonderful new technology—the information-rich. But if previous technologies are anything to go by, this is something which will change fairly rapidly as VR shows its usefulness and as the equipment becomes more affordable. Currently the speed and power of computers roughly doubles about every eighteen months while the price halves. 'Old' computers, unwanted in the information rich worlds, find their way to developing nations giving them low-cost access.

There has been some criticism of the <u>Kyoko Date</u> project to create a virtual pop star (see the links at the end of this document). The worry seems to be that people will be misled by an idealized humanoid. Leaving aside the fact that the Kyoko Date project never tried to palm their creation off as real ('date' is Japanese for 'fake' or 'for show'), such concerns seem to underestimate people's good sense and need for complex, real humans. Kyoko created a sensation for a few weeks in Japan, then people just lost interest in it. We won't have to worry about virtual humans till computers manage to pass the Turing Test, and then our main worry is going to be how to extend our definitions of human rights, and citizenship to include them . . . but that will be decades, perhaps even centuries off yet.

Klein 9
Hawthorne
10

The criticism of such creations as Kyoko could be extended to include avatars such as Summer: the argument being that a veneer of beauty hides the true nature of the human flaws underneath and makes people more intolerant of physical defects. But I would argue exactly the opposite. We already have an incredibly powerful culture of physical beauty which marginalizes, and is terribly oppressive of, those of us who 'don't measure up'. Using avatars as trojan horses we are able to meet people and befriend them before revealing our physical nature. This forces people to admit to themselves that people with different skin colours, different dress styles, different levels of capability (deaf, wheelchair users, blind, etc.) are worthwhile human beings. You can try to reason with someone who is racist or bigoted until you are blue in the face, but the only way to actually convince them is to have one of 'the despised' become their friend. VR manages this in a way few other media have. True, it would be much better if we could simply have more public images of good and worthwhile ugly people, brilliant people in wheelchairs, great people of all races—and I believe that day is coming . . . gradually. But in the meantime we have to work around our petty human failings any way we can.

Why haven't I mentioned the problem of children becoming 'hooked' on VR and losing touch with reality? Because I don't see it as a problem. I don't think VR will be realistic enough to be much of an escape for perhaps another few decades at least—perhaps never—reality is just so very much better! In fact, using VR always makes me realize how incredible the real world is. My appreciation of everyday things is magnified: small weeds growing through cracks in the concrete, the dust motes in a sunbeam from the window, a bird outside my window feeding on nectar from a flower. And computer generated VR just pales in comparison to the escape value of a good book. (I chuckle when I remember being warned by some people when I was a child that I spent too much time reading books.) Books are the ultimate in VR! Films, stage plays, and computer VR experiences have great difficulty conveying what a person thinks and feels, or what their motivation is. These are easily, economically conveyed through the printed word. With a good book you are able to be omniscient, to feel the emotions of perhaps several characters and understand what drives them.

The astonishing thing about online VR communities is that they exist largely in spite of the need to earn their owners an income. There have been a number of extraordinary universes which have imploded under the pressure of finance (OzVirtual, OnliveTraveller, the early AlphaWorld, are three prominent examples). The simple fact is that most virtual worlds are not run by large faceless corporations, but by small groups of visionaries who love to meet and socialize with people, and sculpt 3D artforms.

Ramifications

I would like to close this piece with a quick look at the ramifications of VR and its long-term effect on our society.

Using VR to see the unseeable is bound to have some large effects on research at some points in the future. Things which have always been impossible to visualize will become open to understanding in new ways.

Nobody can foresee what this will illuminate. It could finally lead to an understanding of protein folding, or how the brain organizes itself, or how room-temperature superconductivity might be achieved. It could open new windows onto understanding the weather, or the operation of the immune system. It is conceivable it could spark whole new industries. Few things have this kind of potential.

Most air pollution is produced by the common motor car, usually driven by one person to and from work each day. Virtual reality holds out the prospect that many people may be able to avoid this costly waste of time and money each day. This would free up the roads for those who still need them, making them less dangerous as well as less frustrating. At the moment it is not unusual for people to spend three or four hours each day just travelling to and from work! The cost of petrol and wear and tear on vehicles must be a huge expense in the economy, aside from the tragedy of death and injury from road accidents. Funds currently spent building giant arterial roads would find other uses too.

National borders will become immaterial when interacting with other people. It won't matter if the people in your conference room are from the same city as yourself or whether they're talking with you from points scattered all over the Earth; it is all the same to someone in VR. The familiarity with other cultures that this brings will make it very difficult to support the insanity that is racism, and will help to heal the intolerance that springs from xenophobia.

Epidemics spread extremely easily through any large society where there is a lot of personal contact. The telephone began the technological trend to interpersonal communication without physical contact. VR can only enhance this. Human contact is a necessary part of society and will never be replaced by VR, but unwanted or unnecessary contact is a waste of time and, as the threat of new infections grows, it may become an avoidable risk.

Fletcher 14

Most people with disabilities are as capable of performing work inside VR as anybody else. This makes possible the integration of a very marginalized group into the mainstream of productive society. For people whose ability to move is severely restricted, new work on getting signals direct from the brain offers the prospect of minimizing their dependency on other people and enhancing their lifestyle. For people who have one or more senses missing or severely diminished, there is hope of receiving direct input to their brains—replacing or augmenting those senses. If you find this a gruesome thought, consider how you would feel if you fell tomorrow and broke your neck, or if you lost your sight due to glaucoma as do thousands of people every year. If you were offered the ability to resume your social and working life, through using a computer in this way instead of being reliant on somebody else for much of the rest of your life, would you consider it perverse? . . . or liberating?

The structure of cities will undergo some change as most office work will take place at home instead of in the city. People will go to the city specifically to meet people and for entertainment. The cities will become more service-industry based. Manufacturing will change later when telepresence becomes common. After that people will be able to control factory machines from home.

Some of us will always be the pioneers, with a desperate need to search for new horizons, but as the planet is more and more affected by people, what little that remains of wilderness becomes too valuable to intrude upon. As space travel recedes ever further into the future, where can the pioneers go? VR offers an infinite multitude of universes.

References

Books

Rheingold, Howard. 1991, 1992. *Virtual Reality*. London: Mandarin Paperbacks.
Still the best for an entertaining and down-to-earth, backgrounder on the concepts and major developments in VR, though with the sudden rise of multi-user virtual worlds and VRML in the last couple of years it is getting a little dated.

Hartman, Jed & Wernecke, Josie. 1996. *VRML 2.0 Handbook*. Reading, Massachusetts: Addison-Wesley.
The ultimate resource for those interested in learning how to build worlds using VRML (Virtual Reality Modeling Language).

Wilcox, Sue Ki. 1998. *Web Developer.com Guide to 3D Avatars*. New York: John Wiley & Sons, Wiley Computer Publishing.
A guide to the main software available for building avatars. It has a practical and a commercial approach. Comes with a CD-ROM containing demo software and avatar models. There is also a Web site with updates.

Roehl, Bernie; Justin Couch; Cindy Reed-Ballreich; Tim Rohaly and Geoff Brown. 1997. *Late Night VRML 2.0 with Java*. Emeryville, CA: Macmillan Computer Publishing, Ziff-Davis Press.
This enormous tome covers tutorials on textures and sound in VRML worlds, the Living Worlds and Humanoid Animation standards, and using the Java programming language to make multi-user worlds.

On the Internet

(These sites are all current as of this writing, but the Web changes constantly so don't expect all to be current years later.)

Active Worlds

<<u>http://www.activeworlds.com/</u>>

This phenomenal universe of worlds has the fastest, and most feature-packed interface to date. The also have by far the greatest number of worlds and the greatest number of inhabitants.

Aussiecon-VR

<<u>http://www.outerworlds.com/worldcon/</u>>

This project will present more than 50 virtual worlds in about nine virtual universes during the 57th World Science Fiction Convention being held in Melbourne in September 1999. This is the first of what I expect will be annual VR restivals. A team of almost 100 people (mostly volunteers) are producing this event.

Avatars98 Homepage

<<u>http://www.ccon.org/conf98/</u>>

You can see pictures and reports of what went on during the day.

Biota/Artificial Life

<<u>http://www.biota.org/</u>>

This is a working group—a bunch of volunteers who do this purely as an interest, trying to develop standards and new artforms (and lifeforms).

Blaxxun Interactive Virtual Worlds

<<u>http://www.blaxxun.com/</u>>

This is probably the best known multi-user virtual world on the Internet. You will need to download a fairly large (free) program to enter the world though.

Construct

<<u>http://www.construct.net/</u>>

Lisa Goldman is the president of this amazing company in USA. They have a lot of useful information online.

CosmoPlayer

<<u>http://cosmosoftware.com/</u>>

The most-used VRML viewer for the Internet. It is freely downloadable, and plugs in to become a part of your Web browser which may be Netscape Navigator (or Communicator), or Microsoft's Internet Explorer.

DeepMatrix

<<u>http://www.geometrek.com/</u>>

DeepMatrix is a multi-user virtual world system which, like VNet, doesn't require any special download. It improves upon VNet however, in two main areas: it offers shared objects, and the ability to have more people in a world simultaneously than VNet.

Focus on Web3D

<<u>http://web3d.about.com/</u>>

Sandy Ressler has made this a central clearing-house for all manner of news and information relating to VRML.

Jeff Sonstein's list of VNet Worlds

<<u>http://ariadne.iz.net/~jeffs/vnet/</u>>

Information about VNet, including a list of current VNet worlds on the Web that you can visit. Remember that a VNet world requires no special software other than a standard VRML viewer in your Web browser.

Kyoko Date

<<u>http://www.dhw.co.jp/horipro/talent/DK96/index_e.html</u>>

<http://www.etud.insa-tlse.fr/~mdumas/kyoko.html>
  Japanese project to create a virtual pop star.
Miriam's Home Page
<http://werple.net.au/~miriam/>
  My pages contain some VRML avatars and worlds and many lists of links. Take the
  Virtual Reality link to find more links to things VR.
Out Of The Blue
<http://www.outoftheblue.com/>
  Linda Hahner is president and CEO of this, the company to make the world's first VR
  banner ads. They have also been doing a lot of work on educational stuff for kids in
  VRML.
Pond World
<http://www.contentcreator.com/PondR01b.wrl>
  Tracey Bezesky's cute pond world.
Rendering Revealed
<http://www.parc.xerox.com/red/members/stone/vrml-cfwg/rendering/>
  Maureen Stone's tutorial on lighting in VRML worlds.
Sony Community Place
<http://sonypic.com/>
  This is another well-known multi-user world on the net, but with a very large (freely
  downloadable) program required to gain entry.
Summer's page at Millennium Co
<http://millenium.simplenet.com/summer.htm>
  Summer is the avatar by Victoria D'Onofrio (MyTwoKeys) and Rodolfo Galeano
  (Netropolis) which won the Avatars98 grand prize.
Texture Mapping in VRML
<http://www.ywd.com/cindy/vrml_tex.html>
  Written by Cindy Reed-Ballreich, this is the ultimate reference on using textures in
  VRML.
The Web 3D Consortium
<http://www.web3d.org/>
  This is the nerve centre for VRML.
VRML97
<http://www.web3d.org/Specifications/VRML97>
  This is a complete specification of VRML 97 (Virtual Reality Modeling Language
  version 2). It enables you to build virtual worlds using just a text editor.
www-vrml
<www-vrml-request@web3d.org>
  This is the main VRML mailing list. To subscribe (it costs nothing), send an email
  with 'info' in the main part of the text (without the quotes).

thirteen

The Nickelodeon Days of Cyberspace

by Kathy Mueller

In the 1990s cyberspace, multimedia, the Internet and online communication have been appropriated by the masses as their latest entertainment obsession. Multi-player games, chat-rooms and search engines offer a variety of distractions to the end-user.

It has been exactly one hundred years since the last mass frenzy over a media innovation. In the 1890s, the magic of film was introduced by the Lumière brothers in France when they screened a train rapidly approaching the audience. In this historic moment, half the audience ran screaming from the hall, for fear that they would be run down . . . but they kept coming back for more . . . and flooded the penny arcades to watch the hand-cranked machines[1] show simulations of the animated physical world on the moving screen.

The filmic medium is about the manipulation of the physical dimension: the impact of image size, the dynamics of movement, the variation of points of view, and their juxtaposition so that the sequence of images creates an impact upon the viewer's consciousness and emotional state.

Cyberspace, which involves multimedia, the Internet and online engagement, is a medium about the manipulation of the mental dimension. Its strongest impact is on the subconscious, rather than the conscious. I have yet to come across a dictionary definition of cyberspace, but if we accept that it has to do with the mental dimension, then the definition of cybernetics should suffice as a starting point. *The Macquarie Dictionary* describes cybernetics as:

---

[1]. See Kevin Brownlow (1968) for a detailed description of the development of the filmic medium.

the scientific study of those methods of communication and control which are common to living organisms and machine, especially as applied to the analysis of the operations of machines such as computers.

Hence <u>cyberspace</u> could equate to head-space or mental space, as in the exploration of the nature of interaction, both internally and externally, so as to methodically communicate within systems or groups in an effective pattern. Mental constructs, our assumptions, our deep-seated beliefs and expectations, our personal boundaries, our sense of self, our mental processes, are all called into play. How is this so? Because we directly engage in an interactive process which takes place within a digital medium wherein we reveal aspects of our mental processes through language/text, image, roles engaged in, and interlock with others who are also revealing aspects of their mental dimension.

Fletcher 14

Without the presence of the physical dimension to signal us, our expectation of true identity and reality (both our own and others!) is challenged. The imagination, without the containment of the physical, can go wild: self can become anything or anyone. There are stories of men posing as women (and vice versa) in online chat-groups. There are stories of older people posing as younger people in lonely hearts chat-rooms in order to relive moments of romance and passion. Initially this identity swapping caused a huge furore. There are stories of people feeling <u>betrayed</u> and outraged by the discovery that those online identities that they had 'bonded with', turned out to be totally opposite to what had been presented in text. There were cries of invasion, overstepping the boundaries, of 'mind-fucking', a total warping of the concept of identity and truth. But what is self? What is identity? What is that distasteful invasion of the mind all about? And what is truth and whose truth is it?

Klein 9

Yes, these are the 'Nickelodeon Days' of cyberspace. Just as audiences of the 1890s were caught off guard by the startling dynamism of film sequences: the oncoming train, the roller coaster sequence, or the sea waves sequence—sequences which shattered the audience's barriers of defence—so too, the confronting range of roles and misrepresentation of identity, image and illusions of reality in cyberspace have caught the masses off guard. Despite their plea for protection from the insincere, they are nonetheless addicted[2] to this new form of communication. How quickly it has become acceptable to take on multiple identities without anyone thinking the worst of you.

Sherry Turkle (1985, 1995) has done extensive research into the effects that computers and online interactions have on the individual. She expresses a concern for understanding the changing sense of self in an increasingly complex world. Turkle sees Self as multiple and the multiplicity of selves required to deal with the multiplicity of systems, roles and functions needs to be accepted in order for the individual to become fully developed. Turkle observes that in online computer interaction the self is constructed and transformed by language.[3]

The exploration of the multiplicity of selves is better known in drama circles as role-play. I see role-play as the key to the creation of an online industry that will encompass entertainment, mental health, education, the solving of political and social problems and the sorting of conflict.

With cyberspace in its infancy, the doors are wide open to creative uses of its rich convergence of arts, science and technology. In the past five years I have been investigating a wide range of disciplines in order to come to terms with the convergence that creates cyberspace: psychology, mythology, anthropology, game theory, interface design, graphic design, navigation design, communication theory,

---

2. This latest addiction was confirmed when a self-help group, 'chatrooms anonymous', set themselves up online to try to understand what had happened to them. Many had lost their jobs, some had lost their partners due to their online addiction.

3. What strikes me about online interaction, especially chat-rooms, is that people are riveted by the sense of community and interaction at the very time when their external 'real' worlds have ceased to promote a sense of community or a sense of place for the individual. In an online interaction, one speaks through text and another acknowledges those thoughts with a response. As simple as this 'cause and effect' may seem, many people do not experience this sense of acknowledgement or balanced interaction in their lives. It is understandable how our need for 'acknowledgement' can become an addiction.

instructional design, information design, computer systems architecture, databases, data processing and tracking systems.

Cyberspace has the potential for integrating polarities, dualities and multiplicities. On the one hand it supports the feminine notion of <u>connectivity</u>, networking, team process, and the dialectical process of asynchronous online dialogues with flexible work hours from flexible locations. On the other, it is built upon the masculine notion of logic and precision programming which make it possible to wire the variety of computer hardware and software combinations in order to connect with people from around the world. And the great news is, by careful appropriation of masculine and feminine mental constructs, we are capable of realigning to true creativity.

Hawthorne
6

<u>Creativity</u> is about bringing into existence that which has not yet been thought of. It is a product of the mental dimension, especially of the imaginative faculty. In my experience, the creative process begins with an awareness of the physical dimension we live within, and an awareness of what is lacking within the physical dimension. It is the need to deal with this lack that spurs on the creative process. Creativity often begins by isolating known components of patterns and rearranging those components into different and new combinations.

Arnold 11

How can cyberspace promote creativity, when I define cyberspace as being of the mental dimension rather than the physical dimension where creativity starts? Here is the wonderful catch: humans have the unique ability to take abstract concepts and find physical representations for them. Mythology and archetypal images, stories and characters are the most enduring representations of complex, abstract themes and issues. The narrative structure of storytelling sets up the situation, builds the conflicts through obstacles in the way of intended goals, and finally presents the resolution of issues arising from the situation.

If we approach <u>storytelling</u> from a Jungian perspective, all story elements are figurative metaphors and concrete devices which reconstruct the internal process of discovering one's inner potential, the inner landscape and mental constructs. All the characters in a

Namjoshi
17
Hawthorne
19
Fletcher 14

dramatic story are aspects of self. The tasks which the hero must engage in to reach the ultimate goal are metaphors for the 'process' of empowerment. The obstacles in the path of the hero are physical representations of internal conflicts which keep us from achieving our full potential.

So where does storytelling intersect with cyberspace? Through the engagement in online role-play. This may be in free-form text games such as Dungeons and Dragons adventure role-play, or it can be in the future developments of interactive soap opera and melodrama wherein players take on prestructured character types who work together or against each other to achieve their character goals.

Carol Pearson[4] talks about six kinds of heroes evident in everyday lives: the innocent, the orphan, the martyr, the magician, the warrior, and the wanderer. We see these characters pop up time and time again in our favourite movies, and feel comforted by stories that reflect our inner struggle with the human condition. But there is a difference between watching the role modeling of hero journeys within movies and actually engaging in the heroic tasks within a role-play environment.

English 12

While there will be many extraordinary uses made of the Internet, one of the most useful and creative developments of cyberspace could be the design of an online role-play methodology which promotes the discovery of one's inner potential through game play interactions. I believe it is possible to design a process whereby each individual could track their own mental processes, analyse whether their own strategies are useful in terms of achieving a given task, and diagnose how best to make the required changes for self-empowerment.

In England, game theorist Nigel Howard (1989) and his colleagues have recently been exploring the intersection of game

---

[4.] In her preface, Carol Pearson suggests that we would not be able to solve the great political and social problems of our time if we persisted in seeing the hero as 'out there' beyond ourselves. She echoes the Jungian concept for the need to take the journey that is innate in our species.

If we do not risk, if we play prescribed social roles instead of taking our own journeys, we feel numb, we experience a sense of alienation, a void, an emptiness inside.

theory with drama theory. A glance at the glossary terms for his drama theory reveals how all the elements of drama and its unpredictability could be programmed into computer role-play. Similarly, in the USA, Chris Crawford has developed an online game structure outlining a storytelling device Erazmatron, that defines character, objects, goals and emotional unpredictability.

Unlike game theory, where winning and losing are defined by the rules of the game, drama theory accepts that outcomes of dramatic crisis can be unpredictable and are seldom played out according to the rules. In other words, drama theory embraces the irrational element of being human. It is often the irrational elements within each of us that allows us to survive when the chips are down and we are facing annihilation, whether that annihilation manifests itself physically, mentally or emotionally.

Some drama theorists believe that all stories can be described in terms of <u>mathematical formula</u>.[5] If this is true, then the marriage of game theory and drama theory holds great promise for exploring the unpredictable elements of the mind . . ., and with this promise comes the pioneering of tandem industries in entertainment, mental health and social politics.[6]

Hawthorne
19

Games and game play create a safe containment that one does not often have access to in real life. Self-expression can be explored since

---

5. In an entertaining letter to the editor of *New Scientist Magazine*, Stan Hayward—film writer, drama theorist and scientist—responds to the work of Nigel Howard's marriage of game theory and drama theory by defining the mathematical models of drama theory which include linear (sequential), zigzag (non-sequential), domino (one event sets off others in a line), and ripple (one event spreads out in all directions), shunting (an event effecting others but indirectly), and bus stop (characters changing as the story moves along). Hayward also outlines character objectives as being 'the game', and suggests that players are divided into those who promote the objective and those who hinder it.

6. The gateway to these online industries is the formulation of meta-data: meta-models of communications, meta-games, meta-patterns, meta-tracking and meta-processing. The ability to see what meaning really lies beneath the language, what meaning lies within the game or the shift in the games being played, the ability to see the patterns of interaction and assess the <u>frame of reference</u> from which to interpret interaction, has gradually been building over the past decades with the work of neurolinguistic programmers who study models of interaction and define the elements of interaction. Since this work can be described in terms of input and output, it can be translated to 'computer speak' and at present is limited only by the knowledge one has of programming.

Namjoshi
17

the containment within game rules creates a separation from reality. Players may be encouraged to engage in a wide range of emotional responses, including the 'darker' emotions of anger, jealousy, fear, guilt, betrayal, etc. Games can also create a catalyst for ego-enhancement. Issues concerning competition, self-esteem, power and helplessness, and risk-taking may come to the fore in a game. The game structure provides an opportunity to confront, work through, and gain mastery over uncomfortable feelings. And games can create an environment for cognitive repatterning skills. Concentration, memory, anticipating consequences of one's behaviour, reflectivity, and creative problem-solving, can be developed through game play.[7]

Fletcher 14

The rules of game play are constructed around the same elements found in <u>stories and storytelling</u>. Games are developed around themes, there is a clear set-up or starting point, a clear goal or ending point, a clear set of character roles, and the elements of conflict and obstacle are clearly signalled.

The kinds of character roles in any given game dictates the level of complexity it expects the player to engage in. Some role-plays are straight forward. The role of the guard in a football game is to guard the goal posts, to keep the ball from entering between the posts. This must be done at any cost. On the other hand, if a player takes on the role of the detective who must solve a crime in a mystery game, then more complex patterns of mental processes must be engaged in.

It is these more complex interactions that interest me, for they demand the examination of player strategies, tactics and meta-communication patterning that goes beyond the present online games which clutter the multi-player arena. It forces the question: can we track online player interaction so as to present the appropriate 'pay-off' sequences for given scenarios and assess the outcomes?

For player interactions to be tracked, the nuts and bolts of communication theory need to be accepted. Data is information

---

7. See Charles Schaefer and Steven E. Reid (1986) on the full range of life skills that one could master from engaging in game play.

which is potential knowledge. Data information flows in a particular direction (or directions). Data can be defined as input or output. Data can be processed. Data can flow intermittently, can be withheld, can be conditional. Data can be networked and systematized. Data needs to be analysed within given contexts.[8]

Although the theory of communication and learning may appear to be dry, the case studies are anything but dull. If we apply communication theory to human relationships the results are explosive. Gregory Bateson (1972)[9] explores the making of a schizophrenic over three generations, as an issue of communication patterning. When input and output are scrambled, and neither is acknowledged for what it is, that is, the context is constantly shifting, then disjuncture results. Complex mental patterning disintegrates into a chronic state of defence. It becomes clear that mental patterns are a key feature in communication, mental health and learning (Bateson 1972; Schank and Riesbeck 1981).[10] It is Bateson's, and Schank's and Riesbeck's work that inspired me to look further into <u>mental mapping</u>.

Arnold 11
Hawthorne 19
Fletcher 14

Throughout this discourse I refer to mental maps, mental constructs, mental models and mental patterns. Basically all these terms are subsets of an individual's thinking process. It includes their belief systems, attitudes, values, behaviours, fears, hopes, dreams, goals and ambitions. The thinking process is revealed through actions and reactions (physical, verbal, emotional) and the

---

8. See Bonnie Nardi (1995), research Scientist in advanced technology at Apple Computer, on 'activity theory' as a means of structuring human-computer interaction. Activity theory provides a hierarchical framework for describing human activity and offers a set of perspectives for its use in many areas of human need, including health and education.

9. *Steps to an Ecology of Mind* is a revolutionary approach to man's understanding of himself in which social anthropologist and mental health advocate Gregory Bateson describes the unconscious level of the mind as being inaccessible except by icons and metaphors (1972: 142). Meta-messages are signalled during interchanges which provide more trustworthy comment than the verbal message.

10. Roger Schank and C.K. Riesbeck propose that learning involves memory, memory involves story or narrative, and that we store data bits of 'story memory' so as to create mental patterns which in time become our beliefs which inform our attitudes and behaviour responses.

contradictions within these combinations. Because I am interested in tracking online role-play interaction, an understanding of mental constructs is important. Computer-devised characters can be mapped, and their relationships between each other can be mapped. But how is the player's mental process tracked? The live-online player is given choices of ways to respond depending on what role they are playing. These choices need to be signalled through a communication interface which best helps the player identify her/his own mental processes, at the same time allowing the computer to track those mental patterns and offer solutions accordingly.

So how do we move from the Nickelodeon Days of cyberspace to a more sophisticated use of cyberspace? What shift needs to take place in human thinking in order to fully maximize its potential? Cognitive scientists, psychodramatists and clinical psychologists have led the way in defining human nature, identifying the elements of human interaction, human needs and behavioural patterns. But an elitist's 'knowing' about human thinking and communication does not create a change in the thinking of the masses. The knowledge must be structured in a form that is useful to the masses. It is only when the masses themselves embrace the concept of mental constructs through personal usefulness, that an evolution (or indeed revolution) in mental processes can take place. Lead on role-play!

The Beginnings of Interactive Soap Opera and Melodrama
All the people I know who 'hang out' in online chat-rooms love the verbal engagement with a wide range of colourful characters. However, the one thing that everyone eventually seems to desire is that something dramatic happen: some dramatic event that galvanizes those in the chat-room to act together to achieve something.

This desire is really about wanting to engage in adventure role-play. Humans have a natural desire to engage in situations where some goal or intention is achieved and everyone feels a sense of completion, fulfilment and in many cases exhilaration. And it can be a safe way to bond with others. It is also about the desire to explore aspects of self, often aspects of self that are not permissible in the 'real world'. I have a friend who takes on a lot of responsibility in her real life job, but when she gets on the Internet she loves taking on the role of the delinquent, or the outrageous one. In real life she is a model citizen and highly regarded by her peers, but in an online chat-room she can be obnoxious to the point where online viewers dismiss her as an angry young male.

So what would happen if there were online interactive soap operas and melodramas where players could, on a regular basis, take on roles which suited their moods, inclinations and desires? At present there are a number of online adventure role-play games in the form of <u>MUDs</u> *(Multi-User-Dungeons or Dimensions whereby players meet online and engage in role-plays within a text-based description of an environment)* but the interactions take place by typing in text rather than being entertained by a stunning graphical interface. What I am proposing is that story-lines around a variety of dramatic characters, themes and genres be prestructured so that players can take on a role and explore dimensions of themselves which may not be possible in the real world, by dealing with dramatic situations online.

Montgomery 5
English 12

Interactive soapies and melodramas are one of the futures of online entertainment. For every kind of TV drama you watch, there could be a simulated online role-play whereby, instead of passively watching or vicariously experiencing, you learn by doing, you gain insights and wisdom through the experience of making the decisions, 'sweating' over the choices, feeling the mistakes and celebrating the victories.

The beginnings of interactive soap could start out with something simple: Live-Online-Little-Interactive-Episodic-Serials.

A player would log on to a given Web site, choose a character, receive instructions as to the character's intended goal, and then engage with other characters (players) from around the world in order to achieve the character's goal. Players could explore playing hero roles of which they never thought they were capable. Players get hooked into the role-play when the central question is asked: Will I achieve my goal or will I be led astray, seduced by the devious

(Image by Kiera Poelsma)

intentions of others? Players could also choose to explore the Villain, the shady aspects of self that they dare not explore in real life. Again, the central question hooks the player into a learning curve: Will evil triumph or will the villain be foiled by the noble deeds of others? And by the way, What was that neat strategy that character used to deflect negative criticism?!

The engagement in role-play brings an immediacy to situations and an intimacy between parties despite the tyranny of distance. Not only does it hold a future for entertainment, but the same principles can be used for social politics, simulation training, education and mental health. The mental health industry is a growing area worldwide and is badly understaffed. In creating an interactive structure which puts players in charge of their own learning about self and mental processes, preventative measures can be taken to alleviate an area of growing social unrest: family dysfunction, workplace dysfunction, communication breakdown, and youth suicide.

The Dovetailing of Entertaining Role-Play and Mental Health

Earlier I implied that games and role-play promote the self-discovery process. Living in an era where 'body image' defines acceptability and the lack of an acceptable body image promotes low self-esteem and self-worth, games and role-play are vital tools in discovering what really matters about self and human interaction.

A sense of Self is born out of three developmental discoveries: the **concept of secrets** (the creation of an internal boundary where precious information is stored), the **concept of intimacy** (sharing secrets as the way of bonding others to our internal secret world, of extending boundaries to those we trust) and the **concept of manipulating the external world** (Piaget 1929, 1932, 1951, 1954; Winnicott 1953, 1962, 1974; Meares 1992).

These three concepts form the basis for much human conflict, and hence are central to role-play development. If we tease out these concepts into personal issues, they may translate into the following:

The concept of secrecy would relate to issues of personal power and safety, the concept of intimacy to issues of discernment and trust: whom to trust with the sharing of self-knowledge. And the concept of manipulation would relate to issues of action, effecting change, making decisions, doing, achieving, controlling the outer world to get our needs met.

Secrecy, intimacy and manipulation are powerful concepts, and yet these concepts often become taboo in our social structure. A child who keeps a secret from his/her parents can be labelled as sneaky, untrustworthy, or bad! A child who has a mind of her/his own can be seen as 'difficult' to control and therefore dangerous. For the authoritarian parent, this presents a threat to parental control, and therefore the child must be punished.

If we compare parental feedback to notions of game play feedback, we might have a better understanding of how a child becomes disempowered. Both parental feedback and the rules of game play define the parameters for what is considered an acceptable 'win' situation, and what responses will create a 'lose' situation.

The name of the game is 'communication': visual, auditory, kinaesthetic (feeling) messages about how to deal with problems and what is considered an acceptable solution. Just as in game play feedback, parental feedback may be spoken rules, unspoken rules, unspoken expectations, voiced expectations, examples and role modelling, mood or tone. But the difference between game play feedback and parental feedback can be huge. The rules within a game structure are programmed and fed back to the player in clear terms of cause and effect and with clear win/lose parameters. But the rules of parental control often imply mixed signals, confused feedback wherein one message contradicts another. Thus a verbal message may be structured with positive words but the unspoken message (the tone) may be negative. These mixed messages can create a situation whereby the child can never win, and thus can never feel empowered within the relationship.

Westwood and Kaufmann 15

Unfortunately the social/familial influences on how one communicates are long lasting, and are embedded into the individual's psyche or mental patterns until some other structure or mental pattern is introduced in such a way as to allow the individual to explore other ways of dealing, thinking, and strategizing. Research reveals that kids love playing games because once they learn the rules, they can win: something they never get to do in their real lives. Thus we have an opportunity through games and role-plays to undo some of the communication dysfunction created by real life.

Role-play enhances communication skills and survival strategies. The willingness to engage in a variety of character roles increases awareness of different thinking, different attitudes and different coping strategies. Role-play scenarios create a safe containment for players to explore aspects of themselves: aspects which are revealed by how they interact with other characters. Players taking on a role are clearly guided as to what aspect of themselves they are playing, what their primary objective is, and what attributes their character role possesses in order to overcome obstacles and achieve their goals.

This kind of clarity and focus can be highly entertaining and creatively addictive! It encourages playfulness and spontaneity, especially in playing out roles which are normally taboo in social situations. Much to the consternation of parents many players of adventure role-play games love engaging in the role of the 'baddie'— what Jungians would call the 'shadow side'. However, if the safe containment of a role-play game does not allow us to explore the darker side of our natures and understand its consequences, how will we ever come to know our selves fully? The energy of the unexplored aspects of self lies dormant until a force outside of self stirs it, and then it will be projected out onto another who could use that power against us because we have failed to understand its dynamic and we fear its power and strangeness.

Human beings at their most creative moments are inquisitive. When certain aspects of self are denied or forbidden, that is, the shadow side, or darker emotions, then Self continues on the journey of self-evolution with fewer resources, less feeling, and less inquisitiveness. Unfortunately the politics of denial are rife in our society. When the president of a nation lies in public under oath about his behaviour, what chance does the average person have for gaining a role model who acknowledges all aspects of self? Our socialization process encourages minimization of the important feelings and of personal issues through quiet omission, or even blatant lies. If the price of denial is loss of feelings, then an emptiness builds up inside the self, an emptiness created by frozen feelings. Alternative realities are constructed in an attempt to fill the void: fantasy worlds that further betray our perception of what is really happening (Milburn *et al*. 1996).

Schaefer (1986) nominates the offspring from 'authoritarian' parents as those who have much to gain from game play and role-play:

> Authoritarian parents discourage a free flow of ideas in the family and pre-empt most decision-making power. They exercise social power through coercion, threats and punishments (Schaefer 1986: 131).

This observation dovetails neatly with Melbourne psychologist Russell Meares's (1992: 74) notion that 'those with disorders of self usually live in a state of chronic disjunction'. Curiosity, inquisitiveness and the flow of exploration has been curtailed and a sense of isolation follows.

In designing role-play, it is important to encourage a free flow of ideas (the good, the bad and the ugly) within a safe containment of rules and role-play, with continuity of feedback both from other 'characters' as well as from computer 'help' guides. This approach not only enhances the entertainment value, but is also vital for the development of those with social difficulties.

The principles of symbolic role-play games and rule-based games are thematically similar to real life situations and provide an avenue for development of self. Piaget (1951, 1959) describes symbolic play as the mingling of magic and reality. The inanimate real world is given attributes of life. The child's ability to imagine animation in inanimate objects is paralleled by a magical omnipotence: we believe that human activity determines universal events. This magical system of thinking involves a sense of power as well as terror. In a computer role-play game, the player engages with the notion of symbolic play, assigns power to the graphics on the screen, and endows them with power. The player can genuinely become fearful when the 'baddie' threatens her/him.

The Principles of Drama: Real life and fantasy

Every good dramatist is familiar with Psychologist Abraham Maslow's Hierarchy of Human Needs: Survival, Safety and Security, Love and Belonging, Esteem and Self-Respect, Knowledge and Understanding, and Self-Actualization. This hierarchy reveals what motivates us, and what's at stake if we don't get our basic needs met. At the core of any good role-play situation is one of these basic needs. It is worth spending some time exploring these basic needs, since mental patterns and coping strategies develop around these needs. This discussion will distil in the reader an understanding of some of the elements that must be tracked in order to interpret a player's motivation, mental constructs and meta-patterns.

The need for survival is the most fundamental human need, for without it, nothing else matters, nothing else is possible. This need for survival is about mental and emotional survival as well as physical survival. Sadly, many individuals do not survive the mental and emotional scarring of early life experiences in any form that allows them the freedom to discover their full potential. Yes, they may survive physically, but their lives may be reduced to an empty shell, and they may live with the mentality of a prisoner within their own minds: minds that were patterned on mental constructs which abhorred the full exploration of self. Given this situation, if a player feels that survival is at stake during the role-play interaction, this may trigger some unpredictable responses.

The need for safety and security brings a sense of well-being which allows an individual to develop a sense of trust, intimacy and discernment regarding the best options for pursuing one's full potential. Again safety and security can refer to the physical needs such as a roof overhead or shelter from aggressors, but also refers to the notion of mental and emotional safety and security: a need for order, a need for personal boundaries, the right to one's own feelings

---

11. Personal Integrity is about getting one's needs met without having to betray self to the demands of others. Personal integrity is a hard nut to crack if the sense of self has been curtailed at an early age. Sylvia Brinton Perera cites scapegoating within families to be a major cause of disempowerment. Development of self is

skewed towards that of the alienated fragmented, passive victim . . . instinctive energies are not tamed or integrated: they remain split, eruptive and frightening (Brinton Perera 1986: 30).

The scapegoated individual is unable to develop a personal identity due to aspects of self being denied, repressed or dissociated by parents. There can be no sense of personal integrity when one does not know who one is!

and opinions without fear of retaliation. When this basic need is not met, it is difficult to maintain one's personal integrity,[11] for the basic instinct for survival dictates that one will do anything—including disowning parts of self, rather than risk total annihilation. In online chat-rooms the need for safety and security is pretty well met by the structure of the site, so users enjoy the freedom to play, to flirt, to bond, or just share information. In an online role-play, the boundaries of the game create a safe and secure containment, so a player is free to reveal or share information that will help him/her reach a goal. Notions of secrecy, intimacy and manipulation can be explored. For some players this brings a huge development in their socialization process.

The need for love and belonging, as in partner bonding or in belonging to a community or a cause, brings with it a healthy development of complex emotions involving notions of loyalty, commitment and betrayal. This need also enhances the ability to discover self and express self through interaction with others. When this need for love and belonging is not met, intense behavioural dysfunction or perversion may develop: obsessions, possessiveness, sadistic or masochistic tendencies, etc. Role-play will certainly bring to the fore any hidden anxieties but due to the 'safe containment' of the game structure, the function of the role-play and the device of computer feedback, the player is given the opportunity to come to grips with the deeper issues if they should wish to investigate their feelings and look at the computer tracked meta-patterns of their interactions.

The need for esteem and self-respect comes about as a result of one's engagement with others. It is about the need to feel one's place within the group, to acknowledge one's own strengths, uniqueness and to accept recognition from others. With esteem and self-respect comes the ease of being able to acknowledge and support others. One of the saddest indications of how our society is unable to help the individual meet this basic need comes from watching first-time mothers ask for help from their mothers, and hearing those newly-made grandmothers tell their daughters that they will just have to learn to cope on their own with their newly born child, just as every generation of woman has had to. This admonishment smacks of bitterness and punishment. Since *their* basic need for esteem and self-respect as mothers was ignored, their minimization of worth is passed down through the generations. In online role-play, the computer tracking system gives constant feedback without the judgements of conventional value systems. Feedback affirms player action in terms of whether they have moved closer or further from their intended goal. Players in need of advice or options can enter the 'emotional first-aid kit' and explore issues, emotions, situations with the acknowledgement that there is no one right answer, only a range of options which may be more or less in line with the integrity of what that character needs to achieve.

The need to know and understand is one of the most powerful driving forces behind creative endeavour. Even when mental and emotional abuse create setbacks in childhood, the thirst for knowledge, the spark of understanding, the joy of creating a difference with knowledge gained, has indeed set many a tortured soul free from the chains of their mental prisons. It is particularly through this basic human need that role-play can have a lasting effect on the individual's mental constructs and increase one's options and adaptability.

The need for self-actualization: Every individual yearns to develop, to evolve from what she/he is, to what she/he could become, to reach one's full potential. Just as the pauper dreams of becoming the prince, the prince dreams of being free of the throne and its rules and responsibilities. To reach full potential, individuals must be willing to undertake activities and complete tasks to claim their intended goal.

Tasks and activities is where role-play begins. There is no role-play without a clear sense of who is who, who wants what, what the situation is (goal, obstacle and task) and where the scenario takes place.

The Place of Archetypal Characters and Stereotypes in Role-play Development

In online role-play, a character role resonates with a particular energy and conjures up particular kinds of expectation. When a player accepts a role he/she intuitively understands the territory that goes with playing that character. Despite cries that archetypal and stereotypical characters are simplistic, their singularity is their strength. The player has the opportunity to explore one particular aspect of themselves by engaging in this character role. Character roles may be modern naturalistic types or fantasy based. The role of the godmother is gentle, nurturing and protective, while the role of the stepmother may be comprised of bitterness, manipulation and selfish thwarting. Thus two Characters may be two sides of the same coin, but by separating them out to their simplest form, clear exploration of mental constructs is encouraged. On the other hand, character roles may be complementary in how they help each other to achieve their goals. The goal of the 'orphan' may be to gain his/her rightful inheritance to the throne; the goal of the 'warrior' may be to quest for justice; the 'orphan' and the 'warrior' may help each other to achieve their goals; an 'obstacle' to them achieving their goal could be the 'Ice Queen' whose goal is to protect her castle from all intruders.

Location or setting, too, plays a big part in player expectation: locations may be archetypal in their particular energy and may conjure up in the player particular kinds of feelings and expectation. The Castle, The Graveyard, The Wastelands, The Fork in the Road, all present different resonances and expectations.

Situation is perhaps the most crucial part of developmental role-plays. If the goal and the obstacle to the goal are not clearly presented, then the player will be left with a feeling of incompleteness in their exploration. They will feel they have 'failed to achieve' something of worth. They will be prevented from gaining insights into character behaviour because they will not have pitted themselves against all odds, they will not have 'sweated' as the stakes were raised. For maximum effect, the situations will always involve a threat to one or more of the basic human needs as described above. It is through the struggle to get these basic needs met, that character (and the player's sense of self) is developed, both internally and externally. It is through our engagement in this process of interaction that the human developmental process unfolds.

Role-play Scenarios and Mental Constructs

If we accept that role-play scenarios are best situated around a dramatic engagement to get our basic needs met, then we can look at the mental and emotional struggle the individual engages in order to achieve her/his goal. Let us look at the mental stages and emotional milestones of human development, so we can track the progress toward self empowerment or personal power. Personal power is manifest through the following abilities, which build upon each other: the ability to trust, discern, achieve, develop intimacy, individuate, socialize, maintain integrity and generativity.

The ability to trust: Since survival issues come to the fore in the life of a newly born infant, notions of trust and mistrust become the first most important stage in human development. Will I survive? Will I be fed if I cry to signal my hunger? Or will I be abused for upsetting the household? The patterns of cause and effect between child and parent during this period play an important role in shaping mental constructs around the notion of trust. Is this a safe world? Is this a consistently ordered or chaotic world? Is it dangerous out there?

What do I need to do to survive? Issues of trust can continue on into the formative years when the child expresses her/his feelings and these feelings are minimized or forbidden by an authority figure. The child learns not to trust what she/he feels. The child learns that parts of self are not acceptable and need to be rejected if one wants the love of a parent or other love object. Feelings of shame and self-esteem are formed early and are deeply entrenched within the child's mental constructs of the world and self within the world.

Without a sense of trust in Self's feelings, thoughts and desires, all further stages of personal development are impaired in some sense or other. One of the ways to establish trust is through consistent rules. Gameplay and role-play can provide this foundation and back it up with feedback which reinforces those rules. Consistent cause and effect can re-pattern cognitive disorders and build a sense of trust in self's choices. Role-play can catalyse a 'switching on' of some of the aspects of self which have been 'switched off' or repressed. During role-play all the complexities of life, all the confused messages and mixed signals, are simplified into one focus: achieve your goal.

The ability to discern is an important stage of personal development. The ability to see the pattern within the chaos, the ability to make sense and meaning of the patterns, the ability to make choices appropriate to getting one's needs met, is critical to the journey towards personal empowerment. Unfortunately, the inability to trust self and one's intuitions creates a partial shutdown of self, which in turn creates confusion, lack of clarity and ultimately a sense of powerlessness to make useful decisions. This is particularly so where the child has authoritative parents who make all the decisions and do not see the child as having an inner life. Personal boundaries are invaded and the individual cannot separate personal feelings from those of the parents.

The confidence to achieve is another important stage with which many people struggle until the day they die. The ability to identify, express and act to have one's needs met is crucial to quality of life. If the child does not receive feedback which affirms their right to have their needs met then the child falters in their sense of self, and their sense of place in the world. Sometimes the ability to express what is important is crushed under the fear of annihilation. The ability to adapt between discipline and diversion to achieve one's own potential is lost in a haze of uncertainty. The relative simplicity of the tasks and goals in role-play, helps to rebuild confidence and identify options to act upon.

The ability to develop intimacy in relationships: The lack of trust in self makes it difficult to trust one's own judgment about who one can trust to share one's inner most self. The lack of trust in self means one is unable to be in touch with all the aspects of self, since some aspects of self such as the darker feelings may not be acceptable and have therefore been isolated and ostracized from self. Thus, the inability to accept self, the inability to accept all facets of self, jeopardize one's ability to be honest with others. Feelings of isolation are magnified and attempts to assuage one's yearning heart are found in casual sex where the sharing of feelings and real intimacy have no place.

The ability to individuate: To discover and maintain one's own identity is an important step in self-empowerment. But since the need for love and belonging plays such an important part in the formative years of the child, there is always the danger that in surrendering self to another, one could jeopardize the process of discovering one's personal identity. In a healthy relationship where both parties have a strong sense of self, this is not a danger since the dialectic of interaction suggests an exploration of all offers made in the interaction. However, in an unhealthy relationship, one party's identity may be subsumed by the personality of the other. When self is lost, role-play is a good way to explore aspects of self that have been lost in the dysfunction.

Individuation is the process whereby an individual moves from an acceptance of tribal values towards a questioning of the status quo, and experimenting with what feels appropriate and acceptable to Self, based on one's life direction, life purpose or intended goals. The individuation process is also the self-discovery process whereby the individual learns the ability to stand up for personal needs and desires even if they clash with the status quo. In the process the individual develops a personal moral code.

The ability to engage in the socialization process: Since the basic human need for esteem and self-respect comes through one's engagement with others, it is an important developmental stage to be able to discern the meta-games, the meta-patterns and meta-messages of various social contexts in order to receive the positive strokes required for personal esteem. Without this ability to engage discerningly in social situations, inappropriate behaviour may result with shame following shortly after. Those who do not have the ability to discern the meta-games of socialization often isolate themselves for fear of humiliation. The inability to engage in the socialization process often leaves one feeling they have no place in society. Anxiety and loneliness are camouflaged by other more acceptable addictions such as workaholism or, in some circles, drug taking.

The ability to maintain integrity and generativity: The ability to maintain a life lived with integrity comes from listening to one's own intuitions and articulating one's own needs. This relationship with self puts one in a state of flow which promotes the creative process and hence promotes a sense of generativity or personal output, creative expression, a point of view on the world at large. Those who have not been able to honour self may discover health problems or breakdowns where internal blockages were created long ago. This setback, sometimes known as the mid-life crisis, is a common occurrence since the first half of our lives we spend serving family and community, and it is only by struggling with our internal conflicts regarding how the world should or could be, that we come to honour

our own unique thoughts and processes. Role-play is a useful way of rediscovering personal integrity. Each character role is unique in his or her intention and goal. That goal must be reached if the player is going to achieve a sense of satisfaction regarding the exploration of that role. Achieving a goal within a role-play situation generates options around how one could get one's needs met, and if the connection is made between online role-play and real life role-plays then that person has a better chance of getting her/his needs met and generating further options for self and others. So what does all this have to do with online role-play?

Story Plots and Character Plotting for online role-play

Someone once told me that there are only seven major plots or themes around which stories are created. Although I never could find the 'magical seven plots' in a book, most writers agree there are roughly a dozen archetypal situations with which we humans seem to struggle, and hence we are riveted by stories which resonate with these themes. If we look at the plot patterns, it becomes clear that they reflect Maslow's hierarchy of basic human needs. The themes are universal, but 'how' characters deal with the unfolding of the theme is really about character motivation and character strategies to have their needs met in dealing with the success pattern; the love pattern; the cinderella/ugly duckling pattern; the triangle pattern; the return home pattern; the revenge/justice pattern; or the Faustean pattern. All these themes are the basis for plot and unique unfoldings of individual characters.

If we accept the premise that every dramatic story has a set-up, an escalation of conflict, and a resolution of the conflict, and if we view character role-play in the same terms, then the structure for an online methodology begins to take shape. Having outlined both the elements of drama and the elements of the self-discovery process, I will now outline the elements of a data processing system which can track player interactions and give progress on their playing strategies.

The Need for a Conceptual Model for Tracking Online Role-play Interactions

In the past three years I have been developing a conceptual model for tracking online role-play. At present, the three areas I have identified as crucial to its success are: (1) <u>interface design</u> for communication tracking, (2) meta-game design for strategy tracking, and (3) role-play design for player selfdevelopment. The further I delve into these areas, the more labyrinths will be discovered, but that's just part of the excitement of being around in the Nickelodeon Days of cyberspace!

Westwood and Kaufmann 15

Interface Design for Communication Tracking

In order to track role-play interactions it is necessary to define the terms so that the player as well as the computer can see the patterns of strategic engagement. In order for the player to see the patterns of strategic engagement, they need to be presented with a communication interface which defines the terms of engagement in iconic and metaphoric form.[12]

This demand for a patterned communication interface, rules out NLP (Natural Language Parsing) systems which are used in free form text writing. NLP systems do not allow either computer or user to track the meta-messages or strategies that a role-play game would require in order to bring about a satisfactory pay-off in story terms. Whilst I would prefer the freedom of free text flow rather than drop-down menus wherein players choose preset words, phrases or

---

[12.] In studies of perception and cognition it is common practice to use symbols, images, objects as an anchor for mental coding, and in game development this concept is extended to mental mapping of character behaviour and motivation.

sentences, the most important thing is to be able to track the overall shape of the interactions, which means developing some meta-pattern controlling device beyond natural free flow of text.

Since role-play interaction requires the player to speak, to share feelings and thoughts, or to withhold hidden agendas from other players, the communication interface must define the elements necessary to create fairly sophisticated communication, but must also present those elements in a fairly minimalist way so as to allow 'head-space' for the player to mix and match the elements in a way which best suits what they are trying to communicate.

But language can be a minefield. Psychologically words are loaded with a 'charge' or resonance that carries a message, which in turn carries an image or <u>association</u>. Unfortunately, the same word can trigger different images or associations for different people: hence confusion, sometimes anxiety or even outrage can result from an interaction. Example, when I say 'dog', what image comes to mind? a collie? a cattle dog? a prison informer? other? It differs for each of us, because we each interact with that word from different contexts or consciousness.

Namjoshi
17
Hawthorne
19

The great thing about games is that they create a 'containment and context' for ideas and interactions so that players have a common play space to explore. However, in investigating online 'role-play' games wherein the verbal interactions play a major part in the outcome, the choice of 'words' and 'language patterns' for a given character is crucial, and must be pre-written. So how are all the interactions pre-written, without pre-empting what a player might want to say or do? How does one organize thoughts, concepts and words so as to give the player maximum freedom to explore, yet still be able to tag the meta-communication and track their meta-strategies?

After much musing and reflection I went back to my training in family systems psychology and looked at the communication model presented by Virginia Satir (1972, 1983; Satir *et al.* 1976). Satir talks about the defence positions used in families. She divides defence positions into four quadrants: the Blaming Preacher, the Avoiding

Distracter, the Detached Expert, and Pacifier. The first step in using the Satir model was to define its polar opposites so that I could track not only defence strategies but also positive initiations and supportive interactions.

My polarity response for Blaming and Preaching became Listening and Acknowledging. My polarity response for Avoid and Distract became Focus and Gather Information. My polarity response for the Detached Expert was to Explore Options. My polarity response for the Pacifier was to Share one's Own Feelings and Thoughts.

But still this did not give me the level playing field I needed to track player interaction. The polarity response had quickly set up a value system based on dualities. The 'either/or' mental construct created little option beyond positive or negative, influence or defend, good or bad, right or wrong. The implication was that influence and support were good and defence was bad. To become truly empowered in any interaction it is necessary to move beyond notions of good and bad, right or wrong, to choose whatever response is appropriate to maintain personal integrity.

What became important was to explore a way of allowing the user to discover the appropriate time to defend self, the appropriate time to admit vulnerability, and the appropriate time to influence someone. If this was not achieved then the role-play interactions could hardly support the process of selfdevelopment, nor could it create anything beyond simplistic story lines and characters.

Finally, another communication model evolved after studying animal behaviour. As I watched a friend's dog, suddenly the meta-pattern of human behaviour became clear. If we accept that, like primitive animals, we 'move towards' or *approach* those with whom we want to bond, that we 'move away' from or *back off* from those we wish to disengage from, that we 'move against' or *attack* those who threaten our sense of self, and that we 'move around' or *explore* those about whom we are not sure but remain curious, then we can create a model of interaction which honours the notion that any direction is appropriate in given situations depending upon what we need. Getting our needs met is the end result of being empowered.

Within the meta-pattern of interaction there are meta-strategies for each of the four directions. If a player chooses to 'move against' another player, then choices must be made as to how (strategy) one will signal to the other that she/he is moving against: will it be a quiet *challenge* thus allowing the other party some dignity? Will it be a bold *confrontation* which stops players in their tracks? Will it be a *minimization* tactic which deflates the other's intention? Will it be a *ridicule* tactic which humiliates the other? Or will it be a *bullying* tactic which threatens to annihilate?

Every direction in the interaction signals something about how the player is strategically dealing with the other player in order to achieve her/his goals within the role-play scenario. These 'moves' can be tracked by the computer, and can start to build a picture of the expected outcomes. Is the player moving closer to or further from intended goals?

Context is all important in interpreting these player moves. Character, location, obstacle, and goal are important factors to consider. But context and consciousness of strategies leads on to the next area of research: how does one design the games within games so the player movements can be tracked without placing a value judgement on them?

Meta-Game Design

Classic game theory posits that within the rules of the game, an outcome is defined as a win or loss by calculating the points which have been gained or lost based on a zero-sum equation: in other words, one person's gain is another person's loss—the 'scarcity' model rather than the 'abundance' mental construct. Now, in real life, functional relationships tend to move into 'win/win' games rather the 'win/lose' games. But this is more difficult to track in computer games, especially role-play games, since the computer is tracking digits rather than values.

So where do we go from here? This is where game theory intersects with drama theory. The key component to drama theory is that, given the game on offer, one party refuses to play the 'game', and thus will not abide by the rules. They do something that is not within the rules, which escalates the 'drama', and that action precipitates a change in the game. If the other party responds by joining the new game, then the new game continues until another juncture is reached, when, again, the game may change. However, one party may not join the other in the new game, and may initiate the 'stalemate' game or the 'scapegoat' game, etc.

If we accept for the purposes of role-play that all interactions can be seen as a game, then the next thing to decide is how to classify interactions, nominate the games that are being played, and define what action constitutes a shift in the game play. Drama theorist and scientist Stan Hayward defines the common ground between game theory and drama theory as 'the decision'. If we accept the 'decision' as the key to engaging in game play, then what we have to be very clear about is, 'What is at stake for the player?' The 'stakes' dictate the decisions most likely to be made in the game-playing process.

Let us go back to the earlier discussion of psychology where I outlined the basic human needs as being Survival, Bonding, Self Respect, Knowledge and Understanding, Self-Actualization, etc. If a player is to achieve her/his goal in the game, the first thing they need to do is to survive. The 'survival game' is the most basic game, and when under threat of annihilation, the 'orphan' in search of his rightful place on the throne will abandon the 'self-respect game', or the 'self-actualization game', and simply engage in the 'survival game'.

The overriding game or meta-game is based on the player's driving need at that moment of play, depending upon their goal and the type of character they are pitted against at any given moment. Within the meta-game are smaller games within the interactions. For instance, in the 'greeting' game, the 'conversation' game, or the 'farewell' game, information may be withheld, or, indeed, players may mislead other characters so as to protect their meta-game position.

Given the context of character, situation and location, the computer can second guess the kind of meta-game at stake for the players, but it is the individual interactions of players which signal how they are dealing with the meta-game. Conceptually these games and meta-games will be triggered by what happens in the 'pools' of interaction. It is these 'pools' of interaction which hold the language patterns. The language patterns are like the alphabet of the game-play communication. Every interaction is tagged for a variety of contexts (character, situation, location, goal, etc). Every 'pool' will have an entry code and exit code which activates a 'gate' which takes characters into or out of a given 'pool' of interaction as they move from one game to another. The strategies which players take, or the 'moves' which they decide upon, triggers the release of the 'gates' and catapults the player into other games with different content and sometimes different language patterns.

Role-Play Design for Player Self-Development

Role-play characters must be designed for easy, accessible recognition of character type. In online game play, the player receives the 'image' of what a character looks like as the starting point for taking on that role-play. That image must 'resonate' with an expectation of how one will behave and possibly even what kind of goals that character aspires to. Once the player chooses the character, based on an image, then they receive the character's goals, motivation and back story.

So in a medieval fantasy role-play, the 'Orphan Prince' in search of his rightful place as heir to the throne, will be presented visually very differently from the 'Ice Queen', who must protect her castle from all invaders, especially the 'Orphan Prince'. What follows from the image is an expectation of how the character will speak. The 'Orphan Prince', who looks a bit naive and waif-like, has some of the language patterns of the 'victim' mentality. However, the 'Orphan Prince' also has a sense of humour, unlike the 'Ice Queen', who appears immaculate and supercilious. She has the language patterns of the persecutor and the seductress. She is sophisticated in how she bullies, humiliates and manipulates others.

Image and language are inextricably fused in this conceptual role-play model. Information has a life of its own and what people do with it depends upon a whole lot of variables. When Neurolinguistic Programming was introduced by Grinder and Bandler,[13] many people attacked the information about language patterns as dangerous and evil. These people saw the information as dangerous in the wrong hands, and therefore wanted to ban its knowledge from everyone. I see that same information as a useful tool for empowering others because it reveals the patterns by which others interact to influence each other. Through role-play design, mental constructs can be explored. Through role-play design, databases can track 'language patterns' as 'information' about the 'mental states' of characters, including their motivation and how they get their needs met. This awareness of mental states is useful for players to absorb and use in their daily lives.

In role-play interactions two aspects of information need to be differentiated: information as 'message' (a tone or gesture which implies 'I don't like you') and information as 'language pattern'. So given a situation wherein the 'Ice Queen' wants to dissuade the 'Orphan Prince' from staying at the castle, she might 'threaten' him with the message embedded within the following language pattern: 'If I were you I'd be careful . . .', whereas the 'fugitive', who hides in the tunnel, warns the orphan prince with the information: 'Your life is in danger' . . . Both characters are giving the 'orphan prince' valuable information, but one message is more direct than the other. Both are giving the orphan prince a clear message, but they have different motivations and intentions for speaking, hence their language patterns differ.

[13.] In the 60s and 70s, John Grinder and Richard Bandler modelled the communication patterns and techniques of successful communication experts, such as family therapist Virginia Satir and hypnotherapist Milton Erickson, to distil the elements and influences of communication.

Many language patterns imply a tone. Where tone is not implied, the interface will give the player options to add tone by choosing a face: angry, sad, happy, fearful, etc. Within the drama of conflict, language is normally tied up with intention (motivation) and context (character and situation) to present information. These discreet responses should be able to be placed in a database to be used for other contexts and intentions.

Let's look at a role-play situation with two very different types of characters with different kinds of goals. Let's take the character of the 'Amazon Warrioress', whose goal is to save her village from the onslaught of the enemy. The game she is engaging in is a 'quest' game of saving. She will win self-respect and admiration if she succeeds in her quest. Now let's look at another character, the 'Casanova', whose goal is to win the affections of unattainable women, to make them conquests, perhaps even casualties, through the game of seduction. In this scenario, the 'Casanova' will attain self-respect and admiration if he is able to seduce the unattainable 'Amazon Warrioress'. When these two characters meet they enter into a third game called the 'game of distraction'. She may be distracted from her quest by him, and he may spend all his time trying strategies to seduce her and thereby double his kudos. She may even allow him to bed her, if she feels this will allow her greater access to enemy secrets or maybe even produce an ally to help her in her quest. When she enters into this game with him, she may not have enough information about him to know if he is a potential enemy or ally, so she is taking a big risk to achieve her goal. Being a Warrioress, her very nature precludes her falling for him, but in being bedded by such a character, she also opens up the possibility of betrayal, in more than one sense, which could jeopardize her chances of obtaining her goal. Hence bedding down with the enemy is a dangerous but plausible strategy.

Now, if an online player who was role-playing the 'Amazon Warrioress' did become smitten by the player who was role-playing the 'Casanova', then there would have to be a role-play mechanism whereby the 'Amazon Warrioress' could put aside her overriding goal and take on the role of 'The Lover', or some such exotic character, so as to explore the feelings, mental states and strategies related to flirting, seduction and titivation. Likewise, the player engaging in the character of the 'Casanova' might like to explore notions of loyalty and commitment by taking on the role of the 'Faithful Servant' or 'Honourable Husband'.

The process of how all this is tracked by the computer is part of my research. The ability to make up lists and cross-reference those lists for possible outcomes between characters, motivations, games, game shifts, language patterns and options is where the fun begins. The basic dramatic principle is the 'what if . . .' principle. Take the dozen thematic plot patterns, add the basic human needs, the principle of self-development, and map it out in language patterns, and we're halfway home. Place all these concepts within specific 'pools' and code the 'gates' to open as the player moves towards their goal, and we're on the home stretch.

References

Bateson, Gregory. 1972. *Steps to an Ecology of Mind, a Revolutionary Approach to Man's understanding of Himself.* New York: Chandler Publishing, Ballantine Books.

Brownlow, Kevin. 1968. *The Parade's Gone By.* Great Britain: Martin Secker & Warburg Ltd.

Hayward, Stan. 1998. Letter to the editor. *New Scientist Magazine, 160* (2158) 62, October 31.
<www.newscientist.com>

Howard, Nigel. 1989. N-soft person games. *Journal of the Operational Research Society,* 49, p.144.
<http://www.nhoward.demon.co.uk>

Meares, Russell. 1992. *The Metaphor of Play, On Self, the Secret and The Borderline Experience.* Melbourne: Hill of Content.

Milburn, Michael A. and Sheree D. Conrad. 1996. *The Politics of Denial.* Cambridge, Massachusetts: MIT Press.

Nardi, Bonnie. 1995. *Context and Consciousness, Activity Theory and Human Computer Interaction.* Cambridge, Massachusetts: MIT Press.

Pearson, Carol, S. 1989. *The Hero Within.* San Francisco: Harper.

Perera, Sylvia Brinton. 1986. *The Scapegoat Complex, towards a mythology of Shadow and Guilt.* Toronto: Inner City Books.

Piaget, Jean. 1929. *The Child's Conception of the World.* London: Routledge and Kegan Paul.

Piaget, Jean. 1932. *The Moral Judgement of the Child*. London: Routledge and Kegan Paul.

Piaget, Jean. 1951. *Play, Dreams and Imitation in Childhood*. London: Heinemann.

Piaget, Jean. 1954. *The Construction of Reality in the Child*. New York: Basic Books.

Piaget, Jean. 1959. *The Language and Thought of the Child*. London: Routledge and Kegan Paul.

Satir, Virginia. 1972. *People Making*. Palo Alto, CA: Science and Behaviour Books.

Satir, Virginia. 1983. *Conjoint Family Therapy*. Palo Alto, CA: Science and Behaviour Books, Inc., 3rd edition.

Satir, Virginia, R. Bandler and J. Grinder, 1976. *Changing with Families*. Palo Alto, CA: Science and Behaviour Books Inc.

Schaefer, Charles and Steven E. Reid (Eds.), 1986. *Game Play: Therapeutic uses of childhood games*. New York: John Wiley & Sons.

Schank, Roger, and Robert P. Abelson, 1977. *Scripts, Plans, Goals and Understanding: An inquiry into human knowledge structures*. New Jersey: Lawrence Erlbaum Associates.

Schank, Roger and C.K. Riesbeck. 1981. *Scripts and Stereotypes: Programming common sense*. New Jersey: Lawrence Erlbaum Associates.

Turkle, Sherry. 1985. *The Second Self: Computers and the human spirit*. New York: A Touchstone Book, Simon & Schuster, Inc.

Turkle, Sherry. 1995. *Life on the Screen: Identity in the age of the Internet*. New York: Simon & Schuster, Inc.

Winnicott, Donald W. 1953. Transitional Objects and Transitional Phenomena. *International Journal of Psychoanalysis 34*, 89-97.

Winnicott, Donald W. 1962. Ego Integration in Child Development. In *The Maturational Processes and the Facilitating Environment*. New York: International Universities Press.

Winnicott, Donald W. 1974. *Playing and Reality*. Harmondsworth: Penguin.

fourteen

Cyberfiction: a Fictional Journey into Cyberspace (or How I Became a CyberFeminist)

Beryl Fletcher

Introduction

I am a feminist novelist writing about the lives of contemporary women. Until recently, cyberfiction has been the exclusive preserve of science fiction writers (usually male) but cyberspace is fast becoming an everyday reality in the lives of many women. To me, cyberspace is an exciting Real Place where women live and work and play, a place that is ripe for representation within realist feminist fiction. This is the story of how I came to write my novel *The Silicon Tongue* and how I fell in love with the Internet. I explore the themes that came to fascinate me during the writing of *The Silicon Tongue*: the transformation of women's stories and memories from private speech to public (cyber)space; the political and technological manipulation of women's fertility; the possibility of a reconciliation between body and mind in cyberspace.

Cyberpunks

One day in 1993 I wandered into a bookstore and saw a copy of *Wired* Magazine. On the cover was a group of young Americans with stark white faces and bar codes tattooed on their foreheads. They were called cyberpunks. As a writer of contemporary fiction, I am always on the lookout for the emergence of radical movements outside the dominant culture and the place of women within them.

Was this a new subculture? I looked around the nightclubs and the streets of Auckland. No cyberpunks. I searched the Net. Plenty of self-defined Geeks and Nerds[1] but still no cyberpunks in New Zealand. One Auckland man claimed that he knew some in the UK. They were the same old punks, he claimed, but wired. Then he tried to sell me a bulletproof jacket (via email) that he had illegally imported into New Zealand. I abandoned the search.

At this stage I decided that cyberpunk was more a collection of ideological ideals, *a state of mind* rather than a definable alternative community.[2] Cyberpunk combines the potential use of new information technology with traditional anarchistic values. Two of the major ideas that shaped the cyberpunk movement grabbed my attention. Briefly, these were:

> 1. Information wants to be free. That is, that everyone has the right to generate, receive and *tamper with* information, and everyone has right of access to new information technologies. Once data goes digital it belongs to everyone. This is why the cyberpunk movement is associated with hackers, crackers and phreaks.[3]

[1.] The terms Nerds and Geeks, once derogatory, are now used with pride by persons heavily involved in cyberculture. Douglas Coupland, in his novel *Microserfs* (Coupland 1995) provides us with the useful information that in the USA, a Geek is considered to be a Nerd with a job!

[2.] 'Spurred on by cyberpunk literature in the mid 1980s certain groups of people started referring to themselves as cyberpunks . . .' These include hackers, and artists and musicians using the new computer technology . . .

> However, one person's 'cyberpunk' is another's everyday obnoxious teenager with some technical skill thrown in, or just someone looking for the latest trend to identity with. Also, there are those who claim that 'cyberpunk' is undefinable (which in some sense it is, being concerned with outsiders and rebels), and resent the mass media's use of the label, seeing it as a cynical marketing ploy. (Schneider, in FAQ sheet from <alt.cyberpunk: erich@bush.cs.tamu.ed>).

[3.] Hackers are computer outlaws who break into security codes of information systems, sometimes for fun, sometimes to show that they have the expertise to do it, sometimes to make the point that security systems are just another form of bureaucratic oppression by the powerful. Cracking is a more serious form of hacking: breaking into military security systems etc. Phreaks are people who do similar things with the telephone system. (FAQ sheet from alt.cyberpunk, assembled by Erich Schneider). Pixel, my cyberpunk character in *The Silicon Tongue*, hacks into state bureaucratic databases to obtain vital information: the name and address of her birth grandmother. She also plants a virus into the computer network of her grandmother's boss as an act of revenge.

2. Stay at the margins of the social world and disrupt the authoritarian centre.

I asked myself: what would a character look like who espoused these political ideas? What would she look like? And where did she come from? I gave her changeable tattoos including a barcode, a tax number and an email number, I dressed her in black, and I gave her a <u>cyborg</u> origin.[4]

Klein 9
Hawthorne
10

Thus my character from *The Silicon Tongue*, Pixel, was created. To develop the notion of cyborg hybridity, I gave her a complicated conception and birth. The egg and sperm from her genetic parents were joined together before they died in an air crash. They left a will leaving a large sum of money to their adopted daughter Marlene if she would consent to be implanted with the frozen embryo. This means that Pixel was a two-year-old *orphan* before she was born. She grew to birth size within the surrogate womb of her adopted sister. If you think this is impossible, you are wrong. Bizarre twists of kinship and *belonging* are now common in the high-tech world of <u>Assisted Reproduction Techniques</u> (ART).

Klein 9

I had already decided that my third novel would be based on the complex and rapidly changing relationships between women's stories, women's bodies and technology but I did not want to write within the genre of science fiction or the recently named subgenre of sci-fiberpunk.[5]

The more I read about the new technologies, both in ART and in the development of cyberspace, the more I became spooked by a strange and ironic reversal between the realms of fiction and truth.

---

4. I am using cyborg here in the sense of the interface between human life and technology rather than in the sense of an implant or mechanical addition to a body. I am aware that the notion of cyborg also refers to a hybrid subjectivity. Pixel claims that hybridity is her natural state, directly caused by the duality and confusion in her kinship lines. Donna Haraway makes the point that to exist outside the narratives of kinship is to be at some level 'nonhuman'. (Haraway 1991: 11).

5. The term sci-fiberpunk refers to a type of fiction where the subject matter and themes of science fiction are integrated with new technologies especially the Internet. Sci-fiberpunk is more to do with near-future or extant technologies and their possible outcomes for social and political life on earth rather than inter-planetary travel (see Shiner 1992: 21–3).

Technological truths have become fantastical, fictional, mythical. I never in my wildest dreams (or nightmares) ever thought that I would read a Bill presented to the New Zealand Government in 1996 that stated, in official bureaucratic style, that babies should not be allowed to be bred from *unborn foetal mothers* or that women should not give birth to *animals*.[6] So if the technology has become the fiction, then fiction needs to become more realistic. I decided that I could write realist narrative that could dwell with comfort in cyberspace.

Although my novel *The Silicon Tongue* can be classified as realist cyberfiction rather than cyberpunk, I do borrow some elements from the genre, especially with my character Pixel. In the body of fiction referred to as cyberpunk, silicon chips are sometimes embedded in the wetware (the brain) of an individual but I chose the tongue. The tongue is the physical site of human speech and also another word for language in English (that is, the mother tongue). A poetic and loquacious person is sometimes said to have a silken tongue. The metaphor of a silicon chip implanted in the tongue broadens the possibility of speech beyond bodily contact and names the incredibly expanding sites of human chatter and gossip via email and Real Time Chat on the Net. In my view, it is the *tongue* rather than the *mind* that has taken flight.

I believe that ancient forms of oral exchange and storytelling and mythology are shaping the language of cyberspace and not the other way around. That is, the technology provides new systems of communication but human beings are doing the same old thing. Narrative is narrative is narrative. Period.

---

6. From the Human Assisted Reproductive Technology Bill, presented by Dianne Yates, MP, to the New Zealand Parliament, August 1996.

No person shall place or cause to be placed, in a woman—

(a) a live embryo other than a human embryo

(b) any live gamete other than human gametes: or—

(c) any eggs from any human foetus or any embryo created using eggs from any human foetus (pp. 4–5).

There is of course one vital difference: you do not need to be present in the body to have speech exchanges or to co-create worlds of visual and textual fantasy with other people. There can be virtual intimacy in real time without the necessity of physical travel. This realisation has produced a huge amount of theory ranging from dire warnings of the imminent death of the body in cyberspace to the utopian view that, at last, we are free of the tyranny of the solipsistic mind, we can join together in one huge pulsating sentient cyber-mind, we can rise above the limitations of time and place and space.

This may be so, but cyberspace is a social construct, and is plagued by the same inequalities that we encounter in our everyday reality. I agree with Dale Spender's analysis of the Net as a gendered space, in her recent book *Nattering on the Net*. I go into the Net as a feminist just as I do in my everyday life. I couldn't make any sense of it otherwise. Or cope with the blatant and sometimes vicious misogyny. Conversely, I find that the Net can be a restful place for me as a woman precisely because of the absence of the body. I can say and do as I please and nobody can see my age, my disability, my vulnerability. So too for my characters Pixel and Joy in *The Silicon Tongue*. They pay back Joy's abusive ex-boss by infecting his computer with a virus (Our Lady of Revenge) without ever taking the physical risks that endanger women when confronting a man face-to-face.

For me, the process of writing a novel begins with a growing fascination with something new and strange that demands my attention. The second stage is one of creating the characters and events that match my current obsession. During my research for my novel, I became aware of cyberspace as a new novelistic landscape, a new country to be explored, a place that is at once both very familiar and very alien, a place just as real as beaches, shops, houses and mountains. I asked myself a set of questions that had arisen through months of indulging my obsession through talking, reading, surfing and lurking around cyberspace. And I nagged others for stories about their experiences on the Net.

I came up with three central problems:

a) Can I write a novel where one woman travels from speech to books to <u>virtual reality</u> in one lifetime?

b) If the main drawback of cyberspace is a further tragic fragmentation between the body (experience) and the mind (ideas), how can I represent this battle in fiction without becoming didactic?

c) And last but not least, is there any hope of a reconciliation between body and mind in cyberspace?

Theme One: The journey from oral representation and communication to cyberspace

In chapter one of *The Silicon Tongue* we meet the main protagonist Alice. She has agreed to allow a mysterious historian make an oral history of her life.

> The first problem is the tape recorder. She can't get it to work properly. The girl fiddles with it, asks me to speak slowly into the microphone, then she rewinds the tape and plays it back. Nothing. She tries again. This time, a faint hiss, a whisper.
>
> 'I was born Alice Nellie Smallacomb . . .'
>
> My voice sounds strange. I had imagined a deepening with age, a richness. But it squeaks and crackles like a young lad in puberty, and the words come out differently from how they sound in my head. Maybe I have lived too long in this warm island wind. Deep grooves in my skin and now these thin quavers. I never thought my voice would pass away before I did (Fletcher 1996: 1).

The woman doing the taping offers Alice five hundred dollars for each session. Alice is surprised that her spoken words have any value. She has exceptional recall of events in her life but is reluctant at first to divulge her unique memory system to the strange young woman.

How can I get my early years across to her? I have been alive for seventy-five years. It is like looking back over a vast and sullen ocean towards a single candle about to flicker out at the edge of the horizon. Dead time, frozen in history. At least, this is how she will see it. I don't know if she will believe that I have total recall of every important conversation and event that has shaped my life. It's too soon to tell her about my system for storing memories. She may think I'm a crazy woman, with my talk of beads and kaleidoscopes and coded colours, red for life, white for death, black for renewal. (*Ibid*: 2).

Alice has developed her system for storing oral and visual memories along similar lines to classical mnemotechnics, the art of artificial memory. The ancients perfected a method called architectural memory where the practitioner constructed rooms in an imaginary palace and stored information in the appropriate place. They could recall events, artifacts and oral interaction at will.[7]

I found the similarity between this ancient method of memory and what I had seen in cyberspace exciting. It provided the link that I was looking for in order to trace the continuity between oral communication and memory and virtual reality.

Alice decided to train her memory when she was taken from London to New Zealand against her will at the age of fourteen. She was afraid that if she forgot her past, she too would disappear.

I leaned on the windowsill and I swore never to forget anything that ever happened to me. I would remember everything: weather, colours, words, faces, the feel of cloth, the shape of particular clouds, the taste of particular foods. I would remember every journey I ever made, every person I ever met. I would become both witness and chronicler of my own experience.

And I began that very night to train my memory. This is how I do it. I rehearse the happenings, the feelings of the day, and I put it into the context of the past. I visualise the pattern of the kaleidoscope that I saw long ago at the Warrington's. Diagonal forms, each one filled with glass

---

7. See Yates (1966) for a fascinating account of people who perfected the art of classical mnemotechnics.

beads shaped like multi-coloured tears. I colour code the memories and place them into the appropriate bead . . . .

My interest lies in the relationship between yesterday and the day before not today and tomorrow. I let the future lie, I see it as a building that is just out of my peripheral vision. I don't want to know whether it is constructed out of brick or stone or wood, I centre my attention onto the building I have just left and how it lies in relation to the multiple rooms that stretch back to my first memories of the special quality and movement of light. The flame of candles flickering on the rosy wet face of my mother, the pool of electric light over the kitchen table, the glistening spirals of apple skins, the yellow eggs and sugar, the glazed fruit buns.

Every night of my life, no matter how tired I am, I re-experience my stories. Not as anecdotes but as feelings. I transfer the work of the mind into the storehouse of the body (*Ibid*: 50).

Later in the novel Alice meets her great-grand-daughter Pixel, the cyberpunk. Pixel listens to the audiotapes of Alice's life and turns words into visions by constructing a virtual reality game. Pixel claims that if words/visions become public *and potentially interactive* on the Internet, we can be freed from the lonely prison-house of interior monologue.

Pixel has taught me this: *if you can see what I mean you can be me* . . . .

Then she shows me the kaleidoscope on the computer screen, rolling and changing with each turn, primitive, unformed, but unmistakably the same patterns that I saw over seventy years ago. I am dumbfounded, lost for words. Something has been taken from my head and placed into the outside world, colour by colour, shape by shape . . .

I have taught Pixel this: if you experience what I experience, you can be me (*Ibid*: 222–3).

Theme Two: Alice as a metaphor of body and Pixel as mind

I constructed Pixel as a character who lives a life of duality, both in her uncertain kinship origin where the links between blood and family are fractured and in her life on the Net.

> . . . I am making a virtual reality game out of my known ancestors. I have two lines, my nurture line and my biological line. Unlike non-surrogates, my family tree has a double strand. There is the line back from Marlene, the nurture line of caring and feeding and sleepless nights. But none of this would be possible without the alchemy that turns eggs and sperm into flesh. So you see I have to do everything twice (*Ibid*: 209).

> The redundant mythology of giving birth. A non-issue for the likes of me and my compatriots. Cast adrift birthless in the land of the unknown warrior. The egg as passive victim, the sperm as spear. The new mythology of conception. Who laid your egg? Who projected your sperm? Who or what brought the two of you together in the bridal suite at the Hotel Petrie?

> The great leveller of the clinic. A holy place of hushed voices and white coats. Fertility chants performed over flushed ova and glaciated sperm. Christ was born in a stable. I was conceived along with the cows and sheep and other unmentionables. Does this make me a special woman, the daughter of a new God? (*Ibid*: 174)

> I hate living in the body, it is too demanding, too there. One day, I will achieve the ultimate detachment, I will scatter across the Net so far and wide that the filaments of skin and bone will stretch into nanothreads of the purest gossamer, sweet strings waiting to be played, my lyre, myself . . . .

> It's the sweat I hate and the blood and the yellow cells of fat and gristle and the discordant tunes, the groans, the cries, the whimpers. I refuse to live solely within the confines of this hardware and I refuse to conform to wetware rules no matter what the method of creation, either cloned or formed in vitro or brought into being by a mindless fuck (*Ibid*: 111).

I constructed Alice as a character who validates experience (the body) above all else. She wants to remember *what really happened to her*, not someone else's version. Not only does she crave remembrance, she wants to become the carrier of a truthful family history. She embraces cyberspace as a superior form of memory production. In virtual reality, *being there* is an added dimension. She can, through the medium of the virtual kinship game, share more than an oral description of her past with her family. Alice hopes that her daughter Joy will at last believe her stories.

> I want Joy to be the first player, I want her to understand the horrors of my childhood. I was there, I had to live through it, moment by moment, day by day. I want her to apologise for her accusation that I have stolen my childhood from the fictional stories of others. If I can compel Joy to play this game, we will become closer, I am certain of it (*Ibid*: 232).

Mueller 13

Theme Three: The reconciliation of body and the mind in cyberspace

A sub-text of *The Silicon Tongue* is the acting out of the war that is currently being fought over the various forms of postmodern theory where the experience/identity of the author becomes subservient (sometimes to the point of obliteration) to the text. Language becomes disembodied from experience, the text can be spoken by anyone, anywhere. Experience, emotional intelligence, the past, history, all are swept away. There is an obvious parallel between these extreme forms of abstract theory and a life lived entirely in cyberspace. Pixel's life is a metaphor of the perceived evils of cyberspace. She hates the body and lives as far apart from it as possible.

Yet Alice, who lives in the body, who remembers everything about the past, who fears that when her body is gone her experience will have been suffered *for nothing* is also a victim of circumstance and history. I showed Alice at the mercy of her body in that she had no choice in being brought to New Zealand as a servant, no choice in bearing the child of an unknown rapist, no choice in becoming married to a man who 'rescued' her from shame. In some ways, Pixel has had more choices. She lives in a generation of young women who do not perceive sex as the primary factor in a fixed biological and cultural fate. (Thou art woman, therefore thou shalt . . . .)

Pixel had no choice about her bodily *origins* as a frozen embryo but in all other aspects of her life she created her own version of the relationship between her body and mind. She gives up on the body because of her peculiar biological origins and lives entirely within cyberspace. Towards the end of the novel, Alice takes Pixel from her isolated room into the outside world. Pixel rides in a car and paddles at the edge of the sea for the first time. Although this does not offer a resolution to the contradiction between experience and abstract ideas, it does offer a hope that the body-mind difference (as exemplified by the lives of Alice and Pixel) can at least be partially resolved. The point that I make in the novel is that Alice and Pixel are able to find a common ground through a retrieval of a shared past: a past that Alice painfully lived through, moment by moment, a past that was necessary for the nurture, but not the high-tech origin, of Pixel. Without the life of Alice, without her nurture of Joy, there would be no Pixel. Without stories and recorded memories of the past lives of women there can be no coherence in the present moment. The present is rendered senseless.

Practical Uses of the Internet for Fiction Writers

There is a practical element to cyberspace that is proving to be invaluable to me in my work as a novelist. I have an enormous library at my fingertips that I can consult every day. This library is interactive: that is, I can interact with the writers or providers of information in a way that goes way beyond merely consulting a book. For example, I have just completed my fourth novel *The*

Bloodwood Clan (1999). This novel is set both in New Zealand and Australia. In an early chapter, I have one of the main characters Eliza hiding in the bush near Mudgee, New South Wales, spying on a man. Eliza is an expert on the local flora and fauna and she knows that there is some danger to her when lying low in the undergrowth. There are deadly funnel-web spiders here and she may be covering the entrance to a burrow with her bare skin. At any moment, an irate spider may emerge and give her the kiss of death. But would it?

I wondered if it was true that this spider is actually present in the central west of the State. I am very familiar with the habits of the funnel-web spider from living in the bush myself for many years in southern New South Wales. One of my tasks was to clear the ground of these spiders near my house every few months to make sure that there was no danger to my children. I had learned that if one of us was bitten, we could die within twenty minutes. This was in the days before there was an antidote available. Checking the beds and shoes inside the house were daily rituals. I must have killed fifty spiders inside the house over the years. The presence of this frightening spider in my environment shaped my daily actions so I knew that my character would also be very aware of what could happen to her if she was bitten far away from help.

Before cyberspace, it would have taken me weeks to find out if funnel-webs were present in the Mudgee district. There were no books on Australian spiders in my local library in Hamilton, New Zealand. No problem! I asked the World Wide Web and instantly found the home page of the NSW Neurotoxin Research Group at the University of Technology in Sydney. I emailed my request. Within two hours I had my answer. Yes, *Atrax robustus* (funnel-web) can be found as far north as the Hunter River. Problem solved. I returned to my text, confident that I was not creating a *faux pas*.

Conclusion: Cyberfeminism and Creativity

Namjoshi
17

Cyberspace does not exist apart from <u>culture</u>, it is an analogue or mirror of culture. Like culture, cyberspace is constantly in the process of procreation, shifting, fluid, never fixed. So if it's nothing new, why do writers and other artists find it so mind blowing? Why the excitement? When I made my first tentative journey into cyberspace I had an experience similar to my 75-year-old character Alice. I suddenly felt part of something that was at once both very familiar yet very strange. I saw meanings as collective entities, I *saw* culture, outside of my head, in the public space. In a peculiar sort of way it was the end of aloneness, forever.

Understanding the processes and artifacts of cyberspace is like suddenly *visualising* what language is and what language *can do*.[8] Just as the invention of writing and the printed word expanded the possibilities of the creation and shared experience of new language forms and meanings so will cyberculture take language to the limit. This has got to be good news for both fiction writers and feminists. Language has always been a primary preoccupation of feminists, scholars and creative artists alike. The politics of naming, the formation of identity, the interpretation of literature, all have been subject to intense feminist scrutiny. The freedom and anarchistic possibilities inherent in cyberspace provide a wonderful opportunity for feminists to confront patriarchal structures, not as artifacts frozen in space and time and tradition but at the very moment of generation, at the actual place and time where ideas, words, meanings and actions that are culture forming and culture maintaining are in the process of becoming. I am thankful that this technology arrived two decades after the beginning of the contemporary feminist revolution. It is frightening to think what could have happened if cyberspace had been firmly entrenched before the massive outpouring of <u>feminist scholarship</u> and activism changed the world forever.

Stafford 7

---

8. I am using language in its widest sense: words, symbols, pictures, glyphs etc. that create and convey forms of shared human meanings and intentions.

The wall between public and private is being relentlessly broken down. Once data goes digital it is potentially in the public realm. Hackers, crackers and phreaks are always technically one step ahead of the technocrats. Legal and moral issues surrounding private information, secrets, ownership of ideas, words, scripts, all must be rewritten. The old relationships between language and power, the gatekeeping practices that kept women out of the centre, are crumbling.

I am an absolute beginner in cyberspace, both technically and creatively. The truth is that we all are. It is challenging, joyful, sometimes frightening, but never dull. For creative writers, cyberspace is a garden of delights. Cyberspace has the potential to stretch imagination and language to the limit; it is a vast library of information, a gossip session, a politically charged emotional landscape. In short, a perfect place for feminists.

References

Coupland, Douglas. 1995. *Microserfs*. London: Flamingo.
Fletcher, Beryl. 1996. *The Silicon Tongue*. Melbourne: Spinifex Press.
Fletcher, Beryl. 1999. *The Bloodwood Clan*. Melbourne: Spinifex Press.
Haraway, Donna. 1991. The Actors are Cyborgs. In Contance Penley and Andrew Ross (Eds.), *Technoculture*. Minneapolis: University of Minnesota Press.
Schneider, Erich. 1996. *Frequently Asked Questions (FAQ) on alt.cyberpunk* <http://bush.cs.tamu.edu/~erich/alt.cp.faq.html>
Shiner, Lewis. 1992. Inside the Movement: Past, Present, and Future. In George Slusser and Tom Shippey (Eds.), *Fiction 2000*. Georgia: University of Georgia Press.
Spender, Dale. 1996. *Nattering on the Net*. Melbourne: Spinifex Press.
Yates, A. Frances. 1966. *Art of Memory*. Chicago: Chicago University Press.

fifteen

Making a Multimedia Title

**Virginia Westwood and
Heather Kaufmann**

The transition from teaching to technology

There are two main reasons why we got started in the business of multimedia production and publishing. The first was that Virginia was enjoying her public service job less and less, the other reason related to Heather's background in teaching English as a Second Language (ESL) and adult literacy. For seven or eight years before she resigned, Heather had become more and more interested in the potential for using computers for teaching language and literacy skills.

Heather found, as many others have, that computers are effective resources in adult education and are particularly suitable for second language and literacy learners. She also found—and the published research supports this—that computer-aided learning has a very positive effect on the self-esteem of adults and that it often increases people's motivation to learn. Adults really like the privacy of learning with computers. They like the fact that they have control over their own learning, that it is (or should be) self-paced, and that the self-access aspect lets them fit their learning in around their other commitments. All of this means they can learn in their pre-ferred way: provided, of course, the learner has access firstly, to good computer programs, and secondly, to computers, either privately, or through the organisation they are associated with. We found that there are very few computer programs that are suitable for adult literacy and adult ESL learners in their content's intrinsic usefulness and interest value, and in their language level. So we knew what we wanted to do. We wanted to make good language and <u>literacy</u>

programs for adults and we wanted to make programs that were easy to use, programs that didn't assume any computer literacy skills or English language skills, such as the ability to read complicated instructions. We wanted to make programs that were motivating and educationally sound. We wanted to make programs that people could use on their own. That is, programs that give learners feedback about what they are doing; in other words, programs that are highly interactive.

We also wanted to make programs that would respect the knowledge and interest of adults who have minimal English language and literacy skills. Heather found that many adult literacy and adult ESL teachers were using programs designed for children. Teachers did this because they had no suitable options. However, we think this practice adds to the humiliation of adults who are already disempowered in so many ways. We also wanted our programs to contain positive images of strong women and to reflect our multicultural and multiethnic society.

While we had a very clear idea of what we wanted to do, Heather knew that she couldn't make the programs herself because she doesn't have a programmer's mind. She had proved this to herself twice a long time ago when she did programming courses. Virginia was becoming less and less happy in her public service job, so towards the end of 1994 we decided we would begin making a program. Virginia resigned from her job and started to teach herself how to use the multimedia authoring program we had bought. Then we cleaned up an old mudbrick cottage on our block and called it our office. We bought a couple of desks, a fax machine, a new computer and we registered our business name. We were in business! Heather is a very cautious person. She took six months long service leave, just in case the whole thing was a total disaster and we needed a salary again.

In December 1994 we started work on our first program, *The Alphabet*. Before starting, we made one really important decision and that was to attempt a very, very small project; one that had very specific boundaries and one for which there was an identifiable need.

We published that program in March 1995 and then immediately started work on our second program, *The Interactive Picture Dictionary*; that was published in November 1995. Our third program, *Issues in English*, was published in 1996 and we'll be using examples from it to demonstrate some of the points we are going to make about producing a multimedia title.

The business is . . .

Our office is certainly a very unconventional one. It is very high tech inside although it is low tech outside. We also have a wildlife shelter and this is one of the little kangaroos that hopped up to work with us every day while we were making *Issues in English*.

Neither of us had had any prior experience in multimedia technologies, in programming or in publishing, when we started our business, which we called <u>Protea Textware</u>, in 1994. Virginia's background is in information management and processing at the interface between the computer and users, and Heather, as mentioned, in ESL teaching and adult literacy. Since we began we have produced and published five of our own programs, and our sixth program will

Introduction

be published in 1999. We have also been involved in, and published, publications for external bodies.

After nearly five years, Protea Textware is still just the two of us and we are now an incorporated company. We still do just about everything, from the original concept right through all of the production, resource acquisition and so on, through to marketing and distribution. For the first two or three years, we didn't contract out any part of the process but now we do contract out some tasks. In general, we still do everything ourselves because that's how we like it. We really enjoy being involved with every aspect of the process.

We publish on <u>CD-ROM</u>, and not on the net, and that is mainly because the net is not, at this stage, fast enough for sustained <u>interactive multimedia</u>; it's not fast enough for the sort of inter-activity that is an integral part of our programs. Also, a lot of our users live in remote areas so they don't have good telecommunications access and net access is still unreliable in many of those remote areas.

Guymer 3

Arnold 11

. . . also a wildlife shelter.

It is really important to make the point that CD-ROMs are not the equivalent of multimedia; multimedia doesn't equal CD-ROM. A CD-ROM is simply a big storage disk. There is no intrinsic value in a CD-ROM; it is just that it is convenient to use for multimedia because its storage is so huge and multimedia files—film, video, sound, animations—require a lot of storage space. That is the only connection between CD-ROM and multimedia.

We publish educational interactive multimedia programs. When we talk about interactivity, we are not just talking about navigation and hot links and hot words and so on, we are talking about users actually doing things and the programs responding in a highly context-sensitive way to what is going on.

There are a lot of different kinds of multimedia, different genres of multimedia. There are the entertainment programs and titles, there are edutainment titles: programs that are a crossover between education and entertainment. There are also educational programs for children and for adults, as well as for corporate and other training areas. There are reference multimedia programs such as encyclopaedias, and there are coffee-table presentation multimedia programs. We specialise in producing programs for adult literacy, numeracy and English as a second language, although we have also published a program for teaching Maltese literacy.

It is important to note the differences between these kinds of programs. The whole approach to producing a multimedia title depends on its genre. The differences also reflect the part of the industry that the titles come from. The industry has many disparate constituents. People have come from the games area, film and entertainment, public relations, corporate advertising, marketing, the education and training sector, and book publishing sectors. Then, of course, there are the related areas of the industry including the technical sectors, programming, sound, film, design and graphics.

So, the industry is very diverse; it is still relatively new and it hasn't really got an identity, which is good for us. It means that there are no huge traditional barriers as there would be if it were a coalesced lump of an industry. It is all these little bits, and all the bits

Mueller 13
English 12
Bird 16
Arnold 11

have got different traditions. Even though men dominate nearly every component of the industry, there isn't a whole male tradition in it, in the way we see it anyway, and that view of it has allowed us to get established.

The result is that there is no built model, there is no tradition and it means that there are no rules for producing a multimedia program. That has allowed us to develop our own model. What is really important for women getting into the industry, is that we don't have to follow somebody else's model, there isn't a tradition, we can do it ourselves, we can do it our own way and we can develop the paradigms for ourselves. And we have certainly benefited because we don't come from any of the traditional areas of programming or systems development. We haven't been constrained by any of those things, we knew what we wanted to achieve and so we thought, 'Well, how will we do this?' and 'We will do this our own way'. So who's to argue?

So we have developed our own paradigm. We don't do it the same way as other people whom we know of who produce multimedia titles. It is a really good opportunity for women to get involved in this industry and to build our own paradigms for making multimedia titles. It is an incredibly powerful medium and we think that it's important for women to be part of it. Our methods are non-hierarchical, unstructured and nonlinear. It gives us a very high level of flexibility so that we can remain focused on the end-user throughout the project.

Development by evolution

The first stage in the process of developing a multimedia title is to develop an idea, concept, content, structural design and so on. Figure 1 represents the traditional way of approaching one of these projects. It's linear. You start at the beginning. You work your way through. You sign off each stage before you get to the next bit, and then some time later you come out at the end. Beyond that there is

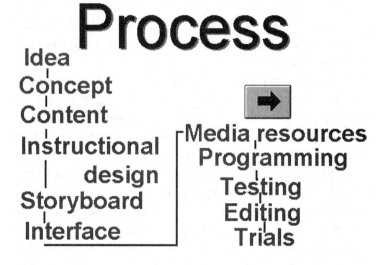

Figure 1: The traditional way . . .

also the marketing and selling. However, when we do it, this is what it looks like. Figure 2 shows our approach. This is the way that we do it and we don't think anyone else does. It is going to be very hard to describe because it is not a linear process. However, as you can see, everything happens more or less at the same time: we do start out with an idea and we do end up finishing the trials at the end of it, but in between we see the production of a multimedia program as a totally organic event. Everything is interwoven, nothing really is complete until the last day before you cut your final mistress copy of the program. And all the way through, the program evolves and develops as we are working through it.

As writing is linear, we will have to deconstruct our process to cover each part but remember that, in our model, there are active connections and overlaps between the parts all the way through the development period.

We mentioned earlier what we want to achieve in our program: accessibility, a high level of interactivity, and sound educational pedagogy. Take *Issues in English*, our third program, as an example.

Figure 2: . . . and Protea's way

We believe that it is an example of an effective language resource which successfully achieves these three outcomes. We developed it to teach and test a wide range of English language skills, including pronunciation, listening, reading and writing, grammar, spelling and vocabulary. We wanted the language activities to be highly contextualised. We wanted it to cover a wide range of skills levels and we wanted to utilise the advantages that video offers language learners. We also wanted to include activities that would be applicable to both English as a Second Language learners as well as English speaking literacy learners.

Concept development

Concept development is a very hard thing to explain. It takes a lot of brain storming, a lot of late nights, a lot of butcher's paper and you end up with something like Figure 3.

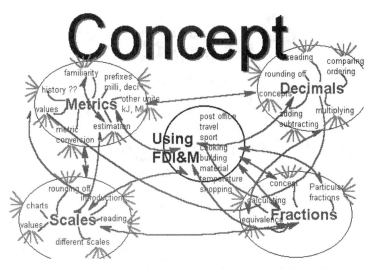

Figure 3 Conceptual development is not straightforward

This is a very summarised, very cleaned-up version of one of our recent projects. About 50% of what is on the real thing is not shown on Figure 3. And of course it is only a two dimensional represent-ation, so if you made it into a 3D image you'd have a better idea of what's going on. Concept development is a long process and we don't finish it before we go onto anything else. Usually concept develop-ment might end about halfway through our whole project dev-elopment. This diagram shows the things that go into concept development. There are the main themes of the program and this, of course, is an educational program. It would be different for other genres of multimedia.

In the diagram, the relationship between the different themes, the relationship between the sub themes, and all of the separate parts, get names like blobs, chunks, slices, slivers and superchunks. We come up with all sorts of things to name the parts and relationships, and it means we have a new set of names every time, to indicate the complexity of the interrelationships within a program.

Development and interactivity

In the case of *Issues in English*, content development involved producing scripts for twenty-four of the thirty-two videos. Very briefly, we have eight issues, each issue at four different levels. For each issue at each level, we have got a video clip of the person presenting an opinion or some information about that issue at that particular language level. Heather wrote the scripts so that we could control the lengths of the sentences, the level of the complexity of the vocabulary and the kinds of grammatical structures that are used. Then she wrote about 600 exercises based around the thirty-two video clips. At Level 4, we had real people from real organisations just come and speak so she didn't need to script that.

It is a different process from producing the content for a book, partly because there isn't the same kind of linearity as there is in a book. Users can do any activity, at any time. They can start anywhere in the program. This raises a number of issues because, on the one hand, there is some kind of logical order associated with the activities but, on the other hand, we are committed to giving the user complete control. We have gone some way towards resolving this issue by suggesting a logical starting point.

Instructional design

Instructional design is a process that applies to educational multimedia programs. It's about developing content and activities so that they are educationally sound and effective in fulfilling the outcomes. The effectiveness of an educational program depends on how interactive it is. Despite what many people say, games developers are about the only multimedia producers who really understand interactivity.

Arnold 11
Mueller 13

Interactivity is another term that is difficult to define and is used very loosely. It often simply means that the user can move from one screen to the next whenever they want, or that they can control the speed or perhaps the order in which things happen. However, we take interactivity to mean much more than that. For us, interactivity means that the user and the computer program interact in a way that is meaningful to the user of the program. For example, it could mean that the computer program sets a task, the user responds by doing something, perhaps by typing something or by selecting one of the alternatives offered. Then the computer immediately responds to the user input by providing some kind of meaningful and context specific feedback which indicates that either the response is correct, or at least acceptable, or that it is not acceptable. In either case the user should be offered some context specific feedback, or help or encouragement.

Navigation

Arnold 11
Hawthorne
19

Navigation is how the user gets from one part of the program to another. It involves making decisions about what other parts of the program you will or won't let the user go to. It means making decisions about how they can get to other parts of the program or which parts we'll encourage them to go to. Decisions about navigation are based on learning paths and learning styles.

Storyboarding

Storyboarding is a process of writing out for the programmer all the elements that are on a screen at any time and specifying the functions of each. So Heather specifies for Virginia, who is the programmer, how she wants each part to work. For example, for the kinds of activities that we have included in our programs, we have had to make decisions about what happens if people select the right word and what happens if they select the wrong word. What happens if they spell a word wrongly? How many tries do you give them when they make a mistake? What sort of feedback do you give them? How can they get help if they don't know what to do?

Mueller 13

We made decisions about when learners might want to go back and have a look at the original videos again. We needed to decide what sort of record keeping we wanted to include and which parts could be printed out. Should there be a formal testing or evaluation part of the program and, if so, how should that part differ from the teaching part? Does the testing part give any feedback? How does

Help work? Are instructions spoken, written or both? We need all the time to keep in mind what is going to be helpful for the user.

Interface design

In broad terms, <u>interface</u> is the combination of the visual and the manipulable elements on the screen which make it possible for the user to interact with the program. One of the first things we work with is a metaphor for the whole program. In *Issues in English* we used talking balloons: these reflect the theme of the program which is about issues of conversations, debating, language skills and so on; that then gives us the beginning of a style to work through for the whole program. It may be a good halfway through the program's development before we know how this image will be used in the program. The metaphor for the interface generally generates itself. We try lots of different things as we work with the program and gain familiarity with the content and type of activities we want. When the metaphor emerges, the style of icons and so on evolve from that.

Mueller 13

One of the hardest challenges in making one of these programs is coming up with your means of allowing users to make choices about which bit of the program they are going to go to at any time. Our problem is particularly difficult because we can't rely on <u>English language</u>, either spoken or written. Also we don't want to make assumptions about the level of computer literacy of our users. So we don't use common computer menuing systems.

Pollock and
Sutton 2

Because we are teaching people English language skills, we have to use visual cues. We have come up with hundreds of metaphors and ideas, a hand of cards, doors, books, signposts, webs, nodes, all sorts of things in order to try to provide an intuitive and unambiguous way in which users can make a choice based on some knowledge; rather than based on a serendipitous action on their part. The development of the interface between all these elements on the screen takes into account our philosophy about access, about the end users, about age, about images which we are portraying; assumptions about the computer skill levels of the users, and so on. We assume that the people who are using these programs want to learn something about English, rather than play with the computer. The computer happens to be convenient and we find it a very powerful medium for presenting this material, but we don't use the standard computer interface models, we don't use the tiny little buttons that require very high levels of motor skills. So our computer programs don't look so much like a computer screen. We have found that our programs reduce adult users' fear of using computers, which is a very positive outcome.

Resources

The actual resources in a multimedia program are often considered to be the guts of a multimedia program. Programs such as the coffee-table or reference works often arise from a collection of resources to which people have access. In our programs, the resources come secondarily, as a way to illustrate and to add meaning to the content and to the language. Resources can take a very long time to get together. We do a lot of the photography ourselves, and we use clip images, we buy photographic images, and we scan still shots. We do most of the sound recording ourselves in-house.

We do some filming with professional actors in studios. In this case, we write the scripts, direct the recordings and the filming but have a professional crew. Sometimes we need to film people who have expertise in language. For these people, we have found the studio situation too intimidating and we have set up to film in-house as well. We then take the raw material back again and capture it, digitise it, edit it and compress it ourselves. So we use the other parts of the industry who are really not multimedia industry, for their skills, and then we take that back, according to our needs.

It is frustrating that while there are a lot of technical skills for the production of resources in the community, there is not a very high level of integration with multimedia, and the requirements for multimedia are different from those for other other media which present the same material. We are really keen to see a lot more women getting involved in technical areas, specialising in multi-media.

Hardware

Our end product is always directed by the end-user. For example, we could utilise full screen, full motion, movies; we could use CD stereo quality sound, we could use 24-bit high resolution graphics; we could use virtual reality. In fact, there is no end to what you can do with the technology but there is a very definite end to what users can accommodate when they are using your program. Most of our users are home users or in educational institutions, they are not games people, they are not people who have bought high end machines to experience the technology. They have standard off-the-shelf machines. When we first started, people didn't even have sound cards. We had to produce our first program on floppy disks and convince people to put a $40 sound card into their computer. As the 'average' level of technology increases, we can include resources that demand more of the computer. So our videos get bigger, sound quality improves, colour depth increases, speech recognition improves. But what we use is always determined by the users' hardware.

Programming

As we mentioned earlier, Virginia had no programming experience. She, too, had failed a course in some very obscure computing language in first year at university. It was on one of those machines where you have a stack of a hundred cards and you put it into the stack every night and every morning it would come back because it was failed on the second card. In a whole term you never get your program to run and Virginia felt that there was no future for her in programming. One never knows what surprises the future may hold!

When we decided to start this business, we bought a multimedia authoring program which Heather had seen and liked. We live a long way out of town and Virginia travelled two hours a day on the train to work, reading the manuals from cover to cover. That's how she learnt to program! To get up to speed with the technology, she read all the trade journals and magazines and still has not done a formal programming course.

However, this background does have its benefits. Because Virginia hadn't learned the traditional systems development model of following very linear paths, we can range all over the place as we develop our programs. It means we have flexibility in our programming which most other development teams don't have. It took a long time to convince Heather that Virginia, in her approach to programming, assumes that the program can be made to do anything that Heather might need it to do. Virginia just works out how to do it when she gets to that point. We're on such a big learning curve—and have been for the last five years, and will be for the next however long we continue in this business—that we don't have time to learn things formally. We can't learn skills at leisure because they may be of interest or of use. It is absolutely learning on a need-to-know basis. When Virginia needs to do something new then she goes and learns about it. That is the only approach we can use to keep up with all of the changes in technology.

Testing and editing

In this medium we test most of our work on the way through, which, again, is quite a different thing from a traditional approach where all the testing is usually done at the end. However, we test as we go along and that approach gets us through about 80% of the problems. Of course, when you are actually building a program and you test it, you test it in the way you expect the end-user to use it. When you are editing a book, you can read through it and pass over the odd typographical error, or even a page substitution and the reader will still get the meaning of what is going on and probably not get too annoyed. If you have one typo in the coding of one of these multimedia programs you can bring the whole program to its knees or, worse still, it just works wrongly and you don't notice. And once more, you don't notice what particular sequence of key strokes it was that might have made it go wrong or where it was that you left out a letter or made a typo or missed a variable or something.

So editing is an absolute nightmare. You have to edit for the unexpected. If you are looking at a book or a film or a recording, you edit what is in front of you. If that's good, then that's good. With multimedia editing, you have to edit for the things you don't particularly want people to do but they might do any way. Heather is known as 'puss fingers' in our organisation because she can bring a program to its knees faster and better and more absolutely than anybody else we know!

In conclusion, we hope that our story convinces women that we can all be involved in this industry. Our experience certainly indicates that it is possible. There aren't high barriers imposed by things like lengthy formal training, and it's really important that we do participate fully. It's an incredibly powerful and accessible medium; it's very influential and there is a lot of it around. We need to make sure that our values, our culture and our histories are being distributed as widely as the others, and the best way for us to do that is to be in there and doing it.

sixteen

Fiction and Interactive Multimedia

Carmel Bird

This story is a personal account of how old-fashioned networking combined with interactive multimedia came to have a dramatic effect on one of my books, *Red Shoes*. Most of the books I write are fiction or manuals on how to write fiction. *Red Shoes* is a novel. The other women involved in the project were both ex-students of the multimedia course at RMIT. Ruth Luxford is an animator, illustrator and programmer, and Jennie Swain, a playwright, actor, musician, singer and songwriter. I met them through a network of mutual friends at RMIT.

In 1994, in Vancouver, I visited a hypertext cafe at a writers' festival. Until then I had not really been aware of the relationship between the way some of my fiction is structured and the way hypertext works. For instance, my novel *The Bluebird Cafe* has a primitive hypertext quality in that there is a long section at the end of the book that lists, like a glossary, some key matters from the body of the work. I imagined, when I saw how electronic hypertext works, that this glossary could have been done electronically. *The Bluebird Cafe* was published first in 1990. At that time I had not even dreamt of hypertext and electronic interactivity, and yet that novel finishes with the section which suggests interactivity and hypertext. There are examples of the same kind of thing throughout my work, but *The Bluebird Cafe* is perhaps the most obvious.

When I read Ilana Snyder's book *Hypertext: The electronic labyrinth* I was finally inspired to develop a hypertext version of *Red Shoes*. This decision quickly led to the idea of making a CD-ROM, not only with hypertext but with multimedia effects as well. The publisher, Random House, agreed to packaging the CD-ROM as a give-away

Namjoshi
17

Mueller 13
Westwood
and Kauf-
mann 15

with the novel. I would fund the making of the CD-ROM, and they would take care of the reproduction and distribution.

In order to make the CD-ROM I needed the expert help of Ruth and Jennie. Because they were interested in doing the work for its own sake, as well as as a job, they agreed to very low rates of pay.

We worked together on the electronic version of the novel for several months. It was a strange and exhilarating thing to see my text becoming hypertext and to see it being presented along with images and sounds. Because I invented them, I believe in the characters and events, but it was strange to work alongside Ruth and Jennie who also spoke of the things in the book as if they were real events and real people. I am so very admiring of the work these two have done, and very grateful to them for their time and patience and brilliance.

Reading the novel as hypertext, with multimedia elements, is different from reading it in hard copy. And if readers don't wish to have a CD-ROM, they don't have to take it. Having taken it, they don't have to use it. The novel itself in hard copy can be read alone. And people who forget to pick up the CD-ROM when they buy the book can contact the publisher and receive a copy. People will use the two media in different ways. It's up to them. I am close to the production of both, so I move easily between the two. The whole text of the hard copy is on the electronic copy, but the electronic effects deliver a different reading experience. Sometimes I think that because of all the beautiful colourful images on the CD-ROM it is a little like reading a magazine, but I don't really know how other people will receive it.

I have been asked why I produced the CD-ROM of *Red Shoes*, and the answer is that I saw the possibilities of the technology for my work, and I am interested in experiments. This was just that, an experiment, and if we had had the time and the money we could have gone on and on adding and perfecting effects.

Producing a book is always nerve-wracking; producing a book and its accompanying CD-ROM is very nerve-wracking indeed. Perhaps some critics will be scornfully dismissive of this project. Be that as it may, I know that the hard copy and the CD-ROM of *Red*

Shoes are another step and a new development in my own exploration of language and storytelling. And the CD-ROM is still just an experiment. Parts of this experiment can be downloaded from my website: <http://www.carmelbird.com>

The technology used in the development of *Red Shoes* lends itself to a playfulness which is one of the elements of my work—even though my subject matter is often serious, there is frequently a ludic quality. So the use of the technology was liberating for me in that it allowed me to demonstrate with image and sound some of the things that my writing does on the page. For one thing, the CD-ROM bursts into song when it feels like it. There are hints of this in my writing, as in my novel *The White Garden*. But the electronic version of *Red Shoes* gave me the opportunity to do it full-on. For instance, the hard copy of the novel contains a recipe for Angel Cake, just printed out as text, as it ought to be. The CD-ROM draws the reader right in to this recipe because Jennie has written a song for it, and Ruth has developed an animation.

The details of the technology used in the creation of *Red Shoes* are as follows:

Programming and authoring—Macromedia Director 6, a multi-media software which is flexible and powerful enough to create projects from corporate presentations to computer games. It does not have hypertext linking, and so a special code was written for the *Red Shoes* project. This code searches for the right screen when any bold is clicked.

Artwork—Adobe Photoshop and Fractal Designs Painter.

Sound—Macromedia Sound Exit 16, as well as software for composing music and synchronising sound effects into soundscapes.

The CD-ROM can be used on PCs and Macs.

References

Bird, Carmel. 1996. *The Bluebird Cafe*. Sydney: Random House Australia.

Bird, Carmel. 1996. *The White Garden*. St. Lucia: University of Queensland Press.

Bird, Carmel. 1998. *Red Shoes*. Sydney: Random House Australia.

Snyder, Ilana. 1996. *Hypertext: The electronic labyrinth*. Melbourne: Melbourne University Press.

carmel@carmelbird.com

<http://www.carmelbird.com>

seventeen

A Meme of Great Power or What the God Vishnu Has to Do With the Internet[1]

Suniti Namjoshi

Hindu tradition, text and technology, implications for global education

There are two sets of ideas really that make it easy for someone with a Hindu background to realise that the Internet is an excellent analogue for the cultural exchange that goes on anyway, whatever the technology; though I would argue that it doesn't need a Hindu to see certain things, any poet would do just as well.

The first set of ideas has to do with assumptions that are not necessarily made: (1) Technology does not equal civilisation, (2) Passage through time does not equal progress, and (3) <u>Literacy</u> does not equal education. To put it more dramatically: India has a highly civilised, highly illiterate population.

Westwood
and Kauf-
mann 15

The other set of ideas has to do with attitudes towards myth. (In this context, of course, Christian theology is also mythology.) Hinduism differs from the religions of the book in that it's permissible for a Hindu to invent stories and myths that try to explain, understand or simply express human experience. Indulging in such invention does not constitute heresy. Well, that's how it was until Hindu fundamentalism came along. Now, here's a fable with the title 'From the

---

[1] Paper given at the Women in Technology section of the LETA (Learning Environment Technology Australia) 96 Conference, Adelaide, 3 October.

Panchatantra', though it soon becomes obvious that fable isn't from *The Panchatantra*, an old and well-known book of fables in Sanskrit.

> In the holy city of Benares there lived a brahmin, who, as he walked by the riverbank, watching the crows floating downstream, feeding on the remains of half-burnt corpses, consoled himself thus: 'It is true that I am poor, but I am a brahmin; it is true that I have no sons, but I, myself, am indisputably a male. I shall return to the temple and pray to Lord Vishnu to grant me a son.' He went off to the temple and Lord Vishnu listened and Lord Vishnu complied, but whether through absent-mindedness or whether for some other more abstruse reason, he gave him a daughter. The brahmin was disappointed. When the child was old enough, he called her to him and delivered himself thus: 'I am a brahmin. You are my daughter. I had hoped for a son. No matter. I will teach you what I know, and when you are able, we will both meditate and seek guidance.' Though only a woman, she was a brahmin, so she learned very fast, and then, they both sat down and meditated hard. In a very short time Lord Vishnu appeared. 'What do you want?' he said. The brahmin couldn't stop himself. He blurted out quickly, 'I want a son.' 'Very well,' said the god, 'Next time around.' In his next incarnation the brahmin was a woman and bore eight sons. 'And what do you want?' he said to the girl. 'I want human status.' 'Ah, that is much harder,' and the god hedged and appointed a commission (Namjoshi 1981/1993a: 1)

It's not just that the fable is not in the *Panchatantra*, it's equally obvious that this particular episode to do with the god, Vishnu, is unlikely to be found anywhere else. It's also obvious that I'm unlikely to be accused of blasphemy for having written it at all. For people from a religious background where there is one sacred text, the problem is trickier.

But what does this have to do with the Internet? Simply this: in a culture with a strong oral tradition there's an awareness that the process of exchanging bits of information and creating new constructs out of the old bits goes on all the time—whatever the technology. It is not necessary to be a poet to see this and to participate in it. Or rather, this is what human beings do anyway. As Saint Suniti says in *Saint Suniti and the Dragon*, 'Poetry is the sound of the human animal.'

When Suniti's friends came upon her soliloquizing yet again, they felt they had better say something.

'Look here,' they scolded. 'Why do you want to be a saint? Why invent devils? Why write poetry?'

'Writing poetry is what human beings do,' Suniti was patient. 'It's like birds, you know. Poetry is the sound of the human animal.'

She had said this with such complete conviction that her friends were silenced, but only for a moment.

'Okay, but why don't you write about concrete, everyday things? Why all this mythicism?'

'Because,' replied Suniti, 'an ordinary person going on and on about angels and devils, that, don't you see, is the human condition.'

'Well, but,'—her friends were unconvinced—'why don't you do something really useful? Take up a trade. You'd feel a lot better.'

'This is my trade!' Suniti snapped. She was getting indignant.

Her friends realized they had gone too far. 'Oh. Well, here we all are. Ply your trade. Entertain us.'

'That's exactly what I have been doing,' Suniti retorted.

Her friends were startled. They did not feel in the least entertained, but they tried again.

'Well, instruct us as well. Give us some answers.'

Suniti was exasperated. 'I've just defined the human condition, and for good measure I've even thrown in the nature of poetry. You too have a part to play, you know. You have a function.' (Namjoshi 1993: 50–51).

In short, engaging in the cultural process is not an unnatural activity. It is, for example, what we're doing at this moment.

There's often some confusion between art form and medium. The new technology is a medium for broadcasting and receiving. In some respects the claims it makes for itself are a shadow of what good listeners or readers of poetry have been doing for centuries. Take the matter of simultaneity and sequence, for example.

A poem on a page of the world wide web can have links to other pages as well as internal links, and it can have graphics and sound. But how is this useful or helpful to writer or reader?

Poetry wasn't always a poem on a page. That was merely the medium for broadcasting. For hundreds of years, and in many different cultures, poems were recited.

The sound was integral to the poem.

Good listeners or readers had an instantly available frame of reference. Later, good students had a range of reference works.

Today, really good readers of poetry hear the sound of the poem as they read it in their head, and they have a frame of reference that makes the resonances of the poem instantly available.

They also ingest the poem as a sequential as well as a simultaneous piece of work. The connections between different bits of the poem aren't just a matter of contiguity. There are links between different sections. And these are held together simultaneously in the head.

Good readers also literally see the poem's images in their head.

But most people are not good readers of poetry. In part, the problem arises because there is no longer a common <u>frame of reference</u>.

So how can the use of an html page help?

Some answers. An html page can:

(1) make the images instantly available (graphics);

(2) make the sound instantly available;

(3) make useful information (that is, the missing frame of reference) instantly available.

These three possibilities just use the technology as a teaching tool, a crutch. They do nothing to the nature of poetry itself. But poetry was never made out of the printed page or a computer screen. Its medium is words, thought. There is, of course, a terrible confusion about the word 'medium' (Namjoshi 1996: xvii–xviii).

Hawthorne
19
Mueller 13

Nevertheless, there is no reason why poetry should not use the new technology for broadcasting and for receiving, why the Internet should not be a 'medium' for poetry in this sense of the word.

When the culture is reasonably homogenous, it's easy to see how the external world reflects the internal, communal mental space. The images of gods and goddesses scattered all over India are reflected on the TV screen, and are also contained in the stories inscribed on people's brain cells. Or again, if you'll forgive an anachronism, I imagine that, in medieval times, Christian cyberspace would have looked very like the inside of a cathedral.

As I see it, cyberspace is simply the communal, cultural space, independent of any particular technology. I think it's the affinity between the computer screen and one's own mind which made it easy to imagine a space in which computers were linked together. What's important to remember though, is that it's the link between human brains that matters, not between computers.

In a period of heterogeneity and change, cyberspace would, of course, reflect the heterogeneity and change. This sounds innocuous, but what it often reflects, of course, is deadly warfare. The speed of the new technologies results in global rather than national cultures. Despite India's vast population, it's possible that more people know about *Star Trek* than the doings of the god, Vishnu. Then when the Americans send the good ship Enterprise, as they did in September 1996 in order to help bomb Iraq, there's a certain resonance!

Introduction

In *Building Babel* I've stolen the word '<u>memes</u>', from Richard Dawkins to stand for bits of culture. What I am saying is that the good ship Enterprise is a meme of great power.

The thing about memes is that they mutate. They battle for survival. Some get transmitted and some don't. The *transmission of memes is the educational process*. When the young are feeling reverent,

A meme of great power—the good ship Enterprise (Suniti Namjoshi)

they say that they are what we have made them. But that's a double-edged remark . . .

In *Building Babel* I've tried to embody the cultural process in the writing of the text; and so I've used characters like Cinders, Little Red and Rap Rap, that is, characters who are themselves obviously memes. They are certainly memes in Medusa's head. Young Medusa is the inheritor of the civilisation that Rap Rap and the others have consciously attempted to create. This process is never smooth, and here are some of the things that they and mad Med have to say about the process.

> SUCCESS SECTION
> But the roar of the guns still outroars.
> Three hags sit about a fire in the middle of a forest. But why these dress ups, set ups, hang ups? The fire is necessary: it keeps them warm. The forest is there: Little Red has saved it for herself. It has a lodge, and the other two are Little Red's guests. As for being old, that is not something Cinders, Rap Rap or Little Red can help. 'We meant well,' Cinders offers. 'What difference does that make?' Rap Rap mutters. Cinders shrugs, 'We'd have done a lot worse if we had meant ill.' Rap Rap glares. Little Red sighs. In a way none of it matters, but she is the hostess.
> Sadly she says, 'Sweet Sister Success doesn't rise ever higher into graceful old age. Crone Kronos comes along. What we had worked for somehow mutates.'
> Rap Rap says, 'Then Mad Med comes along: boisterous, ebullient. 'I am of supreme importance. Where is my inheritance? Where my sustenance?' She snatches our bread. She stomps about. She makes a mockery of all we've made.'
> Cinders sighs, 'She is what we've made.'
> Three old women stare into the fire. There's a crashing in the darkness. Snow White and Rose Green. They want to share the fire. Alice and the fawn. Mad Med & Co. The three old witches are tempted to set the forest alight. Rap Rap brandishes a burning brand, but only in her mind's eye, only for a moment. They break the circle. They shift a little, and make space (Namjoshi 1996: 170–171).

ADVENT
In the difficult distance a dome gleams
        on the sea's horizon.
Babel rising? The sun or the moon?
But no floating city drifts to their shore.
        No metaphors now.
It's Mad Med cradled in an eggshell.
        Awake or sleeping?
    No hi fi blasts the air.
    No seaweeds writhe in her hair.
And the waves are so gentle that the sisters
        expect the sound of a harp,
            well, some heavenly music.
    'Mad Med, welcome ashore!
        Mad Med, you bloody—!'
No, no such sounds, only the sound
        of waves lapping.
Since the sisters keep their grief to themselves,
and forgive Medusa her ignorant beauty (Namjoshi 1996:
174).

'Compleynt, compleynt, I hearde upon a day,'
[Canto 30, Ezra Pound]

So it's my birthday and all these godmothers come to wish me
ill or well—depends on the time of day, and how they're
feeling. Little Red brings a tinder box. I'm supposed to be
grateful? Rap Rap has brains, Rap Rap's a scholar. She brings
a computer. I play games. Rap Rap scowls. She had wanted
me to acquire wisdom and learning. I am learning. And
Cinders is superior. Cinders produces a party dress. That's
more like it. It dazzles and glitters. Sequins and silk. When I
open it up, it disintegrates. Can't even sell it. Well, they meant
well. I'm supposed to smile. I smile a bit. Then I cry. I do what
the young are supposed to do. They smile. They scowl. Two
can play the game. Why not? Solitude brings me her solitude.
The Black Piglet? Tells more stories. Oh well. They bring what
they can. I take what I can. I rip out the sequins. Someday I'll
make a brand new dress—something that fits.
    I DON'T forgive them my impoverishment (Namjoshi
1996: 175).

A TEXT DOESN'T EXIST

The sisters pull themselves together. So much more pleasant to lie in the shade. Let the building of Babel regulate itself. But The Piglet wriggles from the arms of death. Solly and Shy— for a time at least—refrain from gardening. And Rap Rap, Cinders and Little Red present themselves.

. . .

they turn to Mad Med.

>'We gave you Virtue, Truth and Beauty.'
>'We gave you our memes.'
>'We gave you memories.'
>'Our past!'
>'Your future!'

Med just stands there, and scowls at them. As they carry on, her scowl becomes more and more ferocious. The sisters stop. They ask Mad Med, 'Well, what do you want?'

'I want—' Med hesitates. 'I want to take over the building of Babel. I want my friends. I want to find out what I think of Babel. I want—' Here she grins an evil grin—'I want, if necessary, to destroy Babel.'

The sisters brace themselves. If they had glass shields, they would now raise them.

>'But you are ill-tutored.'
>>'Ill-mannered.'
>>>'Illiterate.'

Med glares.

'Your friends would trample on the memes of Babel.'

Med shrugs.

'Babel wasn't built in a day, you know. Are you proposing the Conquest of Babel?'

Med turns away. 'Keep Babel then. Keep it intact. May Crone Kronos and Death, and Mad Mem as well, haunt the ruins of Babel.'

'What are you saying?'

'I am saying,' Mad Med replies instantly, 'that Babel cannot bloom in the desert air, and that a text doesn't exist until it's read.'

The sisters bow their heads. 'Very well,' they say, 'lower the barriers. Open the floodgates. Reveal the text. Let friends enter and barbarians as well. Are you content?'

Mad Med grins. 'Come on,' she cajoles, 'It's not so bad.'

Hawthorne 6

The sisters tremble. Mad Med sets off to inform the world that <u>Babel is now open</u> to touts and tourists, vagrants and visitors, friends and allies, prospective immigrants, long lost citizens, and other pickers up of cultural artefacts. Very few come. Once again, the sisters tremble. They buckle down to help Mad Med (Namjoshi 1996: 179–80).

And so the conservatism of the old guard is broken, and *Building Babel* is opened to the public. It can be reached from the Spinifex Home Page. <<u>http://www.spinifexpress.com.au</u>> and readers are invited to contribute to the memes of Babel.

What's important about the new technology is not that it's good or bad in itself, nor that it's an improvement on the printing press or on an oral tradition. What is important about it is that it's in use.

What is happening on the Internet for better or for worse is a powerful part of the cultural process. My central point here is that educationists, poets, writers—all those of us who are vitally concerned with the process of building culture and community—should learn to use the new technology. As many of you know, it's easy to use, and its effects are multifarious.

References

Namjoshi, Suniti. 1993a. *Feminist Fables*. Melbourne: Spinifex Press. (First published 1981. Sheba Feminist Publishers.)
Namjoshi, Suniti. 1993b. *Saint Suniti and the Dragon*. Melbourne: Spinifex Press.
Namjoshi, Suniti. 1996. *Building Babel*. Melbourne: Spinifex Press.
The Panchatantra. A book of fables in Sanskrit.

eighteen

A Hyperfext Fable and Some Explanation

Suniti Namjoshi

The fable below has been marked up as <u>hypertext</u>. For the purposes of reading it, ignore everything in italics. What remains is what it would look like in a book, or indeed, on the computer screen. The words in bold print are hypertext links. (A bit like footnotes in books.) Below the fable I've explained what the hypertext tags mean. Hypertext Markup Language (HTML) isn't difficult. It does two things: (1) provides formatting tags, so that the text can be formatted, and (2) provides a way of linking words in the text to other pages on the World Wide Web, that is, pages with a URL (Uniform Resource Locator) or address. Browsers or navigators are bits of software that allow you to type in the addresses of pages available on the web (the navigable part of the Internet) and to go there, that is, to read those pages. It is no longer necessary to write the html tags by hand, but understanding how html works is still useful. The new technology is another means of broadcasting and receiving information: it is therefore of considerable importance to the cultural process, that is, to the changing, shifting and building of culture.

<html>
<head>
<title>Other Locations</title>
</head>
<body>
<bodybgcolor='#8F8FBD'>
<p>
<p><aname='11'>
* <h1> <ahreh='#1'>***Other locations***</a></h1> </a>*
<dd> As blood from the sunsets seemed to stain the world repeatedly, and as the world itself wobbled increasingly on an unstable axis, there was a whispering among the people, especially the women, that escape was possible. Some women

Bird 16
Hawthorne 19

scoffed, 'We're not likely to be chosen to <*a href='#2'>***man***>/a*> the spaceships. And as for going as paying passengers, we can't afford it!' But these women were told that access to cyberspace was both cheap and easy, well, relatively cheap, relatively easy, cheaper and easier than going to the moon, and in the end likelier than the moon to provide heart's ease. Some women tried it. 'Zip! Zap! Bing! Bang! Ha ha! Hoo hoo!' Tarzan and the apes having a party and no place for Jane . . .

<*dd*> They were told to try again. There were other locations, playgrounds, not battlegrounds . . . 'Why should we?' they protested, 'We thought cyberspace was a place that was well governed, lawful and orderly . . .' Other women, who had been out there (and lived to tell the tale) explained patiently. 'Unlike India and Australia, and other places which were once seen as colonies, a location in cyberspace, doesn't actually exist until it's perceived. And anyhow just sticking a flag somewhere and saying it's colonised, doesn't mean anything.'

Arnold 11

<*dd*> 'Well then,' asked the women reasonably, 'what does mean something? Why go out there? Why not stay at home peacefully?'

<*dd*> 'Because,' was the answer, 'there's a job to be done. And if it's to be well done, you'll have to do it.'

<*dd*> 'Do what?'

Hawthorne 19 <*dd*> <*ahref='#3">*'Create a pleasant garden,'*</a*> said some.

Namjoshi 17 <*dd*> 'Write poetry,' said others.

Bird 16 <*dd*> 'Exchange recipes,' said still others.

<*dd*> 'Why?' asked the women. 'What has any of this to do with cyberspace?'

<*dd*> 'It's the shared space inside people's heads,' the voyagers replied. 'It has always been there. Bits of it grow, other bits die. If as a species we're to survive, you'll have to work on it.'

<*dd*> The women sighed. A formidable task. But it was, after all, what they had always done: spinning, weaving, managing the <*a href='#2'>*web*</a*>—they would deal with it.<*br*><*br*>

<*center*><*i*>copyright <*ahref='#4'>***Suniti Namjoshi***</a*></i*></center*>
<*br*>
<*br*>
<*br*>
<*br*>

<*aname='1'*> <*dd*>This particular URL is to another place on the same page— very like a footnote. A word or group of words that has a link attached to it is highlighted. Here I'm using bold print. This next link however would take you to <*a href='http://www.spinifexpress.com.au*> **The Spinifex Home Page**</a*> In order to get back you would have to choose 'Back' on your browser.</a*><*br*>

<*center*><*ahref='#11'*>**Return to the top of the page.**</a*></center*>
<*br*><*br*>

*<a name='2'> <dd>*Intentional pun, of course. Just trying to illustrate linking.*</a>
*

   * <ahref='#11'>***Return to the top of the page.***</a> *
*

*

*<a name='3'> <dd>*I was trying to find a suitable link to explain formatting tags, and decided to use gardening imagery. You have to use these peculiar brackets for html tags. After that it's just a matter of typing in a formatting tag, like 'i' for italics, to turn it on and a cancellation, '/i', to turn it off. Some tags, like 'p' for line space or 'br' for line break, don't need turning off. If you want to see how a particular page has been formatted, ask to view the 'source' through your browser. This will reveal the marked up text.*</a>
*

   * <a href='#11'>***Return to the top of the page.***</a> *
*
*
*
*

*<aname='4'> <dd>*Good Luck with all this.*
*
*<dd>*V i s i t   *<a*
href=http://www.ex.ac.uk/~smnamjos/welcome.html'>
my Home Page*</a>* or
<a
href='http://www.sinifexpress.com.au/~women/babelbuildingsite.html'>
The Babel Building Site.*</a>
*
</a>

*<dd>*If you type this page into your computer, starting with 'html' and finishing with '/html', and then open it with the 'Open file' command through your browser, what you see should look like a Web page.
*</a>
*

* <ahref='#11'>***Return to the top of the page.***</a> *
</body>
<html>

nineteen

Unstopped Mouths, and Infinite Appetites: Developing a Hypertext of Lesbian Culture

Susan Hawthorne

> *Caught in moments*
> *on the cusp of millennium,*
> *poetry affords bridges*
> Deborah Staines, *Now Millennium*

Hypertext

Bird 16
Namjoshi
17

In the few years since <u>hypertext</u> has become a familiar word to speakers of English, much has been written on how to define it. Aarseth (1994: 67) defines it quite simply: 'It is merely the direct connection from one position in a text to another.' This definition is clearer than many others I have read. It avoids the pitfall of restricting it to a particular medium.

The scholarship on hypertext is wide ranging, and the prehistory of cyberculture (Tofts and McKeich, 1997) is a long one. Although some, like Gaggi (1998) express the view that it 'will radically alter our whole notion of what a text is—and what reading is' (1998: 102), others such as Suniti Namjoshi, write about the precursors of hypertext, and how there is a long and continuing link between myth, storytelling and cyberculture (1996: ix–xxix). She compares the way in which poetry functions and the 'direct connections' of hypertext. Just as oral literature is still literature, oral literature also shares many features with hypertext. She writes (1996: xvii):

> Poetry wasn't always printed on a page. That was merely the medium for broadcasting. For hundreds of years and in many different cultures poems were recited.

David Porush (1996: 128–30) argues that the Talmud represents an early form of hypertext with the original text at the centre and other spaces set aside for commentary and notes. In the Talmud, the oldest texts are near the centre, with later textual accretions towards the edges. I walked around the Cathedral of the Annunciation in the Kremlin with a guide once, as she showed us the Russian Orthodox paintings lining the walls. Here again, in visual form this time, an image at the centre with small storytelling icons framing it. A hypertext for a largely illiterate populace. Medieval manuscripts take up a position midway between the Talmud and Russian icons, containing both text and images. The stations of the cross in Christian churches take hypertext into an architectural medium. An astrologer can read the marks which indicate a natal chart, can explain the links highlighted by good and bad aspects in a chart. What all these things have in common is a mental symbolic language which is shared by those who inhabit the particular culture, whether it be Jewish, Orthodox or esoteric.

Similarly, the hypertextual nature of <u>traditional</u> and contemporary Aboriginal painting can be explored through excavating the meanings of U shapes, of circles, of certain marks representing plants or animals or topographies of land. These are processes we notice in visual imagery, in a way that we rarely notice in print; although good readers of poetry will follow the symbolic tracks of a poem, in just the same way a good reader of Aboriginal art will read the painting. That we have not noticed this before, is simply that we have adjusted to print and other media and allowed it to construct us. Information technologies will also construct us, but the process is obvious just now because we are having to change our habits.

Arnold 11

One of the significant features of hypertext in its electronic form is its nonlinearity. And this too, is often assumed to have no precursors. One could argue that the Talmud and the stations of the cross are linear narratives, but it is not possible to say that of the Australian

Aboriginal mix of song, dance, story and painting which constitutes traditional lore. Aarseth (1994: 64) puts forward the *I Ching* as an example of a nonlinear text. The reading of the *I Ching* is accompanied by a ritual throwing of coins or yarrow stalks which forces randomness upon the reader, while the open text allows for a multitude of readings, each reader attributing, by association, their own meaning to the text.[1]

Aarseth suggests another metaphor for nonlinear hypertext, that of topology. In this, he draws on standard meanings for topology in mathematics, namely: 'those properties of geometric figures that remain unchanged even when under distortion, so long as no surfaces are torn', and turning this to the study of nonlinear topologies, which he describes as:

Mueller 13

> the study of the ways in which the various sections of a text are connected, disregarding the physical properties of the channel (paper, stone, electromagnetic, and so on) by means of which the text is transmitted (Aarseth 1994: 60).

Topology is not far from the mapping and navigating metaphors so commonly encountered in the literature. The writer's or reader's move across hypertextual links takes on the feel of a journey, with the writer preparing the signposts or diversions for the reader's interest. But Mireille Rosello (1994: 129) is wary of extending the metaphor from navigation and mapping to travel because of its association with mastery and colonisation. She notes that 'the metaphors used in hypermedia are rapidly solidifying and thus escaping scrutiny' (*ibid.*). I'd argue that, in addition, the canon of hypertextual works is also being institutionalised, and much of what passes for exciting new hypertextual work is more of the same with a costume change.

[1.] The I Ching is a traditional Chinese meditation on the future, in a comparable way to the western Tarot or throwing of dice. But instead of using cards, either coins or yarrow stalks are used and from the combination of positions, of which there are sixty-four possible outcomes, the querent is led to read particular passages in the *I Ching* book, otherwise known as *The Book of Changes* (1983).

Other writers have compared hypertext to <u>memory</u>. Suniti
Namjoshi refers to the 'memes', a cultural memory, passed from
generation to generation through the oral literature and the dominant symbols of the culture. Vayu Naidu, in a contribution to the
BabelBuildingSite writes:

Namjoshi
17
English 12

> The contexualisation of memes to poetry and technology can be so
> successfully transposed to the survival of the Indic oral traditions. The
> caste of Bharatas are the memes of Natyashastra across the regions
> while reenacting the mythology of the fire sacrifice and retelling that first
> story about the tug-of-war between deva and asura. Perhaps more than
> that the Vyasas are the memes who have kept the epics pan Indian (sub-
> continental and even south east-asian) and have interpolated political
> and historical inventions over time. This ensures that the maps of the
> epics' universes are intact while containing the vehicles of evolution
> within (Naidu, n.d.).

Beryl Fletcher, drawing on the work of Frances Yates (1978), refers
to an ancient practice called '<u>architectural memory</u>' which assists a
person in memorising very long chains of information such as
speeches or oral stories. The chain of memory pegs, or rooms, or
objects, act as catalysts to the mind and move it on to the next point,
to whatever is associated with that mental link.

Fletcher 14

Hypertext is also associated with webs, matrices, mazes,
labyrinths.

> A labyrinth . . . is a place in which ideally, all the possibilities of choice . . .
> are embodied, and . . . must be exhausted before one reaches the heart
> (Barthes, cited in Snyder 1996: 37).

This is text moving in the opposite direction to the Talmud. Rather
than starting at the centre and moving out, a labyrinth of this kind,
as exemplified by the game *Myst* (1993), moves from the outer
towards the centre or alternate centres. But the problem with
hypertext—in its electronic form—is that it is impossible to know
where in the text one is, since there are no clear boundaries between
the text and others, and often there is no distinguishable point of
ending. Even if one encounters the same material while reading, the

Mueller 13

order of reading and therefore the <u>associational</u> context, will be different. Hypertext reading is more like a journey taken without a map. How do you know when you are halfway? When you have reached a climax? When you have reached the centre? Or whether indeed you have finished reading the text? It is always possible that another reading experience is available. Excessive complexity, therefore, is potentially a problem for writers of hypertext. As Janet Murray (1996: 87) points out:

> hypertext fiction is still awaiting the development of formal conventions of organization that will allow the reader/interactor to explore an encyclopedic medium without being overwhelmed.

The potentially endless web of interconnections can confuse rather than elucidate the text, and although there is an exciting edge to this endless weave of interlinked texts, the excitement is theoretical rather than practical.

Poetry

The earliest human literature is in a poetic form. Poetry has meter, form, metaphor, rhythm and meaning—although not all poems will have all these features.

The following is part of a song from an Australian epic cycle of Arnhem Land.

> We Djanggawul saw the Morning Star shining . . .,
> Saw its shine on the Green-backed turtle, lighting up its throat . . . !
> Paddling, we saw that turtle: saw its eyes open, its flippers outstretched as it floated.
> Sea Water lapped at its shell, spreading across its back,
> Making a sound as it rose above the surface, see the dilly bag at its back!
> It swam through the sea, with shell like a rock, hiding the bag under its flipper.
> 'I have another basket' (the turtle says). 'It is the cuttle fish.'
> (Berndt 1952: 64)

This is an extract from Song 2 of the Djanggawul[2] cycle, and like other ancient epic cycles it includes information about travelling from place to place, about the environment, animals and astronomical events. We know from the poem that the people in it are travelling at dawn, and we also get to find out about the artefacts of the culture: dillybags and baskets are mentioned here, and elsewhere canoes, paddles, mats and poles are mentioned.

Poetry is often very dense, conveying large amounts of information quite briefly. In a period when all cultural information had to be memorised in order to pass it on to the next generation, brevity and density, as well as certain formulaic utterances were important. Similarly, rhythm and meter assist the memory, so song, music and poetry often came together in <u>oral poetic traditions</u>. Alongside this, dance and drama also developed. Poetry, in its origins, crossed many media when it was expressed.

Namjoshi
17

> But Demeter, mistress of fruits in their season, of bright gifts
> The bestower, cared not to sit in the richly made chair,
> But stood there in silence, her beautiful eyes cast downward,
> Till thoughtful Iambe, seeing her, placed for her comfort
> A well-carpented stool and threw upon it a silvery fleece.
> There sat the goddess, concealing her face with her shawl,
> All too long, silently grieving, she crouched on the stool,
> Acknowledging no one either by word or by deed,
> Saddened and still, weak from not having touched food or drink,
> Ceaselessly yearning after her deeply girt daughter.
> (Sargent 1975: 7)

This short section from 'The Homeric Hymn to Demeter' is filled with formulaic phrases and names which you can find repreated throughout Homeric literature. The first line is a standard introductory line for an immortal, listing her attributes 'mistress of fruits in season' and 'of bright gifts the bestower'. The description of Iambe, 'thoughtful Iambe', and the 'silvery fleece', along with 'deeply girt daughter' are standard combinations of compound adjectives

---

2. The Djanggawul are three people: two sisters and a brother.

and nouns throughout the Homeric tradition. In a hypertext version of the poem, they could become links, so that one could trace other tales about Iambe, or Persephone (deeply girt daughter) or other fleeces just by being able to find these words.[3] In Ancient Australia and Ancient Greece, as well as every other known culture, people invented ways of telling history, of speaking about the attributes of deities and of the environment they lived in. The travels of Demeter and of the Djanggawul are vehicles for marking territories, describing the places a particular people live in, as well as significant events and people involved in the culture.

When poetry moves to print, it retains many of these features, but it also develops additional ones. The way a poem looks on a page becomes important, and it becomes possible to invent new complex forms whose patterns are readily shown in visual form: the sonnet, the sestina, the haiku and a whole range of other forms appear, and poetry moves a little away from the formulaic and toward the different, the original or surprising expression. Gradually, poetry becomes more individualised, and becomes a personal expression of events and experiences, although some poetry takes on cultural expression—the works of say, HD (Hilda Doolittle) (1974), or Timoshenko Aslanides (1998) are examples which draw on the representation of cultural history. HD, as Joan Retallack (1985) points out, was addicted to formulas, not surprisingly given how steeped she was in formulaic Ancient Greek poetry. While Aslanides, in a nod towards hypertext, has produced a series of 366 linked poems in print in his collection *AnniVersaries* (1998). At the end of the book the author provides notes on the structure and on the specific links within the text. If this book were produced electronically using hypertext, the links could be made directly into the text, thereby allowing the reader to jump immediately across poems without having to consult the back of the book.[4]

[3.] For more on how scholars working in the field of Classics are using hypermedia see Crane and Mylonas (1991: 205-220).

[4.] A similar note precedes the text in Julio Cortazar's *Hopscotch* (1967).

The twentieth century has seen poetic innovation across a huge array of forms—from Gertude Stein's rhythmically rich works, to the meaninglessness of Dada, the visually powerful concrete poetry, the diverse works of rap, sound and performance poets—just to name a few. And now there is electronic poetry, hypertextual poetry, cyberpoetry, multimedia poetry. How will these new developments change and extend poetry once again?

One direction taken by poets is what performance poet Komninos Zervos[5] calls 'cyberpoetry' but which could also be called 'liquid poetry'. In contrast to concrete poetry, these are poems where the letters flow on the screen, sometimes literally as a way of creating work with consistency of medium and message. A one word poem 'Drip' has a letter which drips as you read it. Another, 'Wave' moves across the screen in a series of wave forms reminiscent of ee cummings. These are poems which can only be produced using electronic means. Such attributes could be accorded to previously 'concrete' poems. One by Cassandra Grahame (1975: 205) I found recently, is halfway there in its print form:

W
O M E N
    S
    T
    R
    U
    A
    T
    E

On his CD-ROM *Cyberpoetry Underground* Komninos Zervos (1998) defines cyberpoetry, using a mix of motion, sound and text with moving letters, as folllows:

---

5. Komninos Zervos' poetry can be found at URL <http://student.uq.edu.au/~s271502>, while other examples can be found in the electronic zine on a website established by Komninos Zervos, as a poet in residence at Melbourne's State Library of Victoria.
<http://emedia.experimedia.vic.gov.au/cyberpoet/>

Cyberpoetry / words in time and space / stimulating imagery / evoking emotion / telling stories in a new way / to suit the new technology

Cyberpoetry / words freed from the page / words in three dimensions / fluid concrete poetry / welded with sounds

Cyberpoetry / words as actors in their own movie

Namjoshi
17
Suniti Namjoshi's BabelBuildingSite (1999) uses a different set of rules. This Web site uses hypertext as its raison d'être, inviting readers to contribute their responses to the book, *Building Babel*, an allegory of Internet culture, or to the material in the final chapter which is included on the Web site. Here you will find visual images as graphics or photographs, a music score, poems, fictions, auto-biographical responses to the work, as well as 'liquid poetry'. An interesting example of the latter jumbles the letters of the word 'Babel' in imitation of its associational meanings.

Hypertext allows both poet and reader to interact with one another, and for that interaction to have an element of transparency about it. The BabelBuildingSite encourages readers to engage with the material in the novel and on the Web site, including suggesting how the material contributed should be linked to others. Namjoshi writes of the interactive process that goes on inside the head of a reader of poetry and compares it to the way in which hypertext works. In an imaginary power struggle between Writer and Reader, she explains to the Reader:

> There's everything left for you to do. At least fifty per cent. All that work is interactive. In the end you recreate the poem in accordance with the contents of your own head. It's not win or lose. You get your individual version of the poem. It sings in your brain. And out of that poem you can, if you like, write another poem (1996: xx).

The strength of using hypertext is that the author can make transparent the process which has been used for thousands of years in storytelling, poetry, music and art. The danger is that it may close off the imagination of the reader. But this will depend on the way the project is undertaken. To what extent are all the gaps filled in? Is there sufficient richness in the material to allow the reader to elaborate imaginatively on the work presented? These are critical questions. The person uploading the content of a Web site or a CD-ROM has to know the difference between answering questions (for an information page) or creating opportunities for further imaginative play (in the case of a work of art).

The writer, like the artist, is constantly creating invisible hyperlinks in poems, either to previous works of her own, or to the poetic heritage she inhabits. With the electronic medium, those hyperlinks can be made visible. The <u>writer can link</u> the phrases to images or to other poems (among many possibilities). What this makes possible is a connection to the inexhaustible resources of the human mind, made even more so with each mind which interacts with the material.

Bird 16

Feminism

It's here that my exploration of new forms for my own poetic expression comes in. I have to acknowledge influences here. My history, poetically speaking, is very much linked to an interest in symbols and myth, alongside political poetry as developed by many lesbian and feminist writers over the past twenty-five years.

There are interesting overlaps between the language of hypertext and feminism. Landow (1992: 2) writes that 'ideas of center, margin, hierarchy, and linearity' are replaced by 'multilinearity, nodes, links and networks'. Apart from multilinearity, these were words in common usage among feminists in the 1970s, and multilinearity certainly describes what we were doing in consciousness-raising groups and collectives. We were privileging the previously unheard, unspoken, unimportant, linking with one another through common or different experience, making associations across those experiences and expanding those associations into a cultural life which was built on a strange scaffold that only we could see as it slowly grew into what we now know as a culture centred on women's experience. Lesbians took it even further, creating communities, music, literature, and art intended for other lesbians.

The problem with most hypertext discourse is that it ignores women's work.[6] Virginia Woolf's work meanders through a labyrinth of sensations and emotions with short pieces like 'Kew Gardens' (1944) or 'Street Haunting' (1930) or 'The Mark on the Wall' (1944) having the wandering quality of some hypertext. Longer works such as *The Waves* (1931) are multilayered and multivocal with no clear endpoint, only an open-ended question of what might be next. Similarly, Gertrude Stein's (1972) work would lend itself extraordinarily well to electronic formats. With her non-linear narrative, her use of rhythm and rhyming constantly forcing the reader to ask questions about the process of reading.[7] Of the feminist generation writing from 1970 on, Monique Wittig (1975, 1979) and Suniti Namjoshi (1993, 1996) have both produced an extraordinary corpus of non-linear texts which exist on a blurred line between poetry and fiction. Heavily allusive, rich in textual associations with eastern and western traditions, these texts predate the move toward nonlinearity in literature. Other writers, such as Gloria Anzaldúa, have also blurred boundaries with their work, and *Borderlands/La frontera* (1987) stands as a fine example of this.

Similarly, a preoccupation with mapping and structure informs recent fictional work by feminist writers, whether it is the path of the taxidriving Iona in Finola Moorhead's *Remember the Tarantella* (1994), the temporal map traversed by Leslie Marmon Silko in *Almanac of the Dead* (1991) or the mental iconic maps in *The Falling Woman* (1992); while in the nonfiction arena, US theorists, Susan Griffin and Mary Daly suggest what is to come in their use of a mix of

---

[6.] There are exceptions to this, of course, and Rosello (1994) and Murray (1996) use examples by women writers.

[7.] See for example her story, 'Many Many Women'. The pages of this piece look like a digital code. The last sentence resembles a binary chant:

> The one who is the one who is that one, any one and any one is one, one is one, one is that one, and any one, any one is one and one is one, and one and one, and one and one and one and one (Stein 1972: 198).

sources and discourses, and an idiosyncratic use of language in their texts. Susan Griffin's mix of poetry and nonfiction in *Woman and Nature* (1978) and Mary Daly's witty neologisms in *Gyn/Ecology* (1978) paved the way for a more playful approach to academic discourse. The serendipitous titles and publication dates indicate that a shift was taking place in the culture, and certainly in feminist culture of the period.

I make the above points to show how hypertext is part of a continuum. Because it is now located in an electronic format, it appears to be a bigger break in the tradition than it is. Indeed, for poets, the shift to hypertext is not a huge one, it is simply a matter of coming to grips with the technology and being prepared to extend poetic thinking into other media.

Unstopped Mouths

In early 1997 I began to work on a series of hypertextual poems.[8] In their print incarnation the hypertext appears as footnotes or annotations to the text. But in the various electronic forms which I have explored (and I am only at the beginning of this process), they appear as a poem with hyperlinks to key words, as maps, as PowerPoint slides, as charts of potential hypertextual pathways; they could also appear as text combined with photographic images or sound, or as moving images, such as animation or QuickTime video, or they could be accompanied by virtual images. These are only the possibilities I have imagined within the capabilities of current technology, although in practice I've not yet produced all of these forms.

---

8. The first poem in the sequence, 'Unstopped Mouths' was published in print in 1997, and in the electronic zine on a CyberPoetry website, <http://emedia.experimedia.vic.gov.au/cyberpoet/zine/hawthorne/index.html> in 1999. Others, including 'In the Convents' (1999) and 'In the Rose Garden' (1998b) appeared subsequently. 'Unstopped Mouths' and 'Carnivale' have been used as the basis of circus theatre in 1997 and 1998 respectively. Several of the poems have been the starting point for songs composed by Dion Kulak.

At the current stage of development, the poems work in several dimensions: as linear text they can be read straight through without the hypertextual links; they also work across the poems, so that certain words recur in several poems. These combined vertical and horizontal readings, are further added to by the links created by the hypertextual footnotes, which may take the reader on to other materials, or through the poems in a different order. The complexity of the project increases with each new poem. The intention which lies behind the multilayering of texts is to allow the reader, in part, to see something of the process of creation. To turn the reader from a passive consumer of poems to an active pursuer of some of the sources of the poems. These sources in turn might generate new links, new insights into the production of culture, in particular, the production of lesbian culture. The final shape of the poem, and its genesis are thereby transparently linked for the reader. The multi-layering, the creation of a matrix of connections, also allows the reader to approach the poem from different directions. The reader could begin with a single word and from there follow the text through a kind of linguistic/poetic labyrinth. The reading of the poem, therefore, shares some of the randomness of the writing of the poem.

Poems look intended; look as though everything is in its place. But many poems arise out of chance; the chance of catching a fleeting thought. In the case of the poems I am writing, the chance of coming across the hypertextual references as I write, some remembered and sought out, some from personal experience or contacts, some stumbled upon at the time of writing or later.

In deciding to write a poem about lesbian culture, I was confronted with the inaccessibility of many of the images I was using. Would any of my readers understand me? Would lesbians understand that the imagery had been chosen specifically to reflect the culture which lesbians have developed, albeit much of it hidden? I introduced the hypertextual element as a way of expanding the number of readings of the poem, a way for the reader to go on exploring.

My starting point was lesbian tradition and culture:

jade-Chinese-silk workers-hair
moon-sleeping alone-night-restless-trees-arms-sky
cows-lovers-horns-sweet peas-cerise
sisters-companions-mangoes-rice wine
stopped mouths-statues-silence-multilingual polyps
stoma-lips-mouth-feasts-tongue
ache-body-absence-distance-hollow of memory-loss-regret
morning-flowers
longing-huddling-squandering time-chamber of the heart
whistling

There are many images in this list which were incorporated into the final poems, and quite a few which weren't. This is because these are starting points and as the poem proceeds, the mind continues its associative processing, adding and subtracting from the list. Some were subtracted because they were images or concepts I had used previously and when a choice appeared I selected the image I had not used.

The title, 'Unstopped Mouths', comes from a phrase in Page duBois' book, *Sappho is Burning* (1995). She describes the 'stopped mouths' (1995: 37) of statues and this immediately made me think of the mouthless cycladic figures (2800–2500 BC) who stand arms folded, eternally silent. This led me, in turn, to the ways in which lesbians have been silenced. So many lesbian writers have used metaphors of mouths and lips to represent sexuality and sensuality; in addition it carries implications of language, speech, writing, of sustenance, and eating. The unstopped mouths of many lesbians over the last couple of decades have transformed lesbian culture. We have invented ourselves, we have excavated the past, and we have reinterpreted much of literature and art.

The hypertextual footnote to the words 'unstopped mouths' is just the beginning, the first reference of many other references to mouths, to sexuality, to eating. And these other references crop up in other poems in the sequence, each resonating with the other, with all the others, becoming almost a chorus. The footnotes are also a kind of history. They range from scholarly to irreverent and whimsical in tone; they cover ancient history and the rigours of contemporary cultures. They include references to visual arts, historical interpretation, slang and quotations from poetry and literature, among other things.

In the following extract a connection is made between words, poultry and lesbian sexuality.

in the parched chook run turkeys gobble their throats wobbling swallowing words *gobbling* half words

> *gobbling*. Christina Rosetti uses the word "goblin" to great effect in her long poem, *Goblin Market*. The old meanings of the word "gob" are interesting, ranging across mouth (as in shut your gob, or the rather large lollies called gob-stoppers), language (as in the gift of the gab), to talk incessantly, (as in gabble). To gobble, means to swallow noisily, rather like a turkey. The word "gob" was in much more frequent use in 1862 when Christina Rosetti published her poem. "Goblin pulp and goblin dew" were the words which prompted these thoughts, but there are other references in the poem which are even more suggestive of lesbian sexuality. "Did you miss me? / Come and kiss me. / Never mind my bruises, / Hug me, kiss me, suck my juices / squeezed from goblin fruits for you, / Goblin pulp and goblin dew. / Eat me, drink me, love me; / Laura, make much of me." Christina Rosetti. 1994. *Goblin Market and other poems*. Mineola, NY: Dover Publications. 13.

The double entendre of goblin—its connection with that old word 'gob' for mouth and 'gobbling' for eating with relish or lust—would not be lost on a poet.

The dense text of lesbian poetry has had a twofold purpose. First of all, the density of poetry lends itself to disguise. Metaphor, allegory, linguistic and structural games are all a part of poetic practice. Secondly, dense text has become a protection, a code. In an effort to hide their meaning many lesbian poets wrote enigmatic, heavily coded, richly textured work.

In writing this series of poems, I have been concerned as much with researching lesbian culture, finding the shards of lesbian traditions in the fragments of Sappho's poems, the small collections of work by Nossis or Erinna, the Sanskrit and <u>Indian traditions</u>, so finely written about by Giti Thadani (1996), and much more besides. I know my work will not be encyclopaedic, it's not intended to be. Rather I want it to be suggestive, to provoke further research, to make lesbians wonder about their history, to open up the field to further speculation and imagination.

Namjoshi
17

For example, on the latter I have used references to Biblical imagery and reinterpreted it, extended it by speaking about things which have been omitted (Hawthorne 1998a: 161).

> some have seen visions a winged woman in scarlet and purple the mother of harlots of lesbians of loose women of carnal lust a friend of the lion the dragon the eagle but not of the lamb we are fallen *Babylon is fallen is fallen* is fallen we anoint our bodies with oil we anoint our heads with oil

> > *Babylon is fallen is fallen*. Revelations 14:8. Babylon is used over and over in the Bible as the archetypal evil city. It is filled with pagans, heathens, idolaters, adulterers, whores, buggers and no doubt, lesbians. Lesbians, like other daughters of Babylon, are fallen women. Anything reeking of women's sexuality is regarded as blasphemous in Biblical, and later Church texts.

This is an echo of an earlier reference in the poem to daughters of Babylon (Hawthorne 1998a: 159):

> we are daughters of Babylon some of us have been whores we have sinned my right hand is cunning my tongue more so have mercy upon us miserable sinners

> > *cunning*. The word "cunning" is related to the Scots ken, to know. This is the same root from which the word "cunt" derives. There is a wonderful idiosyncratic word "cuncti-potent" which means to be powerful in a cuntish sort of way, in other words a woman with power. The derogation which has occurred with the four letter use of the word "cunt" is perhaps an indicator of woman hatred.

This poem is hypertextually linked to others in the series, which at times touch on similar themes. For example, the theme of the closed community is one which reappears throughout the sequence. There are references to schools for girls, to colleges, to convents, to asylums, to gyms and to prisons.

In my poem, Lavender Shift, I write:

there are stories of girls sent away to boarding schools there they will remain pure some of these girls have turned into *wolves* inhabiting the night *baying to the moon* with desire satisfying their *infinite appetites* some have been corrupted by the very ones paid to protect them (unpublished, 1999)

> *wolves. The Wolf Girls of Vassar* were a group of girls at Vassar women's college who cavorted at night dressed in wolf skins. They were perhaps acting out Djuna Barnes' (1936) depiction of lesbian sexuality in *Nightwood*.
>
> *bay to the moon.* "I want to howl at the moon/celebrate her offerings" (Tomiye Ishida. "Tsuki ga Deta". In C. Allyson Lee and Makeda Silvera, Eds. 1995. *Pearls of Passion*. Toronto: Sister Vision Press.).
>
> *infinite appetites.* A reference to Baudelaire's poem *Femmes Damnées*, which novelist Christine Crow cites in her *Miss X or the Wolf Woman* (1990, London: The Women's Press); a novel which explores at length lesbian passion, repression, and the relationship between a headmistress and one of her star pupils.

The appetite of wolves is equated with lesbian sexual desire, but from a non-lesbian perspective it is the ill-fated desire of the outcast, of those who can do nothing more than meet their destiny, with an appetite which is uncontrollable. Appetite, of course, is necessary to live. Without it one wastes away and dies. Towards the end of the novel Mary Wolfe writes: 'Infinite Joy is appetite' (Crow 1990: 232). Acceptance of one's appetite, of one's sexuality and desire is what creates infinite joy.

Coming back to the subject of mouths there is this line in Crow:

the still forbidden turret, yawned like a chasm, darker yet . . . dark, as they say, as the lips of a wolf, dark as a wolf that has lost the tip of its tongue (Crow 1990: 138).

As mentioned earlier, the lips, the mouth are central to lesbian sexuality. And they are an important part of reclaiming lesbian culture. Speaking out, writing, coming out all require speech, the use of the tongue, the unstopping of our mouths.

The poems also deal with contemporary culture, personal experience, the stories of friends and acquaintances. Take the story of Jake (from 'In the Prisons'):

> six foot tall Jake is in because she has hair on her face she wears a *beard* and they arrest her constantly because they think she's an eighteen-year-old youth looking for trouble she's past forty but the skin on her cheeks is as smooth as silk

> > *beard*. Lesbians who have beards because they happen to have more hair grow on their faces than is socially acceptable are sometimes mistaken for young gay men. A women's liberation slogan of the 1970s ran along the lines: we love ourselves only as much as we love our sisters with hair on their faces.

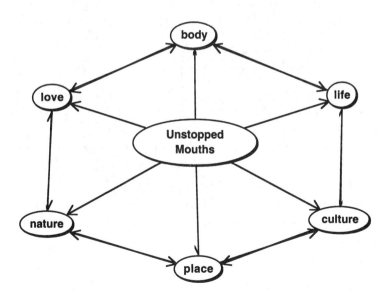

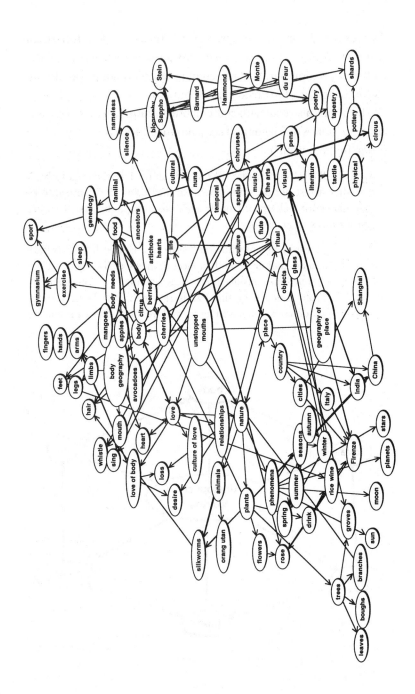

As I move from one poem to the next, I discover yet another rich seam of material, one I hadn't anticipated. And my map of the connections between the poems has become so complex that I have ceased to map the poems on paper, but carry it instead in my head. I have reproduced here a partial map of the first poem, 'Unstopped Mouths', which was produced using StoryVision.

What the map makes clear is the complexity of constucting a crosshatched set of hypertextual links. The hypertextual links, moreover, indicate the poet's intention and these meanings can be made transparent through linking to either a site or another explanatory or associative text, which makes the meaning clear. For all the discussion of the death of the author, there is something to be said for having access to the poet's intention.

Conclusions

The concept of hypertext has given me a way to express a lesbian poetics, using both poetic and academic conventions, two worlds I happen to straddle. Hypertext, along with other electronic interventions and inventions, will open up a huge array of possibilities for poets to explore into the next millennium. Perhaps, as Deborah Staines says, it will create 'bridges'.

References

Aarseth, Espen J. 1994. Nonlinearity and Literary Theory. In George Landow (Ed.), *Hypertext Theory* (pp. 51–80). Baltimore and London: The Johns Hopkins University Press.

Anzaldúa, Gloria. 1987. *Borderlands/La frontera*. New York: Kitchen Table, Women of Color Press.

Aslanides, Timoshenko. 1998. *AnniVersaries: 366 linked poems, one for every day of the Australian year*. Sydney: Brandl and Schlesinger.

Barnes, Djuna. 1936/1974. *Nightwood*. London: Faber and Faber.

Baudelaire, Charles. 1857/1989. *The Flowers of Evil*. In Marthiel Mathews and Jackson Mathews (Eds.), New York: New Directions.

Berndt, Ronald. 1952. *Djanggawul: An Aboriginal religious cult of north eastern Arnhem Land*. Melbourne: F.W. Cheshire.

Bolter, Jay David, Michael Joyce, John B. Smith and Mark Bernstein. 1990–1993. *Storyspace™*. Computer Software. Watertown, MA: Eastgate Systems Inc.

Cortazar, Julio. 1998. *Hopscotch*. London: The Harvill Press.

Crane, Gregory and Elli Mylonas. 1991. Ancient Materials, Modern Media: Shaping the Study of Classics with Hypertext. In Paul Delany and George P. Landow (Eds.), *Hypermedia and Literary Studies* (pp. 205–20). Cambridge, MA and London: MIT Press.

Crow, Christine. 1990. *Miss X or The Wolf Woman*. London: The Women's Press.

Daly, Mary. 1978. *Gyn/Ecology: The metaethics of radical feminism*. Boston: Beacon Press.

Delany, Paul and George P. Landow (Eds.), 1991. *Hypermedia and Literary Studies*. Cambridge, MA and London: MIT Press.

Doolittle, Hilda (H.D.). 1974. *Helen in Egypt*. New York: New Directions.

duBois, Page. 1995. *Sappho is Burning*. London and Chicago: University of Chicago Press.

Fletcher, Beryl. 1996. *The Silicon Tongue*. Melbourne: Spinifex Press.

Gaggi, Silvio. 1998. *From Text to Hypertext: Decentering the subject in fiction, film, the visual arts, and electronic media*. Philadelphia: University of Pennsylvania Press.

Grahame, Cassandra, 1975. Poem. In Kate Jennings (Ed.), *Mother I'm Rooted*. Melbourne: Outback Press.

Griffin, Susan. 1978. *Woman and Nature: The roaring inside her*. New York: Harper and Row.

Hawthorne, Susan. 1992. *The Falling Woman*. Melbourne: Spinifex Press.

Hawthorne, Susan. 1997. Unstopped Mouths. In Susan Hawthorne, Cathie Dunsford and Susan Sayer (Eds.), *Car Maintenance, Explosives and Love and Other Contemporary Lesbian Writings*. Melbourne: Spinifex Press.

Hawthorne, Susan. 1998a. In the Convents. *HEAT 7*.

Hawthorne, Susan. 1998b. In the Rose Garden. *Divan*. An electronic journal of Australian poetry. Box Hill Institute.
    <http://www. bhtafe.edu.au/BHI/VocationalArtsFitness/TM508/divan.htm>

Hawthorne, Susan. 1999. Unstopped Mouths. (Electronic version) *CyberPoetry Site*. State Library of Victoria:
    <http://emedia. experimedia.vic.gov.au/cyberpoet/zine/hawthorne/index.html>

H.D. (Hilda Doolittle). 1974. *Helen in Egypt*. New York: New Directions.

I Ching or Book of Changes. 1983. The Richard Wilhelm Translation, rendered into English by Cary F. Baynes. Third Edition. London: Routledge & Kegan Paul.

Ishida, Tomiye. 1995. Tsuki ga Deta. In C. Allyson Lee and Makeda Silvera (Eds.), *Pearls of Passion*. Toronto: Sister Vision Press.

Landow, George. 1992. *Hypertext: The convergence of contemporary critical theory and technology*. Baltimore, MD: The Johns Hopkins University Press.

MacKay, Anne (Ed.), 1992. *Wolf Girls at Vassar: Lesbian and gay experiences 1930–1990*. New York: St Martins Press.

Miller, Rand and Robyn Miller. 1993. *Myst*. Novato, CA: Broderbund.

Moorhead, Finola. 1994. *Remember the Tarantella*. London: The Women's Press.

Murray, Janet. 1996. *Hamlet on the Holodeck: The future of narrative in cyberspace*. New York: The Free Press.

Naidu, Vayu. n.d. Hindu society particularly has used live brains. *BabelBuildingSite*:
 <http://www.spinifexpress.com.au/babelbuildingsite.htm>
Namjoshi, Suniti. 1993. *St Suniti and the Dragon*. Melbourne: Spinifex Press.
Namjoshi, Suniti. 1996. *Building Babel*. Melbourne: Spinifex Press.
Namjoshi, Suniti. 1999. *BabelBuildingSite*.
 <http://www.spinifexpress.com.au/babelbuildingsite.htm>
Porush, David. 1996. Hacking the Brainstem: Postmodern Metaphysics and
 Stephenson's *Snow Crash*. In Robert Markley (Ed.), *Virtual Realities and their
 Discontents*. Baltimore: The Johns Hopkins University Press.
Retallack, Joan. 1985. H.D., H.D. In *Parnassus: Poetry in review, Spring / Summer / Fall
 / Winter*: 12 (2)–13 (1). 67–88.
Rosello, Mireille. 1994. The Screener's Maps: Michel de Certeau's 'Wandersmänner'
 and Paul Auster's Hypertextual Detective. In George Landow (Ed.) *Hypertext Theory*.
 (pp. 121–158). Baltimore and London: The Johns Hopkins University Press.
Rosetti, Christina. 1994. *Goblin Market and other poems*. Mineola, NY: Dover
 Publications.
Sargent, Thelma. 1975. *The Homeric Hymns*. New York: Norton.
Silko, Leslie Marmon. 1991. *Almanac of the Dead*. New York: Penguin Books.
Snyder, Ilana. 1996. *Hypertext: The electronic labyrinth*. Melbourne: Melbourne
 University Press.
Staines, Deborah. 1993. *Now Millennium*. Melbourne: Spinifex Press. (Published
 jointly with Sandy Jeffs. *Poems from the Madhouse*.)
Stein, Gertrude. 1972. Many Many Women. In *Matisse Picasso and Gertrude Stein with
 two shorter stories*. West Glover, VT: Something Else Press. (This book is also known
 as *GMP*.)
StoryVision, 1.5. Santa Monica, CA: StoryVision.
Thadani, Giti. 1996. *Sakhiyani: Lesbian desire in ancient and modern India*. London:
 Cassell.
Tofts, Darren and Murray McKeich. 1998. *Memory Trade: A prehistory of cyberculture*.
 Sydney: Interface.
Wittig, Monique. 1975. *The Lesbian Body*. Translated by David Le Vay. London: Peter
 Owen.
Wittig, Monique and Sande Zeig. 1979. *Lesbian Peoples: Materials for a dictionary*. New
 York: Avon.
Woolf, Virginia. 1930/1970. Street Haunting. In *The Death of the Moth and other
 Essays*. (pp. 20–36) New York: Harcourt Brace Jovanovitch.
Woolf, Virginia. 1931/1990. *The Waves*. London: The Hogarth Press.
Woolf, Virginia. 1944/1974. Kew Gardens. In *A Haunted House* (pp. 34–42). London:
 Penguin Books.
Woolf, Virginia. 1944/1974. The Mark on the Wall. In *A Haunted House* (pp. 43–52).
 London: Penguin Books.
Yates, Frances. 1978. *The Art of Memory*. Harmondsworth: Penguin Books.
Zervos, Komninos. 1995a. *CyberPoetry Site*. See essay: Techno-literatures on the
 internet. Also see poems.
 <http://student.uq.edu.au/~s271502>
Zervos, Komninos. 1995b. Techno-literatures on the internet. *TEXT*, Vol. 1, No. 1,
 <http://www.ins.gu.edu.au/eda/text/journal.htm>
Zervos, Komninos. 1998. *Cyberpoetry Underground*. Privately produced.

twenty

Glossary

agent an automated series of commands which results in several paths being searched simultaneously. Such search programs are called worms or spiders.

Alternate World Syndrome body amnesia caused by spending prolonged periods in the virtual world (see Michael Heim 1995: 67).

ARPANET a communications network first developed by the US Defense Department, extended to universities, and only in the last decade used by companies and individuals.

atopic no place. In contrast to utopia, a good place. Atopias don't exist, or have no expression in the physical world. Cyberspace is atopic.

avatar a graphical figure operating in virtual reality. It has several features including a nickname, a visual form (specified by VRML), as well as orientation and position. Most avatars have a humanoid form, but this can be decided by the creator. For VRML code on how to create an avatar see Roehl *et al.* (1997: 587–606).

backbone analogous to the human body, the electronic backbone is the main communication line which connects computers to one another.

bandwidth refers to the amount of information which can be passed on in a single interaction. If it is online, wide bandwidth allows the transmission of real time video, images, music etc. Narrow bandwidth results in slow transmission. Reality is described by some as 'very wide bandwidth' (Holmes 1997: 237).

bit the smallest unit of digital data, represented as the binary digits, 0 and 1.

broadcast the means by which one person, or a small group of people, are able to transmit information to a large number of people. Typically it is a means of mass communication programmed to appeal to a very wide audience.

byte each character, such as a letter or a symbol, is made up of a group of bits. Eight such bits make a byte.

carpet bombing a term borrowed from military usage. A site is carpet bombed when numerous—many thousands—of email messages are sent to the one email address. The server is overloaded and the entire system collapses and shuts down.

CD-ROM Compact Disk Read-Only Memory CD-ROM is currently the usual delivery means for interactive multimedia programs. With enough memory to store the equivalent of 1500 floppy disks, it enables the producer to use a mix of video, audio, text and graphics.

chat rooms an online space, rather like a telephone party line, in which participants can communicate through text in real time. Chat rooms tend to bring together people with similar interests. Anyone can set up an Internet Relay Chat line with a few IRC commands. Some chat rooms are operated by commercial Internet providers such as America Online (see also ICQ).

CMC Computer Mediated Conferencing synchronous or asynchronous communication via an online computer.

consciousness-raising (CR) CR groups were an important feature of the Women's Liberation Movement of the late 1960s and early 1970s. A method of group communication borrowed from the Chinese Revolutionaries, it brought together small groups of women (usually not more than ten) who shared their life histories while simultaneously looking at the political dimensions of them. In this way, many women discovered that things which previously they had thought were their own individual problems were in fact shared by many others.

cracker an 'outsider who breaks into (or cracks) computer systems without authorization. A cracker is different from a hacker, who may or may not use her/his computer expertise to gain access to secured computer systems' (Millar 1998: 200).

cyber from the Greek word, κυβερ, kuber, which means steersman. It implies governance (same root as gubernatorial), and resonates with the concept of navigation. In the context of the digital age, it is a prefix signifying a word's connection to the world of the Internet.

cyberculture a diversity of means already exists for this term. In general it points to the 'new forms of social interaction made possible by computer networks' (Tofts and McKeich 1998: 15). In its broadest sense it includes social, political, technological, scientific and cultural activities which involve hypertext, email, the World Wide Web, simulations and virtual worlds. The word's origins can be traced back to the 1960s (Wiener 1968: 173).

CyberFeminist feminists notice injustice in the world in relation to women, and feminism demands of us that we do something to change the situation. Likewise, through CyberFeminism and Cyber-Feminist analysis we are able to perceive the inequalities in the digital culture, including the language used by its controllers. Cyber-Feminists participate in cyberculture, challenging its assumptions, inventing new ways, and becoming online activists.

cyberfiction fiction which intersects with the cyberworld. Cyber-fiction has a range of possible forms, from hypertextual to fiction which uses elements of multimedia. In addition to text, it might also include one or more of sound, graphics, video or virtuality. Cyber-fiction can be read on CD-ROMs as well as on the Internet.

cybernetics coined in 1948 by Norbert Wiener to describe theories of communication and control in both the machine and in living beings (including animals and humans).

cyberpoetry like Cyberfiction, cyberpoetry takes on multiple forms. It includes <u>hypertext</u>, poetry on the <u>World Wide Web</u>, poetry which moves and may take on graphic form. 'Liquid poetry' is an electronic form on concrete poetry, and can move around the viewer's screen.

Mueller 13

cyberspace a non-physical space which denotes the space of connection between networked computers. It has also expanded to mean an imaginary space, a space in the human mind, connected to other minds through <u>digital</u> links. Some argue (Benedikt 1992, cited in Holmes 1997) that cyberspace must include an element of community.

Klein 9
Hawthorne
10

cyborg the cyborg is a body which crosses the boundary between organic substance and machinic substance. This is achieved when there is an insertion into the body of, or surrounding of the body by, a mechanical or informational device.

data glove a glove which is wired to a computer and feeds back information on the body's movement. It is used in <u>virtual reality</u> settings. Similar bioapparatuses include headphones, electronic glasses, and datasuits surrounding the entire body. Such cybernetic clothing allows audible, visual, tactile and proprioceptive feedback.

digital digital information is stored as a string of ones and zeros (digits). It has now been applied to many kinds of media including music, visual images, moving images, text, calculations and the international monetary market. It has also spawned a digital culture and discourse which presents everything digital as better than anything analogue.

disintermediation doing away with the person in the middle who is often an 'expert'. It describes the process of having direct access to information and material. In commercial terms it describes direct digital transactions between producer and consumer over the Internet, thereby removing the need for retailers. In the service area it could remove the need for advisers with expertise in particular areas.

e a prefix indicating that something is taking place in an electronic medium. email, e-commerce, e-cash, e-books etc.

email electronic mail. A system which allows people to send messages back and forth using computer networks via the <u>Internet</u> (Senjen and Guthrey 1996).

emoticon a picture made up of typographical symbols and used to express emotion in an otherwise textual environment. Common examples include :-) smiley, :)) a big smiley, ;-) winking smiley, as in 'I'm only joking', :-(sad, :-/ wry, 8-) smiley with glasses, B-) smiley with horn-rimmed glasses, :-D laughing, :-0 surprised, or horrified, :-P poking tongue out, or chuckle depending on person doing it.

ersatz a German word meaning, 'substitute'. In the context of virtual experience or simulations it expresses the sense of not real, false. An ersatz experience is one which occurs in simulated environments somewhere between the imagined and the real.

firewall a electronic security system. A firewall prevents unauthorised users from getting access to confidential information. Firewalls can be broken through by <u>crackers</u>.

flame a response indicating anger. Flaming can occur through <u>email</u> or more publicly on <u>Newsgroups</u>. The best response to flaming is to delete the message.

game theory developed around role-play games in which participants are able to experience, through play, the role another person has in particular settings. In a workplace, for example, there could be roles such as employer, unionist, human resources personnel, manager, employee. The rules for such games are prescribed, in contrast to the open-ended unprescribed roles of drama theory.

Mueller 13

GATT General Agreement on Tariffs and Trade the Agreement was signed by member countries in 1948. Representing the trade arm of the international monetary and trade institutions, it is a multilateral agreement which assumes equal bargaining power in an unequal world. GATT has been widely criticised for its rhetoric of free trade which disguises a defence of the economic interests of the powerful nations.

goto a search engine.

GPS Global Positioning System a <u>navigational</u> system which uses satellites and makes it possible for users to accurately determine their position anywhere on the globe.

HTML Hyper Text Markup Language document structuring tags which form the basis of Web page design. A tag, such as <html>, indicates that what follows is to be set out as indicated by the tags. The headers, font sizes, colour, as well as where paragraphs begin and end can be readily identified by the computer.

HTTP Hyper Text Transfer Protocol this protocol 'enables users to move hypertext files within the Internet' (Penn 1997: 292).

hyperlinks words on a Web page which are displayed in a different colour, indicating to the viewer the existence of a link to another Web page. When the word is clicked on the link is activated.

hypermedia a document which combines hypertext and multi-media.

hypertext an electronic link to another site or another page or another part of the same page. Hypertext enables the reader to move through a document in a <u>nonlinear</u> fashion. More simply, it is any series of documents connected by links. Footnotes and annotations are a print equivalent to hypertext. In this book the 𓂀 symbol functions as a hypertext operator.

hypertext fiction 'Stories written in hypertext . . . are segmented into generic chunks of information called 'lexias' (or reading units) . . . they occupy a virtual space in which they can be preceded by, followed by, and placed next to an infinite number of other lexias. Lexias are often connected to one another with <u>hyperlinks</u> . . . a single lexia might contain many links, or it may contain no links at all, thereby gluing readers to the page or allowing them to move only

forward or backward, as the pages of a book do. The existence of
hypertext has given writers a new means of experimenting with
segmentation, juxtaposition and connectedness. Stories written in
hypertext generally have more than one entry point, many internal
branches and no clear ending' (Murray 1996: 55–56).

ICQ I seek you (What is it?) is a revolutionary, user-friendly Internet
tool that informs you who's online at any time and enables you to
contact them at will. With ICQ, you can chat, send messages, files
and URLs, play games, or just hang out with other Netters while still
surfing the Net <http://www.icq.com/products/whatisicq.html>

immanence associated with women in western industrial society,
it is equated with wallowing in the mud, although in reality it is
about sustaining life through distribution of essential resources and
the necessities of life.

IMF International Monetary Fund established in 1944 at
Bretton Woods, New Hampshire, one of the three international
monetary and trade institutions (the others are the World Bank and
GATT). The IMF provides lending facilities for 'development' projects
in the so-called Third World. It has also provided 'rescue packages',
usually with harsh economic rationalist conditions attached to the
'rescue package'.

IMMaterial Interactive Multimedia Material in contrast to the
earthbound conditions and structures of our daily lives.

immersion associated with the experience of submersion in water.
Immersion is a comparable psychological state which conveys the
sense of being overwhelmed by another reality. It focuses all our
attention on the other reality, so that we lose perceptual sight of
actual reality. It can be an incredibly pleasurable experience, it could
also be potentially terrifying.

information economy in contrast to the industrial economy
which relies on transport systems, mass production and high labour

costs, the information economy relies on high speed communications systems, globalisation and reduced labour inputs.

interactivity generally interactivity describes the way a user moves from one screen to the next, controlling the speed or direction in which they move. Westwood and Kaufmann suggest a higher level of <u>interactivity</u> so that the 'user and the computer interact in a way which is *meaningful* to the user' (1999: 361).

Westwood and Kaufmann 15

internet thousands of computers linked by networks of mainly telephone lines, now connected to most countries in the world. Originally developed from ARPANET, a communications network first developed by the US Defense Department, extended to universities, and only in the last decade used by companies and individuals.

intranet an internal network which functions in a way comparable to the <u>Internet</u>. Not publicly accessible.

IRC Internet Relay Chat   see Chat rooms.

ISDN Integrated Services Digital Network a telephone line which delivers multiples of 64 kilobits per second. A <u>bandwidth</u> at least double an ordinary telephone wire, it enables the transmission of multimedia, data, voice and video at higher speeds. It makes videoconferencing possible.

LISTSERV an electronic method of mailing list management. <u>Online</u> services, such as *WMST-L*, which allow subscribers to receive automatic <u>email</u>s on particular topics of interest, such as Women's Studies.

Luddite named after Ned Ludd, a leader of an early nineteenth-century political movement whose members protested against the mechanisation of their craft. Such industrial protest was not taken to mean resistance to a new and dispossessing industrial regime, but rather as a sign of antagonism to technology. CyberFeminists who are critical of the new information technologies risk being mislabeled as Luddites.

lurker a person who observes Newsgroups without participating. Some people read and watch for a while before entering, or deciding not to participate, in such a group.

meat the body, in technospeak. The brain is referred to as meat machine; prostituted women have been referred to as meat puppets. A cynical view of humanity is implied.

meme a metaphorical extension of the gene. A meme exists in culture and is passed down from one generation to the next. In western culture, knowledge of Christianity or of capitalism are memes; in Hindu India, *The Panchatantra* is a meme. Iconic elements of the culture tend to become memes.

MIME Multi Internet Mail Extension is a standard which enhances ordinary email so that non-text data such as sound and images can be transmitted.

modem modulator/demodulator A device which enables one to communicate via telephone lines. It makes it possible to receive email, surf the Internet, or communicate through chat rooms, LISTSERVs, Newsgroups and other Internet resources. Modems can be either internal, in which case they are installed inside the computer, or external, in which case they are attached to the computer via the modem port. In order to use a modem, it must be connected to a telephone jack.

morphing computers make it possible to create visual shapeshifting images. By using 'morphing' software, a face can be transformed with a series of minute adjustments to the features so that a baby's face can seem to melt into that of a person much older, and/or of a different ethnicity or sex.

MUDs Multi User Dimensions or Dungeons These are text-only virtual environments in which the player can move about and interact with others. For the most part they are recreational games where people take on different characters or roles. They can also be used for educational purposes or as social spaces.

multimedia a form of communication which uses multiple kinds of media including sound, animation, video and text.

navigation the means by which a user moves from one part of a programme to another. On the <u>World Wide Web</u> it is the series of <u>hyperlink</u>s which a user follows; in a closed <u>CD-ROM</u> environment there are a limited number of navigation links which involve decision making on the part of the user and a knowledge of learning systems on the part of the programmer.

newsgroup an electronic discussion group. The discussion does not take place in real time, rather users post messages to one another. They differ from <u>LISTSERV</u>s because users do not automatically receive the messages but have to visit the site.

nonlinear a narrative structure not dependent on sequences of causality through linear time. A nonlinear text has many possible reading pathways as well as multiple points of entry or exit. Electronic and <u>hypertext</u>ual narratives lend themselves to nonlinearity, but nonlinearity can also be found in print texts.

online being connected or wired. In order to participate in the <u>digital</u> culture, one must first be online.

point-of-view a narrative structure which allows the reader to know whose perspective is being described. The pronouns I, you, he, she, and it usually suggest whose point-of-view it is. Skilful writers can shift point-of-view mid-sentence.

panopticon an all-seeing device. Real-time video allows for the possibility of such a machine which could run and <u>broadcast</u> via the <u>Internet</u>, as video or <u>virtual</u> images.

posthuman a fantasy in which the world is inhabited by digitised minds rather than by human beings.

proprioception a bodily feedback system which passes information about muscle activity, position and the dynamic state of the body to the brain.

Quick Time a <u>Virtual Reality</u> tool which allows the user to rotate the onscreen position 360 degrees, stepping backward and forward in continuous space. The images have a slightly jerky look about them.

RL Real Life.

RWX renderware text file format.

simulation an attempt to imitate real life. Simulations include games, such as *SimCity*, which attempt to replicate real life processes or developments. The more sophisticated the simulation, the more complex styles of playing are possible. Simulators allow the user to experience things which are in a simulated context rather than in reality. They mimic the physical and perceptual experiences. An example is the flight simulator used to train pilots, or the fairground entertainments which take the user through environments such as outer space, the grand canyon or other extreme environments.

snail mail a new word coined since the introduction of <u>email</u>, to mean the normal postal service.

storyboard a storyboard is used by the producer to communicate with the programmer of a multimedia product. All the elements on each screen are specified by the storyboarder. Storyboarding is a process which ensures that all the elements work as they should, even when used improperly or in surprising ways.

transcendence rising above the physical needs of human existence—the body, food, shelter, love—in order to reach perfection. The virtual world is often portrayed these days as a means of attaining this state of being. Transcendence is usually portrayed as a masculine pursuit in contrast to <u>immanence</u>.

URL Uniform Resource Locator a <u>World Wide Web</u> address. For example, the URL for Spinifex is: <<u>http://www.spinifexpress.com.au</u>>

virtual almost real.

virtual reality   virtual reality is a computer-generated 3-D environment designed to <u>simulate</u> real environments. The environment is 'read' by the eyes or body by donning special glasses, <u>dataglove</u>s or bodysuits wired to another computer.

VRML Virtual Reality Modeling Language   a language which enables the programmer to create 3-D virtual worlds.

wired world   the wired world is the new social reality created by the new computer-oriented technologies. It includes <u>cyberspace</u>, <u>virtual</u> worlds as well as the real world and its economy in which the digital culture exists.

www World Wide Web   A visual tool of the <u>Internet</u> which allows people in different locations to retrieve, view or distribute information through a series of linked pages. It is widely used for <u>e</u>-commerce and global publishing.

zines   Independently published electronic magazines published for an electronic audience.

References

Heim, Michael. 1995. The Design of Virtual Reality. In *Body and Society: Cyberspace/Cyberbodies/Cyberpunk: Cultures of Technological Embodiment*, 1 (3–4), 65–77.

Holmes, David (Ed.), 1997. *Virtual Politics: Identity and Community in Cyberspace*. London: Sage Publications.

Millar, Melanie Stewart. 1998. *Cracking the Gender Code: Who Rules the Wired World*. Toronto: Second Story Press.

Murray, Janet H. 1996. *Hamlet and the Holodeck: The Future of Narrative in Cyberspace*. New York: The Free Press.

Penn, Shana. 1997. *The Women's Guide to the Wired World: A User-Friendly Handbook and Research Directory*. New York: The Feminist Press.

Roehl, Bernie, Justin Couch, Cindy Reed-Ballreich, Tim Rohaly, and Geoff Brown. 1997. *Late Night VRML 2.0 with Java*. Emeryville, CA: Ziff-Davis Press.

Senjen, Rye and Jane Guthrey. 1996. *The Internet for Women*. Melbourne: Spinifex Press.

Tofts, Darren and Murray McKeich. 1997. *Memory Trade: A Prehistory of Cyberculture*. Sydney: Interface.

Wiener, Norbert. 1968. *Cybernetics: Control and Communication in the Animal and the Machine*. 2nd Edition. Cambridge, MA: MIT Press.

twenty-one

Notes on Contributors

Dr Josie Arnold is a Senior Lecturer in Media and Multimedia, Swinburne at Lilydale. She is interested in how Australian culture is being affected by globalisation and, in particular, the opportunities this presents for cyber-feminism for electronic deliveries to enhance teaching and learning.

Over thirty years of teaching have led her to an understanding of textuality and discourse in relationship to cultural and curriculum matters. She has produced over forty books, filmscripts and electronic texts and many articles, and her experience in writing and lecturing underpins her interest in feminist positioning in the emergent electronic culture.

She is the co-author of the CD-ROM 1997/8/9 *Oz 21 Australia's Cultural Dreaming* (Josie Arnold, Kitty Vigo and Daniel Green) and the accompanying Web sites point to the difference between print and electronic texts and the possibilities for cultural change in the colonisation of cyberspace. In 1997 she was nominated Teacher of the Year by Swinburne at Lilydale and Swinburne University of Technology and, in 1998, with Kitty Vigo, was nominated Team Teacher of the Year by Swinburne at Lilydale and Swinburne University of Technology.

Carmel Bird's books include the novels *The White Garden*, *Crisis*, and *The Bluebird Cafe*. *Red Shoes* is a novel in print and on CD-ROM. Carmel's short story collections include *Automatic Teller*, *The Common Rat* and *The Woodpecker Toy Fact*. Manuals for writers are *Dear Writer* and *Not Now Jack—I'm Writing A Novel*. She has edited the anthologies *Daughters and Fathers*, *Relations*, and *The Stolen Children*. Her Web site is at <http://www.carmelbird.com>

Miriam English was born in Deniliquin, NSW, spent most of her childhood in the bush around the Hawkesbury north of Sydney, and dropped out of high school to draw cartoons for television. Since then she's had drawings, cartoons, stories and articles published in various places, worked as assistant editor and staff writer for *Australian Multimedia* magazine, and has taught herself about a dozen computer languages. She enjoys modifying her computers (in true computer-geek style). Her favourite computer is the Amiga computer ('amiga' is Spanish for girlfriend). She is relieved that, at long last, she can create virtual worlds on the Internet, instead of just writing stories about it (which she has been doing since a child). She is very proud of the fact that she has no formal qualifications of any kind—she is completely self-taught.

Beryl Fletcher was born in New Zealand. In 1992, her novel *The Word Burners* was awarded the Commonwealth Writer's Prize for the best first book in South Asia and the South Pacific. She has since published three novels, *The Iron Mouth*, *The Silicon Tongue* and *The Bloodwood Clan*.

In 1994, she was chosen to represent New Zealand at the International Writing Program at the University of Iowa, USA. In 1999, she was appointed as Writer in Residence at The University of Waikato, New Zealand. Now sixty, Beryl believes that women who matured Before Feminism have important stories to tell.

Laurel Guymer was born in 1963 in Melbourne. She lectures in Women's Studies at Deakin University, having worked as a Nurse/Midwife in the areas of critical care and women's health for more than ten years. She has a

Master of Arts (1997) in Women's Studies and in late 1997 commenced her PhD on the sexual politics of contraception. Her current research includes feminist investigations of homophobia, sexual coercion and the sex industry, Women's Studies graduates careers and the implications of the pro-euthanasia movement for women. She is an active member of FINRRAGE and is involved in the international campaign against population control and abusive, hazardous contraceptives. Over the past two years she has presented and published internationally a number of papers and written three book chapters. In 1999 with Renate Klein she was awarded a DUTSD (Deakin University Teaching and Staff Development) grant to develop interactive teaching materials (Web site/CD-ROM) based on collaborative interactional feminist pedagogy. She is committed to radical feminism, flexible teaching and learning, which results in her boundless energy and enthusiasm for Women's Studies.

Susan Hawthorne is a writer, publisher and circus performer, and her most recent book is a collection of poems, *Bird*. She has written a novel, performance scripts, poetry and non-fiction, and edited eight anthologies. She has degrees in Philosophy and Ancient Greek Language, and has taught in the fields of Philosophy, Education, Literature and Women's Studies. Her work has been published in journals such as *NWSA Journal* (USA), *Tessera* (Canada), *Women's Studies International Forum* (UK), *Beiträge* (Germany),  *Journal of Australian Lesbian Feminist Studies*, *HEAT* and *Meanjin* (Australia). She is an Academic Associate at Victoria University, St Albans Campus, and writing a PhD in Women's Studies at the University of Melbourne. She has won awards for her poetry, fiction and non-fiction writing and is also working on a collection of hypertextual poems, *Unstopped Mouths*.

Donna M. Hughes was born in USA in 1954. She holds the Eleanor M. and Oscar M. Carlson Endowed Chair in Women's Studies, and is the Director of Women's Studies at the University of Rhode Island, USA. She is the Education and Research Coordinator of the Coalition Against Trafficking in Women. She is the author of *Pimps and Predators on the Internet: Globalizing the Sexual Exploitation of Women and Children*, and the editor of *Making the Harm Visible—The Global Sexual Exploitation of Women and Girls—Speaking Out and Providing Services*.

Renate Klein is internationally known for her research in the areas of Women's Studies theory (*Theories of Women's Studies*, with Gloria Bowles) and feminist critiques of reproductive and genetic engineering (*Test Tube Women: What Future for Motherhood and Infertility: Women Speak Out about their experiences of reproductive medicine*). A biologist by training, she is Associate Professor in Women's Studies and the Director of the Australian Women's Research Centre at

Deakin University in Australia. She is the (co)-author/(co)-editor of five books on reproductive technologies and four books on feminist issues. Renate Klein has degrees in biology, sociology and Women's Studies from Zürich and London Universities and the University of California (Berkeley). In 1996 she published *Radically Speaking: Feminism Reclaimed* (with Diane Bell) and is currently working on the second volume, *Essential Readings: A Source Book of Radical Feminist Writings*.

Joan Korenman is Director of the Center for Women and Information Technology <http://www.umbc.edu/cwit/> and Professor of English at the University of Maryland, Baltimore County (UMBC). From 1982–1998, she directed UMBC's Women's Studies Program. In 1991, she founded *WMST-L*, an electronic forum for Women's Studies teaching, research, and program administration. With more than 4000 subscribers in 48 countries, *WMST-L*

is now the largest women-related academic email forum in the world. She also established and maintains the UMBC Women's Studies Web site <http://www.umbc.edu/wmst/>; it includes annotated, frequently-updated information about women-related email forums, Web sites concerned with women's studies/women's issues, and more.

Professor Korenman is the author of the 1997 book *Internet Resources on Women: Using Electronic Media in Curriculum Transformation*, (updates at <http://www.umbc.edu/wmst/ updates.html>) and articles about computer-mediated communication and online resources for women. She has also given numerous conference talks and workshops on these topics and participated in a panel on 'Doing Women's Studies Research Electronically' at the 1995 Beijing United Nations Conference on Women. In her other life, she writes about American literature.

Alesia Montgomery is a doctoral student in sociology at the University of California, Berkeley. Her research focuses on the ways that everyday contexts and social location (for example, class, race, gender, sexuality) shape technology use.

Kathy Mueller was born in 1948, in Cleveland, Ohio, USA. After graduating from Cleveland State University with a BA and Dip Ed, she migrated to Australia and began teaching high school in a rural NSW town in 1971.

Film-making and stage productions were always part of her teaching and this eventually led to studies in Dramatic Arts and Film and Television at the Victorian College of the Arts. Kathy has won numerous awards for her film directing and writing.

In 1992, feeling limited by narrative structure and the fantasy construct, Kathy began her exploration of interactive drama, beginning with studies in Family Systems Psychology and Neuro-linguistic programming, then moving to the study of gameplay systems and interactive storytelling.

She is a national trainer in interactive script writing for the Australian Film Television and Radio School and is currently designing a conceptual model for tracking online role-play interactions for her PhD.

Suniti Namjoshi was born in India in 1941. She has worked as an officer in the Indian Administrative Service and in academic posts in India and Canada. She has taught in the Department of English at the University of Toronto and now lives and writes in Devon.

She has published numerous poems, fables, articles and reviews in anthologies, collections and journals in India, Canada, the US, Australia and Britain. She has published five books of poetry in India and three in Canada, including *The Authentic Lie* (1982) and *From the Bedside Book of Nightmares* (1984). Her first book of fiction, *Feminist Fables*, was published in 1981; her second, *The Conversations of Cow*, in 1985; and her third, *Aditi and the One-eyed Monkey*, written for children, in 1986. She has written with Gillian Hanscombe the sequence of poems, *Flesh and Paper*, which appeared in print and as an audio tape in 1986. *The Blue Donkey Fables* (1988) was among the top twenty titles selected for Feminist Book Fortnight in 1981. *Because of India: Selected Poems*, which covers a period of over twenty years, was published in 1989, and *The Mothers of Maya Diip*, a satire set on an island off the west coast of India 'where a matriarchy bloomed unashamedly', in the same year. *Saint Suniti and the Dragon* and a new edition of *Feminist Fables* have been published by Spinifex Press, Melbourne (1993) and Virago Press, London (1994).

Her latest book, *Building Babel*, is about the process of building culture under the aegis of Crone Kronos, i.e., time. Spinifex have put the last chapter on the Internet as a kind of building site to which others can contribute. Other Web sites which she has helped to make or made herself include:

Home Page <http://www.ex.ac.uk/~smnamjos/>; Babel Building site <http://www.spinifexpress.com.au/babelbuildingsite. htm>; CyberShapers <http://www.ex.ac.uk/~smnamjos/CYBERSHAPERS/ CYBERSHAPERS.HTML>; 'Commonplace Practice' A Poem for Many Voices for The Commonwealth Institute <http://www.commonwealth. org.uk/vying.htm>

Bandana Pattanaik has taught English language and literature at the tertiary level in India for several years. She did an MA in Women's Studies at Deakin University, Melbourne in 1996–97, and now works in the research unit of the Global Alliance Against Traffic in Women (GAATW), Bangkok.

Scarlet Pollock   Jo Sutton

Scarlet Pollock and Jo Sutton are founders of Women'space, and coordinating editors of *Women'space Magazine*, which is published in print and online. Coming from backgrounds in 'Violence Against Women' and 'Women's Health', they are now involved in the Women's Internet Campaign for women's equal access, involvement and control over new communication technology. Scarlet and Jo coedited *Virtual Organizing, Real*

Change: Women's Groups Using the Internet, Women'space, 1997. Women'space can be visited online at: <http://www.womenspace.ca>

Beth Stafford was born in Joliet, Illinois, and grew up in Chicago. One of the first US academic librarians to establish reference services for feminist scholars, she has published guides and evaluative articles and book chapters on resources for research directories of Women's Studies programs and a keyword-searchable database of such programs and other databases now accessible on Internet.

In 1979 she was responsible for establishing the Women's Studies/Women in International Development Library at the University of Illinois in Urbana-Champaign, which she still directs.

Heather Kaufmann was born in Melbourne in 1948. She has degrees in Psychology and in Teaching English as a Second Language, and her passion in life is travelling (but not in boats!). Together they established Protea Textware, an educational software publishing company, in Melbourne in 1994. They have published six titles. They also run a wildlife shelter for orphaned native animals and their office is often home to kangaroos, wombats and koalas. Their programs often show traces of animal presence!

Heather Kaufmann and
Virginia Westwood

Virginia Westwood was born in Adelaide in 1954. She has a degree in Agricultural Science, and has worked in information technology for nearly twenty years, but her great passion in life is sailing around the Pacific ocean.

Index

OTHER CYBER TITLES FROM SPINIFEX PRESS

Dale Spender
Nattering on the Net: Women, Power and Cyberspace
Top Twenty Title, Listener Women's Book Festival, 1995
The first book to look at women and the cyberworld.
A clarion call for women to get wired.

Hari Kunzru, Wired

ISBN 1-875559-09-4

Rye Senjen and Jane Guthrey
The Internet for Women
An essential tool for any female (or male) user who wants to participate in the future . . .

Sophia Chauchard-Stuart, Independent

ISBN 1-875559-52-3

Suniti Namjoshi
Building Babel
Suniti Namjoshi is an inspired fabulist: she asks difficult questions—about good and evil, about nature and war—unfailingly bracing her readers with her mordant humor and lively play of her imagination.

Marina Warner

A unique book which invites the reader to explore ideas on culture and contribute to the Babel Building Site on the Spinifex Website:
<http://www.spinifexpress.com.au/babelbuildingsite.htm>
ISBN 1-875559-56-6

Beryl Fletcher
The Silicon Tongue
One of the best reads I have ever had. I couldn't put it down, gripped in the exploration of intersecting lives, rejoicing that women in their seventies can fly in cyberspace.

Diane Nason, Hot Gos

ISBN: 1-875559-49-3

*If you would like to know more about Spinifex Press,
write for a free catalogue or visit our Website.*

SPINIFEX PRESS
PO Box 212, North Melbourne
Victoria 3051 Australia
<http://www.spinifexpress.com.au>